"MY FRIEND LUCY WHO SMELLS LIKE CORN"
by Sandra Cisneros

From her celebrated novel Women Hollering Creek, this slice of life featuring two brown-skinned Texan girls evokes the sensuality and intimacy of preadolescent friendships.

from *RIDING IN CARS WITH BOYS*
by Beverly Donofrio

This "bad girl" talks candidly of her sexual awakenings ("By 1963, the fall of the eighth grade, I was ready. I was hot to trot") and the pregnancy that "turns out to be a blessing instead of a curse."

"AUNT MOON'S YOUNG MAN
by Linda Hogan

A love story between a reservation's "medicine woman" and a much younger man is seen through a teenager's eyes as she learns about the community's reaction to this unconventional couple as well as about her own longings.

"WHAT MEANS SWITCH"
by Gish Jen

The romance between a Chinese-American girl and a Japanese boy in an all-American high school is hilarious, insightful, and bittersweet.

AND 19 MORE SUPERB STORIES

SUSAN CAHILL's anthologies include *Women & Fiction: New Women & New Fiction: Mothers: Memories, Dreams, & Reflections by Literary Daughters; and Among Sisters: Short Stories by Women Writers.* She is the author of the novel *Earth Angels* and co-author with Thomas Cahill of *A Literary Guide to Ireland.* A teacher in New York City high schools and colleges, she is currently completing her doctorial dissertation on autobiographies by American women writers since World War II and teaching at Fordham University.

GROWING UP
FEMALE

Stories by Women Writers from the American Mosaic

Edited and with an Introduction by
Susan Cahill

A MENTOR BOOK

MENTOR
Published by the Penguin Group
Penguin Books USA Inc., 375 Hudson Street,
New York, New York 10014, U.S.A.
Penguin Books Ltd, 27 Wrights Lane,
London W8 5TZ, England
Penguin Books Australia Ltd, Ringwood,
Victoria, Australia
Penguin Books Canada Ltd, 10 Alcorn Avenue, Suite 300,
Toronto, Ontario, Canada M4V 3B2
Penguin Books (N.Z.) Ltd, 182–190 Wairau Road,
Auckland 10, New Zealand

Penguin Books Ltd, Registered Offices:
Harmondsworth, Middlesex, England

First published by Mentor, an imprint of New American Library,
a division of Penguin Books USA Inc.

First Printing, September, 1993
10 9 8 7 6 5 4 3 2 1

Copyright © Susan Cahill, 1993
All rights reserved

Permissions to reprint the stories in this volume appear on page 337.

 REGISTERED TRADEMARK—MARCA REGISTRADA

Library of Congress Cataloging Card Number: 93–83710

Printed in the United States of America

PUBLISHER'S NOTE
These are works of fiction. Names, characters, places, and incidents either are the product of the authors' imagination or are used fictitiously, and any resemblance to actual persons, living or dead, events, or locales is entirely coincidental.

For my daughter,
Kristin Maria

CONTENTS

Introduction

❦

The focus of the stories in this collection is the experience of passing from girlhood to womanhood in late twentieth-century, multicultural America. The transitional rites and crises of female adolescence come across in these selections in their many different moods and dimensions; the angle of vision varies, depending on the eye and heart of the writer, and accordingly, the tone of the collection swings dramatically from dark comedy to misery to a wacky or cool realism. Collectively the stories explore—sometimes in a minor key—the passage from childhood to a more complex self-awareness and social consciousness. As realists, the writers do not represent this growth in understanding as a free movement without loss. The recognitions of young maturity cost. Often the stories enact a simultaneous loss and growth, a double movement that in many cases concerns the relationships between young women and their parents and friends, their neighborhoods, their sexual partners, and various institutions, especially the changing family in troubled times. Out of these relationships the complexities of various plots develop: the teenage runaways, pregnancy, promiscuity, loneliness and alienation, ambition, exploitation, childbirth, the movements toward personal freedom, and the transcendence of destructive circumstances and the dependencies of childhood.

The stories and autobiographical narratives reflect the cultural and class diversity that has always been a fact of

American life, though one seldom acknowledged in the table of contents of many fiction anthologies. But in the late twentieth century, more than two hundred years since our multicultural and multivocal beginnings, the heterogeneity of American life has finally entered both the popular and academic American consciousness. As Sacvan Bercovitch writes in *Ideology and Classic American Literature*, "America is many forms of ethnicity, many patterns of thought, many ways of life, many cultures, many American literatures." In *Growing Up Female: Stories by Women Writers from the American Mosaic,* the "mosaic beauty" of America, a phrase first used by Dorothy Canfield Fisher, suffuses the multifarious lives of these stories' adolescent protagonists: the poor rural and/or nomadic whites in the stories of Judy Troy, Donna Trussell, Katherine Dunn, and Joyce Maynard; the inner-city, rural, and middle-class African-Americans in the stories of Paulette Childress White, J. California Cooper, Andrea Lee, and Gloria Naylor; the poor Mexican-Americans and privileged Dominican-Americans in the stories of Sandra Cisneros and Julia Alvarez; the at once oppressed and independent Native Americans in the narratives of Mary Crow Dog and Linda Hogan; the varied backgrounds of the Asian-Americans in the stories of Amy Tan, Yoshiko Uchida, Ruth Sasaki, and Gish Jen; the immigrant and first-generation Jewish-Americans of Anzia Yezierska and Diane Levenberg; the both practicing and renegade Irish-Catholic Americans of Elizabeth Cullinan and Patricia Zelver; the rebellious and resigned Italian-Americans of Beverly Donofrio and Janice Eidus; and the upper-class, so-called mainstream in the New England story of Susan Minot. By virtue of its ethnic and class inclusiveness, this text makes an important contribution to the literary history of American women writers and to cultural studies. For, as Mary Dearborn writes in her study *Pocahontas's Daughters: Gender and Ethnicity in American Culture,* "Literature produced by American ethnic women presents in dramatically high relief aspects not only of the female or ethnic experience in America but of American culture itself."

Money is scarce across the spectrum of this mosaic of young lives and aspirations. Only in the comfortable New England of Minot's "Lust" and the Philadelphia of Lee's

"New African" is it taken for granted. The class gap of contemporary American life—the disproportionate distribution of wealth between the haves and have-nots—figures in these stories to show the ways in which relative degrees of poverty and pinch affect the lives of many girls and women. In real lives, the ones reinvented by the writers in this book, choices exist only in a healthy economic and social context. The inability of some of these protagonists— in the stories by Donna Trussell, Mary Crow Dog, Joyce Maynard, Judy Troy, Paulette Childress White, and J. California Cooper—to exercise life-supporting or wholehearted choices in their youth reveals the thin weave of their fortunes and futures. The impoverished young women of some of these stories must use their wits simply to survive. In late twentieth-century America, the time frame of most of these stories and their writers, choice is a luxury of middle-class territory.

These stories, then, reflect the American scene as readers know it now, on the verge of the next century: that scene is economically constricted and multicultural—according to the Census Bureau, one in four Americans now defines himor herself as Hispanic or nonwhite; the widespread economic constrictions engender stark class divisions.

The adolescent scene in multicultural, class-divided America is also sexually active: according to various social service and health-care agencies, 80% of eighteen-year-olds have had sexual experience, a statistic that perhaps exacerbates the usual conflicts between the mores of young people and those of older, traditional authority figures; it also underscores the moral confusion of a changing America. In the narratives of Beverly Donofrio, Joyce Maynard, and Donna Trussell, for example, their takes on teenage pregnancy illumine the subject from different angles. But the tone of indeterminacy in each of them is profoundly true to the irresolvable and conflicted feelings of the crisis. There is not a triumphant chord sounded in any of the stories concerning the effects of the sexual revolution of the last three decades. Read collectively, the stories suggest that the final chapter of that revolution, designating winners and losers, remains unwritten. Throughout the collection, chords of indeterminacy ring more convincingly than moral certainty. The sexual focus of some of these stories also points up the radical change in adolescent experience since the sixties. To consider the young female protagonists of earlier American fiction by women writers, say, Carson McCullers's Frankie Addams, Katherine Anne Porter's Miranda, or Jean Stafford's Molly Fawcett alongside Gloria Naylor's Kiswana Browne or Janice Eidus's Geraldine or Katherine Dunn's "Dutch" is to understand how utterly life has changed for young women in America.

Contrary to the myths about adolescence given currency in the lyrics of popular music, the experience of romantic love is seldom an end in itself in these stories. Sexual happiness emerges as one of many plots within the search for and construction of personal identity and freedom. Such is the feeling within such culturally different fictions as Sasaki's "First Love," Levenberg's "The Ilui," and Hogan's "Aunt Moon's Young Man." In these stories, romantic love as well as marriage are no longer ends in themselves or means of escape. For some, education and achievement have become as essential as love. The days when love and marriage were conceived of as a young woman's final and best destiny figure in this collection as days of delusion and loss. Yezierska's "The Miracle" and Uchida's "Tears of Autumn" bring us back to the dream-worlds of an earlier, more innocent age. Even the contemporary protagonist of Levenberg's "The Ilui" narrowly escapes the self-sacrifice enacted by the old myth of a totalizing romantic love.

The sadness and loss that characterize growing up female in America often originate in these stories with the older generation. No matter how strong a protagonist's desire for autonomy, she cannot disconnect her unfolding identity from her experience of her parents and her culture. Self-sufficiency is another myth she must un-learn. Elizabeth Cullinan's "The Power of Prayer," Judy Troy's "The Way Things Will Be," and Mary Crow Dog's autobiographical narrative illustrate the power of one generation over another and the older generation itself as a product of its culture, whether the culture of Catholicism, as in Cullinan's story, or the outsider's culture of insecurity and political oppression—a culture of powerlessness—inscribed so poignantly in Troy's story and so starkly in Mary Crow Dog's. As the title of J. California Cooper's story puts it, "Sins Leave Scars." In some of the stories—Lee's, Levenberg's, Donofrio's—the protagonist's sense of loss and anguish derives from her growing consciousness that there still exists a huge gap between the way our culture imagines and treats men and the way it imagines and treats women. The constraints of gender, it seems, are still with us, across lines of class, race, and region: the settings of the stories include both Atlantic and Pacific coasts, New England, the South, the Midwest, cities, small towns, and reservations.

No matter how oppressive or constricting the particular circumstances or cultural inheritance in any of these stories, however, each writer achieves, in varying degrees, a transcendence of wit and understanding. Without such change, no growth would have occurred. The impact of the characters' new understandings is heightened by the voice of some of the stories: like their narrators, the fictional voice is often irreverent, funny, and wonderfully open-minded, in tune with adolescence itself. Yeats was right, of course, when he said, "There can be no literature without praise." It is also true that the literary art collected here resounds with bravery. For these ethnic writers, outsiders almost to a woman, have not invented young female characters who destroy themselves or who are destroyed completely by their circumstances or their marginality. And because the focus of the stories is on a transitional stage of life, the writers' characters are free to defer or mock or ignore the traditional forms of enclosed female selfhood. Without condemning the enclosures and defeats of their mothers' lives, these young women imagine and pursue other lives and visions for themselves. Sis, the narrator of Linda Hogan's "Aunt Moon's Young Man," rejects the influence of the older women in town (they were "cold in the eye and fretted over their husbands"); she hits the road. Both Beverly Donofrio and Katherine Dunn, rejecting patterns of wifely subservience, invent protagonists with the courage to head out for the territory of their own making, on their own terms. The stay-at-home housewives who dominate the imaginations of many American male writers—from James Fenimore Cooper through Mark Twain to John Updike—are now on the move themselves in the imaginations and lives of their daughters. The writers in this anthology invite our consideration of their less emotionally constricted worlds for the women of the next century. The pleasure of their wider prospects, despite their tight finances, is palpable.

This collection offers, then, a rich and varied sample of writing by many new women writers about the experience of growing up female in multicultural, late twentieth-century America. But a sample it remains. Other highly successful stories of adolescence, omitted for the usual reasons of budget and length and heavy current availability in other collections, include excerpts from Paule Marshall's *Brown Girl, Brownstones;* Alice Walker's classic story, "Everyday Use" (available in *Women & Fiction*); Joyce Carol Oates's bitter story of an incommunicado mother and teenage daughter, "Shopping," as well as her "Where Have You Been, Where Are You Going?"; Sandra Cisneros's "Woman Hollering Creek"; Audre Lorde's recollections of realizing her lesbian identity in her autobiographical narrative *ZAMI: A New Spelling of My Name* (available in *Mothers: Memories, Dreams, and Reflections by Literary Daughters*); Tama Janowitz's "Modern Saint #271"; and other selections by various writers such as Ellen Akins, Terry McMillan, Alexis de Veaux, Millicent Dillon, and Patricia Lear.

In the introductions to the stories that follow, I have sketched a few biographical details as well as some intertextual commentary on the critical responses to the writers' work and some suggestions for teachers, readers, and students alike about the similarities of plot and characterization that make many of these stories variations on a common theme. What such an approach highlights is the commonalities that unite rather than separate young women and women writers of the American mosaic. In an interview published in the *Paris Review,* Joyce Carol Oates underscored the fact of an experiential and literary community of the word:

> All of us who write work out of a conviction that we are participating in some sort of communal activity. Whether my role is writing, or reading and responding, might not be very important. I take seriously Flaubert's statement that we must love one another in our art as the mystics love one another in God. By honoring one another's creation we honor something that deeply connects us all, and goes beyond us.

I offer this anthology in honor of the writers who honor it. I submit it, too, in praise of and with wild hopes for the young women of the coming century, the originals for the creations of these writers' generous and heterogeneous imaginations.

JULIA ALVAREZ left the Dominican Republic when she was ten years old and grew up living with her family in the Bronx, attending various New England prep schools, and traveling back to Santo Domingo in the summers. *How the Garcia Girls Lost Their Accents,* the novel from which "Trespass" is taken, focuses on four Dominican sisters as they try to become American; their names are Carla (the eldest and the subject of "Trespass"), Sandra (Sandi), Yolanda (the author's alter ego, and also called Yo, Yoyo, or Joe), and Sofia (Fifi). The poignant stories of the Garcia girls' first year in the U.S. bring to mind other versions of the immigrant family's rites of passage either included or mentioned in this collection: Yoshiko Uchida's, Amy Tan's, Gish Jen's, Anzia Yezierska's, and the title story of Sandra Cisneros's *Woman Hollering Creek.* Alvarez describes the difficulties of adapting to American life and growing up female in a patriarchal household, the girls' embarrassment when friends meet their parents, their anger as they are bullied and called "spics," and their identity confusion following the summer trips to the family compound in the Dominican Republic. The emotional landscape of "Trespass" is particularly troubled: the adolescent Carla's New World consists of Catholic schoolboys hurling racist taunts, and an exhibitionist who follows her in his car as she takes the long walk alone between her strange new school and her new neighborhood. The ambivalence of the girls' adaptation to Anglo-Saxon culture gives this chronicle of growing up female and immigrant a powerful complexity of tone and feeling. Gloria Naylor called Alvarez's first novel, which is really a collection of fifteen interrelated stories, a major achievement: "[She] gives you the privilege of visiting a family presented with such eloquence and such profound honesty you'll want to claim them as yours. Just as with any loving home, you'll want to be asked back again and again."

Julia Alvarez has also taught poetry throughout the United States and in 1986 published her first book of poetry, *Homecoming*. She lives with her husband in Middlebury, Vermont, where she teaches at Middlebury College.

———————————— ❧ ————————————

Trespass
from *How the Garcia Girls Lost Their Accent*

❦

Julia Alvarez
Carla

The day the Garcías were one American year old, they had a celebration at dinner. Mami had baked a nice flan and stuck a candle in the center. "Guess what day it is today?" She looked around the table at her daughters' baffled faces. "One year ago today," Papi began orating, "we came to the shores of this great country." When he was done misquoting the poem on the Statue of Liberty, the youngest, Fifi, asked if she could blow out the candle, and Mami said only after everyone had made a wish.

What do you wish for on the first celebration of the day you lost everything? Carla wondered. Everyone else around the table had their eyes closed as if they had no trouble deciding. Carla closed her eyes too. She should make an effort and not wish for what she always wished for in her homesickness. But just this last time, she would let herself. "Dear God," she began. She could not get used to this American wish-making without bringing God into it. "Let us please go back home, please," she half prayed and half wished. It seemed a less and less likely prospect. In fact, her parents were sinking roots here. Only a month ago, they had moved out of the city to a neighborhood on Long Island so that the girls could have a yard to play in, so Mami said. The little green squares around each look-alike house seemed more like carpeting that had to be kept clean than yards to play in. The trees were no taller than little Fifi. Carla thought yearningly of the lush grasses and thick-limbed, vine-ladened trees around the compound back home. Under the *amapola* tree her best-friend cousin, Lucinda, and she had told each other what each knew about how babies were made. What is Lucinda doing right this moment? Carla wondered.

Down the block the neighborhood dead-ended in abandoned farmland that Mami read in the local paper the developers were negotiating to buy. Grasses and real trees and real bushes still grew beyond the barbed-wire fence posted with a big sign: PRIVATE, NO TRESPASSING. The sign had surprised Carla since "forgive us our trespasses" was the only other context in which she had heard the word. She pointed the sign out to Mami on one of their first walks to the bus stop. "Isn't that funny, Mami? A sign that you have to be good." Her mother did not understand at first until Carla explained about the Lord's Prayer. Mami laughed. Words sometimes meant two things in English too. This trespass meant that no one must go inside the property because it was not public like a park, but private. Carla nodded, disappointed. She would never get the hang of this new country.

Mami walked her to the bus stop for her first month at her new school over in the next parish. The first week, Mami even rode the buses with her, transferring, going and coming, twice a day, until Carla learned the way. Her sisters had all been enrolled at the neighborhood Catholic school only one block away from the house the Garcías had rented at the end of the summer. But by then, Carla's seventh grade was full. The nun who was the principal had suggested that Carla stay back a year in sixth grade, where they still had two spaces left. At twelve, though, Carla was at least a year older than most sixth graders, and she felt mortified at the thought of having to repeat yet another year. All four girls had been put back a year when they arrived in the country. Sure, Carla could use the practice with her English, but that also meant she would be in the same grade as her younger sister, Sandi. That she could not bear. "Please," she pleaded with her mother, "let me go to the other school!" The public school was a mere two blocks beyond the Catholic school, but Laura García would not hear of it. Public schools, she had learned from other Catholic parents, were where juvenile delinquents went and where teachers taught those new crazy ideas about how we all came from mon-

keys. No child of hers was going to forget her family name
and think she was nothing but a kissing cousin to an orang-
utan.

Carla soon knew her school route *by heart,* an expression
she used for weeks after she learned it. First, she walked
down the block by heart, noting the infinitesimal differences
between the look-alike houses: different color drapes, an
azalea bush on the left side of the door instead of on the
right, a mailbox or door with a doodad of some kind. Then
by heart, she walked the long mile by the deserted farmland
lot with the funny sign. Finally, a sharp right down the
service road into the main thoroughfare, where by heart she
boarded the bus. "A young lady señorita," her mother pronounced the first morning Carla set out by herself, her heart
drumming in her chest. It was a long and scary trek, but
she was too grateful to have escaped the embarrassment of
being put back a year to complain.

And as the months went by, she neglected to complain
about an even scarier development. Every day on the playground and in the halls of her new school, a gang of boys
chased after her, calling her names, some of which she had
heard before from the old lady neighbor in the apartment
they had rented in the city. Out of sight of the nuns, the
boys pelted Carla with stones, aiming them at her feet so
there would be no bruises. "Go back to where you came
from, you dirty spic!" One of them, standing behind her in
line, pulled her blouse out of her skirt where it was tucked
in and lifted it high. "No titties," he snickered. Another
yanked down her socks, displaying her legs, which had begun growing soft, dark hairs. "Monkey legs!" he yelled to
his pals.

"Stop!" Carla cried. "Please stop."

"Eh-stop!" they mimicked her. "Plees eh-stop."

They were disclosing her secret shame: her body was
changing. The girl she had been back home in Spanish was
being shed. In her place—almost as if the boys' ugly words
and taunts had the power of spells—was a hairy, breast-
budding grownup no one would ever love.

Every day, Carla set out on her long journey to school
with a host of confused feelings. First of all, there was this
body whose daily changes she noted behind the closed bathroom door until one of her sisters knocked that Carla's turn

was over. How she wished she could wrap her body up the way she'd heard Chinese girls had their feet bound so they wouldn't grow big. She would stay herself, a quick, skinny girl with brown eyes and a braid down her back, a girl she had just begun to feel could get things in this world.

But then, too, Carla felt relieved to be setting out towards her very own school in her proper grade away from the crowding that was her family of four girls too close in age. She could come home with stories of what had happened that day and not have a chorus of three naysayers to correct her. But she also felt dread. There, in the playground, they would be waiting for her—the gang of four or five boys, blond, snotty-nosed, freckled-faced. They looked bland and unknowable, the way all Americans did. Their faces betrayed no sign of human warmth. Their eyes were too clear for cleaving, intimate looks. Their pale bodies did not seem real but were like costumes they were wearing as they played the part of her persecutors.

She watched them. In the classroom, they bent over workbooks or wore scared faces when Sister Beatrice, their beefy, no-nonsense teacher, scolded them for missing their homework. Sometimes Carla spied them in the playground, looking through the chain link fence and talking about the cars parked on the sidewalk. To Carla's bafflement, those cars had names beyond the names of their color or size. All she knew of their family car, for instance, was that it was a big black car where all four sisters could ride in the back, though Fifi always made a fuss and was allowed up front. Carla could also identify Volkswagens because that had been the car (in black) of the secret police back home; every time Mami saw one she made the sign of the cross and said a prayer for Tío Mundo, who had not been allowed to leave the Island. Beyond Volkswagens and medium blue cars or big black cars, Carla could not tell one car from the other.

But the boys at the fence talked excitedly about Fords and Falcons and Corvairs and Plymouth Valiants. They argued over how fast each car could go and what models were better than others. Carla sometimes imagined herself being driven to school in a flashy red car the boys would admire. Except there was no one *to* drive her. Her immigrant father with his thick mustache and accent and three-piece suit would only bring her more ridicule. Her mother did not yet know how to drive. Even though Carla could imagine owning a very expensive car, she could not imagine her parents as different from what they were. They were, like this new body she was growing into, givens.

One day when she had been attending Sacred Heart about a month, she was followed by a car on her mile walk home from the bus stop. It was a lime green car, sort of medium sized, and with a kind of long snout, so had it been a person, Carla would have described it as having a long nose. A long-nosed, lime-green car. It drove slowly, trailing her. Carla figured the driver was looking for an address, just as Papi drove slowly and got honked at when he was reading the signs of shops before stopping at a particular one.

A blat from the horn made Carla jump and turn to the car, now fully stopped just a little ahead of her. She could see the driver clearly, from the shoulders up, a man in a red shirt about the age of her parents—though it was hard for Carla to tell with Americans how old they were. They were like cars to her, identifiable by the color of their clothes and a general age group—a little kid younger than herself, a kid her same age, a teenager in high school, and then the vast indistinguishable group of American grownups.

This grownup American man about her parents' age beckoned for her to come up to the window. Carla dreaded being asked directions since she had just moved into this area right before school started, and all she knew for sure was the route home from the bus stop. Besides, her English was still just classroom English, a foreign language. She knew the neutral bland things: how to ask for a glass of water, how to say good morning and good afternoon and good night. How to thank someone and say they were welcomed. But if a grownup American of indeterminable age asked her for directions, invariably speaking too quickly, she merely shrugged and smiled an inane smile. ''I don't speak very much English,'' she would say in a small voice by way of apology. She hated having to admit this since such an admission proved, no doubt, the boy gang's point that she didn't belong here.

As Carla drew closer, the driver leaned over and rolled down the passenger door window. Carla bent down as if she were about to speak to a little kid and peeked in. The man smiled a friendly smile, but there was something wrong with it that Carla couldn't put her finger on: this smile had a bruised, sorry quality as if the man were someone who'd been picked on all his life, and so his smiles were appeasing, not friendly. He was wearing his red shirt unbuttoned, which seemed normal given the warm Indian-summer day. In fact, if Carla's legs hadn't begun to grow hairs, she would have taken off her school-green knee socks and walked home bare-legged.

The man spoke up. "Whereyagoin?" he asked, running all his words together the way the Americans always did. Carla was, as usual, not quite sure if she had heard right.

"Excuse me?" she asked politely, leaning into the car to hear the man's whispery voice better. Something caught her eye. She looked down and stared, aghast.

The man had tied his two shirtends just above his waist and was naked from there on down. String encircled his waist, the loose ends knotted in front and then looped around his penis. As Carla watched, his big blunt-headed thing grew so that it filled and strained at the lasso it was caught in.

"Where ya' going?" His voice had slowed down when he spoke this time, so that Carla definitely understood him. Her eyes snapped back up to his eyes.

"Excuse me?" she said again dumbly.

He leaned towards the passenger door and clicked it open. "C'moninere." He nodded towards the seat beside him. "C'm'on," he moaned. He cupped his hand over his thing as if it were a flame that might blow out.

Carla clutched her bookbag tighter in her hand. Her mouth hung open. Not one word, English or Spanish, occurred to her. She backed away from the big green car, all the while keeping her eyes on the man. A pained, urgent expression was deepening on his face like a plea that Carla did not know how to answer. His arm pumped at something Carla could not see, and then after much agitation, he was still. The face relaxed into something like peacefulness. The man bowed his head as if in prayer. Carla turned and fled down the street, her bookbag banging against her leg like a whip she was using to make herself go faster, faster.

Her mother called the police after piecing together the breathless, frantic story Carla told. The enormity of what she had seen was now topped by the further enormity of involving the police. Carla and her sisters feared the American police almost as much as the SIM back home. Their father, too, seemed uneasy around policemen; whenever a cop car was behind them in traffic, he kept looking at the rearview mirror and insisting on silence in the car so he could think. If officers stood on the sidewalk as he walked by, he bowed ingratiatingly at them. Back home, he had been tailed by the secret police for months and the family had only narrowly escaped capture their last day on the Island. Of course, Carla knew American policemen were "nice guys," but still she felt uneasy around them.

The doorbell rang only minutes after Carla's mother had called the station. This was a law-abiding family neighborhood, and no one wanted a creep like this on the loose among so many children, least of all the police. As her mother answered the door, Carla stayed behind in the kitchen, listening with a racing heart to her mother's explanation. Mami's voice was high and hesitant and slightly apologetic—a small, accented woman's voice among the booming, impersonal American male voices that interrogated her.

"My daughter, she was walking home—"

"Where exactly?" a male voice demanded.

"That street, you know?" Carla's mother must have pointed. "The one that comes up the avenue, I don't know the name of it."

"Must be the service road," a nicer male voice offered.

"Yes, yes, the service road." Her mother's jubilant voice seemed to conclude whatever had been the problem.

"Please go on, ma'am."

"Well, my daughter, she said this, this crazy man in this car—" Her voice lowered. Carla heard snatches: something, something "to come in the car—"

"Where's your daughter, ma'am?" the male voice with authority asked.

Carla cringed behind the kitchen door. Her mother had promised that she would not involve Carla with the police but would do all the talking herself.

"She is just a young girl," her mother excused Carla.

"Well, ma'am, if you want to file charges, we have to talk to her."

"File charges? What does that mean, file charges?"

There was a sigh of exasperation. A too-patient voice with dividers between each word explained the legal procedures as if repeating a history lesson Carla's mother should have learned long before she had troubled the police or moved into this neighborhood.

"I don't want any trouble," her mother protested. "I just think this is a crazy man who should not be allowed on the streets."

"You're absolutely right, ma'am, but our hands are tied unless you, as a responsible citizen, help us out."

Oh no, Carla groaned, now she was in for it. The magic words had been uttered. The Garcías were only legal residents, not citizens, but for the police to mistake Mami for a citizen was a compliment too great to spare a child discomfort. "Carla!" her mother called from the door.

"What's the girl's name?" the officer with the voice in charge asked.

Her mother repeated Carla's full name and spelled it for the officer, then called out again in her voice of authority, "Carla Antonia!"

Slowly, sullenly, Carla wrapped herself around the kitchen door, only her head poking out and into the hallway. *"¿Sí, Mami?"* she answered in a polite, law-abiding voice to impress the cops.

"Come here," her mother said, motioning. "These very nice officers need for you to explain what you saw." There was an apologetic look on her face. "Come on, Cuca, don't be afraid."

"There's nothing to be afraid of," the policeman said in his gruff, scary voice.

Carla kept her head down as she approached the front door, glancing up briefly when the two officers introduced themselves. One was an embarrassingly young man with a face no older than the boys' faces at school on top of a large, muscular man's body. The other man, also big and fair-skinned, looked older because of his meaner, sharp-featured face like an animal's in a beast fable a child knows by looking at the picture not to trust. Belts were slung around both their hips, guns poking out of the holsters. Their very masculinity offended and threatened. They were so big, so strong, so male, so American.

After a few facts about her had been established, the mean-faced cop with the big voice and the pad asked her if she would answer a few questions. Not knowing she could refuse, Carla nodded meekly, on the verge of tears.

"Could you describe the vehicle the suspect was driving?"

She wasn't sure what a vehicle was or a suspect, for that matter. Her mother translated into simpler English, "What car was the man driving, Carla?"

"A big green car," Carla mumbled.

As if she hadn't answered in English, her mother repeated for the officers, "A big green car."

"What make?" the officer wanted to know.

"Make?" Carla asked.

"You know, Ford, Chrysler, Plymouth." The man ended his catalogue with a sigh. Carla and her mother were wasting his time.

"¿Qué clase de carro?" her mother asked in Spanish, but of course she knew Carla wouldn't know the make of a car. Carla shook her head, and her mother explained to the officer, helping her save face, "She doesn't remember."

"Can't she talk?" the gruff cop snapped. The boyish-looking one now asked Carla a question. "Carla," he began, pronouncing her name so that Carla felt herself coated all over with something warm and too sweet. "Carla," he coaxed, "can you please describe the man you saw?"

All memory of the man's face fled. She remembered only the bruised smile and a few strands of dirty blond hair laid carefully over a bald pate. But she could not remember the word for bald and so she said, "He had almost nothing on his head."

"You mean no hat?" the gentle cop suggested.

"Almost no hair," Carla explained, looking up as if she had taken a guess and wanted to know if she was wrong or right.

"Bald?" The gruff cop pointed first to a hairy stretch of wrist beyond his uniform's cuff, then to his pink, hairless palm.

"Bald, yes." Carla nodded. The sight of the man's few dark hairs had disgusted her. She thought of her own legs sprouting dark hairs, of the changes going on in secret in her body, turning her into one of these grownup persons.

No wonder the high-voiced boys with smooth, hairless cheeks hated her. They could see that her body was already betraying her.

The interrogation proceeded through a description of the man's appearance, and then the dreaded question came.

"What did you see?" the boy-faced cop asked.

Carla looked down at the cops' feet. The black tips of their shoes poked out from under their cuffs like the snouts of wily animals. "The man was naked all down here." She gestured with her hand. "And he had a string around his waist."

"A string?" The man's voice was like a hand trying to lift her chin to make her look up, which is precisely what her mother did when the man repeated, "A string?"

Carla was forced to confront the cop's face. It was indeed an adult version of the sickly white faces of the boys in the playground. This is what they would look like once they grew up. There was no meanness in this face, no kindness either. No recognition of the difficulty she was having in trying to describe what she had seen with her tiny English vocabulary. It was the face of someone in a movie Carla was watching ask her, "What was he doing with the string?"

She shrugged, tears peeping at the corners of her eyes.

Her mother intervened. "The string was holding up this man's—"

"Please, ma'am," the cop who was writing said. "Let your daughter describe what she saw."

Carla thought hard for what could be the name of a man's genitals. They had come to this country before she had reached puberty in Spanish, so a lot of the key words she would have been picking up in the last year, she had missed. Now, she was learning English in a Catholic classroom, where no nun had ever mentioned the words she was needing. "He had a string around his waist," Carla explained. By the ease with which the man was writing, she could tell she was now making perfect sense.

"And it came up to the front"—she showed on herself— "and here it was tied in a—" She held up her fingers and made the sign for zero.

"A noose?" the gentle cop offered.

"A noose, and his thing—" Carla pointed to the policeman's crotch. The cop writing scowled. "His thing was inside that noose and it got bigger and bigger," she blurted, her voice wobbling.

The friendly cop lifted his eyebrows and pushed his cap back on his head. His big hand wiped the small beads of sweat that had accumulated on his brow.

Carla prayed without prayer that this interview would stop now. What she had begun fearing was that her picture—but who was there to take a picture?—would appear in the paper the next day and the gang of mean boys would torment her with what she had seen. She wondered if she could report them now to these young officers. "By the way," she could say, and the gruff one would begin to take notes. She would have the words to describe them: their mean, snickering faces she knew by heart. Their pale look-alike sickly bodies. Their high voices squealing with delight when Carla mispronounced some word they coaxed her to repeat.

But soon after her description of the incident, the interview ended. The cop snapped his pad closed, and each officer gave Carla and her mother a salute of farewell. They drove off in their squad car, and all down the block, drapes fell back to rest, half-opened shades closed like eyes that saw no evil.

For the next two months before Carla's mother moved her to the public school close to home for the second half of her seventh grade, she took Carla on the bus to school and was there at the end of the day to pick her up. The tauntings and chasings stopped. The boys must have thought Carla had complained, and so her mother was along to defend her. Even during class times, when her mother was not around, they now ignored her, their sharp, clear eyes roaming the classroom for another victim, someone too fat, too ugly, too poor, too different. Carla had faded into the walls.

But their faces did not fade as fast from Carla's life. They trespassed in her dreams and in her waking moments. Sometimes when she woke in the dark, they were perched at the foot of her bed, a grim chorus of urchin faces, boys without bodies, chanting without words, "Go back! Go back!"

So as not to see them, Carla would close her eyes and wish them gone. In that dark she created by keeping her eyes shut, she would pray, beginning with the names of her own sisters, for all those she wanted God to especially care for, here and back home. The seemingly endless list of familiar names would coax her back to sleep with a feeling of safety, of a world still peopled by those who loved her.

❦

SANDRA CISNEROS was born in Chicago in 1954 and grew up there, the daughter of a Mexican father and a Mexican-American mother, and sister to six brothers. She began her writing career in poetry—"I think you have to learn how to build a room before you build a house"—and studied at the Iowa Writers' Workshop where she learned "what I didn't want to be, how I didn't want to write." After graduation, according to Rosemary L. Bray in *The New York Times Book Review*, "she returned to the family home in Chicago and spent time in the Pilsen barrio; 'I became fascinated by the rhythms of speech, this incredible deluge of voices.' It is this deluge of voices that Ms. Cisneros so faithfully taps in her work. But she can also trace her love of language to her mother, a self-educated woman who got library cards for the seven Cisneros children long before they could actually read themselves."

Sandra Cisneros has also worked as a teacher of high school dropouts, and recently as a writer-in-residence at California State University at Chico, the University of California at Berkeley and Irvine, and the University of Michigan. The recipient of two NEA fellowships for poetry and fiction, as well as the Lannan Literary Award for 1991, Cisneros is the author of *My Wicked Wicked Ways,* a volume of poetry, *The House on Mango Street,* and *Woman Hollering Creek,* a volume of twenty-two stories about the experiences of Chicanas, women born in the United States whose heritage lies south of the Mexican border. The critic Peter S. Prescott praised *Woman Hollering Creek* (from which the following story is taken): "[The author's] feminist, Mexican-American voice is not only playful and vigorous, it's original—we haven't heard anything like it before. There's nothing cautious about the sketches and stories in *Woman Hollering Creek.* Noisily, wittily, always compassionately, Cisneros surveys woman's condition—a condition that is both precisely Latina and general to women everywhere. Her characters include preadolescent girls, disappointed brides, religious women, consoling partners and deeply cynical women who enjoy devouring men. . . . The book's triumph is its title story, a story good enough to take its place in any anthology of American short stories. . . .'' Of her writing, Cisneros has said, ''I write the kind of stories I didn't get growing up. Stories about . . . people I knew and loved, but never saw in the pages of the books I borrowed from the Chicago Public Library. Now that I live in the southwest, I'm even more appalled by the absence of brown people in mainstream literature and more committed than ever to populating the Texas literary landscape, the American literary landscape with stories about Mexicanos, Chicanos, and Latinos.'' In ''My Lucy Friend Who Smells Like Corn,'' Cisneros evokes the sensuality and intimacy between two preadolescent girls, a recurring theme in the fiction of women writers of many cultures. Patricia Meyer Spacks, writing of the relationships between women in *The Female Imagination*, observed that for Charlotte Bronte, in *Shirley* and *Jane Eyre*, ''intimacy between women may be more profound, more balanced, than any union possible between the sexes.'' Such a view applies, too, to the bond between the narrator and Lucy in the following story.

———————————

❦

My Lucy Friend
Who Smells Like Corn

☙

Sandra Cisneros

Lucy Anguiano, Texas girl who smells like corn, like Frito Bandito chips, like tortillas, something like that warm smell of *nixtamal* or bread the way her head smells when she's leaning close to you over a paper cut-out doll or on the porch when we are squatting over marbles trading this pretty crystal that leaves a blue star on your hand for that giant cat-eye with a grasshopper green spiral in the center like the juice of bugs on the windshield when you drive to the border, like the yellow blood of butterflies.

Have you ever eated dog food? I have. After crunching like ice, she opens her big mouth to prove it, only a pink tongue rolling around in there like a blind worm, and Janey looking in because she said Show me. But me I like that Lucy, corn smell hair and aqua flip-flops just like mine that we bought at the K mart for only 79 cents same time.

I'm going to sit in the sun, don't care if it's a million trillion degrees outside, so my skin can get so dark it's blue where it bends like Lucy's. Her whole family like that. Eyes like knife slits. Lucy and her sisters. Norma, Margarita, Ofelia, Herminia, Nancy, Olivia, Cheli, y *la* Amber Sue.

Screen door with no screen. *Bang!* Little black dog biting his fur. Fat couch on the porch. Some of the windows painted blue, some pink, because her daddy got tired that day or forgot. Mama in the kitchen feeding clothes into the wringer washer and clothes rolling out all stiff and twisted and flat like paper. Lucy got her arm stuck once and had to yell Maaa! and her mama had to put the machine in reverse and then her hand rolled back, the finger black and later, her nail fell off. *But did your arm get flat like the clothes? What happened to your arm? Did they have to pump it with air?* No, only the finger, and she didn't cry neither.

Lean across the porch rail and pin the pink sock of the baby Amber Sue on top of Cheli's flowered T-shirt, and the blue jeans of *la* Ofelia over the inside seam of Olivia's blouse, over the flannel nightgown of Margarita so it don't stretch out, and then you take the work shirts of their daddy and hang them upside down like this, and this way all the clothes don't get so wrinkled and take up less space and you don't waste pins. The girls all wear each other's clothes, except Olivia, who is stingy. There ain't no boys here. Only girls and one father who is never home hardly and one mother who says *Ay! I'm real tired* and so many sisters there's no time to count them.

I'm sitting in the sun even though it's the hottest part of the day, the part that makes the streets dizzy, when the heat makes a little hat on the top of your head and bakes the dust and weed grass and sweat up good, all steamy and smelling like sweet corn.

I want to rub heads and sleep in a bed with little sisters, some at the top and some at the feets. I think it would be fun to sleep with sisters you could yell at one at a time or all together, instead of alone on the fold-out chair in the living room.

When I get home Abuelita will say *Didn't I tell you?* and I'll get it because I was supposed to wear this dress again tomorrow. But first I'm going to jump off an old pissy mattress in the Anguiano yard. I'm going to scratch your mosquito bites, Lucy, so they'll itch you, then put Mercurochrome smiley faces on them. We're going to trade shoes and wear them on our hands. We're going to walk over to Janey Ortiz's house and say *We're never ever going to be your friend again forever!* We're going to run home backwards and we're going to run home frontwards, look twice under the house where the rats hide and I'll stick one foot in there because you dared me, sky so blue and heaven inside those white clouds. I'm going to peel a scab from my knee and eat it, sneeze on the cat, give you three M & M's I've been saving for you since yesterday, comb your hair with my fingers and braid it into teeny-tiny braids real pretty.

We're going to wave to a lady we don't know on the bus. Hello! I'm going to somersault on the rail of the front porch even though my *chones* show. And cut paper dolls we draw ourselves, and color in their clothes with crayons, my arm around your neck.

And when we look at each other, our arms gummy from an orange Popsicle we split, we could be sisters, right? We could be, you and me waiting for our teeths to fall and money. You laughing something into my ear that tickles, and me going Ha Ha Ha Ha. Her and me, my Lucy friend who smells like corn.

J. CALIFORNIA COOPER is the author of three collections of stories—*A Piece of Mine* (1984, from which the following story is taken), *Homemade Love* (recipient of a 1989 American Book Award), and *Some Soul to Keep* (1987). Many of the stories consist of portraits of rural African-American females seeking affection and respect from indifferent lovers and husbands. While suffering disappointments and cruelty in their lives, these women manage to sustain optimism, courage, and a sense of humor. Most of Cooper's stories, as in "Sins Leave Scars," are monologues in which a woman tells of a crisis in the life of a close friend, relative, or acquaintance through homespun observations and energetic colloquial language. Reviewers have strongly praised her authentic rendering of the African-American oral tradition. Alice Walker commented: "In its strong folk flavor, Cooper's work reminds us of Langston Hughes and Zora Neale Hurston. Like theirs, her style is deceptively simple and direct, and the vale of tears in which some of her characters reside is never so deep that a rich chuckle at a foolish person's foolishness can not be heard. It is a delight to read her stories." Terry McMillan observed that her stories— some call them parables—are infused with their author's belief that black people should own their own land and get an education, and that women in particular—no matter what their age—have to learn to deal with being alone. Cooper's women, says McMillan, "don't cry or whine about their condition, but are set on figuring out how to get on with their lives." Ntozake Shange has praised Cooper as an artist: "Her stories, parables, and monologues take flight with truths about being alive, rhythm of folks at ease by the creek and the pool table, songs of love and remorse, syncopated, galloping, and beguilingly genuine."

Cooper has also published a novel, *Family,* and seventeen plays, many of which have been produced on the stage, public television, radio, and college campuses. In 1978, she was named Black Playwright of the Year for *Strangers,* which was performed at the San Francisco Palace of Fine Arts. She has received the James Baldwin Writing Award (1988) and the Literary Lion Award from the American Library Association (1988). Ms. Cooper lives in Texas, and is the mother of a daughter, Paris Williams.

———————————— ❦ ————————————

Sins Leave Scars

❦

J. California Cooper

When Lida Mae was born the ninth of nine children, she had a 90% possibility to do and be anything she would choose. She had a good brain and disposition, good health and body, excellent looks and big legs to come in the future! She was going to be neat, petite and all reet! As they say!

During the first 12 years as she was realizing her world of food, animals, insects, trees and flowers, school and other people, people, mostly men, were realizing her. Even brothers and uncles liked to put their hands and anything else they could where they shouldn't have been. She always had some change to spend and she was generous and kind to everyone and shared always. She liked to laugh. I mean, what did she know to cry about? So she was fun to be with.

Her mother, Sissy, was tired and worn out early from having fun because it seemed every time she had some fun, she had another baby! They were beautiful children though and each one a memory of some good time! The first one was her husband's and maybe one or two of the others. She didn't know and it didn't matter no-way! She had some money from the state and her own little odd jobs (not too many tho, she had been tired a long time now) so that in case, as usual, her husband didn't bring nothing home, she could feed them and him, too. Sissy was like that, treated everybody alike.

So Lida Mae hurried to school and to play, even to household chores with a smile on her pretty face. She lived by rote that way til she was 14 years old and was coming home from school and got a ride from one of her mother's friends, Smokey, who had a run-down raggedy car but acted like it was a new Oldsmobile or something. During the ride he drove real slow, the long way, cause he couldn't get enough of feasting his eyes on Lida Mae and all her innocent peachy splendor. She shone like a brilliant star in that dirty beat-up old pile of junk. She had accepted the ride cheerfully enough so he asked her to accept $1.00 first then changed it to $2.00 to let him touch her in her very own private spot. She seemed disappointed for a moment, but Lida Mae kept looking at the $2.00 on the seat til she said "I ain't gonna pull my panties down!" He said he could manage that and she opened her young legs and he managed it as she picked up her $2.00 and rolled it deep into her fist. She got out at home, at last, and he whispered "Don't tell your mama!" She answered "Are you a fool? I ain't gonna give her my $2.00!" and slammed the door and bounced on in her house!

Now, people don't have to be there to "know," you know? Somehow some people just looked at Lida Mae and knew something from their own experiences. Lida Mae had a few boyfriends her own age she laughed and talked and kissed with and sometimes at a show or playing hide and seek, they did just that: played hide and seek. She was not really a loose young girl or a prudish one, just caught up in the middle of life and didn't know a damn thing about it so she just "felt" her way through. Then, when she was 15 years old she was still a virgin because she also liked her school work, books and the teachers. She knew all about love leading to marriage and all that but she wanted something out of life because her teachers told her there was something to get out of life. She wasn't always thinking about boys.

But the unexpected is so unexpected it's expected! One day going home from school (she was really a doll at 15 going on 16) the man who owned the filling-station called to her and said "Hey, little bit! come over here and have a Coke with me! It's on the house!" Lida Mae, because of her fight for survival at the dinner table at home, seldom refused something to eat or drink for free. She smiled as she turned her feet toward the station, "O.K. Mr. Hammon!'' He grinned down at her. ''Let's sit inside, it's too hot out here!'' ''O.K.'' She smiled as she followed him. He opened the Cokes asking her if she wanted some whiskey in it and when she said ''No thank you'' gave her plain Coke. He sat down in the only chair pulling her by her dresstail down on his lap. ''Sit down here girl, ain't got no other chair for you to sit on.'' Now, Lida had known him all her life it seemed so she wasn't nervous, she sat! He rubbed her leg through her dress while he talked to her, ''Who your boyfriend girl?'' he grinned. (He wasn't a bad looking man.)

''I don't know,'' she said smiling.

''You don't know who you love?'' He looked shocked.

''I don't love none of em, I just like em!'' She took a drink.

''I know they like you.'' He lowered his voice.

''How come?'' She grinned.

''Girl, you know you pretty, pretty as a picture!'' He rubbed her leg. ''Even I could like you!'' He was serious now.

''Oh, Mr. Hammon, you wouldn't! I'm too young for you and Mrs. Hammon wouldn't like that!'' She took another drink.

''Mrs. Hammon don't know everything!'' He smiled then noticed she was almost through with the Coke. ''Wanna nother Coke?''

''No, I got to go now! I'll take one with me if you want to!'' She set the empty bottle down and prepared to get off his lap.

Mr. Hammon moved his knees and Lida Mae almost fell backwards and Mr. Hammon grabbed her around the waist and under her dress as she struggled to get up. He said, ''Oh! Oh! Lookit here what I got my hand on! I didn't mean to do it, but I couldn't let you fall!'' He grinned.

''Well help me up!'' She cried.

''I can't!'' He grinned. ''I can't move my hand!'' But he was moving his hand and when he let Lida Mae up, she was mad! She left there with six Cokes tho and her virginity intact.

Lida Mae didn't play so hard with the boys for the next week or so. Something told her it wasn't so innocent and she felt a little grown up in a way they weren't.

Somehow on the next hot day after school when Lida Mae had no money, her long braids freely flying behind her, she turned into Mr. Hammon's filling-station. He was just a man after all and she felt grown so she went and got her own Coke and sat down in the chair herself! Mr. Hammon watched awhile as he worked on his customer, one of the few in this little small town, then she was leaving with six more Cokes, waving good-by. In a few days she stopped again and reached for a Coke but the Coke freezer was locked. Mr. Hammon walked over to her smiling as he unlocked it and held it open for her and told her to take two out. This day when she sat on his lap, she opened her legs and he smiled with the devil looking out of his eyes and she looked at him with eyes wide open to receive the devil.

It wasn't long before Lida Mae was not a virgin anymore and really liked Mr. Hammon. She had all the Coke she wanted to drink and kept a nice little piece of change in her pockets. She had new sweaters, blouses, skirts and shoes to wear. Things she had never had too much of except at Christmas, maybe. She didn't play with the boys her age anymore cause "she had a MAN," a grown man with money! She felt above her friends, girls and boys, until sometimes she forgot and played as hard as they did at games the way a young girl her age should have!

Mr. Hammon didn't care nothing bout no school; sometimes he told his wife he was going fishing instead of working and closed the garage and Lida Mae skipped school. He and Lida Mae stayed in back of the garage on the little cot Mr. Hammon had kept for such purposes for the last 20 years anyway. They drank Coke, only now they had whiskey in it and Lida Mae would get home drunk but nobody paid it no mind, there was so much else to pay attention to in a house full of nine grown and half grown kids: some of the older ones coming in drunk too. There were still some there that were 25 years old or bout! Just lazy, do-nothings most of them. Some bringing a wife or husband home or go live off with one and be back and forth so you sometimes didn't know who was living at home and who was not! Sissy didn't get drunk so much anymore after the doctor warned her. Just laid around and never smiled, eating and sleeping and getting fat, but when she did get drunk they gave her plenty space cause she would tell them to get their grown asses out of her house! Then, she would grab her coat and stagger out the door to they didn't know where and they didn't care where! Just don't mess with their lives! I'm sure the devil used to look in on the situation and be amused!

Lida Mae liked herself because she had more sense than to settle for boys who could only make babies. Mr. Hammon wouldn't do that to her! He gave her money too! Now, how you like that!? She smiled to herself. SHE had a future! She was gonna stop cutting school too! The teachers had spoken to her and she was getting ready to graduate, but she had missed a few tests and things that she had to make up! So! This was the last day she was going to let him talk her into cutting class in the afternoon, she thought to herself as she turned into the filling-station.

She was telling him that as he was undressing her, he was already undressed when he let her in the back door. She was also taking a drink of her Coke and whiskey as he laid her down and was kissing her beautiful body all over, loving its smoothness and softness. He excited her body and she put the drink down tho she wished he wouldn't hurry so! They were moving up an old road for him and a new and unfamiliar one for her.

BAM! The window next to the door was broken in and Mrs. Hammon looked through the opening! "Andy! Open this got-damn door!" She screamed, looking like a crazy woman in a frame. Mr. Hammon was speechless and could only stare at the broken window and shift his gaze to the door as she kicked it! He wished he could stop moving on top of Lida Mae, who was trying to push him off, but he couldn't. Lida was scared and wanted to run but he wouldn't stop and she began to have a climax just as Mrs. Hammon came through the window and lifted her knife and started trying to cut Lida Mae's face (which Lida hid with her arms) but cut her arms instead; then her husband was reaching for her, trying to stop her and hollering to Lida Mae to run! Get her things and run! Which Lida Mae, wide-eyed and frightened nearly to death and bleeding from numerous cuts, tried to do! She had to grab clothes, dodge the knife, open the door all at the same time. She was crying too and couldn't always see. Finally she got the door open and there were all those people who had heard the noise and come to see what was happening. Lida was naked and bleeding . . .

what a sight! She had just begun to run when the knife
flicked across her buttocks and she screamed as she ran into
the arms of Smokey who "just happened" to be standing
there with what looked like hate in his face. He grabbed her
and helped fight Mrs. Hammon off because Mr. Hammon
couldn't stay outside long with no clothes on, til he hit her
on the chin, knocking her out, and put Lida Mae in his car
to take her to the hospital.

They were almost there when he stopped the car near a
wooded area. He slapped her already bloody face saying
"Whatcha wanna go with that sucker for? I'm glad I told
on you cause that'll keep your ass away from there!!!" She
was in shock, so she couldn't say nothin as he wiped the
blood away from her face and kissed her as he removed
the clothes from her, laying her back. She started to struggle
and he said "I just saved your life, bitch!" He slapped her
again so hard her earring flew off through the window. He
made sex with her, dirty as she was, and bloody, then drove
her to the hospital and helped her go in. Needless to say she
carried those scars the rest of her life, the ones outside . . .
and the ones inside.

Lida Mae didn't get to her graduation. She did not want
anyone to see her again, ever. The doctor had sewn her up;
72 stitches on her arms and buttocks. They had also decided
to fix her insides (since she had already started trouble so
young) so she would not be bothering the state with bills
for children. She didn't know it, no one but the doctor and
the nurse did.

When she went home, she was so unhappy there, her
mother sent her to live with a sister of hers about 15 miles
away in another little town. Lida Mae was glad to go. She
packed her new long-sleeved blouses and the rest of her
things and left without looking back.

She was very quiet the first month or two she lived in the
new town. Going to church with her aunt who was very
religious. School was out, so she helped around the house
and with the few animals they had. Everything was fine and
Aunty was pleased cause Lida was no trouble at all and she
must be a good person cause the preacher started stopping
by two or three times a week to visit and he never had
before. He was watching his flock . . . he said.

Lida Mae knew why he was coming by cause he was

always touching her when it was accompanied by words of the Lord. But, she wasn't having any of that! She thought about the graduation she had missed and her future that had stopped. She didn't want to be a domestic or a waitress so she had to think of going back to school or something! Well, "something" came up first, in the person of a friend of her uncle's. A nice older man about 55 years old, James Winston. His wife had passed on and he had a house, car, some land and some money and even tho he had another girl friend, Josie B., he was falling in love with Lida Mae. He wanted to marry her.

Lida Mae took about a week to think about it. She kept picturing the house and the car. She could have her OWN! Her aunt kept urging her by saying, "HOUSE, HOUSE, HOUSE." Her uncle kept saying, "Money, money, money." So Lida Mae took her young, inexperienced, naive self and married him and went home to her house!

Now, in the country, if you don't work or have something to do, the time stretches out long, long, long. You fill the days with eating, gossip or making love. Lida Mae's largest outlet was gossip! She didn't really know she was gossiping, she thought she was just telling a friend the truth about what she thought. But people can take your truth and stretch it, twist it, tear it apart, turn it inside out and when you get it back, you are making enemies and when you try to straighten it out, you talk a whole lot more and give the people new ammunition to shoot back at you and then you have made more enemies! So the days come to be filled with stinky shit and then you don't feel so good (unless it's natural to you) and you don't always know why. Then, you go to church and sing and shout and get a little off your chest and then feel better all day Sunday . . . for awhile.

It wasn't long before Lida Mae was going with the preacher. She just seemed to move naturally into situations without much forethought, but she really hadn't ever known anyone who gave her any idea of how or why this was done; only a few teachers in school regarding the future through education, and there was so much in her life that diluted those urgings to wise decisions.

Lida Mae was kind tho, she was good to her husband. The house was clean, his meals were cooked, his clothes were clean, but he drank quite a bit now and was usually

sleeping it off nights. She was drinking more now and with
some kind of confrontation at least three times a week on
account of her mouth, she naturally turned to the preacher.
It made her feel the affair was O.K. with God. It wasn't
O.K. with God and it wasn't O.K. with Mrs. Preacher either
cause one night she came over to see Lida Mae and when
Lida Mae came to the door, Mrs. Preacher threw a pot full
of lye water in Lida's face. It was a good thing her aunt was
there; she cared for Lida's face and got her taken to the
doctor. Lida's skin was young and healed well but her eyes
were affected and they were cloudy and dim when she came
from the hospital. I went by to see her and she said to me
"Well, here I am, still young, done been cut up and now
almost had my eyes burnt up! I can see, but not much. Not
the things I want to see. Not the pretty world outside and
not my pretty clothes. I don't want to go anywhere again.
But, this is my house! I have given up a lot for it and done
a lot to it and I don't want to leave it again ever, tho I do
want to leave this town. I don't want no more of Mr.
Preacher either! Oh he calls, and comes around! But I
wouldn't open the door and if my husband let him in I went
in my bedroom and shut the door til he was gone!''

But time passed and soon everything was back to "normal?'' Lida Mae thought of school only briefly, just couldn't
get the grit up to go. Thought of eye operations, but since
she had to go out to some big city and she didn't want to
do that either and her husband didn't want to spend all his
money (course they wasn't his eyes) she didn't go. She seem
to be seeing a little better every day anyway.

Time went by and this Josie B., who used to be Lida's
husband's girl-friend, came to be friends with Lida Mae. I
could have told Lida she didn't mean her no good cause
Josie B. was still mad bout losing that house and money and
a man. But Lida Mae seem to listen to you, then when she
talked back to you seem like she ain't heard nothing you
said! Anyway they became friends and they started going
out together to these juke joints that they have round here.
Between that gossip and liquor and backbiting, Josie somehow got things fixed so one day when Lida Mae was high
and sitting on a stool in one of those joints, Leella and
Bertha jumped on her and beat Lida up! Even busting a
bottle cross her mouth so that she lost four or five teeth

right there in front. Well Lida Mae went right back in the
house again and stayed there and in church for three or four
months. She was about 20 years old now, but drinking so
heavy (used to send her husband to the liquor store every
day!) she looked like she was 50! Skin still smooth and all
but them eyes and that mouth and them scars! Lord have
mercy!

Then, one day, her husband stepped on a nail and only
soaked his foot and in two weeks he was dead! Josie B. and
Bertha came and sat outside the cemetery and laughed,
drinking in their car with hatred in Josie B.'s eyes. I went
to see Lida after the funeral, she was sitting on the screened
in front porch still in her black dress with a record playing
real loud saying "The sun gonna shine in my backdoor some
day!" I talked to her awhile and she said one thing; she say
"You know, I got this house, I got some money and a car
. . . but I keep trying to see, in my mind, would I rather
have my eyes, and my teeth . . . and my looks back and all
these scars off . . . I believe I rather have nothing if I could
just have myself back. OR SOME REAL LOVE! Ain't nothin
left for me but love. I'm all gone."

She was young, but she was old! And through! But somewhere inside of me I didn't think she had to be.

Something good happens to everybody and about a year
or so later a man came back to this town who had grown up
here. He came to see his mama and saw Lida Mae at church
(that's the only day she sobered up) and gave her his heart
and stayed longer than he had planned. She took him in,
used him, abused him . . . just tried to use that poor man
up! She seemed to be mean, mean, mean! He was a neat,
clean person with a little money, I guess, cause he was
always running to the liquor store for Lida or bringing her
candy, flowers and sweaters and things. Got her car fixed
and all the work in her house that needed a man's touch.
But she put him out every day when she through needing
him for that day, cussing him. Now, she was playing that
record bout the sunshine was coming in her back door some
day and here the sunshine was coming in her front door and
she didn't see it! Well, she was making him eat shit and
nothing but a fool want to eat the same thing every day so
he finally kissed his mama good-by and left, looking back,

but leaving anyway! Lida Mae say "He'll be back! I put some of this good stuff on him! He be back!"

But he never came back.

The years have passed and we have really sure nuff got old. Lida Mae looks like she is 150 years old and she is only 45 or so. I stop over to see her on my way to my son's house to get my grandchild sometime and she still be setting on the porch, drinking and she say things I don't know if I believe them. She say, "Life ain't shit, you know that? It ain't never done a fuckin thing for me!!"

When I leave, thoughts be zooming round in my head and I think of those words I got on a 15¢ postcard go like this:

Some people watch things happen.
Some people make things happen.
Some people don't even know nothing happened.

Then I go on over to pick up my grandbaby and thank God, ugly as I may be, I am who I am.

ELIZABETH CULLINAN grew up in New York City and environs, graduated from Marymount College in Manhattan, and went to work at *The New Yorker* for fiction editor William Maxwell. She says, "Working for William Maxwell was like nothing in this world except reading his novels; it made me a writer." Her first short story was published in *The New Yorker*, and since then she has published two volumes of short stories, *A Time of Adam*, from which "The Power of Prayer" is taken, and *Yellow Roses*. Her work has also been included in *The Best American Short Stories*, *Women & Fiction 2*, and *The Substance of Things Hoped For*. Her first novel, *House of Gold*, was awarded a Houghton Mifflin Literary Fellowship. In his review in *The New York Times*, Richard Elman praised the novel's Joycean rendering of the textures of ordinary lives. Maeve Brennan defined Cullinan's gift most precisely: she writes "a contemplative prose." Of the collection *Yellow Roses*, critic John Leonard wrote: "This book makes me feel better about the world. It hedges, as though to hide behind that hedge while careless thugs on black horses gallop by, but it seems essentially to endorse the uses of intelligence and the stamina of love. . . . When you can say in eight pages what most novelists have never been able to say at all . . . you are a first-rate writer. Elizabeth Cullinan is a first-rate writer."

While writing her most recent book, *A Change of Scene*, a novel reflecting the years Cullinan lived in Ireland, the writer received grants from The National Endowment for the Arts and the Carnegie Fund. She has taught at the Iowa Writers' Workshop, the University of Massachusetts, and Fordham University. The story that follows, "The Power of Prayer," shows her ability to trace the engraving and painful experiences of a young girl's perception of her parents' marriage. With a vision as bleak and as truthful as anything in Beckett (or, for that matter, in her fellow Irish-

Americans, William Kennedy, Ellen Currie, and F. Scott
Fitzgerald), Cullinan shows, too, the connection between
the girl's private domestic territory and the larger culture
beyond, of school and church.

———————————
❧

The Power of Prayer

❦

Elizabeth Cullinan

Nothing in their lives was natural any longer—that was what it amounted to. Nothing that touched them did not take on a certain kind of strangeness. That morning, the cold woke Aileen. She raised her head from the pillow and held it stiffly, straining her neck. Her eyes and her ears, her arms and legs and stomach—particularly her stomach—all were involved in the act of listening. There was no sound in the house, nothing but silence. A car passed. Three blocks away, on South Street, a bus went by. Aileen fell back onto her face, burrowing into the pillow and under the covers, tunneling down into softness and warmth.

"It's ten of seven," her mother said from the doorway. She stood there a moment, almost as though she were not quite sure what her next move should be, and then, when she saw Aileen push back the covers, she left.

The house was full of winter, the accumulated stuffiness of the long, cold months. Aileen stepped out of bed, picked up her underwear, and went out into the hall, looking neither to the left nor to the right, as though this were a strange house and she a timid guest. Safely inside the bathroom, she turned the big old-fashioned key in the lock; avoiding the face that looked out at her from the mirror, she ran the scalding hot and cloudy cold water, dipping her facecloth in one and then the other and rubbing it with a sliver of soap. She washed her face carelessly but gave great attention to the cleaning of her teeth, using a long ribbon of toothpaste and brushing hard, as though they would never be clean enough to suit her. Not taking any notice of her body (she was too thin, they told her—thin as a rail, skin and bones), she put on her underwear, threw her pajama coat about her shoulders, left the bathroom, and went over to her parents' bedroom. The bed was empty, and only one pillow had been slept on. The door of the spare room yawned upon a bed that hadn't been slept in at all.

So he hadn't come home; her father hadn't come home.

Feeling more at ease, she went back to her room and took a navy serge jumper and gray cotton blouse from their hanger. When she put on this drab uniform, the material fell into pleats where none were called for, and the sash went twice around her waist. (Too thin, she thought; too thin, too thin.) She combed her hair carefully, and left the room to begin the long descent through the house.

The kitchen, dining room, and furnace room were on the first floor, which was not quite as low as a basement but low enough to make it cold and damp and dark there. The second floor consisted of a front porch and two adjacent parlors separated by brocade portières. When Aileen came to the first parlor, where, the day before, she had left her school hat, she looked in and then sucked in a great breath of horror. There, fully dressed, his coat over him, his mouth open, sleeping deeply, snoring lightly, lay her father.

The wild scream of the teakettle rose and immediately was cut off. Aileen stepped back and closed the parlor door. The second flight of stairs was dark and crooked. At the bottom she stood perfectly still, listening to the silence that seemed about to break the house apart, and then she walked down the narrow hall and looked through the little diamond-shaped window in the upper part of the door. Her mother was sitting at the kitchen table. She held a glass of tomato juice in one hand; the other supported her head. Aileen went in and put her hand on her mother's back. Without looking up, Mrs. Driscoll took Aileen's other hand, rubbing her thumb over it and pressing the fingers between her own.

Aileen produced the words that the occasion demanded but that were, today, such a bad joke. "Happy birthday."

On the first Friday of every month at the Academy of St. Monica, Mass in honor of the Sacred Heart was celebrated in the school auditorium for the benefit of the students, the nuns having already attended their own service in the small chapel on the second floor of the convent. For most of the girls, this meant getting up half an hour earlier, leaving the house without eating, and spending the rest of the day in a state that was not dizziness, nor hunger, nor headache, nor nausea, but seemed to draw upon all of these and was in no way alleviated by the sweet bun and container of milk that the nuns distributed after Mass by way of breakfast.

Aileen had missed the seven-o'clock bus, and was the only girl from St. Monica's on the seven-fifteen. She would be late for Mass, she thought, as she fell into an empty seat. Damp air blew in through the open window, and Aileen could feel the curl leaving the ends of her hair. She raised her hands to her head to protect it, and rested her elbows on the stack of books that were balanced so carefully—first the loose-leaf, then the health book, then the thick English readings, and next to it the smaller grammar and Latin and algebra texts. As they rode up the slope of South Street, between the rows of frame houses, Aileen began to go over the story around which was built her first year of high school: My father doesn't come home . . .

The windows of the houses did not blink. The blinds were not flicked shut.

He doesn't come home until very late and sometimes not at all. I'd almost rather he *didn't* come at all, because then there isn't a quarrel. When there's a quarrel, they don't ever seem to remember me. It doesn't matter to them that I can hear the things they say. Sometimes I have to cover my ears.

The bus entered Main Street, but the sight of the stores did not distract her.

It started when he left his job at the insurance company, she went on. My uncle built two apartment houses, and he made my father the manager of one. He was going to manage the other, too—after a while—and then they were supposed to build some more together. They were going to be partners, and we were going to be very well fixed. But instead, just the opposite happened. We never have enough money, and we're way in debt. The thing is, she added, almost ashamed to be telling herself, my father goes to horse races. And he drinks. And my mother says there may be some woman . . .

After she had admitted those facts, she went over them
again, but they were still hard to believe. Those were things
she had heard people joke about—drinking, and gambling, and
the other. They weren't things that happened; they weren't
more powerful than love in a family, and a happy life . . .
My mother thinks we should leave him, she went on, enter-
ing the next phase of the story. Maybe she's right. I don't
know. I'm only fourteen. And he's my father . . . Waves of
self-pity began to rise inside her—high wave after high wave.
Only fourteen, she cried to herself. I'm only fourteen and
my father doesn't come home.

The bus passed Jessup Park, where two flocks of pigeons, rising into the air, began to drift over the trees in
wide, separate circles; then, they merged and flew together.
Aileen's arms were stiff from holding her hair in place, and
so she drew them down. The damage was done. It was already quite straight. As she watched the birds' exact, aimless flight, the force of her own unhappiness gradually
seemed to diminish and, almost calmly, she thought, If my
mother gets a separation, there'll only be one signature on
my report card. Mid-terms are next month. Everyone will
know.

Beyond the next corner was St. Monica's. Aileen stood
up and, trying to balance herself and the books, pulled the
cord and started toward the rear exit. She jumped from the
bus, then ran hard through the iron gates, under the arch of
St. Augustine, up the hill, past the statue of the Sacred Heart
that spread its arms in welcome, past the summerhouse at
the top of the hill, and over to the school building.

As the heavy door crashed behind her, the warning bell
rang from the auditorium ahead. Aileen slipped into one of
the back rows and dropped to her knees on the stone floor
just as the priest bent over the altar. The three long bells of
the Consecration rang. Make him come home tonight,
Aileen said again and again, as though concentration itself
were successful prayer. I beg of You. I plead with You.
Make him come home. Make him come home. *Tonight*.

A finger drummed sharply on Aileen's shoulder. Sister
Alphonsus Liguori stood over her, holding out a scrap of
thick net veiling. ''Where is your uniform hat, Miss Driscoll?'' the nun whispered.

* * *

Freshman Latin was the first class of Sister Alphonsus Liguori's day—the very worst time and the very least challenging subject, as far as she was concerned. On First Fridays the hour was almost more than she could endure. The girls who were not dozing were overexcited. The brash ones became reckless, the quiet ones dazed. The bright grew cocky and the slow seemed to come to a standstill. Sister Alphonsus waited outside the room until the class had filed in, and then she entered, hoping, as she always did, that the noise would automatically cease but it continued.

"Please, class," she said, tapping the bell that stood by her right hand. "The period has begun." She raised her hand to her forehead, waiting for the girls to follow the gesture. "In the name of the Father . . ." she began.

Until the year before, Sister Alphonsus had taught poetry at the College of St. Cecilia, which was near Ossining, and her work there had been remarkably successful. It was seldom that her students came away without at least honorable mention in any contests they entered.

However, she became, quite suddenly, subject to dizzy spells. She would have to leave a class and go to her room. Naturally, as she was first to recognize, the girls' work suffered. Sister Alphonsus' family was wealthy. Her brother wanted to send her to some convent abroad for a period of rest, and went so far as to draft a letter to the Mother Superior of the eastern province, but Sister Alphonsus decided against the plan. "I have taken the vow of poverty," she wrote him, "and it must now take me wherever it will."

She was sent to the Order's House of Rest on the tip of Long Island, and after a year there returned to teaching but on a different level. Mother General had decided that high school Latin would not be such a strain on Sister Alphonsus. The little girls required a much less strenuous program—their minds were less demanding. Sister would find them charming, and it would be in the nature of a homecoming for her to be stationed in Queens—just across the river from New York City, where she had grown up.

Elmhurst was not, of course, the world into which Sister Alphonsus Liguori had been born, and the little girls were, she soon discovered, timid or brazen, hostile or indifferent, dull or hypersensitive, but they had yet to show her their charm. Where was innocence, she wondered time and again.

Where were the open hearts and honest faces she had known as a girl? Sister Alphonsus was certainly no advocate of cosmetics for the young, and yet, as she looked at the rows of drab faces before her, she remembered that a little lipstick had always heightened the features of the older girls' faces. But these children—so unattractive, so intractable— what was *she* to do with them? She held her long, thin fingers pointed up in the attitude of prayer, then she drew her *Latin: The First Year* toward her and opened it to the third trial of Hercules. "In the words of the poet Vergil," she began, " *'Arma virumque cano,'* or 'I sing of arms and the man.' " It would do them no harm to encounter ahead of time what waited for a few (a very few) in Latin IV. "The assignment for today was, I believe, 'Hercules and Cacus.' Will everyone turn to page one hundred and fifty-seven, please?" Sister Alphonsus ran her hands over the glossy pages, pressing them down. "Ellen Gleason," she called. "Would you read for us the passage beginning with line three hundred and seventy-two?"

A tall girl with badly blemished skin stood up and began haltingly, " 'Leander,' he cried, hitting himself a blow to the forehead."

"One moment, Ellen." The nun ran her finger along the inside of her coif. "We must bear in mind, young ladies, a fact which I notice is in constant danger of slipping away from us—that is, that the Romans spoke as intelligently and as fluently in their language as we do in ours. Now, we wouldn't say today that someone hit himself a blow to the forehead, would we?" Sister Alphonsus realized, too late, that perhaps the gesture itself was eccentric. "Moreover," she went on, "we are dealing with literature, which is even more refined than ordinary speech. I think that a more accurate translation of the line, Ellen, would be, ' "Leander," he cried, smiting his forehead.' " She looked around at the class and saw a piece of paper fall to the floor and a hand reach down to retrieve it. Oh, the furtiveness of adolescence, she thought with despair.

"Will the young lady behind Miss Gleason be good enough to bring me the piece of paper she's holding?"

Sister Alphonsus watched Aileen Driscoll rise and come forward. It was always the bright students, she thought. That was the pity of it. Mixing with the bold ones, wasting their intelligence in proving themselves no better than the rest. "May I have the note?" the nun asked, holding out her hand to receive the scrap of loose-leaf paper. Sister Alphonsus opened it with great dignity. "Ha, ha," she read, "look who's singing of arms and men." She folded the note and tucked it up her sleeve. "Perhaps you could manage to come and see me, Aileen, at three o'clock, after your last class?"

"I have glee club, Sister."

"Well, immediately *after* that I should like you to report here to me." Sister Alphonsus wondered if the girl were going to burst into tears. Her eyes seemed quite terrified. But then again, the nun remembered, they could be callous enough when they wanted. "May I remind you, class," she said, "that this is a short period, to begin with. Please to waste no more of my time."

The sounds of the dispersing glee club were left behind as Aileen walked past the empty classrooms toward the one that was Sister Alphonsus Liguori's. The light of the overcast day threw the palest of shadows on the wide corridor, and the quiet of the cloister seemed to be seeping over into the school. The academy had been tacked onto what was once the strictly cloistered Convent of St. Monica, and the floor of the school wing sloped at the junction of the two parts. Aileen coasted down the slight grade and, looking up as she came to the door, saw the thin, waxen face of Sister Alphonsus Liguori.

"I wonder, Aileen," said the nun, "that you can't put your high spirits to some better uses than those you find at present." When she spoke, her eyebrows rose slightly as her face strained against the bandaging of her coif.

Aileen followed her into the room and waited while the nun stepped onto the platform and settled herself at the desk as though for class. With her waxen fingers, she folded back the wide sleeves of her habit. "The only excuse I can find for your actions of this morning is the one Our Lord Jesus Christ once offered on behalf of *His* detractors—that you knew not what you did." Sister Alphonsus thrust her chin out over the stiff white shelf beneath it. "*Do* you have any idea what this message involves?" She held out the note.

It didn't involve her, Aileen thought. She hadn't sent it, only received it.

"Since you don't seem to know whether you do or not, let me ask you another question. Can you tell me what is meant by sacrilege?"

"Destroying something that belongs to God," Aileen said.

"Can you give me an example?"

"Stealing a chalice, Sister?"

"That would be an instance, though a rather uncommon one. Wouldn't you say that nuns and priests belong to God more truly than any other person does? More truly, certainly, than a chalice?"

"Yes, Sister," said the girl. She often found it difficult to associate the nuns—their complicated clothes, their sweet smell of hand lotion, and the clatter of their rosary beads—with anything in her own mortal existence.

"Well, in view of this, do you realize how far more serious a remark of this sort is?" Holding the note between her first and second fingers, Sister Alphonsus Liguori wagged it in the air. "You see, it isn't my feelings alone that are involved. It's of little importance how this makes *me* feel. Look up, please, Aileen, when I speak to you." The nun pressed the tips of her fingers together. "It is your own immortal soul that is at stake."

Tears filled Aileen's eyes. She held her arm in front of her face.

"I'm gratified to see that you seem to recognize your error. That, of course, is the first step toward atonement." In the face of what might be genuine remorse, the nun was troubled. "Have you a handkerchief?" she asked.

Aileen shook her head.

Sister Alphonsus took an immaculate, perfectly folded linen square from some secret pocket in the skirt of her habit and held it out to Aileen. "The danger with *feelings* of penitence," she began kindly, "is that we allow them to take the place of those actions that are its true manifestation." She looked away while the girl blew her nose. "I know you're sorry for this insult, but now you must prove it. First of all, I should like to know, if you can tell me, why you're so ashamed."

Suddenly it seemed to Aileen that the story that lay in

readiness ought to be told. She was no ordinary offender. She came from a broken home. That was important. It made all the difference. "My father—" she began, but the words took her breath away. She had to stop.

Sister Alphonsus gave a short, discouraged sigh. "I'm afraid I don't see what your father has to do with it," she said. It was the deviousness of high school children that she detested most, and she had learned to be always on guard against it. "Well?"

Balanced on that narrow ledge hundreds of feet above the nun's upturned face, Aileen turned and crawled back to safety. "He's sick, Sister," she said. It couldn't be spoken about—not now, not ever.

Sister Alphonsus Liguori removed a speck of lint from the gaping jaw of her great sleeve. "I'm sorry to hear that," she said. "Is it a serious illness?"

"Yes, Sister."

"And is he in the hospital?"

"No, he's home."

"Just what seems to be the trouble?"

"They don't know, Sister."

"No diagnosis?" The nun raised her eyebrows, pushing her forehead into fold after fold of shining skin.

"Not yet."

"How long has he been stricken?"

"About six months."

"Six months and no diagnosis." The nun clicked her tongue. After all, it made no difference just now whether the father were sick or not. Her responsibility, in any case, was clear—contrite enough a moment ago, the child had now turned rather sullen. "Well, Aileen, it's a great pity that your father is unwell, and I hope he recovers quickly. I shall remember him in my prayers. But for the moment we must put this aside and return to our original purpose. Three times today you have offended against the virtue of reverence. You were late for Mass, your head was uncovered, and then this. Do you pray often?"

"Some." Aileen looked toward the gray-and-brown landscape outside. The rain had come. Against the background of the building she could see the first light drops.

"Not enough, I imagine. Like most of us, you probably don't spend nearly enough time at prayer. And so, instead of asking that you tell me whether or not you are the author of this message, and, if you're not, who is—instead of giving you a lesson to learn, and keeping you here for an hour—I'm going to have you accompany me to chapel, where you will please say a rosary in petition for an understanding of this important virtue of reverence. In addition,'' she added, ''you might offer up the time for the swift recovery of your father.''

The chapel was empty except for a nun who knelt before the altar with her arms outstretched in the form of a cross. Everything glittered or shone or was stiff and crisp, as though the nuns vied among themselves in the polishing of the sacred vessels. Sister Alphonsus blessed herself with holy water and turned to Aileen. "I leave you on your honor," she whispered, and then left.

Aileen knelt down in the second pew from the rear, and as she made the sign of the cross saw the penitent nun sway, then recover and straighten her position. Against the virtuosity of that prayer, she felt cheap and dishonorable, for what did she ever offer God but selfish petitions? She never prayed as the nuns recommended, for the missionaries, or the conversion of Russia, for the souls in Purgatory, or the poor and oppressed of the world. She asked nothing but favors for herself, and each time one was granted, she produced another—more difficult, more urgent. She leaned back against the bench, with her elbows on the pew in front. "Let me be reverent," she tried now, but the prayer flew off as she thought it. There was only one thing she could ask, one thing to pray about. She would have to take the chance. "Just this once," she said, "and I'll promise not to beg again. But let him come home tonight. Please, let him come home."

They waited dinner until seven-thirty. That was the far edge of their endurance—beyond that they could not hope. The two of them had learned how to pick their way through those long evenings of sadness, and the fact that it was Mrs. Driscoll's birthday did not interfere with their usual pattern but, instead, made the pattern more important. They ate fried fillet of sole with mashed potatoes that had stuck to the pot and string beans that were overcooked, too. Then, from a pound cake, Mrs. Driscoll cut one piece for Aileen and a sliver for herself, and while the girl ate away at hers, Mrs. Driscoll opened the flat package Aileen had put at her place. When she drew out the silk scarf, she began to cry, wiping her eyes with it.

Aileen stared across the table. All her feelings were pity and rage; all her thoughts were desperate. She wanted to rip the scarf in two and throw it away.

"What are we going to do?" moaned Mrs. Driscoll.

"If only there were something we could get him interested in—something we could all do together."

"What?" said her mother. "All he cares about is horse racing."

"Maybe *that*," Aileen said. "We could get him to take *us*."

"Why should I lower myself?"

"It might work."

"It wouldn't be worth it."

The pity and rage became loyalty. "We could try." He was her father. He *was* worth it. "And we could keep a lot of liquor in the house. Then he wouldn't have to go out."

"I always had such high ideals," Mrs. Driscoll said.

"It's going to be all right soon," Aileen said. She could never keep her mother interested in solutions; the trouble itself absorbed and distracted her. "It can't last," she added. "It has to stop sometime." She did feel that very strongly.

They did the dishes and then went upstairs, shutting off the lights behind them as though they were destroying clues. Only the hall lamp was left burning, to shed a pale orange light on the porch door and the staircase behind it. At the top of the last flight, Aileen kissed her mother. On a stand attached to the opposite wall was a statue of the Infant of Prague, dressed in real robes of taffeta and velvet, his tiny hand raised in a blessing. Perhaps He was the one she should have prayed to, Aileen thought. God had so many aspects, how could you choose among them—the Father, the Son, or the Holy Ghost; Jesus on the cross, Christ the King, transfigured and radiant, or the Sacred Heart, opening his chest for all to see the bleeding heart. "I think you ought to take a pill," she told her mother.

"I must. If I don't get some sleep I'll be physically unable to go on."

"Good night," Aileen said. She didn't mention the birthday; she would not have the tears start again. In her room she took off the uniform and, instead of putting on her bathrobe, got out her good outfit—a short black velveteen jacket and full blue tweed skirt—and put that on. Going over to the mirror, she ran the comb through her long hair—her very straight hair—and then began to pin it up. He had forgotten the birthday, she thought. That was it. When he remembered, he would realize what a terrible thing that was—so terrible that nothing could possibly ever be so bad again. When her hair was all pinned up, she took it down to try it another way—in a soft roll over each ear. If things could never again be this bad, they would have to get better. Her father was, after all, not as bad as some fathers, who were terribly strict and unfair. Sometimes, when she listened to him talking to people or watched the way he smoked a cigarette, she was very proud that he was her father; she loved him very much then. And besides he knew just how to make her laugh, and he had always been very kind. Aileen put the last pin in the right-hand bun, then looked straight at herself. He would be kind again. She would love him again.

She was feeling confident and almost easy when she heard the car door slam in front of the house. She went to the window and saw her father come up the path, bending against the rain but walking steadily. Her chest began to burn with unhappiness, and the bones of her back and shoulders seemed intensely painful to her. Oh, she thought, what a way to answer the prayer, God—to let him come home early, but not early enough!

The front door was shut hard, and Aileen heard him go downstairs. He would be checking the back door and the gas stove; even now he was very careful about those things. She listened as he began traveling up through the old house, putting out the hall light, moving on toward where she was. Well, she wouldn't notice him. She didn't have to. She went back to her dresser and picked up the hand mirror to look at the back of her hair. The part was crooked, and strands that were too short to be folded in with the buns hung untidily around her neck. It was not right, she saw. Not right at all.

He had climbed the second flight of stairs. He was there

at the top of the house now, and she heard him coming toward her room. He pushed the door open gently.

"Well, if it isn't Aileen," he said and smiled at her.

She would not be won by teasing. "Hello," she said quietly. She put down the hand mirror and, turning to the mirror on the dresser, seeing him and herself there, began to unpin the rolls over her ears. Wronged, waiting to be allowed to forgive, her feelings were suspended.

"Is your mother in bed?" he asked.

"Yes," Aileen said. She looked full at him and saw that he hadn't been drinking; there wasn't even that excuse.

"Asleep already?" His voice was mocking, and seemed to include her in the mockery.

"She took a pill." He had just forgotten. But she would not tell him. She would not be the one to accuse him. She was his daughter. She was only fourteen.

With his dark hooded eyes still on her, he yawned, then spoke gravely and, so it seemed, deliberately, as though they were discussing serious matters that would be important to her later on when she was older, when she was a woman. "How was the birthday?" he asked her.

MARY CROW DOG, née Mary Brave Bird, grew up fatherless in a one-room cabin, without plumbing or electricity, on a Sioux reservation in South Dakota. Her autobiography, *Lakota Woman,* records her memories of the oppression of Native Americans, the forms of self-destruction enacted by her people, and the liberation from this legacy of despair through the empowering practice of Native American religion and activist politics. The excerpt that follows here focuses on the spirit-killing rituals of growing up female and Native American on the impoverished margins of a racist mainstream America: the aimless drinking, high-speed car rides, petty thievery, and empty, random sex. Eventually Mary Crow Dog rejects these dead-end rites of passage and joins AIM, the new movement of tribal pride that swept Native American communities in the sixties and seventies. She marries Leonard Crow Dog, the movement's chief medicine man, who revived the sacred but outlawed Ghost Dance. *Lakota Woman* is an important document in Native-American literature, a story of determination against all odds, of the cruelties perpetrated against America's First Peoples for centuries, of a young woman's triumphant struggle to save herself in a hostile world. Phoebe-Lou Adams, reviewing *Lakota Woman* in *The Atlantic,* identified the source of Mary Crow Dog's transformation from a passive, exploited girl into a brave young woman: "As the wife of Leonard Crow Dog, the author knows a great deal about the revival of traditional religious practices which he leads, and her explanations of the purposes and effects of Indian rites are invariably interesting, because they introduce the reader to a system of belief that is, however unfamiliar, coherent and attractively generous." From the horrors of her childhood and adolescence, Mary Crow Dog saves herself—and is saved—by a connection with a spirit world unboundaried by self and historical bitterness. This straight-

forward narrative is well suited to accompany the study of
American history, Native American literature, women's literature, and eco-feminism. The author's recollections ex-
emplify the Cheyenne proverb that introduces her story: "A
nation is not conquered until the hearts of its women are on
the ground." Like Linda Hogan's story "Aunt Moon's
Young Man," this autobiography is an in-your-face response to the deterministic interpretations of oppressed and
marginalized cultures: Mary Crow Dog grows up uncon-
quered, a free spirit. As she puts it, "I am Mary Brave Bird.
After I had my baby during the siege of Wounded Knee they
gave me a special name—Ohitika Win, Brave Woman, and
fastened an eagle plume in my hair, singing brave-heart
songs for me."

Aimlessness

from *Lakota Woman*

❦

Mary Crow Dog

St. Francis, Parmelee, Mission, were the towns I hung out in after I quit school, reservation towns without hope. Towns that show how a people can be ground under the boot, ground into nothing. The houses are made of tar paper and almost anything that can be scrounged. Take a rusty house trailer, a small, old one which is falling apart. Build onto it a cube made of orange crates. That will be the kitchen. Tack on to that a crumbling auto body. That will be the bedroom. Add a rotating wall tent for a nursery. That will make a typical home, larger than average. Then the outhouse, about fifty feet away. With a blizzard going and the usual bowel troubles, a trip to the privy at night is high adventure. A big joke among drunks was to wait for somebody to be in the outhouse and then for a few guys to root it up, lift it clear off the ground, and turn it upside down with whoever was inside hollering like crazy. This was one of the amusements Parmelee had to offer.

Parmelee, St. Francis, and Mission were drunk towns full of hang-around-the-fort Indians. On weekends the lease money and ADC checks were drunk up with white lightning, muscatel—mustn't tell, purple Jesus, lemon vodka, Jim Beam, car varnish, paint remover—anything that would go down and stay down for five minutes. And, of course, beer by the carload. Some people would do just about anything for a jug of wine, of mni-sha, and would not give a damn about the welfare of their families. They would fight constantly over whatever little money they had left, whether to buy food or alcohol. The alcohol usually won out. Because there was nobody else, the staggering shapes took out their misery on each other. There was hardly a weekend when somebody did not have an eye gouged out or a skull cracked. ''Them's eyeballs, not grapes you're seeing on the floor,'' was the standing joke.

When a good time was had by all and everybody got slaphappy and mellow—lila itomni, as they said—they all piled into their cars and started making the rounds, all over the three million acres of Rosebud and Pine Ridge, from Mission Town to Winner, to Upper Cut Meat, to White River, to He-Dog. To Porcupine, Valentine, Wanblee, Oglala, Murdo, Kadokah, Scenic, Ghost Hawk Park—you name it. From one saloon to the other—the Idle Hour, Arlo's, the Crazy Horse Cafe, the Long Horn Saloon, the Sagebrush, the Dew-Drop Inn, singing forty-niner songs:

> Heyah-heya, weyah-weya,
> give me whiskey, honey,
> Suta, mni wakan,
> I do love you,
> Heya, heyah.

Those cars! It was incredible how many people they could cram into one of their jalopies, five of them side by side and one or two on their laps, little kids and all. The brakes were all gone, usually, and one had to pump them like crazy about a mile before coming to a crossing. There were no windshield wipers. They were not needed because there were no windshields either. If one headlight was working, that was cool. Often doors were missing, too, or even a tire. That did not matter because one could drive on the rim. There were always two cases of beer in the back and a few gallons of the cheapest California wine. The babies got some of that too. So they took off amid a shower of beer cans, doing ninety miles with faulty brakes and forty cans of beer sloshing in their bellies. A great way to end it all.

At age twelve I could drink a quart of the hard stuff and not show it. I used to be a heavy drinker and I came close to being an out-and-out alcoholic—very close. But I got tired of drinking. I felt it was all right to drink, but every morning I woke up sick, feeling terrible, with a first-class hangover. I did not like the feeling at all but still kept hitting the bottle. Then I stopped. I haven't touched a drop of liquor for years, ever since I felt there was a purpose to my life, learned to accept myself for what I was . . .

I started drinking because it was the natural way of life. My father drank, my stepfather drank, my mother drank—not too much, but she used to get tipsy once in a while. My older sisters drank, Barbara starting four years before me, because she is that much older. I think I grew up with the idea that everybody was doing it. Which was nearly true, even with some of the old traditionals who always pour a few drops out of their bottles and glasses, sprinkle it on the floor or into corners for the spirits of their departed drinking companions, saying in Sioux, "Here, cousin, here is a little mni-sha for you, savor it!"

I started drinking when I was ten, when my mother married that man. He was always drinking, so I would sneak in and help myself to some of his stuff. Vodka mostly—that's what he liked. In school I crept into the vestry and drank the church wine, Christ's blood. He must have understood, hanging out with people like us. At any rate no lightning struck me. The first time I got drunk was when some grown-up relatives had a drinking party. One woman asked me, "Do you want some lemonade?" I said yes and she gave me a big, tall glass of lemonade and put some of that stuff in it. That was my first time. I was trying to walk across the room and could not, just kept falling down, while everybody laughed at me.

Liquor is forbidden on the reservation, which is something of a joke, and drinking it is illegal. But towns like Winner, St. Francis, and Mission have a population which is almost half white and the wasičuns want to have their legal booze. So they incorporated these towns, which are within the reservation, putting them under white man's law. Which means that you have bars there and package stores. Also all around the reservation are the white cow towns with their saloons. Even if you are stuck in the back country, you can always find a bootlegger. My sister Barb was my best friend, the one who really loved me. She was the one who got me up in the morning and put clothes on me, watched over me. One day a boy took me to a John Wayne movie. Afterward we went "uptown" to hustle some hard stuff.

The town hardly had four or five streets, two of them paved, and maybe two dozen shacks and mobile homes sprinkled around, but it had an "uptown," and a "downtown." So uptown we went to the cabin of a half-blood bootlegger, getting ourselves a pint of moonshine, the kind they call "liquid TNT, guaranteed to blow your head off," and a small bottle of rum. As we were coming out of the door we collided with Barb, who had come to get her ration of wet goods. She made a face as if she couldn't believe her eyes and said, "What in hell are you doing here?"

I answered, "What are *you* doing here? I didn't know you patronized this place."

She got really mad. "It's all right for me. I am seventeen. But you are not supposed to be doing that. You are too young!" She took the bottles away from us, threatening to crack the head of the boy if he dared to interfere. In her excitement she smashed the bottles against the corner of the log cabin instead of saving them for herself and her friends.

Another time, after a school dance, I was sitting with a boy I liked, smoking a cigarette, and out of nowhere suddenly there was Barbara yanking the cigarette out of my mouth. She threw it on the floor and stomped on it right in front of everybody. I hit her, yelling, "But you do it." And again she said, "Yeah, but I'm older." We used to fight a lot, out of love and desperation.

After I quit school the situation at home got worse and worse. I had nothing but endless arguments with my mother and fights with my stepfather. So I ran away. At first only for two weeks to a place that was not very far, just a few miles, then I stayed away for months, and in the end, altogether. I drank and smoked grass all the time. At age seventeen that was just about all I did. Whiskey, straight whiskey, and not Johnny Walker or Cutty Sark either. Then I changed over to gin because I liked the taste. How I survived the wild, drunken rides which are such an integral part of the reservation scene, I don't know. One time we were coming back from Murdo at the usual eighty miles an hour. The car was bursting at the seams, it was so full of people. In the front seat were two couples kissing, one of the kissers being the driver. One tire blew out. The doors flew open and the two couples fell out arm in arm. The girls were screaming, especially the one at the bottom who was bleeding, but nobody was seriously hurt. I must have lost more than two dozen relatives and friends in such accidents. One of those winos was out in his car getting a load on. He had a woman with him. His old lady was in another car, also getting smashed. Somebody told her he was making it with that other woman. So she started chasing them all over Pine Ridge. In the end she caught up with them. I do not think they were lovers. He was at that stage where the bottle was his only mistress. His wife shook her fists at them, screaming, "I smash you up! I total you!" All the other drivers on the road who watched those cars drunkenly lurching about scrambled to get out of the way, running their cars off the highway into the sagebrush. Well, the wife succeeded in bringing about a head-on collision at full speed and all three of them were killed.

Supposedly you drink to forget. The trouble is you don't forget, you remember—all the old insults and hatreds, real and imagined. As a result there are always fights. . .

It seemed that my early life, before I met Leonard and before I went to Wounded Knee, was just one endless, vicious circle of drinking and fighting, drinking and fighting. Barb was caught up in the same circle, except that she was running with a different crowd most of the time. She was unusual in that she could drink just one beer or one glass of wine and then stop if she wanted to. Most of us at that stage could not do that. . . .

People talk about the "Indian drinking problem," but we say that it is a white problem. White men invented whiskey and brought it to America. They manufacture, advertise, and sell it to us. They make the profit on it and cause the conditions that make Indians drink in the first place. . . .

I was a loner, always. I was not interested in dresses, makeup, or perfume, the kinds of things some girls are keen on. I was scared of white people and uneasy in their company, so I did not socialize with them. I could not relate to half-bloods and was afraid that full-bloods would not accept me. I could not share the values my mother lived by. For friends I had only a few girls who were like me and shared my thoughts. I had no place to go, but a great restlessness came over me, an urge to get away, no matter where. Nowhere was better than the place I was in. So I did what many of my friends had already done—I ran away. Barbara,

being older, had already set the precedent. A clash with my
mother had sent Barb on her way. My mother was, at that
time, hard to live with. From her point of view, I guess, we
were not easy to get along with either. We didn't have a
generation gap, we had a generation Grand Canyon. Mother's values were Puritan. She was uptight. I remember when
Barbara was about to have her baby, mom cussed her out.
Barb was still in high school and my mother was cursing
her, calling her a no-good whore, which really shook my
sister up. Barb said, "I'm going to have your grandchild, I
thought you'd be happy," but my mother was just terrible,
telling Barb that she was not her daughter anymore. My
sister lost her baby. She had a miscarriage working in a
kitchen detail one morning. They gave her a big, heavy
dishpan full of cereal to carry and that caused it right there.
She lost the baby. She could not get over mother's attitude.

My older sister, Sandra, when she was going to have her
eldest boy, Jeff, my mother did the same thing to her, saying, "What the hell are you trying to do to me? I can't hold
up my head among my friends!" She was more concerned
about her neighbors' attitude than about us. Barb told her,
"Mom, if you don't want us around, if you are ashamed of
your own grandchildren, then, okay, we'll leave."

I understood how mom was feeling. She was wrapped up
in a different culture altogether. We spoke a different language. Words did not mean to her what they meant to us. I
felt sorry for her, but we were hurting each other. After
Barbara lost her baby she brooded. It seemed as if in her
mind she blamed mother for it, as if mother had willed that
baby to die. It was irrational, but it was there all the same.
Once mother told us after a particularly emotional confrontation, "If you ever need any help, don't come to me!" Of
course she did not mean it. She will stick up for us, always,
but looking over her shoulder in case her friends should
disapprove. To be able to hold up your head among what is
called "the right kind of people," that is important to her.
She has a home, she has a car. She has TV and curtains at
the windows. That's where her head is. She is a good, hardworking woman, but she won't go and find out what is really
happening. For instance, a girl who worked with mother
told her she couldn't reach Barbara at work by phone. Immediately mom jumped to the conclusion that Barb had quit

her job. So when my sister got home, she got on her case right away: "I just don't give a damn about you kids! Quitting your job!" continuing in that vein.

Barb just rang up her boss and handed the phone to mom, let her know from the horse's mouth that she had not quit. Then she told mother: "Next time find out and make sure of the facts before you get on my case like that. And don't be so concerned about jobs. There are more important things in life than punching a time clock."

There was that wall of misunderstanding between my mother and us, and I have to admit I did not help in breaking it down. I had little inclination to join the hang-around-the-fort Indians, so one day I just up and left, without saying good-bye. Joining up with other kids in patched Levi's jackets and chokers, our long hair trailing behind us. We traveled and did not give a damn where to.

One or two kids acted like a magnet. We formed groups. I traveled with ten of those new or sometimes old acquaintances in one car all summer long. We had our bedrolls and cooking utensils, and if we ran out of something the pros among us would go and rip off the food. Rip off whatever we needed. We just drifted from place to place, meeting new people, having a good time. Looking back, a lot was based on drinking and drugs. If you had a lot of dope you were everybody's friend, everybody wanted to know you. If you had a car and good grass, then you were about one of the best guys anybody ever knew.

It took me a while to see the emptiness underneath all this frenzied wandering. I liked pot. Barb was an acid freak. She told me she once dropped eight hits of LSD at a time. "It all depends on your mood, on your state of mind," she told me. "If you have a stable mind, it's going to be good. But if you are in a depressed mood, or your friend isn't going to be able to handle it for you, then everything is distorted and you have a very hard time as that drug shakes you up."

Once Barb took some acid in a girl friend's bedroom. There was a huge flag on the wall upside down. The Stars and Stripes hanging upside down used to be an international signal of distress. It was also the American Indian's sign of distress. The Ghost Dancers used to wrap themselves in upside-down flags, dancing that way, crying for a vision until they fell down in a trance. When they came to, they always said that they had been in another world, the world as it was before the white man came, the prairie covered with herds of buffalo and tipi circles full of people who had been killed long ago. The flags which the dancers wore like blankets did not prevent the soldiers from shooting them down. Barb was lying on the bed and the upside-down flag began to work on her mind. She was watching it and it was just rippling up the wall like waves; the stripes and the stars would fall from the flag onto the floor and would scatter into thousands of sprays of light, exploding all over the room. She told me she did not quite know whether it was an old-fashioned vision or just a caricature of one, but she liked it.

After a while of roaming and dropping acid she felt burned out, her brain empty. She said she got tired of it, just one trip after the other. She was waiting, waiting for something, for a sign, but she did not know what she was waiting for. And like her, all the other roaming Indian kids were waiting, just as the Ghost Dancers had waited for the drumbeat, the message the eagle was to bring. I was waiting, too. In the meantime I kept traveling.

I was not into LSD but smoked a lot of pot. People have the idea that reservations are isolated, that what happens elsewhere does not touch them, but it does. We might not share in all the things America has to offer some of its citizens, but some things got to us, all right. The urban Indians from L.A., Rapid City, St. Paul, and Denver brought them to us on their visits. For instance, around 1969 or 1970 many half-grown boys in Rosebud were suddenly sniffing glue. If the ghetto Indians brought the city with them to the reservation, so we runaways dragged the res and its problems around with us in our bedrolls. Wherever we went we formed tiny reservations.

"You are an interesting subculture," an anthropologist in Chicago told me during that time. I didn't know whether that was an insult or a compliment. We both spoke English but could not understand each other. To him I was an interesting zoological specimen to be filed away someplace; to me he was merely ridiculous. But anthropologists are a story in themselves.

It is hard being forever on the move and not having any

money. We supported ourselves by shoplifting, "liberating" a lot of stuff. Many of us became real experts at this game. I was very good at it. We did not think that what we were doing was wrong. On the contrary, ripping off gave us a great deal of satisfaction, moral satisfaction. We were meting out justice in reverse. We had always been stolen from by white shopkeepers and government agents. In the 1880s and '90s a white agent on the reservation had a salary of fifteen hundred dollars a year. From this salary he managed to save within five or six years some fifty thousand dollars to retire. He simply stole the government goods and rations he was supposed to distribute among the Indians. On some reservations people were starving to death waiting for rations which never arrived because they had been stolen. In Minnesota the Sioux died like flies. When they complained to their head agent, he told them to eat grass. This set off the so-called Great Sioux Uprising of the 1860s, during which the Indians killed that agent by stuffing earth and grass down his throat.

Then the peddlers arrived with their horse-drawn wagons full of pins and needles, beads and calico, always with a barrel of Injun whiskey under the seat. In no time the wagons became log-cabin stores, the stores shopping emporiums which, over the years, blossomed into combination supermarkets-cafeterias-tourist traps-Indian antiques shops-craft centers-filling stations. The trading post at Wounded Knee which started with almost nothing was, after one short generation, worth millions of dollars.

It did not take a genius to get rich in this business. There was always only one store in any given area. You got your stuff there or you did not get it at all. Even now, trading posts charge much higher prices than stores in the cities charge for the same articles. The trading posts have no competition. They sell beads to Indian craftworkers at six times the price of what they buy them for in New York and pay the Indian artists in cans of beans, also at a big markup. They give Indians credit against lease money coming in months later—at outrageous interest rates. I have seen traders take Indian jewelry and old beadwork in pawn for five dollars' worth of food and then sell it for hundreds of dollars to a collector when the Indian owner could not redeem the article within a given time. For this reason we looked

upon shoplifting as just getting a little of our own back, like
counting coup in the old days by raiding the enemy's camp
for horses.

I was built just right for the job. I looked much younger
than I really was, and being so small I could pretend that I
was a kid looking for her mother. If my friends were hungry
and wanted something to eat, they would often send me to
steal it. Once, early in the game, I was caught with a package of ham, cheese, bread, and sausages under my sweater.
Suddenly there was this white guard grabbing me by the
arm: "Come this way, come this way!" He was big and I
was scared, shaking like a leaf. He was walking down the
aisle ordering me to follow him, looking over his shoulder
every two or three seconds to make sure that I was still
behind him. Whenever he was not looking at me I threw
the stuff back into the bins as I was passing them. Just threw
them to both sides. So when I finally got to the back they
searched me and found nothing. I said: "You goddam red-
neck. Just because I'm an Indian you are doing this to me.
I'm going to sue you people for slander, for making a false
arrest." They had to apologize, telling me it had been a
case of mistaken identity. I was fifteen at the time.

There was a further reason for our shoplifting. The store
owners provoked it. They expected us to steal. Being Indian, if you went into a store, the proprietor or salesperson
would watch you like a hawk. They'd stand next to you, two
feet away, with their arms crossed, watching, watching.
They didn't do that with white customers. If you took a little
time choosing an item they'd be at your elbow at once, hovering over you, asking, "May I help you?" Helping you
was the furthest from their mind.

I'd say, "No, I'm just looking." Then if they kept standing there, breathing down my neck, I'd say, "Hey, do you
want something from me?" And they answer, "No, just
watching."

"Watching what? You think I'm gonna steal something?"

"No. Just watching."

"Well, don't stare at me." But still they were standing
there, following every move you made. By then the white
customers would be staring, too. I didn't mind, because I
and the store owners were in an open, undeclared war, a
war at first sight. But they treated even elderly, white-haired,

and very respectable Indians the same way. In such situations even the most honest, law-abiding person will experience a mighty urge to pocket some article or other right under their noses. I knew a young teacher, a college graduate, who showed me a carton of cigarettes and a package of Tampax with that incredulous look on her face, saying, "Imagine, I stole this! I can't believe it myself, but they made it impossible for me not to steal it. It was a challenge. What do I do now? I don't even smoke." I took it as a challenge, too.

While I was roving, an Indian couple in Seattle took me in, giving me food and shelter, treating me nice as if they had been my parents. The woman's name was Bonnie and we became close friends in no time. I managed to rip off the credit card of a very elegant-looking lady—the wife of an admiral. Ship ahoy! I at once took my friend to a fancy store and told her to take anything she wanted. I "bought" her about two hundred dollars' worth of clothes, courtesy of the navy. Another time I pointed out a similarly well-dressed woman to a store manager, saying, "I work for that lady over there. I'm supposed to take these packages to the car. She'll pay you." While the manager argued with the lady, I took off with the packages down the road and into the bushes.

Once I got a nice Indian turquoise ring, a bracelet, and a pin. I always admired the beautiful work of Indian artists, getting mad whenever I saw imitations made in Hong Kong or Taiwan. I learned to watch the storekeepers' eyes. As long as their eyes are not on you, you are safe. As long as they are not watching your hands. You can also tell by the manner in which they talk to you. If they concentrate too much on your hands, then they won't know what they are saying. It helps if you have a small baby with you, even a borrowed one. For some reason that relaxes their suspicions. I had no special technique except studying them, their gestures, their eyes, their lips, the signs that their bodies made.

I was caught only twice. The second time I happened to be in Dubuque, Iowa. That was after the occupation of Alcatraz, when the Indian civil rights movement started to get under way, with confrontations taking place between Indians and whites in many places. I had attached myself to a

caravan of young militant skins traveling in a number of cars
and vans. While the caravan stopped in Dubuque to eat and
wash up, I went to a shopping mall, saw a sweater I liked,
and quickly stuffed it under my Levi's jacket.

I got out of the store all right, and walked across the
parking lot where the caravan was waiting. Before I could
join it, two security guards nabbed me. One of them said,
"I want that sweater." I told him, "But I don't have no
sweater." He just opened my jacket and took the sweater
from under my arm. They took me back to the office, going
through my ID, putting down my name, all that kind of
thing. They had a radio in the office going full blast and I
could hear the announcer describing the citizens' concern
over a huge caravan of renegade Indians heading their way.
One of the guards suddenly looked up at me and asked,
"Are you by any chance one of those people?"

"Yeah," I told him. "They're just half a mile behind me
and they'll be here soon, looking for me."

He said, "You don't have to sign your name here. Just
go. You can take that damn sweater too. Just get out of
here!"

The incident made me realize that ripping off was not
worth the risks I took. It also occurred to me there were
better, more mature ways to fight for my rights. . . .

Sexually our roaming bands, even after we had been po-
litically sensitized and joined AIM, were free, very free and
wild. If some boy saw you and liked you, then right away
that was it. "If you don't come to bed with me, wincincala,
I got somebody else who's willing to." The boys had that
kind of attitude and it caused a lot of trouble for Barb and
myself, because we were not that free. If we got involved
we always took it seriously. Possibly our grandparents' and
mother's staunch Christianity and their acceptance of the
missionaries' moral code had something to do with it. They
certainly tried hard to implant it in us, and though we fu-
riously rejected it, a little residue remained.

There is a curious contradiction in Sioux society. The
men pay great lip service to the status women hold in the
tribe. Their rhetoric on the subject is beautiful. They speak
of Grandmother Earth and how they honor her. Our greatest
culture hero—or rather heroine—is the White Buffalo
Woman, sent to us by the Buffalo nation, who brought us

the sacred pipe and taught us how to use it. According to
the legend, two young hunters were the first humans to meet
her. One of them desired her physically and tried to make
love to her, for which he was immediately punished by
lightning reducing him to a heap of bones and ashes.

We had warrior women in our history. Formerly, when a
young girl had her first period, it was announced to the
whole village by the herald, and her family gave her a big
feast in honor of the event, giving away valuable presents
and horses to celebrate her having become a woman. Just
as men competed for war honors, so women had quilling
and beading contests. The woman who made the most beautiful fully beaded cradleboard won honors equivalent to a
warrior's coup. The men kept telling us, "See how we are
honoring you . . ." Honoring us for what? For being good
beaders, quillers, tanners, moccasin makers, and child-
bearers. That is fine, but . . . In the governor's office at
Pierre hangs a big poster put up by Indians. It reads:

> WHEN THE WHITE MAN
> DISCOVERED THIS COUNTRY
> INDIANS WERE RUNNING IT—
> NO TAXES OR TELEPHONES.
> WOMEN DID ALL THE WORK—
> THE WHITE MAN THOUGHT
> HE COULD IMPROVE UPON
> A SYSTEM LIKE THAT.

If you talk to a young Sioux about it he might explain:
"Our tradition comes from being warriors. We always had
to have our bow arms free so that we could protect you.
That was our job. Every moment a Pawnee, or Crow, or
white soldier could appear to attack you. Even on the daily
hunt a man might be killed, ripped up by a bear or gored
by a buffalo. We had to keep our hands free for that. That
is our tradition."

"So, go already," I tell them. "Be traditional. Get me a
buffalo!"

They are still traditional enough to want no menstruating
women around. But the big honoring feast at a girl's first
period they dispense with. For that they are too modern. I
did not know about menstruating until my first time. When

it happened I ran to my grandmother crying, telling her, "Something is wrong. I'm bleeding!" She told me not to cry, nothing was wrong. And that was all the explanation I got. They did not comfort me, or give horses away in my honor, or throw the red ball, or carry me from the menstruation hut to the tipi on a blanket in a new white buckskin outfit. The whole subject was distasteful to them. The feast is gone, only the distaste has remained.

It is not that a woman during her "moontime" is considered unclean, but she is looked upon as being "too powerful." According to our old traditions a woman during her period possesses a strange force which could render a healing ceremony ineffective. For this reason it is expected that we stay away from all rituals while menstruating. One old man once told me, "Woman on her moon is so strong that if she spits on a rattlesnake, that snake dies." To tell the truth I never felt particularly powerful while being "on my moon." . . .

. . . Looking back upon my roving days, it is hard to say whether they were good or bad, or whether I accomplished or learned anything by being endlessly, restlessly on the move. If nothing else, my roaming gave me a larger outlook and made me more Indian, made me realize what being an Indian within a white world meant. My aimlessness ended when I encountered AIM.

BEVERLY DONOFRIO grew up in Wallingford, Connecticut in a conventional and sexist Italian-American family. When she was in the tenth grade, her mother told her she would not be going to college. She urged her smart daughter, who wanted to go to the University of Connecticut and had the grades, to aspire to be a typist.

"Somebody would have to pay," thought the infuriated daughter.

Riding in Cars With Boys: Confessions Of A Bad Girl Who Makes Good, from which the following selection is taken, is the daughter's memoir of her teenage rebellion against sexual stereotyping, a dominating policeman-father and a subservient housewife-mother. Instead of becoming a typist, Donofrio turned up pregnant in her senior year of high school. Then she married and a short time later divorced. Her autobiographical narrative charts the zigzags of her growing up, alongside her young son, in and out of patterns of self-destruction and-creation. As a single mother, she constructed her salvation—and her child's—out of education, the old dream of the sassy tenth-grader. She went to a community college, transferred, with scholarship and son in hand, to Wesleyan, graduated, moved to New York, became a freelance writer, saw her son through Stuyvesant High School, and drove him off to college.

This story of teenaged pregnancy and single motherhood offers a darkly comic and painful experience of "family values" in the real context of small-town and urban, working-class America. In an article in *The Village Voice*, "Bad Girls Like Me" (January 21, 1992), Donofrio writes of the relevance of her story to contemporary teenagers:

Back in 1968, I became one of those infamous girls who got pregnant in high school. The experience was so traumatic I spent 10 years sorting out my feelings then spilling them on paper to write a memoir of my life as a teen mother and hippie on welfare who hits rock bottom before she finds a way to get herself to college. The book came out last year, and a little later I received a phone call from a woman with a distinct Long Island accent who introduced herself as Joanne Savio and told me she'd read *Riding in Cars With Boys* and wanted to invite me to read at her school.

The school is called EPPPA, Educational Program for Pregnant and Parenting Adolescents. What Donofrio told its students is the core wisdom of her book:

"Let's face it," I said, "you're handicapped, so you need to give yourself an edge." Basically, I told them that edge was education. . . . Education had saved my life.

Susan Minot, whose prep-school teenagers in her story "Lust" (page 203) offer an interesting contrast to the high school hoods of Donofrio's Wallingford, wrote of *Riding in Cars With Boys:* "A wonderful book! Beverly Donofrio writes with heart and a mischievous sense of humor. Her story has all the bad girl freshness and vitality to make it true to the bone."

❧

from *Riding in Cars With Boys: Confessions of a Bad Girl Who Makes Good*

❦

Beverly Donofrio

Trouble began in 1963. I'm not blaming it on President Kennedy's assassination or its being the beginning of the sixties or the Vietnam War or the Beatles or the make-out parties in the fallout shelters all over my hometown of Wallingford, Connecticut, or my standing in line with the entire population of Dag Hammarskjold Junior High School and screaming when a plane flew overhead because we thought it was the Russians. These were not easy times, it's true. But it's too convenient to pin the trouble that would set me on the path of most resistance on the times.

The trouble I'm talking about was my first real trouble, the age-old trouble. The getting in trouble as in "Is she in Trouble?" trouble. As in pregnant. As in the girl who got pregnant in high school. In the end that sentence for promiscuous behavior, that penance (to get Catholic here for a minute, which I had the fortune or misfortune of being, depending on the way you look at it)—that kid of mine, to be exact—would turn out to be a blessing instead of a curse. But I had no way of knowing it at the time and, besides, I'm getting ahead of myself.

By 1963, the fall of the eighth grade, I was ready. I was hot to trot. My hair was teased to basketball dimensions, my 16 oz. can of Miss Clairol hairspray was tucked into my shoulder bag. Dominic Mezzi whistled between his teeth every time I passed him in the hallway, and the girls from the project—the ones with boys' initials scraped into their forearms, then colored with black ink—smiled and said hi when they saw me. I wore a padded bra that lifted my tits to inches below my chin, and my father communicated to me only through my mother. "Mom," I said. "Can I go to the dance at the Y on Friday?"

"It's all right with me, but you know your father."

Yes, I knew my father. Mr. Veto, the Italian cop, who never talked and said every birthday, "So, how old're you anyway? What grade you in this year?" It was supposed to be a joke, but who could tell if he really knew or was just covering? I mean, the guy stopped looking at me at the first appearance of my breasts, way back in the fifth grade.

In the seventh grade, I began to suspect he was spying on me, when I had my run-in with Danny Dempsey at Wilkinson's Theater. Danny Dempsey was a high school dropout and a hood notorious in town for fighting. I was waiting in the back of the seats after the lights dimmed for my best friend, Donna Wilhousky, to come back with some candy when this Danny Dempsey sidled up to me and leaned his shoulder into mine. Then he reached in his pocket and pulled out a knife, which he laid in the palm of his hand, giving it a little tilt so it glinted in the screen light. I pressed my back against the wall as far away from the knife as I could, and got goosebumps. Then Donna showed up with a pack of Banana Splits and Mint Juleps, and Danny Dempsey backed away. For weeks, every time the phone rang I prayed it was Danny Dempsey. That was about the time my father started acting suspicious whenever I set foot out of his house. He was probably just smelling the perfume of budding sexuality on me and was acting territorial, like a dog. Either that or maybe his buddy Skip Plotkin, the official cop of Wilkinson's Theater, had filed a report on me.

Which wasn't a bad idea when I think of it, because I was what you call boy crazy. It probably started with Pat Boone when I was four years old. I went to see him in the movie where he sang "Bernadine" with his white bucks thumping and his fingers snapping, and I was in love. From that day on whenever "Bernadine" came on the radio, I swooned, spun around a couple of times, then dropped in a faked-dead faint. I guess my mother thought this was cute because she went out and bought me the forty-five. Then every day after kindergarten, I ran straight to the record player for my dose, rocked my head back and forth, snapped my fingers like Pat Boone, then when I couldn't stand it another second, I swooned, spun around, and dropped in a faked-dead faint.

I was never the type of little girl who hated boys. Never. Well, except for my brother. I was just the oldest of three girls, while he was the Oldest, plus the only boy in an Italian family, and you know what that means: golden penis. My father sat at one end of the table and my brother sat at the other, while my mother sat on the sidelines with us girls. You could say I resented him a little. I had one advantage though—the ironclad rule. My brother, because he was a boy, was not allowed to lay one finger on us girls. So when his favorite show came on the TV, I stood in front of it. And when he said, "Move," I said, "Make me," which he couldn't.

But other boys could chase me around the yard for hours dangling earthworms from their fingers, or call me Blackie at the bus stop when my skin was tanned dirt-brown after the summer, or forbid me to set foot in their tent or play in the soft-, kick-, or dodgeball games. They could chase me away when I tried to follow them into the woods, their bows slung over their shoulders and their hatchets tucked into their belts. And I still liked them, which is not to say I didn't get back at them. The summer they all decided to ban girls, meaning me and Donna, from their nightly softball games in the field behind our houses, Donna and I posted signs on telephone poles announcing the time of the inoculations they must receive to qualify for teams. On the appointed day they stood in line at Donna's cellar door. Short ones, tall ones, skinny and fat, they waited their turn, then never even winced when we pricked their skin with a needle fashioned from a pen and a pin.

By the summer of 1963, my boy craziness had reached such a pitch that I was prepared to sacrifice the entire summer to catch a glimpse of Denny Winters, the love of my and Donna's life. Donna and I walked two miles to his house every day, then sat under a big oak tree across the street, our transistor radio between us, and stared at his house, waiting for some movement, a sign of life, a blind pulled up or down, a curtain shunted aside, a door opening, a dog barking. Anything. Denny's sister, who was older and drove a car, sometimes drove off and sometimes returned. But that was it. In an entire summer of vigilance, we never saw Denny Winters arrive or depart. Maybe he had mononucleosis; maybe he was away at camp. We never saw him mow the lawn or throw a ball against the house for practice.

What we did see was a lot of teenage boys sitting low in cars, cruising by. Once in a while, a carload would whistle, flick a cigarette into the gutter at our feet, and sing, "Hello, girls." Whenever they did that, Donna and I stuck our chins in the air and turned our heads away. "Stuck up," they hollered.

But we knew the cars to watch for: the blue-and-white Chevy with the blond boy driving, the forest-green Pontiac with the dark boy, the white Rambler, the powder-blue Camaro, the yellow Falcon. I decided that when I finally rode in a car with a boy, I wouldn't sit right next to him like I was stuck with glue to his armpit. I'd sit halfway there— just to the right of the radio, maybe.

My father, however, had other ideas. My father forbade me to ride in cars with boys until I turned sixteen. That was the beginning.

"I hate him," I cried to my mother when my father was out of the house.

"Well, he thinks he's doing what's best for you," she said.

"What? Keeping me prisoner?"

"You know your father. He's suspicious. He's afraid you'll get in trouble."

"What kind of trouble?"

"You'll ruin your reputation. You're too young. Boys think they can take advantage. Remember what I told you. If a boy gets fresh, just cross your legs."

It was too embarrassing. I changed the subject. "I hate him," I repeated.

By the time I turned fourteen, the next year, I was speeding around Wallingford in crowded cars with guys who took corners on two wheels, flew over bumps, and skidded down the road to get me screaming. Whenever I saw a cop car, I lay down on the seat, out of sight.

While I was still at Dag Hammarskjold Junior High School, I got felt up in the backseat of a car, not because I wanted to exactly, but because I was only fourteen and thought that when everybody else was talking about making out, it meant they got felt up. That was the fault of two girls from the project, Penny Calhoun and Donna DiBase, who were always talking about their periods in front of boys by saying their *friend* was staying over for a week and how their *friend* was a *bloody mess*. They told me that making out had three steps: kissing, getting felt up, and then Doing It. Next thing I knew, I was at the Church of the Resurrection bazaar and this cute little guy with a Beatles haircut sauntered up and said, "I've got a sore throat. Want to go for a ride to get some cough drops?" I hesitated. I didn't even know his name, but then the two girls I was with, both sophomores in high school, said, "Go! Are you crazy? That's Skylar Barrister, the president of the sophomore class." We ended up with two other couples parked by the dump. My face was drooly with saliva (step one) when "A Hard Day's Night" came on the radio and Sky placed a hand on one of my breasts (step two). Someone must've switched the station, because "A Hard Day's Night" was on again when his hand started moving up the inside of my thigh. I crossed my legs like my mother said, but he uncrossed them. Lucky for me, there was another couple in the backseat and Sky Barrister was either too afraid or had good enough manners not to involve them in the loss of my virginity or I really would've been labeled a slut. Not that my reputation wasn't ruined anyway, because sweetheart Sky broadcast the news that Beverly Donofrio's easy—first to his friends at the country club and then, exponentially, to the entire town. Hordes of boys called me up after that. My father was beside himself. I was grounded. I couldn't talk on the phone for more than a minute. My mother tried to intervene. "Sonny," she said. "You have to trust her."

"I know what goes on with these kids. I see it every day, and you're going to tell me?"

"What's talking on the phone going to hurt?" my mother asked.

"You heard what I said. I don't want to hear another word about it. You finish your phone call in a minute, miss, or I hang it up on you. You hear me?"

I heard him loud and clear, and it was okay with me—for a while, anyway, because my love of boys had turned sour. Sophomore year in high school, my English class was across the hall from Sky Barrister's and every time I walked by, there was a disturbance—a chitter, a laugh—coming from the guys he stood with. My brother was the captain of the football team and I wished he was the type who'd slam Sky Barrister against a locker, maybe knock a couple of his teeth out, but not my brother. My brother was the type who got a good-citizenship medal for never missing a single day of high school.

Meanwhile, his sister began to manifest definite signs of being a bad girl. My friends and I prided ourselves on our foul mouths and our stunts, like sitting across from the jocks' table in the cafeteria and giving the guys crotch shots, then when they started elbowing each other and gawking, we shot them the finger and slammed our knees together. Or we collected gingerbread from lunch trays and molded them into shapes like turds and distributed them in water fountains.

The thing was, we were sick to death of boys having all the fun, so we started acting like them: We got drunk in the parking lot before school dances and rode real low in cars, elbows stuck out windows, tossing beer cans, flicking butts, and occasionally pulling down our pants and shaking our fannies at passing vehicles.

But even though we were very busy showing the world that girls could have fun if only they'd stop acting nice, eventually it troubled us all that the type of boys we liked—collegiate, popular, seniors—wouldn't touch us with a ten-foot pole.

One time I asked a guy in the Key Club why no guys liked me. "Am I ugly or stupid or something?"

"No." He scratched under his chin. "It's probably the things you say."

"What things?"

"I don't know."

"You think it's because I don't put out?"

"See? You shouldn't say things like that to a guy."

"Why?"

"It's not right."

"But why?"

"I don't know."

"Come on, is it because it's not polite or because it's about sex or because it embarrasses you? Tell me."

"You ask too many questions. You analyze too much, that's your problem."

To say that I analyzed too much is not to say I did well in school. Good grades, done homework—any effort abruptly ended in the tenth grade, when my mother laid the bad news on me that I would not be going to college. It was a Thursday night. I was doing the dishes, my father was sitting at the table doing a paint-by-numbers, and we were humming "Theme from Exodus" together. My mother was wiping the stove before she left for work at Bradlees, and for some reason she was stinked—maybe she had her period, or maybe it was because my father and I always hummed while I did the dishes and she was jealous. Neither of us acknowledged that we were basically harmonizing. It was more like it was just an accident that we were humming the same song. Our favorites were " 'Bye 'Bye Blackbird," "Sentimental Journey," "Tonight," and "Exodus." After "Exodus," I said, "Hey, Ma. I was thinking I want to go to U Conn instead of Southern or Central. It's harder to get into, but it's a better school."

"And who's going to pay for it?"

It's odd that I never thought about the money, especially since my parents were borderline paupers and being poor was my mother's favorite topic. I just figured, naively, that anybody who was smart enough could go to college.

"I don't know. Aren't there loans or something?"

"Your father and I have enough bills. You better stop dreaming. Take typing. Get a *good* job when you graduate."

"I'm not going to be a secretary."

She lifted a burner and swiped under it. "We'll see," she said.

"I'm moving to New York."

"Keep dreaming." She dropped the burner back down.

So I gritted my teeth and figured I'd have to skip college and go straight to Broadway, but it pissed me off. Because I wasn't simply a great actress, I was smart too. I'd known this since the seventh grade, when I decided my family was made up of a bunch of morons with lousy taste in television. I exiled myself into the basement recreation room every night to get away from them. There were these hairy spiders down there, and I discovered if I dropped a Book of Knowledge on them they'd fist up into dots, dead as doornails. Then one night after a spider massacre, I opened a book up and discovered William Shakespeare—his quality-of-mercy soliloquy, to be exact. Soon I'd read everything in the books by him, and then by Whitman and Tennyson and Shelley. I memorized Hamlet's soliloquy and said it to the mirror behind the bar. To do this in the seventh grade made me think I was a genius. And now, to be told by my mother, who'd never read a book in her life, that I couldn't go to college was worse than infuriating, it was unjust. Somebody would have to pay.

That weekend my friends and I went around throwing eggs at passing cars. We drove through Choate, the ritzy prep school in the middle of town, and I had an inspiration. "Stop the car," I said. "Excuse me," I said to a little sports-jacketed Choatie crossing Christian Street. "Do you know where Christian Street is?"

"I'm not sure," he said, "but I think it's that street over there." He pointed to the next road over.

"You're standing on it, asshole!" I yelled, flinging an egg at the name tag on his jacket. I got a glimpse of his face as he watched the egg drool down his chest and I'll remember the look of disbelief as it changed to sadness till the day I die. We peeled out, my friends hooting and hollering and slapping me on the back.

I thought I saw a detective car round the bend and follow us down the street, but it was just my imagination. Now that my father'd been promoted from a regular cop to a detective, it was worse. Believe me, being a bad girl and having my father cruising around in an unmarked vehicle was no picnic. One time, I'd dressed up as a pregnant woman, sprayed gray in my hair, and bought a quart of gin, then went in a motorcade to the bonfire before the big Thanksgiving football game. We had the windows down even though it was freezing out and were singing "Eleanor Rigby" when we slammed into the car in front of us and the car in back slammed into us—a domino car crash. We all got out; there was no damage except a small dent in Ronald Kovacs's car in front. He waved us off, and we went to the bonfire.

Back home, I went directly to the bathroom to brush my teeth when the phone rang. In a minute my mother called, "Bev, your father's down the station. He wants to see you."

My heart stalled. "What about?"

"You know him. He never tells me anything."

I looked at myself in the mirror and said, "You are not drunk. You have not been drinking. You have done nothing wrong, and if that man accuses you, you have every reason in the world to be really mad." This was the Stanislavsky method of lying, and it worked wonders. I considered all my lying invaluable practice for the stage. There were countless times that I maintained not only a straight but a sincere face as my mother made me put one hand on the Bible, the other on my heart, and swear that I hadn't done something it was evident to the entire world only I could have done.

My father sat me in a small green room, where he took a seat behind a desk. "You were drinking," he said.

"No I wasn't," I said.

"You ever hear of Ronald Kovacs?"

"Yes. We were in a three-car collision. He slammed on his brakes in the middle of the motorcade, and we hit him."

"It's always the driver in the back's fault, no matter what the car in front does. That's the law. Maybe your friend wasn't paying too much attention. Maybe you were all loaded."

"You always think the worst. Somebody hit us from behind too, you know."

"Who was driving your car?"

"I'm not a rat like that jerk Kovacs."

"That's right. Be a smart ass. See where it gets you. I already know who was operating the vehicle. You better be straight with me or your friend, the driver, might end up pinched. It was Beatrice?"

"Yes."

"She wasn't drinking but you were?"

"*No*! Did you ever think that maybe Ronald Kovacs was drinking? Did you ever think that maybe he's trying to cover his own ass?"

"Watch your language."

I put on my best injured look and pretended to be choking back tears. It was easy because I was scared to death. Cops kept passing in the hall outside the door to the office. I was going out on a limb. If they found concrete evidence that I'd been drinking, my father would really be embarrassed. He might hit me when we got home, and I'd definitely be grounded, probably for the rest of my life.

"They're setting up the lie detector in the other room. We got it down from Hartford for a case we been working on," he said. "Will you swear on the lie detector that you're telling the truth?"

A bead of sweat dripped down my armpit. "Good. And bring in Ronald Kovacs and make him take it, too. Then you'll see who's a liar."

Turns out there was no lie detector; it was a bluff and I'd won the gamble.

When I got him, I played it for all it was worth with my mother. "He never trusts me. He always believes the worst. I can't stand it. How could you have married him?"

"You know your father. It's his nature to be suspicious."

"I wish he worked at the steel mill."

"You and me and the man in the moon. Then maybe I could pay the doctor bills. But that's not your father. He wanted to be a cop and make a difference. He didn't want to punch a time clock and have a boss looking over his shoulder."

When I was four, before my father became a cop, he pumped gas at the garage on the corner, and every day I brought him sandwiches in a paper bag. He'd smile like I'd just brightened his day when he saw me, then I sat on his lap while he ate. Sometimes I fell asleep, leaning my head against his chest, lulled by the warmth of his body and the rumble of trucks whooshing past. Sometimes I traced the red-and-green American Beauty rose on his forearm. I thought that flower was the most beautiful thing in the world back then. Now it was gray as newsprint, and whenever I caught a glimpse of it, I turned my eyes.

"You should've told him not to be a cop," I said. "It's ruining my life."

"It's not up to the wife to tell the husband what to do," my mother said.

"He tells you what to do all the time."

"The man wears the pants in the family."

"I'm never getting married."

"You'll change your tune."

"And end up like you? Never in a million years."

"You better not let your father catch you talking to me like that."

KATHERINE DUNN writes of her youth in the afterword of her most recent novel *Geek Love,* which was nominated for the National Book Award:

My background is standard American blue collar of the itchy-footed variety. We're new world mongrels. The women in the family read horoscopes, tea leaves, coffee bubbles, Tarot cards, and palms. My mother is an escaped farm girl from North Dakota and a self-taught artist and painter. My dad was a third-generation printer and linotype operator, by all accounts a fabulous ballroom dancer. He was jettisoned from the family before I was two and I have never met him and have no memory of him. The story is that my older brother, 13 or so at the time, ran him out of the house with a kitchen knife for speaking roughly to our beloved Mom. I was born in Garden City, Kansas, on the day the U.N. treaty was signed, October 24, 1945, the only girl in a family of boys who spoiled me and taught me to swim, use a slingshot (for keeping one's distance in a fight), climb trees, and ride motorcycles. We were migrant workers during my early years. . . .

Dunn now lives in Portland, Oregon where she attended Reed College and which is also the hometown of her fictional alter ego Jean "Dutch" Gillis, the protagonist of the novel *Truck,* from which the following excerpt is taken. Dunn's published writing includes the novels *Attic* (1970), *Truck* (1971), and *Geek Love* (1989). All her fiction has been highly praised for its tremendous force, its bawdy and bitter imagination, and its dangerous realism. Dunn has written of her work: "I have been a believer in the magic of language since, at a very early age, I discovered that some words got me into trouble and others got me out. . . .

There are other inclinations that have shaped the form and direction of my work: rampant curiosity, a cynical inability to accept face-values balanced by lunatic optimism, and the preoccupation with the effervescing qualities of truth that is probably common to those afflicted by absent-mindedness, prevarication, and general unease in the presence of facts. But the miraculous nature of words themselves contains the discipline. Writing is, increasingly, a moral issue for me. . . . The determination required for honest exploration and analysis of the human terrain is often greater than I command. But the fruits of that determination seem worthy of all my efforts.''

In the novel *Truck,* Dunn takes us on a journey into the mind of a feisty, adventurous adolescent nicknamed ''Dutch'' who goes ''trucking'' from Portland to Los Angeles on a quest in search of herself. In the words of the reviewer in *The New Yorker,* the novel comes alive in its rendering of the confusion and volatile feelings of youth, when sex is a mystery waiting to be understood. *Truck* is ''a modern classic,'' in the words of another critic, ''insistently, almost overwhelmingly real.'' Readers might enjoy comparing Dunn's runaway with the other protagonists in this collection who hit the road or leave behind dead-end lives or relationships: see the selections by Beverly Donofrio (page 67), Linda Hogan (page 117), R.A. Sasaki (page 226), and Diane Levenberg (page 179).

❧

from *Truck*

🐾

Katherine Dunn

H e's gone. Left today. Took the bus to L.A. Two and a half months till school lets out. Got to get money. Got to get out of here. Two and a half months. Get out the lists and unfold them.

Ways to make money

Sell things I have
Steal things and sell them
Put jars in the halls with "Save Dutch Fund" on 'em
Lunch money
Pop bottles
Old tires to recapper
Copper wire
Write papers for people
Mow lawns
Baby-sit

Things to steal and sell

Books (from school and downtown library to kids and secondhand bookshops)
Cakes (from cake sales to wrestling team after they weigh in)
Hubcaps (from parking lot during games etc. to??)
Nylons (from dept. stores to girls at school)
Cigarettes (to boys at school)

Typewriter? (from old Birdsing—pawnshop?)
Also: nick change while tending popcorn stand at home
games

Things to take along

      hatchet
      matches (waterproof and regular)
      rope
x   string
      back pack
x   extra socks (two pair)
x   sweatshirt
x   extra dungarees
x   Band-aids
x   antiseptic (iodine, alcohol, something for burns,
      vaseline)
      knife
      canteen
x   underpants (two pair)
      sleeping bag
      compass
      fishhooks
      poncho
x   needle and strong thread
      boots (good hiking boots)
x   flashlight (batteries)
      jacket
      notebook (pencils)

x   —things I have or can get from home

Wait till it's almost time to start accumulating things.
Some of it too noticeable around the house. Could keep it
in my locker at school. Do that. Keep it there till the very
end. Leave right after school lets out. No use hanging
around after. Maw'd just start making plans for me.

Sold the skates to the rink today. Fifteen dollars. Minus
bus fare, $14.70.

Jake doesn't notice anything. Carry books out by the armload and he just sits there playing with his tie. A good *Crime
and Punishment, Don Quixote, The Great Books: Marx.*

School library books are easier to cover up than the downtown library's. Downtown they put a stamp on damn near every page. Six dollars from the secondhand bookstore on Third Avenue. $5.85 in the pot.

Fourteen pairs of nylons. Size 8, 10 and 11, medium. $7.00 in the pot.

The jars in the hall are amazing. A steady fifty cents a day. Maybe they don't read the card and think it's for a worthy cause. Maybe they think it's a good joke. Just pennies. Once in a while a nickel or a dime. All adds up.

Gave Monica her take-off on Charles Lamb today. All about how Joe Nestle, the cowherd, got drunk and let the cows eat cocoa beans. Milk came out brown. Villagers punished him by making him drink the spoiled milk. Eureka! Disgusting. Monica loved it. Get her a B if she fixes up the spelling and punctuation. $5.00.

Tried to get a typewriter out of the Business classes tonight. Birdsing always leaves the window open a little. Walked all the way out there. Got in O.K. But the typing room was locked. Tried an adding machine instead. Ninety pounds. Got it out the window and into the trees. Took me about an hour. Dragged it part way. Dirt and shit in the works. Probably no good now. Left it in some bushes. Even if it doesn't do me any good it'll hassle old "J.K.L. Semi" Birdsing. Nothing in the pot though.

Sixty-four dollars. Had it in an old shoe in my closet. Dumb. Maw found it today cleaning and came into the living room waving it and looking hysterical. "Where did you get this much money?" She thought I stole it from Dad or robbed a bank or something. I was sitting in the fireplace picking my nose. "Well, Maw, I've been saving it for a long time. From the telephone job and lunch money sometimes. Stuff like that. It's for my education." Very clever I think. True too. My education. She got all happy I'm being so wise. Sits down on the floor in front of the fireplace with her bandanna wrapped around her head like Aunt Jemima. Am I going to college or what? Yeah, maybe, or art school.

Haven't really decided. We sat jawing about things like that till she hadda get up get dinner. Gave me back the sixty-four dollars. Find a better place to put it.

I told Leben I'm running away. Made her swear not to tell of course. If anybody asks her she'll blab her brains. Told her I was going to the Mission Mountains in Montana. Near a little town called St. Ignatius. Saw the mountains on the map when I was looking to see Missoula, where Heydorf was. St. Ignatius is just about a ghost town. Looked him up. Patron saint of thieves and travelers. That's me. Told her all about how I'd live in the mountains. Build a log cabin. Fish and hunt and trap. Be a hermit. Got kind of excited about it. Do all that, only down south.

Cecilia, Vince's little sister, bought four paperbacks and my transistor radio when I told her about running away to the Mission Mountains. She swore not to tell. Holy hair. Probably won't. She goes hiking a lot. Says she's got boots I can borrow. She's a lot taller. Five six maybe. But her feet are the same size as mine. Look at the boots tomorrow. Get her money.

Great boots. Infantry boots, high ankles, thick hard rubber soles, hooks for the laces and two leather straps around the top. Great. Told her I'd get 'em from her just before school lets out. They just fit. A dollar for the paperbacks and three-fifty for the radio. She got a letter from Vince in the navy. He likes it. Shoulda known.

Pietila called me in again about wearing dungarees to school. Told him I was poor and he said he'd be glad to arrange for clothes from some charity or other. Said thanks but I don't take charity. Got a roll of air mail stamps out of his petty cash drawer while he was making a call. Six dollars from Mrs. Martin at the grocery store. Told her it was for a charity. People are dumb.

Lot of trips to the secondhand bookstore. The guy in the Green Dolphin got suspicious. Won't take anymore. Have to go all the way across town to the Academy.

* * *

There's going to be an end of the year party. Mostly seniors but underclassmen can go too. Two days at Mt. Hood. Whole ski lodge. Swimming pool. Lots of food. Tobogganing. Figure I'll tell Maw I'm going to that. Have two days' head start before they start looking for me. Twenty-five dollars a head.

Told Maw about the party. She didn't like it at first but I explained how it's sponsored by the school and loaded with chaperones and all that. Told her it was ten dollars and I'd pay it myself out of my savings. She wanted to pay it but I said I wanted to and now she wants to buy me a dress for it. Aarg. Get out of that somehow. Tell her everybody's wearing pants. Something.

Time running short. Letter from Heydorf. He's staying at the Pasadena Y.M.C.A. Told me to call him when I get into the bus station. "And watch out for Mexicans who want to sell you a diamond ring for sixty bucks. They might rob you and whatever else they do to girls." So he'll meet me. It's easier that way. Feel all mushy toward Maw lately. Try to be good to her since I'm leaving.

Everybody's gone but me. Vince in the navy. Fred and Pete off in college. Heydorf in L.A. All these turds in school really get on my nerves. Never go back to school again. Sit off in my cozy cabin with a kerosene lamp and a fire and read whatever I want. Never have to count the iambic this-and-thats. Never diagram another sentence. Never try to figure out what some asshole teacher thinks is the meaning of a story. "The river is life and the river is death." My ass. My royal Irish asshole. Stupid sons of bitches. I'm passing everything but P.E. and Algebra. Two Cs, three Ds, and two Fs. That's the way it looks now. Might run into trouble.

Teddie Mote decided he's my friend. He hunts and fishes and goes camping a lot so I told him how I'm running off to the Mission Mountains. He thinks it's fantastic. Swore not to tell. He will when they ask but he's loaning me all sorts of camping gear. Told me how more than anything else he wants a son. I didn't laugh because he's loaning me all this stuff.

Maw wouldn't listen to reason about the party dress. Took me downtown after school today and bought it. I wouldn't look at 'em. She picked it out and made me try it on and she bought it. Pink. Cotton at least but pink. No sleeves. My freckledy old arms stick out like a turd in a pan of milk. At least it hasn't got any gewgaws on it and there's a pretty good pocket. I suppose I'll have to wear the damn thing to leave in. White god-awful shoes. Gold heels and pointy toes. Fall off when I walk fast. Hurt my toes. And this underskirt with lace on it and darts for tits. An insult. But she couldn't find any with lace that didn't have the tits in. I kept telling her everybody was wearing pants but she called Leben's mother and they conspired. She gave up trying to make me wear skirts to school a long time ago. I kept skipping. Hid down under the bridge all day so nobody'd see me in a skirt. But she figures this once I'll wear a pretty pink dress. That'll learn her.

Dad's brandy about half water now. Have to lay off it. The football team isn't even used to beer. Watered-down apricot brandy knocks them on their asses. $20.00.

All my books gone. Maw asked what I did with them. Told her I'd loaned some out and given the rest to the Fireman's Christmas Fund. She gave me some of hers to donate. Down to the secondhand bookstore again.

Letter from Heydorf. He's getting a .22 pistol. Wants me to get a pile of ammo from his basement to bring to him. Have to raid the place. His mother doesn't like me. Thinks I'm a bad influence. Get Teddie Mote to drive me out. Very handy since he's decided he's my friend.

"You gotta stay right here. Keep the motor running. Getaway car. See?" He's chicken shit. Two blocks away and his face is white and his eyes are bugging. Dark and I run soft on the sidewalk. A little white house. A little grass and a lot of other little white houses. Down the driveway. Concrete steps down to the basement. Dark. Window isn't latched. Slip the screwdriver under and there's no car in the drive. Gone to the movies. Window's up and I slide in. Sink. My feet in a big zinc sink. Step out and down a long ways. Turn on the flashlight. Shelves of canned fruit. Peaches and pears and cherries all golden and pink and cobwebs. Cement floor. Over against the wall, rake hanging up and hose and beneath, on the floor, two piles. A tarp over each one. A little card pinned to each one. The one to the left reads "Leave me." Heydorf's square printing. The one on the right says "Take me." He planned it before he left. Spread out the tarp. Boxes and boxes of shells. ".22" with an eagle's head on each box. Heavy. A big fishing reel. Fold-up fishing pole. Pile it all on the tarp. Wrap it up. Dark and the air is dusty. "What are you doing?" The voice is hard and the light clicks on. Bare bulb and dust everywhere. Dust on my pant legs. The flashlight gives no light in the whiteness. She's standing on the steps. I can see all of her. All the inner tube rolls in a pink knit. Little gold circle pin on her shoulder. "I asked what you were doing." Very cold. Not even angry. Just disgusted. I stand up and get the letter out of my pocket. "He asked me to get this stuff and send it to him." Holding out the letter but she doesn't take it. She walks down the steps slowly. The steps bend and groan. She's very fat. The makeup pale on her face and dark on her mouth and little eyes lost in the hot fat. "I couldn't get here any other time and I thought you weren't home when I came so I thought I'd just take it and leave a note." It's bad. Strained. I'm sweating and shaking. She's not angry. She's cold. "Well, I think you had best go and leave these things where they are. If my son wants them he can write to me and I'll send them." She goes to the door and opens it. I turn off the flashlight and walk past her out the door. It takes two steps to pass her. She smells warm and sweet. Some sweet thing and she's cold. She closes the door and I look through the window as I go and she is wider than the door and she's pink and soft and very cold. Ugh. Get Teddie to buy me a hamburger. Warm me up.

Had to take all the jars out of the hall. Pietila finally noticed and called me in. Told him it was a joke. He said it was probably illegal or something. Doesn't matter. Too late. Already cleaned up. Nearly time now. Four days.

* * *

Report cards. F in social studies too. Maw worried I won't be able to go to college like I want to. Told her I'd do better next year.

Derry Ragel's O.K. Has a car. Told him about the Mission Mountains. He's wild to help but has a date to go to the party. Teddie's going too. Derry'll get his friend Bryce to drive me into town to the bus station. Bryce is high society. Good grades. Escort to the May Fete princess, letterman, René Van Den Bosch's boy friend. Hotsy-totsy, I'm a Nazi.

Cecilia brought the boots today. Put 'em in my locker. Teddie will bring the pack with the stuff I asked for tomorrow. Put it all in my locker and get it out the night of the party. Maw will drive me to school, see the buses loading for the party, drive off. I'll run in and pick up the stuff and meet Bryce out behind the cafeteria.

There's a bus at nine. Express to L.A. Perfect. Leave the school around seven-thirty. Plenty of time to get into town, buy the ticket and get on the bus. Then I'm gone. Out of it. I went away.

Dear Maw,

I am in Montana in the mountains. I'm fine and am a hermit now. Don't try to find me. I am really all right. I'll write again soon.

> *Love to Dad and Nick*
> *your daughter*
> *Jean*

I lick it all up and put it in an envelope. Already stamped. Already addressed. Put it into the larger envelope with the note.

Postmaster,
St. Ignatius, Montana

Dear Sir,

I am an avid collector of postmarks and am interested in obtaining the St. Ignatius postmark. I would appreciate your forwarding this letter with the appropriate stamp to my home.

yours truly,
my father's name

I know the letter is hokey as hell but a person writes hokey things to their mother. She'll know it's me. Does the job.

I've never really given her any trouble before. Tried not to shit on her. Nothing ever gets back to her of what I do. Never ran away before. That was because I was chicken shit. Not because of her. That time when we were in Nevada and I was going to ride my bike to Oregon and live in a hollow tree. Had it all planned out. What I needed to take. How much money I'd have to have. How long it would take me. Didn't have the money. Never even started. Kept thinking how obvious I'd be on the road on my bike. Too scared to hitchhike. Kept seeing my scraggy body laid out on a rock in the desert with snakes crawling all around it and flies buzzing over it. Too easy to get caught and dragged back. Never even started. Never even tried. Too many consequences. All planned out now. Has to work. If I've got the guts. If I start thinking about consequences now it'll make me sick. I'll end up being a good girl and staying here. Stop going out at night. Stop walking on the tracks. Stop laying under the trestle when the freights come through. Stay here with Mama and let my hair grow. Get a job at the supermarket and never nick anything. Never pocket any change. Spend all my money on clothes and sit at night with Maw in front of the TV sewing on my hope chest and waiting for the right Flying A man to come along. Too much. Too much to stand. I really would end up killing somebody. Feeling the knife one day and red and anger and all the lost minutes and wasted hours come pouring out. It'd be whoever was there. It wouldn't matter who. Just whoever was in the room and I'd put my monster face on and not laugh

and not take it off when they laughed. They'd take too long
to know it wasn't a joke and by then it'd be too late. Too
late for them. Too late for me a long time before. Maybe
I'd learn to embroider. Dish towels and pillowcases and
monogrammed handkerchiefs. Once I found out what the
monogram would be. But it'd be too late and the knife would
come into my hand and somebody's true blood would fall
all over my embroidery. I have to go. I have to. Doesn't
need guts anymore. I've got the machine moving and so
many people know a version. Can't back out now. I've got
some pride. I've set it up so I don't have to worry about
having the guts. I'll go because going is easier than staying.
It's good. I did good. Still, I wonder if I'll do it.

Thursday. Last day of school. No use going to class.
Speeches and bullshit. Cutesy farewells. Drag all the stuff
out of my locker and into the nearest can. Boots and Teddie's pack and all the stuff from home. Brought out in little
bags and pockets and folded between books. Relayed for
weeks. All here. No good jacket. No sleeping bag. Get 'em
in L.A. Less to carry for a while anyway. Sit touching it
and packing and repacking. Good Japanese army knife.
Teddie's old man's souvenir. Heavy and black-bladed for
night fighting. No shine to shoot at. A heavy webbed belt
with holes for the canteen and the knife. No vaseline at
home. Out lately. Got Vicks VapoRub. Probably no good
for burns. Burn more than the burn. Throw it in. Never
know. All smooth and tight. Shove it in hard and pound it
all smooth. A back pack and a side pack to hang on one
shoulder. Across the shoulder maybe. All there. All finished. Nothing more to do. Put it all into the locker. Efficient looking. Smooth. Go wandering around the halls. A
few other people wandering around. Laughter and speeches
coming from behind the doors . . . Though I've overworked
and failed you, though I've bitched at you and jailed
you . . . Very cute. Everybody jolly and sweetly melancholy
at parting. Lovely. Big reunion in the fall . . . My, what a
fantastic tan! You've changed your hair! It's beautiful! Don't
you think she's gained a lot of weight? Of course I'm taking
all enriched courses this year . . . already accepted at Oregon State and the U. of O. but I'd really like to go to . . .
But I won't see it or hear it. I'll never have to hear it again.

Never have to be in it and cold and outside in it. Never again. Go down to the gym. All the mats empty. Trampoline's down. Get up on it with my sneakers on. Not allowed but there's nobody around. Walk around. Springing, flying, jump and jump and the floor goes away and my head is wild and my arms move the right way without thinking about it. Fly and the harder I fall the higher I fly. Fly clear away and my foot goes between the springs and I fall flat and still bouncing and it's nice and easy and feels good. I was ready to stop anyway. Get down and go rustle around in the equipment cupboards. Bats and helmets and spikes and pads and gloves and wrist guards and bows and arrows. I was always pretty good with the bow. If we'd had archery all the time I might have passed Phys Ed. They're green fiberglass twenty-pound bows and fiberglass arrows with a plastic fletch and slightly pointed target tips. Take one along. Anybody tries to take me back I'll get 'em in the balls with my trusty bow 'n' arrow. Take a bow with a good string and a handful of arrows. A strap to hold the arrows. Amble down the hall and stow it in the locker. Long day. Nothing doing. Everything already done. Go sleep in the back of the library. Rest up for the trip.

❦

JANICE EIDUS grew up on Gun Hill Road in the Bronx. She is the author of *Faithful Rebecca*, a novel, and *Vito Loves Geraldine*, a collection of stories. The title story of that collection, which follows here, won an O. Henry award in 1990. Her short fiction has appeared in numerous anthologies and magazines such as *The Village Voice*, *North American Review*, and *Mississippi Review*, and has been translated and published abroad. She has taught writing at The Writer's Voice in New York City and Parson's School of Design. She currently resides in the city and teaches writing workshops privately.

❦

Vito Loves Geraldine

❦

Janice Eidus

Vito Venecio was after me. He'd wanted to get into my pants ever since tenth grade. But even though we hung around with the same crowd back at Evander Childs High School, I never gave him the time of day. I, Geraldine Rizzoli, was the most popular girl in the crowd, I had my pick of the guys, you can ask anyone, Carmela or Pamela or Victoria, and they'll agree. And Vito was just a skinny little kid with a big greasy pompadour and a cowlick and acne and a big space between his front teeth. True, he could sing, and he and Vinny Feruge and Bobby Colucci and Richie DeSoto formed a doo-wop group and called themselves Vito and the Olinvilles, but lots of the boys formed doo-wop groups and stood around on street corners doo-wopping their hearts out. Besides, I wasn't letting any of them into my pants either.

Carmela and Pamela and Victoria and all the other girls in the crowd would say, "Geraldine Rizzoli, teach me how to tease my hair as high as yours and how to put my eyeliner on so straight and thick," but I never gave away my secrets. I just set my black hair on beer cans every night and in the morning I teased it and teased it with my comb until sometimes I imagined that if I kept going I could get it high enough to reach the stars, and then I would spray it with hairspray that smelled like red roses and then I'd stroke on my black eyeliner until it went way past my eyes.

The kids in my crowd were the type who cut classes, smoked in the bathroom, and cursed. Yeah, even the girls cursed, and we weren't the type who went to church on Sundays, which drove our mothers crazy. Vito was one of the worst of us all. He just about never read a book or went to class, and I think his mother got him to set foot in the church maybe once the whole time he was growing up. I swear, it was some sort of a holy miracle that he actually got his diploma.

Anyway, like I said, lots of the boys wanted me and I liked to make out with them and sometimes I agreed to go steady for a week or two with one of the really handsome ones, like Sally-Boy Reticliano, but I never let any get into my pants. Because in my own way I was a good Catholic girl. And all this time Vito was wild about me and I wouldn't even make out with him. But when Vito and the Olinvilles got themselves an agent and cut a record, "Teenage Heartbreak," which Vito wrote, I started to see that Vito was different than I'd thought, different than the other boys. Because Vito had an artistic soul. Then, on graduation night, just a week after Vito and the Olinvilles recorded "Teenage Heartbreak," I realized that, all these years, I'd been in love with him, too, and was just too proud to admit it because he was a couple of inches shorter than me, and he had that acne and the space between his teeth. There I was, ready for the prom, all dressed up in my bright red prom dress and my hair teased higher than ever, waiting for my date, but my date wasn't Vito, it was Sally-Boy Reticliano, and I wanted to jump out of my skin. About halfway through the prom, I couldn't take it anymore and I said, "Sally-Boy, I'm sorry, but I've just got to go over and talk to Vito." Sally-Boy, who was even worse at school than Vito, grunted, and I could tell that it was a sad grunt. But there was nothing I could do. I loved Vito and that was that. I spotted him standing alone in a corner. He was wearing a tux and his hair was greased up into a pompadour that was almost as high as my hair. He watched me as I walked across the auditorium to him, and even in my spiked heels, I felt as though I was floating on air. He said, "Aay, Geraldine, how goes it?" and then he took me by the arm and we left the auditorium. It was like he knew all along that one day I would come to him. It was a gorgeous spring night, I could even see a few stars, and Vito put his arm around me, and he had to tiptoe a little bit to reach. We walked over to the

Gun Hill Projects, and we found a deserted bench in the
project's laundry room, and Vito said, "Aay, Geraldine
Rizzoli, I've been crazy about you since tenth grade. I even
wrote 'Teenage Heartbreak' for you."

And I said, "Vito, I know, I guessed it, and I'm sorry
I've been so dumb since tenth grade, but your heart doesn't
have to break anymore. Tonight I'm yours."

And Vito and I made out on the bench for a while, but it
didn't feel like just making out. I realized that Vito and I
weren't kids anymore. It was like we had grown up all at
once. So I said, "Vito, take me," and he said, "Aay, Geraldine Rizzoli, all right!" He had the keys to his older
brother Danny's best friend Freddy's car, which was a beat-
up old wreck, but that night it looked like a Cadillac to me.
It was parked back near the school, and we raced back along
Gun Hill Road, hoping that Sally-Boy and the others
wouldn't see us. Even though Vito didn't have a license, he
drove the car a few blocks away into the parking lot of the
Immaculate Conception School. We climbed into the backseat and I lifted the skirt of my red prom dress and we made
love for hours. We made sure I wouldn't get pregnant, because we wanted to do things just right. Like I said, I was
a good Catholic girl, in my own way. Afterward he walked
me back to Olinville Ave. And he took out the car keys and
carved VITO LOVES GERALDINE in a heart over the door of
the elevator in my building, but he was careful to do it on
another floor, not the floor I lived on, because we didn't
want my parents to see. And then he said, "Aay, Geraldine
Rizzoli, will you marry me?" and I said, "Yeah, Vito, I
will." So then we went into the staircase of the building
and he brushed off one of the steps for me and we sat down
together and started talking seriously about our future and
he said, "Aay, you know, Vinny and Bobby and Richie and
me, it's a gas being Vito and the Olinvilles and singing
those doo-wop numbers, but I'm no fool, I know we'll never
be rich or famous. So I'll keep singing for a couple more
years, and then I'll get into some other line of work and
then we'll have kids, okay?" And I said sure, it was okay
with me if he wanted to sing for a few years until we started
our family. Then I told him that Mr. Pampino at the Evander
Sweet Store had offered me a job behind the counter, which
meant that I could start saving money right away. "Aay,

Geraldine, you're no fool," he said. He gave me the thumbs-up sign and we kissed. Then he said, "Aay, Geraldine, let's do it again, right here in the staircase," and he started pulling off his tux, but I said I wasn't that kind of girl, so he just walked me to my door and we said goodnight. We agreed that we wouldn't announce our engagement until we each had a little savings account of our own. That way our parents couldn't say we were too young and irresponsible and try to stop the wedding, which my father, who was very hot-tempered, was likely to do.

The very next morning, Vito's agent called him and woke him up and said that "Teenage Heartbreak" was actually going to get played on the radio, on WMCA by the Good Guys, at eight o'clock that night. That afternoon, we were all hanging out with the crowd and Vito and Vinny and Bobby and Richie were going crazy and they were shouting, "Aay, everyone, WMCA, all right!" and stamping their feet and threatening to punch each other out and give each other noogies on the tops of their heads. Soon everyone on Olinville Ave. knew, and at eight o'clock it was like another holy miracle, everyone on the block had their windows open and we all blasted our radios so that even the angels in Heaven had to have heard Vito and the Olinvilles singing "Teenage Heartbreak" that night, which, like I said, was written especially for me, Geraldine Rizzoli. Vito invited me to listen with him and his mother and father and his older brother Danny in their apartment. We hadn't told them we were engaged, though. Vito just said, "Aay, Ma, Geraldine Rizzoli here wants to listen to 'Teenage Heartbreak' on WMCA with us, okay?" His mother looked at me and nodded, and I had a feeling that she guessed that Vito and I were in love and that in her own way she was saying, "Welcome, my future daughter-in-law, welcome." So we sat around the kitchen table with the radio set up like a centerpiece and his mother and I cried when it came on and his father and Danny kept swearing in Italian and Vito just kept combing his pompadour with this frozen grin on his face. When it was over, everyone on the block came pounding on the door, shouting, "Aay, Vito, open up, you're a star!" and we opened the door and we had a big party and everyone danced the lindy and the cha-cha all over the Venecios' apartment.

Three days later "Teenage Heartbreak" made it to number one on the charts, which was just unbelievable, like twenty thousand holy miracles combined, especially considering how the guidance counselor at Evander Childs used to predict that Vito would end up in prison. The disc jockeys kept saying things like "These four boys from the streets of the Bronx are a phenomenon, ladies and gentleman, a genuine phenomenon!" Vito's mother saw my mother at Mass and told her that she'd been visited by an angel in white when she was pregnant with Vito and the angel told her, "Mrs. Venecio, you will have a son and this son shall be a great man!"

A week later Vito and the Olinvilles got flown out to L.A. to appear in those beach party movies, and Vito didn't even call me to say goodbye. So I sat in my room and cried a lot, but after a couple of weeks, I decided to chin up and accept my fate, because, like Vito said, I was no fool. Yeah, it was true that I was a ruined woman, labeled forever as a tramp—me, Geraldine Rizzoli, who'd made out with so many of the boys at Evander Childs High School but who'd always been so careful never to let any of them into my pants, here I'd gone and done it with Vito Venecio, who'd turned out to be a two-faced liar, only interested in money and fame. Dumb, dumb, dumb, Geraldine, I thought. And I couldn't tell my parents because my father would have taken his life savings, I swear, and flown out to L.A. and killed Vito. And I couldn't even tell Pamela and Carmela and Victoria because we'd pricked our fingers with sewing needles and made a pact sealed in blood that although we would make out with lots of boys, we would stay virgins until we got married. So whenever I got together with them and they talked about how unbelievable it was that skinny little Vito with the acne and the greasy pompadour had become so rich and famous, I would agree and try to act just like them, like I was just so proud that Vito and Vinny and Bobby and Richie were now millionaires. And after a month or so I started feeling pretty strong and I thought, Okay, Vito, you bastard, you want to dump Geraldine Rizzoli, tough noogies to you, buddy. I was working at the Evander Sweet Store during the day and I'd begun making out with some of the guys in the crowd in the evenings again, even though my heart wasn't in it. But I figured that one day someone else's kisses might make me feel the way that Vito's kisses had made me feel, and I'd never know who it would be unless I tried it.

And then one night I was helping my mother with the supper dishes, which I did every single night since, like I said, in my own way, I was a good Catholic girl, when the phone rang and my mother said, "Geraldine, it's for you. It's Vito Venecio calling from Los Angeles," and she looked at me like she was suspicious about why Vito, who'd been trying to get into my pants all those years when he wasn't famous and I wouldn't give him the time of day, would still be calling me at home, now that he was famous and could have his pick of girls. When she'd gone back into the kitchen, I picked up the phone, but my hands were so wet and soapy that I could hardly hold onto the receiver. Vito said, "Aay, Geraldine Rizzoli," and his voice sounded like he was around the corner, but I knew he was really three thousand miles away, surrounded by those silly-looking bimbos from the beach party movies. "Aay, forgive me, Geraldine," he said, "I've been a creep, I know, I got carried away by all this money and fame crap, but it's you I want, you and the old gang and my old life on Olinville Ave."

I didn't say anything, I was so angry and confused. And my hands were still so wet and soapy.

"Aay, Geraldine, will you wait for me?" Vito said, and he sounded like a little lost boy. "Please, Geraldine, I'll be back, this ain't gonna last long, promise me, you'll wait for me as long as it takes."

"I don't know, Vito," I said, desperately trying to hold onto the phone, and now my hands were even wetter because I was crying and my tears were landing on them, "you could have called sooner."

"Aay, I know," he said, "this fame stuff, it's like a drug. But I'm coming home to you, Geraldine. Promise me you'll wait for me."

And he sounded so sad, and I took a deep breath, and I said, "I promise, Vito. I promise." And then the phone slipped from my grasp and hit the floor, and my mother yelled from the kitchen, "Geraldine, if you don't know how to talk on the phone without making a mess all over the floor, then don't talk on the phone!'' I shouted, "I'm sorry, Ma!'' but when I picked it up again, Vito was gone.

So the next day behind the counter at the Evander Sweet Store, I started making plans. I needed my independence. I knew I'd have to get an apartment, so that when Vito came back, I'd be ready for him. But that night when I told my parents I was going to get my own apartment they raised holy hell. My mother was so furious she didn't even ask whether it had something to do with Vito's call. In fact, she never spoke to me about Vito after that, which makes me think that deep down she knew. The thing was, whether she knew or didn't know, seventeen-year-old Italian girls from the Bronx did not leave home until a wedding ring was around their finger, period. Even girls who cut classes and smoked and cursed. My parents sent me to talk to a priest at the Immaculate Conception Church, which was right next door to the Immaculate Conception School, the parking lot of which was where I gave myself to Vito in the backseat of his older brother Danny's best friend Freddy's car, and the priest said, "Geraldine Rizzoli, my child, your parents tell me that you wish to leave their home before you marry. Child, why do you wish to do such a thing, which reeks of the desire to commit sin?''

I shrugged and looked away, trying hard not to pop my chewing gum. I didn't want to seem too disrespectful, but that priest got nowhere with me. I was going to wait for Vito, and I needed to have my own apartment ready for him, so the instant he got back we could start making love again and get married and start a family. And besides, even though the priest kept calling me a child, I'd been a woman ever since I let Vito into my pants. I ran my fingers through my hair, trying to make the teased parts stand up even higher, while the priest went on and on about Mary Magdalene. But I had my own spiritual mission, which had nothing to do with the Church, and finally I couldn't help it, a big gum bubble went *pop* real loudly in my mouth and the priest called me a hellion and said I was beyond his help. So I got up and left, pulling the pieces of gum off my lips.

The priest told my father that the only solution was to chain me up in my bedroom. But my mother and father, bless their hearts, may have been Catholic and Italian and hot-tempered, but they were good people, so instead they

got my father's best friend, Pop Giordano, who'd been like
an uncle to me ever since I was in diapers, to rent me an
apartment in the building he owned. And the building just
happened to be on Olinville Ave., right next door to my
parents' building. So they were happy enough. I insisted on
a two-bedroom right from the start, so that Vito wouldn't
feel cramped when he came back, not that I told them why
I needed that much room. "A two-bedroom," my mother
kept repeating. "Suddenly my daughter is such a grown-up
she wants a two-bedroom!"

So Pop gave me the biggest two-bedroom in the building
and I moved in, and Pop promised my father to let him
know if I kept late hours, and my father said he'd kill me if
I did, but I wasn't worried about that. My days of making
out with the boys of Olinville Ave. were over. I would
wait for Vito, and I would live like a nun until he returned to
me.

My mother even ended up helping me decorate the apartment, and to make her happy I hung a velour painting of
Jesus above the sofa in the living room. I didn't think Vito
would mind too much, since his mother had one in her living room too. I didn't intend to call Vito or write him to
give him my new address. He'd be back soon enough and
he'd figure out where I was.

And I began to wait. But a couple of weeks after I moved
into the apartment I couldn't take not telling anyone. I felt
like I'd scream or do something crazy if I didn't confide in
someone. So I told Pop. Pop wore shiny black suits and
black shirts with white ties and a big diamond ring on his
pinky finger and he didn't have a steady job like my father,
who delivered hot dogs by truck to restaurants all over the
Bronx, or like Vito's father, who was a construction worker.
I figured that if anyone knew the way the world worked, it
was Pop. He promised he'd never tell, and he twirled his
black mustache and said, "Geraldine Rizzoli, you're like
my own daughter, like my flesh and blood, and I'm sorry
you lost your cherry before you got married, but if you want
to wait for Vito, wait."

So I settled in to my new life and I waited. That was the
period that Vito kept turning out hit songs and making beach
party movies and I'd hear him interviewed on the radio and
he never sounded like the Vito I knew. It sounded like

someone else had written his words for him. He'd get all
corny and sentimental about the Bronx, and about how his
heart was still there, and he'd say all these sappy things
about the fish market on the corner of Olinville Ave., but
that was such crap, because Vito never shopped for food.
His mother did all the shopping, Vito wouldn't be caught
dead in the Olinville fish market, except maybe to mooch a
cigarette off of Carmine Casella, who worked behind the
counter. Vito didn't even like fish. And I felt sad and worried for him. He'd become a kind of doo-wop robot, he and
the Olinvilles, mouthing other people's words. I noticed that
he'd even stopped writing songs after "Teenage Heartbreak." Sometimes I could hardly stand waiting for him.
But on Olinville Ave., a promise was a promise. People had
been found floating facedown in the Bronx River for breaking smaller promises than that. Besides, I still loved Vito.

Pamela married Johnny Ciccarone, Carmela married
Ricky Giampino, and Victoria married Sidney Goldberg,
from the Special Progress Accelerated class, which was a
big surprise, and they all got apartments in the neighborhood. But after a year or two they all moved away, either to
neighborhoods where the Puerto Ricans and blacks weren't
starting to move in, or to Yonkers or Mount Vernon, and
they started to have babies and I'd visit them once or twice
with gifts, but it was like we didn't have much in common
anymore, and soon we all lost touch.

And Vito and the Olinvilles kept turning out hits, even
though, like I said, Vito never wrote another song after
"Teenage Heartbreak." In addition to the doo-wop numbers, Vito had begun letting loose on some slow, sexy bal-
lads. I bought their forty-fives and I bought their albums
and every night after work I would call up the radio stations
and request their songs, not that I needed to, since everyone
else was requesting their songs, anyway, but it made me
feel closer to Vito, I guess. And sometimes I'd look at Vito's photograph on the album covers or in the fan magazines
and I'd see how his teeth and hair and skin were perfect,
there was no gap between his front teeth like there used to
be, no more acne, no more cowlick. And I kind of missed
those things, because that night when I gave myself to Vito
in the backseat of his older brother Danny's best friend
Freddy's car, I'd loved feeling Vito's rough, sandpapery skin

against mine and I'd loved letting my fingers play with his cowlick and letting my tongue rest for a minute in the gap between his front teeth.

So, for the next three, four years, I kind of lost count, Vito and the Olinvilles ruled the airwaves. And every day I worked at the Evander Sweet Store and every night I had dinner with my parents and my mother would ask whether I was ever going to get married and have babies and I'd say, "Come on, Ma, leave me alone, I'm a good Catholic girl, of course I'm gonna have babies one day," and my father would say, "Geraldine, if Pop ever tells me you're keeping late hours with any guys, I'll kill you," and I'd say, "Come on, Pa, I told you, I'm a good Catholic girl," and then I'd help my mother with the dishes and then I'd kiss them good-night and I'd go visit Pop for a few minutes in his apartment on the ground floor of the building and there would always be those strange men coming and going from his apartment and then I'd go upstairs to my own apartment and I'd sit in front of my mirror and I'd tease my hair up high and I'd put on my makeup and I'd put on my red prom dress and I'd listen to Vito's songs and I'd dance the lindy and the cha-cha. And then before I went to sleep, I'd read through all the fan mags and I'd cut out every article about him and I'd paste them into my scrapbook.

Then one day, I don't remember exactly when, a couple of more years, maybe three, maybe even four, all I remember is that Carmela and Pamela and Victoria had all sent me announcements that they were on their second kids, the fan mags started printing fewer and fewer articles about Vito. I'd sit on my bed, thumbing through, and where before, I'd find at least one in every single mag, now I'd have to go through five, six, seven magazines and then I'd just find some real small mention of him. And the radio stations were playing Vito and the Olinvilles less and less often and I had to call in and request them more often because nobody else was doing it, and their songs weren't going higher than number fifteen or twenty on the charts. But Vito's voice was as strong and beautiful as ever, and the Olinvilles could still do those doo-wops in the background, so at first I felt really dumb, dumb, dumb because I couldn't figure out what was going on.

But I, Geraldine Rizzoli, am no fool, and it hit me soon

enough. It was really simple. The girls my age were all
mothers raising kids, and they didn't have time to buy records and dance the lindy and the cha-cha in front of their
mirrors. And the boys, they were out all day working and
at night they sat and drank beer and watched football on
TV. So a new generation of teenagers was buying records.
And they were buying records by those British groups, the
Beatles and the rest of them, and for those kids, I guess, an
Italian boy from the Bronx with a pompadour wasn't very
interesting. And even though I didn't look a day older than
I had that night in the backseat of Vito's older brother Dan-
ny's best friend Freddy's car, and even though I could still
fit perfectly into my red prom dress, I had to face facts too.
I wasn't a teenager anymore.

So more time went by, again I lost count, but Pop's hair
was beginning to turn gray and my father was beginning to
have a hard time lifting those crates of hot dogs and my
mother seemed to be getting shorter day by day, and Vito
and the Olinvilles never got played on the radio at all, period. And I felt bad for Vito, but mostly I was relieved,
since I was sure then that he would come home. I bought
new furniture, Pop put in new windows. I found a hairspray
that made my hair stay higher even longer.

But I was wrong. Vito didn't come home. Instead, according to the few fan mags that ran the story, his manager
tried to make him into a clean-cut type, the type who ap-
peals to the older Las Vegas set. And Vito left the Olinvilles, which, the fan mags said, was like Vito had put a
knife through their hearts. One mag said that Vinny had
even punched Vito out. Anyway, it was a mistake on Vito's
part not to have just come home right then. He made two
albums and he sang all these silly love songs from the twen-
ties and thirties, and he sounded really off-key and miserable. After that, whenever I called the disc jockeys, they just
laughed at me and wouldn't even play his records. I'd have
to go through ten or fifteen fan mags to find even a small
mention of Vito at all. So I felt even worse for him, but I
definitely figured he had to come home then. Where else
could he go? So I bought a new rug and Pop painted the
wall. And I sat in front of my mirror at night and I teased
my hair and I applied my makeup and I put on my red prom
dress and I danced the lindy and the cha-cha and I played

Vito's albums and I'd still cut out the small article here and there and place it in my scrapbook. And I hadn't aged a day. No lines, no wrinkles, no flab, no gray hair. Vito was going to be pleased when he came home.

But I was wrong again. Vito didn't come home. He went and got married to someone else, a skinny flat-chested blond model from somewhere like Iowa or Idaho. A couple of the fan mags ran little pieces, and they said she was the best thing that had ever happened to Vito. Because of his love for her he wasn't depressed anymore about not having any more number one hits. "Aay," he was quoted, "love is worth more than all of the gold records in the world." At first I cried. I kicked the walls. I tore some of the articles from my scrapbook and ripped them to shreds. I smashed some of his albums to pieces. I was really really angry, because I knew that it was me, Geraldine Rizzoli, who was the best thing that had ever happened to him! That blond model had probably been a real goody-goody when she was growing up, the type who didn't cut classes or smoke or tease her hair or make out with lots of guys. No passion in her skinny bones, I figured. And then I calmed down. Because Vito would still be back. This model, whose name was Muffin Potts, was no threat at all. Vito would be back, a little ashamed of himself, but he'd be back.

Soon after that, Vito's mother and father died. A couple of fan mags carried the story. They died in a plane crash on their way to visit Vito and Muffin Potts in Iowa or Idaho or wherever she was from. I didn't get invited to the funeral, which was in Palm Beach. Vito's parents had moved there only six months after "Teenage Heartbreak" became number one. Five big moving vans had parked on Olinville Ave., and Vito's mother stood there in a fur coat telling everybody about the angel who'd visited her when she was pregnant with Vito. And I'd gone up to her and kissed her and said, "Goodbye, Mrs. Venecio, I'm going to miss you," and she said, "Goodbye, Carmela," like she was trying to pretend that she didn't remember that I was Geraldine Rizzoli, her future daughter-in-law. The fan mags had a picture of Vito at the funeral in a three-piece suit, and the articles said he cried on the shoulder of his older brother Danny, who was now a distributor of automobile parts. There were also a couple of photos of Muffin Potts looking very bored.

Then I started to read little rumors, small items, in a few of the magazines. First, that Vito's marriage was on the rocks. No surprise to me there. I was surprised that it lasted an hour. Second, that Vito was heavy into drugs and that his addiction was breaking Muffin's heart. Really hard drugs, the mags said. The very worst stuff. One of the mags said it was because of his mother's death and they called him a "mama's boy." One said he was heartbroken because of his breakup with the Olinvilles and because Vinny had punched him out. And one said he'd been doing drugs ever since Evander Childs High School, and they had the nerve to call the school a "zoo," which I resented. But I knew a few things. One, Vito was no mama's boy. Two, Vito and the Olinvilles still all loved each other. And, three, Vito had never touched drugs in school. And if it was true that he was drowning his sorrows in drugs and breaking Muffin Potts's heart, it was because he missed me and regretted like hell not coming home earlier!

Soon after that I read that Muffin had left him for good and had taken their child with her. Child? I stared at the print. Ashley, the article said. Their child's name was Ashley. There was no photo, and since Ashley was a name with zero personality, I wasn't sure whether Ashley was a girl or boy. I decided it was a girl, and I figured she looked just like her mother, with pale skin and a snub nose and milky-colored hair, and I wasn't even slightly jealous of that child or her mother because they were just mistakes. True, Vito kept acting dumb, dumb, dumb, and making some big fat mistakes, but I didn't love him any less. A promise was a promise. And I, Geraldine Rizzoli, knew enough to forgive him. Because the truth was that even I had once made a mistake. The way it happened was this. One day out of the blue, who should come into the Evander Sweet Store to buy some cigarettes but Petey Cioffi, who'd been one of the guys in our crowd in the old days. A couple of years after graduation he married some girl from the Grand Concourse and we all lost touch. But here he was in the old neighborhood, visiting some cousins, and he needed some cigarettes. Anyway, when he walked in, he stopped dead in his tracks. I could tell he was a little drunk, and he said, "Aay, Geraldine Rizzoli, I can't believe my eyes, you're still here, and you're gorgeous, I'm growing old and fat, look at this belly, but not you, you're like a princess or something." And it was so good to be spoken to like that, and I let him come home with me. We made out in my elevator, and I felt like a kid again. I couldn't pretend he was Vito, but I could pretend it was the old days, when Vito was still chasing me and trying to get into my pants. In the morning, Petey said goodbye, looked at me one last time, shook his head and said, "Geraldine Rizzoli, what a blast from the past!" and he slipped out of the building before Pop woke up. He probably caught holy hell from his wife and I swear I got my first and only gray hair the next morning. But my night with Petey Cioffi made it easier to forgive Vito, since I'd made my mistake too. And I kept waiting. The neighborhood changed around me. The Italians left, and more and more Puerto Ricans and blacks moved in, but I didn't mind. Because everyone has to live somewhere, I figured, and I had more important things on my mind than being prejudiced.

Then I pretty much stopped hearing about Vito altogether. And that was around when my father, bless his heart, had the heart attack on the hot dog truck and by the time they found him it was too late to save him, and my mother, bless her heart, followed soon after. I missed them so much, and every night I came home from work and I teased my hair at the mirror, I put on my makeup, I put on my red prom dress, I played Vito's songs, I danced the lindy and the cha-cha, and I read through the fan mags, looking for some mention of him, but there wasn't any. It was like he had vanished from the face of the earth. And then one day I came across a small item in the newspaper. It was about how Vito had just gotten arrested on Sunset Strip for possession of hard drugs, and how he was bailed out by Vinny of the Olinvilles, who was now a real estate salesman in Santa Monica. "I did it for old times' sake," Vinny said, "for the crowd on Olinville Ave."

The next morning, Pop called me to his apartment. He had the beginnings of cataracts by then and he hardly ever looked at the newspaper anymore, but of course, he'd spotted the article about Vito. His face was red. He was furious. He shouted, "Geraldine Rizzoli, you're like my own daughter, my own flesh and blood, and I never wanted to have to say this to you, but"—he waved the newspaper ferociously, which was impressive, since his hands shook, and he weighed all of ninety pounds at this point, although he still dressed in his shiny black suits and those strange men still came and went from his apartment—"the time has come for you to forget Vito. If he was here I'd beat the living hell out of him." He flung the paper across the room and sat in his chair, breathing heavily.

I waited a minute before I spoke, just to make sure he was going to be okay. When his color returned to normal, I said, "Never, Pop. I promised Vito I'd wait."

"You should marry Ralphie."

"Ralphie?" I asked. Ralphie Pampino, who was part of the old crowd, too, had inherited the Evander Sweet Store from his father when Ralphie Sr. died the year before. It turns out that Ralphie Jr., who'd never married, was in love with me, and had been for years. Poor Ralphie. He'd been the kind of guy who never got to make out a whole lot. I'd always thought he looked at me so funny because he was constipated or had sinuses or something. But Pop told me that years ago Ralphie had poured out his heart to him. Although Pop had promised Ralphie that he'd never betray his confidence, the time had come. It seemed that Ralphie had his own spiritual mission: he was waiting for me. I was touched. Ralphie was such a sweet guy. I promised myself to start being nicer to him. I asked Pop to tell him about me and Vito, and I kissed Pop on the nose and I went back upstairs to my apartment and I sat in front of my mirror and I teased my hair and I put on my makeup and I put on my red prom dress and I listened to Vito's songs and I danced the lindy and the cha-cha.

The next day, Ralphie came over to me and said, "Geraldine Rizzoli, I had no idea that you and Vito . . ." and he got all choked up and couldn't finish. Finally, he swallowed and said, "Aay, Geraldine, I'm on your side. I really am. Vito's coming back!" and he gave me the thumbs-up sign and he and I did the lindy together right there in the Evander Sweet Store and we sang "Teenage Heartbreak" at the top of our lungs and we didn't care if any customers came in and saw us.

But after that there wasn't any more news about Vito, period. Most everyone on the block who'd known Vito and the Olinvilles was gone, and I just kept waiting. Just around that time an oldies radio station, WAAY, started up and it was pretty weird at first to think that Vito and the Olinvilles and all the other groups I had spent my life listening to were considered "oldies" and I'd look at myself in the mirror and I'd think, Geraldine Rizzoli, you're nobody's oldie, you've got the same skin and figure you had the night that you gave yourself to Vito. But after a while I got used to the idea of the oldies and I listened to WAAY as often as I could. I played it every morning first thing when I woke up and then Ralphie and I listened to it together at the Evander Sweet Store, even though most of the kids who came in were carrying those big radio boxes turned to salsa or rap songs or punk and didn't seem to have any idea that there was already music on. Sometimes when nobody was in the store, Ralphie and I would just sing Vito's songs together. There was one deejay on the station, Goldie George, who as on from nine in the morning until noon and he was a real fan of Vito and the Olinvilles. The other deejays had their favorites too. Doo-Wop Dick liked the Five Satins, Surfer Sammy liked the Beach Boys, but Goldie George said he'd grown up in the Bronx just two subway stops away from Olinville Ave. and that he and his friends had all felt as close to Vito as if they'd lived on Olinville Ave. themselves, even though they'd never met Vito or Vinny or Bobby or Richie. I liked Goldie George, and I wished he'd been brave enough to have taken the subway the two stops over so that he could have hung around with us. He might have been fun to make out with. One day Goldie George played thirty minutes straight of Vito and the Olinvilles, with no commercial interruptions, and then some listener called in and said "Aay, whatever happened to Vito anyway, Goldie George, he was some sort of junkie, right?"

"Yeah," Goldie George said, "but I'm Vito's biggest fan, like you all know, because I grew up only two subway stops away from Olinville Ave. and I used to feel like I was a close buddy of Vito's even though I never met him, and I happen to know that he's quit doing drugs and that he's found peace and happiness through the Chinese practice of T'ai Chi and he helps run a mission in Bakersfield, California."

"Aay," the caller said, "Goldie George, you tell Vito for me that Bobby MacNamara from Woodside says, 'Aay, Vito, keep it up, man!' "

"I will," Goldie George said, "I will. I'll tell him about you, Bobby, because, being so close to Vito in my soul when I was growing up, I happen to know that Vito still cares about his loyal fans. In fact, I know that one of the things that helped Vito to get through the hard times was knowing how much his loyal fans cared. And, aay, Bobby, what's your favorite radio station?"

"WAAY!" Bobby shouted.

And then Goldie George played another uninterrupted thirty minutes of Vito and the Olinvilles. But I could hardly hear the music this time. I was sick to my stomach. What the hell was Vito doing in Bakersfield, California, running a mission? I was glad he wasn't into drugs anymore, but Bakersfield, California? A mission? And what the hell was T'ai Chi? I was so pissed off. For the first time I wondered whether he'd forgotten my promise. I was ready to fly down to Bakersfield and tell him a thing or two, but I didn't. I went home, played my albums, danced, teased my hair, frowned at the one gray hair I'd gotten the night I was with Petey Cioffi, and I closed my eyes and leaned my head on my arms. Vito was coming back. He just wasn't ready yet.

About two weeks later I was behind the counter at the Evander Sweet Store and Ralphie was arranging some Chunkies into a pyramid when Goldie George said, "Guess what, everyone, all of us here at the station, but mostly Vito's biggest fan, me, Goldie George, have arranged for Vito to come back to his hometown! This is Big Big Big Big News! I called him the other day and I said, 'Vito, I grew up two subway stops from you, and like, you know, I'm your biggest fan, and you owe it to me and your other loyal fans from the Bronx and all the other boroughs to come back and visit and sing "Teenage Heartbreak" for us one more time,' and I swear Vito got choked up over the phone and he agreed to do it, even though he said that he usually doesn't sing any more because it interferes with his T'ai Chi, but I said, 'Vito, we love you here at WAAY, man, and wait'll you hear this, we're going to book Carnegie Hall for you, Vito, not your grandmother's attic, but Carnegie Hall!' How about that, everyone. And just so you all know, the Olinvilles are all doing their own things now, so it'll just be Vito alone, but hey, that's okay, that's great, Vito will sing the oldies and tickets go on sale next week!''

And I stood there frozen and Ralphie and I stared at each other across the counter, and I could see a look in his eyes that told me that he knew he'd finally lost me for good this time.

Because Vito was coming back. He may have told Goldie George that he was coming home to sing to his fans, but Ralphie and I both knew that it was really me, Geraldine Rizzoli, that he was finally ready to come back to. Vito worked in mysterious ways, and I figured that he finally felt free of the bad things, the drugs and that boring Muffin Potts and his own arrogance and excessive pride, and now he was pure enough to return to me. I wasn't wild about this T'ai Chi stuff, whatever it was, but I could get used to it if it had helped Vito to get better so he could come home to me.

Ralphie sort of shook himself like he was coming out of some long sleep or trance. Then he came around the counter and put his arm around me in this brotherly way. "Geraldine Rizzoli," he said really softly, "my treat. A first row seat at Carnegie Hall."

But I wouldn't accept, even though it was such a beautiful thing for Ralphie to offer to do, considering how he'd felt about me all those years. I got teary-eyed. But I didn't need a ticket, not me, not Geraldine Rizzoli. Vito would find out where I lived and he'd come and pick me up and take me himself to Carnegie Hall. He'd probably come in a limo paid for by the station, I figured. Because the only way I was going to the concert was with Vito. I went home after work and I plucked the one gray hair from my scalp and then I teased my hair and I put on my makeup and I put on my red prom dress and I danced and sang.

All week Goldie George kept saying, "It's unbelievable, tickets were sold out within an hour! The calls don't stop coming, you all remember Vito, you all love him!"

On the night of the concert Pop came by. He had to use a walker to get around by then and he was nearly blind and lots of things were wrong. His liver, gall bladder, stomach, you name it. He weighed around seventy-five pounds. But he still wore his shiny black suits and the men kept coming in and out of his apartment. And he sat across from me on my sofa, beneath the velour painting of Jesus, and he said in a raspy voice, "Geraldine Rizzoli, I didn't ever want to

have to say this, but you're like my own daughter, my own
flesh and blood, and as long as Vito wasn't around, I figured, Okay, you can dance to his albums and tease your hair
and wear the same clothes all the time and you're none the
worse for it, but now that he's coming home I've got to tell
you he won't be coming for you, Geraldine, if he cared a
twit about you he would have flown you out to L.A. way
back when and I'm sorry you let him into your pants and
lost your cherry to him, but you're a middle-aged lady now
and you're gonna get hurt real bad and I'm glad your mother
and father, bless their souls, aren't around to see you suffer
the way you're gonna suffer tonight, Geraldine, and I don't
wanna see it either, what I want is for you to drive down to
Maryland tonight real fast, right now, and marry Ralphie,
before Vito breaks your heart so bad nothing will ever put
it together again!''

I'd never seen Pop so riled up. I kissed him on the nose
and I told him he was sweet, but that Vito was coming. And
Pop left, shaking his head and walking slowly, moving the
walker ahead of him, step by step, and after he left, I played
my albums and I teased my hair and I applied my lipstick
and I danced the lindy and the cha-cha and I waited. I figured that everyone from the old crowd would be at the concert. They'd come in from the suburbs with their husbands
and their wives and their children, and even, I had to face
facts, in some cases, their grandchildren. And just then there
was a knock on my door and I opened it and there he was.
He'd put on some weight, but not much, and although he'd
lost some hair he still had a pompadour and he was holding
some flowers for me, and I noticed that they were red roses,
which I knew he'd chosen to match my prom dress. And he
said, ''Aay, Geraldine Rizzoli, thanks for waiting.'' Then
he looked at his watch. ''All *right*, let's get a move on!
Concert starts at nine.'' And I looked in the mirror one last
time, sprayed on a little more hairspray, and that was it.
Vito took my arm just the way he took it the night I gave
myself to him in the backseat of his older brother Danny's
best friend Freddy's car, and we went downtown by limo to
Carnegie Hall, which was a real treat because I didn't get
to go into Manhattan very often. And Carnegie Hall was
packed, standing room only, and the crowd was yelling,
''Aay, Vito! Aay, Vito! Aay, Vito!'' and Pamela and Car-

mela and Victoria were there, and all the Olinvilles came
and they hugged Vito and said there were no hard feelings,
and Vinny and Vito even gave each other noogies on the
tops of their heads, and everyone said, "Geraldine Rizzoli,
you haven't aged a day." Then Goldie George introduced
Vito, and Vito just got right up there on the stage and he
belted out those songs, and at the end of the concert, for
his finale, he sang "Teenage Heartbreak" and he called me
up onstage with him and he held my hand and looked into
my eyes while he sang. I even sang along on a few of the
verses and I danced the lindy and the cha-cha right there on
stage in front of all those people. The crowd went wild,
stamping their feet and shouting for more, and Goldie
George was crying, and after the concert Vito and I went
back by limo to Olinville Ave. and Vito gave the limo driver
a big tip and the driver said, "Aay, Vito, welcome home,"
and then he drove away.

And ever since then Vito has been here with me in the
two-bedroom apartment. He still does T'ai Chi, but it's really no big thing, an hour or two in the morning at most.
Pop died last year and Vito and I were with him at the end
and his last words were "You two kids, you're like my own
son and daughter." Vito works in the Evander Sweet Store
now instead of me because I've got to stay home to take
care of Vito Jr. and Little Pop, who have a terrific godfather
in Ralphie and a great uncle in Vito's older brother Danny.
And, if I'm allowed to do a little bragging, which seems
only fair after all this time, Vito Jr. and Little Pop are very
good kids. They go to church on Sundays and they're doing
real well in school because they never cut classes or smoke
in the bathroom or curse, and Vito and I are as proud as we
can be.

LINDA HOGAN, a member of the Chickasaw people, on her way to becoming the writer of international reputation she is today, has worked variously as a nurse's aide, dental assistant, waitress, homemaker, secretary, teacher's aide, library clerk, freelance writer, poet-in-schools in Colorado and Oklahoma, and assistant professor at Colorado College. She is currently professor of American and American Indian studies at the University of Minnesota. She is the author of several books of poetry, one of which, *Seeing Through the Sun*, received an American Book Award from the Before Columbus Foundation. Her short fiction includes *That Horse* and *The Big Woman*. Her fiction and poetry have been included in a number of anthologies: *I Tell You Now*, *What Moves Me Brings Me to Myself*, and *Talking Leaves: Contemporary Native American Short Stories*. Of herself as a writer, Linda Hogan says: "My writing comes from and goes back to the community, both the human and the global community. I am interested in the deepest questions, those of spirit, of shelter, of growth and movement toward peace and liberation, inner and outer. My main interest at the moment is in wildlife rehabilitation and studying the relationship between humans and other species, and trying to create world survival skills out of what I learn from this." A recipient of an NEA grant, a Minnesota Arts Board Grant, and a Colorado Writer's Fellowship, Hogan has served on the National Endowment for the Arts poetry panel for two years and is involved in wildlife rehabilitation as a volunteer.

In her introduction to her anthology *That's What She Said: Contemporary Poetry and Fiction by Native American Women*, editor Rayna Green states that the writing of contemporary Native women varies between re-creating the consciously Indian world, retelling the old stories, and the strategy of harking back to the traditional world but then moving on to "the referential framework of contemporary life." The latter approach characterizes "Aunt Moon's Young Man," the story that follows here, as well as the perception that Green reads in all modern Indian writing by women: "the harsh knowledge that race and gender superimpose on experience." In the face of that knowledge, the young protagonist of the story takes to the road, having learned from Aunt Moon that more than one's Indian ancestry (or whatever one's ethnic background) "for people out on the edge," in Green's words, "identity is a matter of will, a matter of choice, a face to be shaped in a ceremonial act."

🐚

Aunt Moon's Young Man

❦

Linda Hogan

That autumn when the young man came to town, there was a deep blue sky. On their way to the fair, the wagons creaked into town. One buckboard, driven by cloudy white horses, carried a grunting pig inside its wooden slats. Another had cages of chickens. In the heat, the chickens did not flap their wings. They sounded tired and old, and their shoulders drooped like old men.

There was tension in the air. Those people who still believed in omens would turn to go home, I thought, white chicken feathers caught on the wire cages they brought, reminding us all that the cotton was poor that year and that very little of it would line the big trailers outside the gins.

A storm was brewing over the plains, and beneath its clouds a few people from the city drove dusty black motorcars through town, angling around the statue of General Pickens on Main Street. They refrained from honking at the wagons and the white, pink-eyed horses. The cars contained no animal life, just neatly folded stacks of quilts, jellies, and tomato relish, large yellow gourds, and pumpkins that looked like the round faces of children through half-closed windows.

"The biting flies aren't swarming today," my mother said. She had her hair done up in rollers. It was almost dry. She was leaning against the window frame, looking at the ink-blue trees outside. I could see Bess Evening's house through the glass, appearing to sit like a small, hand-built model upon my mother's shoulder. My mother was a dreamer, standing at the window with her green dress curved over her hip.

Her dress was hemmed slightly shorter on one side than on the other. I decided not to mention it. The way she leaned, with her abdomen tilted out, was her natural way of standing. She still had good legs, despite the spidery blue veins she said came from carrying the weight of us kids inside her for nine months each. She also blamed us for her few gray hairs.

She mumbled something about "the silence before the storm" as I joined her at the window.

She must have been looking at the young man for a long time, pretending to watch the sky. He was standing by the bushes and the cockscombs. There was a flour sack on the ground beside him. I thought at first it might be filled with something he brought for the fair, but the way his hat sat on it and a pair of black boots stood beside it, I could tell it held his clothing, and that he was passing through Pickens on his way to or from some city.

"It's mighty quiet for the first day of fair," my mother said. She sounded far away. Her eyes were on the young stranger. She unrolled a curler and checked a strand of hair.

We talked about the weather and the sky, but we both watched the young man. In the deep blue of sky his white shirt stood out like a light. The low hills were fire-gold and leaden.

One of my mother's hands was limp against her thigh. The other moved down from the rollers and touched the green cloth at her chest, playing with a flaw in the fabric.

"Maybe it was the tornado," I said about the stillness in the air. The tornado had passed through a few days ago, touching down here and there. It exploded my cousin's house trailer but it left his motorcycle, standing beside it, untouched. "Tornadoes have no sense of value," my mother had said. "They are always taking away the saints and leaving behind the devils."

The young man stood in that semi-slumped, half-straight manner of fullblood Indians. Our blood was mixed like Heinz 57, and I always thought of purebloods as better than us. While my mother eyed his plain moccasins, she patted her rolled hair as if to put it in order. I was counting the small brown flowers in the blistered wallpaper, the way I counted ceiling tiles in the new school, and counted each step when I walked.

I pictured Aunt Moon inside her house up on my mother's shoulder. I imagined her dark face above the yellow oilcloth, her hands reflecting the yellow as they separated dried plants. She would rise slowly, as I'd seen her do, take a good long time to brush out her hair, and braid it once again. She would pet her dog, Mister, with long slow strokes while she prepared herself for the fair.

My mother moved aside, leaving the house suspended in the middle of the window, where it rested on a mound of land. My mother followed my gaze. She always wanted to know what I was thinking or doing. "I wonder," she said, "why in tarnation Bess's father built that house up there. It gets all the heat and wind."

I stuck up for Aunt Moon. "She can see everything from there, the whole town and everything."

"Sure, and everything can see her. A wonder she doesn't have ghosts."

I wondered what she meant by that, everything seeing Aunt Moon. I guessed by her lazy voice that she meant nothing. There was no cutting edge to her words.

"And don't call her Aunt Moon." My mother was reading my mind again, one of her many tricks. "I know what you're thinking," she would say when I thought I looked expressionless. "You are thinking about finding Mrs. Mark's ring and holding it for a reward."

I would look horrified and tell her that she wasn't even lukewarm, but the truth was that I'd been thinking exactly those thoughts. I resented my mother for guessing my innermost secrets. She was like God, everywhere at once knowing everything. I tried to concentrate on something innocent. I thought about pickles. I was safe; she didn't say a word about dills or sweets.

Bess, Aunt Moon, wasn't really my aunt. She was a woman who lived alone and had befriended me. I liked Aunt Moon and the way she moved, slowly, taking up as much space as she wanted and doing it with ease. She had wide lips and straight eyelashes.

Aunt Moon dried medicine herbs in the manner of her parents. She knew about plants, both the helpful ones and the ones that were poisonous in all but the smallest of doses.

And she knew how to cut wood and how to read the planets. She told me why I was stubborn. It had to do with my being born in May. I believed her because my father was born a few days after me, and he was stubborn as all get out, even compared to me.

Aunt Moon was special. She had life in her. The rest of the women in town were cold in the eye and fretted over their husbands. I didn't want to be like them. They condemned the men for drinking and gambling, but even after the loudest quarrels, ones we'd overhear, they never failed to cook for their men. They'd cook platters of lard-fried chicken, bowls of mashed potatoes, and pitchers of creamy flour gravy.

Bess called those meals "sure death by murder."

Our town was full of large and nervous women with red spots on their thin-skinned necks, and we had single women who lived with brothers and sisters or took care of an elderly parent. Bess had comments on all of these: "They have eaten their anger and grown large," she would say. And there were the sullen ones who took care of men broken by the war, women who were hurt by the men's stories of death and glory but never told them to get on with living, like I would have done.

Bessie's own brother, J.D., had gone to the war and returned with softened, weepy eyes. He lived at the veterans hospital and he did office work there on his good days. I met him once and knew by the sweetness of his eyes that he had never killed anyone, but something about him reminded me of the lonely old shacks out on cotton farming land. His eyes were broken windows.

"Where do you think that young man is headed?" my mother asked.

Something in her voice was wistful and lonely. I looked at her face, looked out the window at the dark man, and looked back at my mother again. I had never thought about her from inside the skin. She was the mind reader in the family, but suddenly I knew how she did it. The inner workings of the mind were clear in her face, like words in a book. I could even feel her thoughts in the pit of my stomach. I was feeling embarrassed at what my mother was thinking when the stranger crossed the street. In front of him an open truck full of prisoners passed by. They wore large white shirts and pants, like immigrants from Mexico. I began to count the flowers in the wallpaper again, and the truckful of prisoners passed by, and when it was gone, the young man had also vanished into thin air.

Besides the young man, another thing I remember about the fair that year was the man in the bathroom. On the first day of the fair, the prisoners were bending over like great white sails, their black and brown hands stuffing trash in canvas bags. Around them the children washed and brushed their cows and raked fresh straw about their pigs. My friend Elaine and I escaped the dust-laden air and went into the women's public toilets, where we shared a stolen cigarette. We heard someone open the door, and we fanned the smoke. Elaine stood on the toilet seat so her sisters wouldn't recognize her shoes. Then it was silent, so we opened the stall and stepped out. At first the round dark man, standing by the door, looked like a woman, but then I noticed the day's growth of beard at his jawline. He wore a blue work shirt and a little straw hat. He leaned against the wall, his hand moving inside his pants. I grabbed Elaine, who was putting lipstick on her cheeks like rouge, and pulled her outside the door, the tube of red lipstick still in her hand.

Outside, we nearly collapsed by a trash can, laughing. "Did you see that? It was a man! A man! In the women's bathroom." She smacked me on the back.

We knew nothing of men's hands inside their pants, so we began to follow him like store detectives, but as we rounded a corner behind his shadow, I saw Aunt Moon walking away from the pigeon cages. She was moving slowly with her cane, through the path's sawdust, feathers, and sand.

"Aunt Moon, there was a man in the bathroom," I said, and then remembered the chickens I wanted to tell her about. Elaine ran off. I didn't know if she was still following the man or not, but I'd lost interest when I saw Aunt Moon.

"Did you see those chickens that lay the green eggs?" I asked Aunt Moon.

She wagged her head no, so I grabbed her free elbow and guided her past the pigeons with curly feathers and the turkeys with red wattles, right up to the chickens.

"They came all the way from South America. They sell for five dollars, can you imagine?" Five dollars was a lot

for chickens when we were still recovering from the Great
Depression, men were still talking about what they'd done
with the CCC, and children still got summer complaint and
had to be carried around crippled for months.

She peered into the cage. The eggs were smooth and resting in the straw. "I'll be" was all she said.

I studied her face for a clue as to why she was so quiet,
thinking she was mad or something. I wanted to read her
thoughts as easily as I'd read my mother's. In the strange
light of the sky, her eyes slanted a bit more than usual. I
watched her carefully. I looked at the downward curve of
her nose and saw the young man reflected in her eyes. I
turned around.

On the other side of the cage that held the chickens from
Araucania was the man my mother had watched. Bess pretended to be looking at the little Jersey cattle in the distance, but I could tell she was seeing that man. He had a
calm look on his face and his dark chest was smooth as oil
where his shirt was opened. His eyes were large and black.
They were fixed on Bess like he was a hypnotist or something magnetic that tried to pull Bess Evening toward it,
even though her body stepped back. She did step back, I
remember that, but even so, everything in her went forward,
right up to him.

I didn't know if it was just me or if his presence charged
the air, but suddenly the oxygen was gone. It was like the
fire at the Fisher Hardware when all the air was drawn into
the flame. Even the chickens clucked softly, as if suffocating, and the cattle were more silent in the straw. The pulse
in everything changed.

I don't know what would have happened if the rooster
hadn't crowed just then, but he did, and everything returned
to normal. The rooster strutted and we turned to watch him.

Bessie started walking away and I went with her. We
walked past the men and boys who were shooting craps in
a cleared circle. One of them rubbed the dice between his
hands as we were leaving, his eyes closed, his body's tight
muscles willing a winning throw. He called me Lady Luck
as we walked by. He said, "There goes Lady Luck," and
he tossed the dice.

At dinner that evening we could hear the dance band tun-
ing up in the makeshift beer garden, playing a few practice

songs to the empty tables with their red cloths. They played "The Tennessee Waltz." For a while, my mother sang along with it. She had brushed her hair one hundred strokes and now she was talking and regretting talking all at the same time. "He was such a handsome man," she said. My father wiped his face with a handkerchief and rested his elbows on the table. He chewed and looked at nothing in particular. "For the longest time he stood there by the juniper bushes."

My father drank some coffee and picked up the newspaper. Mother cleared the table, one dish at a time and not in stacks like usual. "His clothes were neat. He must not have come from very far away." She moved the salt shaker from the end of the table to the center, then back again.

"I'll wash," I volunteered.

Mother said, "Bless you," and touched herself absently near the waist, as if to remove an apron. "I'll go get ready for the dance," she said.

My father turned a page of the paper.

The truth was, my mother was already fixed up for the dance. Her hair looked soft and beautiful. She had slipped into her new dress early in the day, "to break it in," she said. She wore nylons and she was barefoot and likely to get a runner. I would have warned her, but it seemed out of place, my warning. Her face was softer than usual, her lips painted to look full, and her eyebrows were much darker than usual.

"Do you reckon that young man came here for the rodeo?" She hollered in from the living room, where she powdered her nose. Normally she made up in front of the bathroom mirror, but the cabinet had been slammed and broken mysteriously one night during an argument so we had all taken to grooming ourselves in the small framed mirror in the living room.

I could not put my finger on it, but all the women at the dance that night were looking at the young man. It wasn't exactly that he was handsome. There was something else. He was alive in his whole body while the other men walked with great effort and stiffness, even those who did little work and were still young. Their male bodies had no language of their own in the way that his did. The women themselves seemed confused and lonely in the presence of the young man, and they were ridiculous in their behavior, laughing too loud, blushing like schoolgirls, or casting him a flirting eye. Even the older women were brighter than usual. Mrs. Tubby, whose face was usually as grim as the statue of General Pickens, the Cherokee hater, played with her necklace until her neck had red lines from the chain. Mrs. Tens twisted a strand of her hair over and over. Her sister tripped over a chair because she'd forgotten to watch where she was going.

The men, sneaking drinks from bottles in paper bags, did not notice any of the fuss.

Maybe it was his hands. His hands were strong and dark.

I stayed late, even after wives pulled their husbands away from their ball game talk and insisted they dance.

My mother and father were dancing. My mother smiled up into my father's face as he turned her this way and that. Her uneven skirt swirled a little around her legs. She had a run in her nylons, as I predicted. My father, who was called Peso by the townspeople, wore his old clothes. He had his usual look about him, and I noticed that faraway, unfocused gaze on the other men too. They were either distant or they were present but rowdy, embarrassing the women around them with the loud talk of male things: work and hunting, fights, this or that pretty girl. Occasionally they told a joke, like, "Did you hear the one about the traveling salesman?"

The dancers whirled around the floor, some tapping their feet, some shuffling, the women in new dresses and dark hair all curled up like in movie magazines, the men with new leather boots and crew cuts. My dad's rear stuck out in back, the way he danced. His hand clutched my mother's waist.

That night, Bessie arrived late. She was wearing a white dress with a full gathered skirt. The print was faded and I could just make out the little blue stars on the cloth. She carried a yellow shawl over her arm. Her long hair was braided as usual in the manner of the older Chickasaw women, like a wreath on her head. She was different from the others with her bright shawls. Sometimes she wore a heavy shell necklace or a collection of bracelets on her arm. They jangled when she talked with me, waving her hands to make a point. Like the time she told me that the soul is a small woman inside the eye who leaves at night to wander new places.

No one had ever known her to dance before, but that night the young man and Aunt Moon danced together among the artificial geraniums and plastic carnations. They held each other gently like two breakable vases. They didn't look at each other or smile the way the other dancers did; that's how I knew they liked each other. His large dark hand was on the small of her back. Her hand rested tenderly on his shoulder. The other dancers moved away from them and there was empty space all around them.

My father went out into the dark to smoke and to play a hand or two of poker. My mother went to sit with some of the other women, all of them pulling their damp hair away from their necks and letting it fall back again, or furtively putting on lipstick, fanning themselves, and sipping their beers.

"He puts me in the mind of a man I once knew," said Mrs. Tubby.

"Look at them," said Mrs. Tens. "Don't you think he's young enough to be her son?"

With my elbows on my knees and my chin in my hands, I watched Aunt Moon step and square when my mother loomed up like a shadow over the bleachers where I sat.

"Young lady," she said in a scolding voice. "You were supposed to go home and put the children to bed."

I looked from her stern face to my sister Susan, who was like a chubby angel sleeping beside me. Peso Junior had run off to the gambling game, where he was pushing another little boy around. My mother followed my gaze and looked at Junior. She put her hands on her hips and said, "Boys!"

My sister Roberta, who was twelve, had stayed close to the women all night, listening to their talk about the full-blood who had come to town for a rodeo or something and who danced so far away from Bessie that they didn't look friendly at all except for the fact that the music had stopped and they were still waltzing.

Margaret Tubby won the prize money that year for the biggest pumpkin. It was 220.4 centimeters in circumference and weighed 190 pounds and had to be carried on a stretcher by the volunteer firemen. Mrs. Tubby was the town's chief social justice. She sat most days on the bench outside the grocery store. Sitting there like a full-chested hawk on a fence, she held court. She had watched Bess Evening for years with her sharp gold eyes. "This is the year I saw it coming," she told my mother, as if she'd just been dying for Bess to go wrong. It showed up in the way Bess walked, she said, that the woman was coming to a no good end just like the rest of her family had done.

"When do you think she had time to grow that pumpkin?" Mother asked as we escaped Margaret Tubby's court on our way to the store. I knew what she meant, that Mrs. Tubby did more time with gossip than with her garden.

Margaret was even more pious than usual at that time of year when the green tent revival followed on the heels of the fair, when the pink-faced men in white shirts arrived and, really, every single one of them was a preacher. Still, Margaret Tubby kept her prize money to herself and didn't give a tithe to any church.

With Bess Evening carrying on with a stranger young enough to be her son, Mrs. Tubby succeeded in turning the church women against her once and for all. When Bessie walked down the busy street, one of the oldest dances of women took place, for women in those days turned against each other easily, never thinking they might have other enemies. When Bess appeared, the women stepped away. They vanished from the very face of earth that was named Comanche Street. They disappeared into the Oklahoma redstone shops like swallows swooping into their small clay nests. The women would look at the new bolts of red cloth in Terwilligers with feigned interest, although they would never have worn red, even to a dog fight. They'd purchase another box of face powder in the five and dime, or drink cherry phosphates at the pharmacy without so much as tasting the flavor.

But Bessie was unruffled. She walked on in the empty mirage of heat, the sound of her cane blending in with horse hooves and the rhythmic pumping of oil wells out east.

At the store, my mother bought corn meal, molasses, and milk. I bought penny candy for my younger sisters and for Peso Junior with the money I earned by helping Aunt Moon with her remedies. When we passed Margaret Tubby on the way out, my mother nodded at her, but said to me, "That pumpkin grew fat on gossip. I'll bet she fed it with nothing but all-night rumors." I thought about the twenty-five-dollar prize money and decided to grow pumpkins next year.

My mother said, "Now don't you get any ideas about growing pumpkins, young lady. We don't have room enough. They'd crowd out the cucumbers and tomatoes."

My mother and father won a prize that year, too. For dancing. They won a horse lamp for the living room. "We didn't even know it was a contest," my mother said, free from the sin of competition. Her face was rosy with pleasure and pride. She had the life snapping out of her like hot grease, though sometimes I saw that life turn to a slow and restless longing, like when she daydreamed out the window where the young man had stood that day.

Passing Margaret's post and giving up on growing a two-hundred-pound pumpkin, I remembered all the things good Indian women were not supposed to do. We were not supposed to look into the faces of men. Or laugh too loud. We were not supposed to learn too much from books because that kind of knowledge was a burden to the soul. Not only that, it always took us away from our loved ones. I was jealous of the white girls who laughed as loud as they wanted and never had rules. Also, my mother wanted me to go to college no matter what anyone else said or thought. She said I was too smart to stay home and live a life like hers, even if the other people thought book learning would ruin my life.

Aunt Moon with her second sight and heavy breasts managed to break all the rules. She threw back her head and laughed out loud, showing off the worn edges of her teeth. She didn't go to church. She did a man's work, cared for animals, and chopped her own wood. The gossiping women said it was a wonder Bessie Evening was healthy at all and didn't have female problems—meaning with her body, I figured.

The small woman inside her eye was full and lonely at the same time.

Bess made tonics, remedies, and cures. The church women, even those who gossiped, slipped over to buy Bessie's potions at night and in secret. They'd never admit they swallowed the "snake medicine," as they called it. They'd say to Bess, "What have you got to put the life back in a man? My sister has that trouble, you know." Or they'd say,

"I have a friend who needs a cure for the sadness." They bought remedies for fever and for coughing fits, for sore muscles and for sleepless nights.

Aunt Moon had learned the cures from her parents, who were said to have visited their own sins upon their children, both of whom were born out of wedlock from the love of an old Chickasaw man and a young woman from one of those tribes up north. Maybe a Navajo or something, the people thought.

But Aunt Moon had numerous talents and I respected them. She could pull cotton, pull watermelons, and pull babies with equal grace. She even delivered those scrub cattle, bred with Holsteins too big for them, caesarean. In addition to that, she told me the ways of the world and not just about the zodiac or fortune cards. "The United States is in love with death," she would say. "They sleep with it better than with lovers. They celebrate it on holidays, the Fourth of July, even in spring when they praise the loss of a good man's body."

She would tend her garden while I'd ask questions. What do you think about heaven? I wanted to know. She'd look up and then get back to pulling the weeds. "You and I both would just grump around up there with all those righteous people. Women like us weren't meant to live on golden streets. We're Indians," she'd say as she cleared out the space around a bean plant. "We're like these beans. We grew up from mud." And then she'd tell me how the people emerged right along with the crawdads from the muddy female swamps of the land. "And what is gold anyway? Just something else that comes from mud. Look at the conquistadors." She pulled a squash by accident. "And look at the sad women of this town, old already and all because of gold." She poked a hole in the ground and replanted the roots of the squash. "Their men make money, but not love. They give the women gold rings, gold-rimmed glasses, gold teeth, but their skin dries up for lack of love. Their hearts are little withered raisins." I was embarrassed by the mention of making love, but I listened to her words.

This is how I came to call Bessie Evening by the name of Aunt Moon: She'd been teaching me that animals and all life should be greeted properly as our kinfolk. "Good day,

Uncle,'' I learned to say to the longhorn as I passed by on the road. "Good morning, cousins. Is there something you need?'' I'd say to the sparrows. And one night when the moon was passing over Bessie's house, I said, "Hello, Aunt Moon. I see you are full of silver again tonight.'' It was so much like Bess Evening, I began to think, that I named her after the moon. She was sometimes full and happy, sometimes small and weak. I began saying it right to her ears: "Auntie Moon, do you need some help today?''

She seemed both older and younger than thirty-nine to me. For one thing, she walked with a cane. She had developed some secret ailment after her young daughter died. My mother said she needed the cane because she had no mortal human to hold her up in life, like the rest of us did.

But the other thing was that she was full of mystery and she laughed right out loud, like a Gypsy, my mother said, pointing out Bessie's blue-painted walls, bright clothes and necklaces, and all the things she kept hanging from her ceiling. She decorated outside her house, too, with bits of blue glass hanging from the trees, and little polished quartz crystals that reflected rainbows across the dry hills.

Aunt Moon had solid feet, a light step, and a face that clouded over with emotion and despair one moment and brightened up like light the next. She'd beam and say to me, "Sassafras will turn your hair red,'' and throw back her head to laugh, knowing full well that I would rinse my dull hair with sassafras that very night, ruining my mother's pans.

I sat in Aunt Moon's kitchen while she brewed herbals in white enamel pans on the woodstove. The insides of the pans were black from sassafras and burdock and other plants she picked. The kitchen smelled rich and earthy. Some days it was hard to breathe from the combination of woodstove heat and pollen from the plants, but she kept at it and her medicine for cramps was popular with the women in town.

Aunt Moon made me proud of my womanhood, giving me bags of herbs and an old eagle feather that had been doctored by her father back when people used to pray instead of going to church. "The body divines everything,'' she told me, and sometimes when I was with her, I knew the older Indian world was still here and I'd feel it in my skin and hear the night sounds speak to me, hear the voice of water tell stories about people who lived here before, and the deep songs came out from the hills.

One day I found Aunt Moon sitting at her table in front of a plate of untouched toast and wild plum jam. She was weeping. I was young and didn't know what to say, but she told me more than I could ever understand. "Ever since my daughter died," she told me, "my body aches to touch her. All the mourning has gone into my bones." Her long hair was loose that day and it fell down her back like a waterfall, almost to the floor.

After that I had excuses on the days I saw her hair loose. "I'm putting up new wallpaper today," I'd say, or "I have to help Mom can peaches," which was the truth.

"Sure," she said, and I saw the tinge of sorrow around her eyes even though she smiled and nodded at me.

Canning the peaches, I asked my mother what it was that happened to Aunt Moon's daughter.

"First of all," my mother set me straight, "her name is Bess, not Aunt Moon." Then she'd tell the story of Willow Evening. "That pretty child was the light of that woman's eye," my mother said. "It was all so fast. She was playing one minute and the next she was gone. She was hanging on to that wooden planter and pulled it right down onto her little chest."

My mother touched her chest. "I saw Bessie lift it like it weighed less than a pound—did I already tell you that part?"

All I had seen that day was Aunt Moon holding Willow's thin body. The little girl's face was already gone to ashes and Aunt Moon blew gently on her daughter's skin, even though she was dead, as if she could breathe the life back into her one more time. She blew on her skin the way I later knew that women blow sweat from lovers' faces, cooling them. But I knew nothing of any kind of passion then.

The planter remained on the dry grassy mound of Aunt Moon's yard, and even though she had lifted it, no one else, not even my father, could move it. It was still full of earth and dead geraniums, like a monument to the child.

"That girl was all she had," my mother said through the steam of boiling water. "Hand me the ladle, will you?"

The peaches were suspended in sweet juice in their clear jars. I thought of our lives—so short, the skin so soft around us that we could be gone any second from our living—

thought I saw Willow's golden brown face suspended behind glass in one of the jars.

The men first noticed the stranger, Isaac, when he cleaned them out in the poker game that night at the fair. My father, who had been drinking, handed over the money he'd saved for the new bathroom mirror and took a drunken swing at the young man, missing him by a foot and falling on his bad knee. Mr. Tubby told his wife he lost all he'd saved for the barber shop business, even though everyone in town knew he drank it up long before the week of the fair. Mr. Tens lost his Mexican silver ring. It showed up later on Aunt Moon's hand.

Losing to one another was one thing. Losing to Isaac Cade meant the dark young man was a card sharp and an outlaw. Even the women who had watched the stranger all that night were sure he was full of demons.

The next time I saw Aunt Moon, it was the fallow season of autumn, but she seemed new and fresh as spring. Her skin had new light. Gathering plants, she smiled at me. Her cane moved aside the long dry grasses to reveal what grew underneath. Mullein was still growing, and holly.

I sat at the table while Aunt Moon ground yellow ochre in a mortar. Isaac came in from fixing the roof. He touched her arm so softly I wasn't sure she felt it. I had never seen a man touch a woman that way.

He said hello to me and he said, "You know those fairgrounds? That's where the three tribes used to hold sings." He drummed on the table, looking at me, and sang one of the songs. I said I recognized it, a song I sometimes dreamed I heard from the hill.

A red handprint appeared on his face, like one of those birthmarks that only show up in the heat or under the strain of work or feeling.

"How'd you know about the fairgrounds?" I asked him.

"My father was from here." He sat still, as if thinking himself into another time. He stared out the window at the distances that were in between the blue curtains.

I went back to Aunt Moon's the next day. Isaac wasn't there, so Aunt Moon and I tied sage in bundles with twine. I asked her about love.

"It comes up from the ground just like corn," she said. She pulled a knot tighter with her teeth.

Later, when I left, I was still thinking about love. Outside where Bess had been planting, black beetles were digging themselves under the turned soil, and red ants had grown wings and were starting to fly.

When I returned home, my mother was sitting outside the house on a chair. She pointed at Bess Evening's house. "With the man there," she said, "I think it best you don't go over to Bessie's house anymore."

I started to protest, but she interrupted. "There are no ands, ifs, or buts about it."

I knew it was my father who made the decision. My mother had probably argued my point and lost to him again, and lost some of her life as well. She was slowed down to a slumberous pace. Later that night as I stood by my window looking toward Aunt Moon's house, I heard my mother say, "God damn them all and this whole damned town."

"There now," my father said. "There now."

"She's as dark and stained as those old black pans she uses," Margaret Tubby said about Bess Evening one day. She had come to pick up a cake from Mother for the church bake sale. I was angered by her words. I gave her one of those "looks could kill" faces, but I said nothing. We all looked out the window at Aunt Moon. She was standing near Isaac, looking at a tree. It leapt into my mind suddenly, like lightning, that Mrs. Tubby knew about the blackened pans. That would mean she had bought cures from Aunt Moon. I was smug about this discovery.

Across the way, Aunt Moon stood with her hand outstretched, palm up. It was filled with roots or leaves. She was probably teaching Isaac about the remedies. I knew Isaac would teach her things also, older things, like squirrel sickness and porcupine disease that I'd heard about from grandparents.

Listening to Mrs. Tubby, I began to understand why, right after the fair, Aunt Moon had told me I would have to fight hard to keep my life in this town. Mrs. Tubby said, "Living out of wedlock! Just like her parents." She went on, "History repeats itself."

I wanted to tell Mrs. Tubby a thing or two myself. "History, my eye," I wanted to say. "You're just jealous about the young man." But Margaret Tubby was still angry that her husband had lost his money to the stranger, and also because she probably still felt bad about playing with her necklace like a young girl that night at the fair. My mother said nothing, just covered the big caramel cake and handed it over to Mrs. Tubby. My mother looked like she was tired of fools and that included me. She looked like the woman inside her eye had just wandered off.

I began to see the women in Pickens as ghosts. I'd see them in the library looking at the stereopticons, and in the ice cream parlor. The more full Aunt Moon grew, the more drawn and pinched they became.

The church women echoed Margaret. "She's as stained as her pans," they'd say, and they began buying their medicines at the pharmacy. It didn't matter that their coughs returned and that their children developed more fevers. It didn't matter that some of them could not get pregnant when they wanted to or that Mrs. Tens grew thin and pale and bent. They wouldn't dream of lowering themselves to buy Bessie's medicines.

My mother ran hot water into the tub and emptied one of her packages of bubble powder in it. "Take a bath," she told me. "It will steady your nerves."

I was still crying, standing at the window, looking out at Aunt Moon's house through the rain.

The heavy air had been broken by an electrical storm earlier that day. In a sudden crash, the leaves flew off their trees, the sky exploded with lightning, and thunder rumbled the earth. People went to their doors to watch. It scared me. The clouds turned green and it began to hail and clatter.

That was when Aunt Moon's old dog, Mister, ran off, went running like crazy through the town. Some of the older men saw him on the street. They thought he was hurt and dying because of the way he ran and twitched. He butted right into a tree and the men thought maybe he had rabies or something. They meant to put him out of his pain. One of them took aim with a gun and shot him, and when the storm died down and the streets misted over, everything returned to heavy stillness and old Mister was lying on the edge of the Smiths' lawn. I picked him up and carried his heavy body up to Aunt Moon's porch. I covered him with sage, like she would have done.

Bess and Isaac had gone over to Alexander that day to sell remedies. They missed the rain, and when they returned, they were happy about bringing home bags of beans, ground corn, and flour.

I guess it was my mother who told Aunt Moon about her dog.

That evening I heard her wailing. I could hear her from my window and I looked out and saw her with her hair all down around her shoulders like a black shawl. Isaac smoothed back her hair and held her. I guessed that all the mourning was back in her bones again, even for her little girl, Willow.

That night my mother sat by my bed. "Sometimes the world is a sad place," she said and kissed my hot forehead. I began to cry again.

"Well, she still has the burro," my mother said, neglecting to mention Isaac.

I began to worry about the burro and to look after it. I went over to Aunt Moon's against my mother's wishes, and took carrots and sugar to the gray burro. I scratched his big ears.

By this time, most of the younger and healthier men had signed up to go to Korea and fight for their country. Most of the residents of Pickens were mixed-blood Indians and they were even more patriotic than white men. I guess they wanted to prove that they were good Americans. My father left and we saw him off at the depot. I admit I missed him saying to me, "The trouble with you is you think too much." Old Peso, always telling people what their problems were. Margaret Tubby's lazy son had enlisted because, as his mother had said, "It would make a man of him," and when he was killed in action, the townspeople resented Isaac, Bess Evening's young man, even more since he did not have his heart set on fighting the war.

Aunt Moon was pregnant the next year when the fair came around again, and she was just beginning to show. Margaret Tubby had remarked that Bess was visiting all those family sins on another poor child.

This time I was older. I fixed Mrs. Tubby in my eyes and

I said, "Mrs. Tubby, you are just like history, always repeating yourself."

She pulled her head back into her neck like a turtle. My mother said, "Hush, Sis. Get inside the house." She put her hands on her hips. "I'll deal with you later." She almost added, "Just wait till your father gets home."

Later, I felt bad, talking that way to Margaret Tubby so soon after she lost her son.

Shortly after the fair, we heard that the young man inside Aunt Moon's eye was gone. A week passed and he didn't return. I watched her house from the window and I knew, if anyone stood behind me, the little house was resting up on my shoulder.

Mother took a nap and I grabbed the biscuits off the table and snuck out.

"I didn't hear you come in," Aunt Moon said to me.

"I didn't knock," I told her. "My mom just fell asleep. I thought it'd wake her up."

Aunt Moon's hair was down. Her hands were on her lap. A breeze came in the window. She must not have been sleeping and her eyes looked tired. I gave her the biscuits I had taken off the table. I lied and told her my mother had sent them over. We ate one.

Shortly after Isaac was gone, Bess Evening again became the focus of the town's women. Mrs. Tubby said, "Bessie would give you the shirt off her back. She never deserved a no good man who would treat her like dirt and then run off." Mrs. Tubby went over to Bess Evening's and bought enough cramp remedy from the pregnant woman to last her and her daughters for the next two years.

Mrs. Tens lost her pallor. She went to Bessie's with a basket of jellies and fruits, hoping in secret that Bess would return Mr. Tens's Mexican silver ring now that the young man was gone.

The women were going to stick by her; you could see it in their squared shoulders. They no longer hid their purchases of herbs. They forgot how they'd looked at Isaac's black eyes and lively body with longing that night of the dance. If they'd had dowsing rods, the split willow branches would have flown up to the sky, so much had they twisted around the truth of things and even their own natures. Isaac was the worst of men. Their husbands, who were absent, were saints who loved them. Every morning when my mother said her prayers and forgot she'd damned the town and everybody in it, I heard her ask for peace for Bessie Evening, but she never joined in with the other women who seemed happy over Bessie's tragedy.

Isaac was doubly condemned in his absence. Mrs. Tubby said, "What kind of fool goes off to leave a woman who knows about tea leaves and cures for diseases of the body and the mind alike? I'll tell you what kind, a card shark, that's what."

Someone corrected her. "Card *sharp,* dearie, not *shark.*"

Who goes off and leaves a woman whose trees are hung with charming stones, relics, and broken glass, a woman who hangs sage and herbs to dry on her walls and whose front porch is full of fresh-cut wood? Those women, how they wanted to comfort her, but Bess Evening would only go to the door, leave them standing outside on the steps, and hand their herbs to them through the screen.

My cousins from Denver came for the fair. I was going to leave with them and get a job in the city for a year or so, then go on to school. My mother insisted she could handle the little ones alone now that they were bigger, and that I ought to go. It was best I made some money and learned what I could, she said.

"Are you sure?" I asked while my mother washed her hair in the kitchen sink.

"I'm sure as the night's going to fall." She sounded light-hearted, but her hands stopped moving and rested on her head until the soap lather began to disappear. "Besides, your dad will probably be home any day now."

I said, "Okay then, I'll go. I'll write you all the time." I was all full of emotion, but I didn't cry.

"Don't make promises you can't keep," my mother said, wrapping a towel around her head.

I went to the dance that night with my cousins, and out in the trees I let Jim Tens kiss me and promised him that I would be back. "I'll wait for you," he said. "And keep away from those city boys."

I meant it when I said, "I will."

He walked me home, holding my hand. My cousins were

still at the dance. Mom would complain about their late city hours. Once she even told us that city people eat supper as late as eight o'clock P.M. We didn't believe her.

After Jim kissed me at the door, I watched him walk down the street. I was surprised that I didn't feel sad.

I decided to go to see Aunt Moon one last time. I was leaving at six in the morning and was already packed and I had taken one of each herb sample I'd learned from Aunt Moon, just in case I ever needed them.

I scratched the burro's gray face at the lot and walked up toward the house. The window was gold and filled with lamplight. I heard an owl hooting in the distance and stopped to listen.

I glanced in the window and stopped in my tracks. The young man, Isaac, was there. He was speaking close to Bessie's face. He put his finger under her chin and lifted her face up to his. He was looking at her with soft eyes and I could tell there were many men and women living inside their eyes that moment. He held her cane across the back of her hips. With it, he pulled her close to him and held her tight, his hands on the cane pressing her body against his. And he kissed her. Her hair was down around her back and shoulders and she put her arms around his neck. I turned to go. I felt dishonest and guilty for looking in at them. I began to run.

I ran into the bathroom and bent over the sink to wash my face. I wiped Jim Tens's cold kiss from my lips. I glanced up to look at myself in the mirror, but my face was nothing, just shelves of medicine bottles and aspirin. I had forgotten the mirror was broken.

From the bathroom door I heard my mother saying her prayers, fervently, and louder than usual. She said, "Bless Sis's Aunt Moon and bless Isaac, who got arrested for trading illegal medicine for corn, and forgive him for escaping from jail."

She said this so loud, I thought she was talking to me. Maybe she was. Now how did she read my mind again? It made me smile, and I guessed I was reading hers.

All the next morning, driving through the deep blue sky, I thought how all the women had gold teeth and hearts like withered raisins. I hoped Jim Tens would marry one of the

Tubby girls. I didn't know if I'd ever go home or not. I had Aunt Moon's herbs in my bag, and the eagle feather wrapped safe in a scarf. And I had a small, beautiful woman in my eye.

❦

GISH JEN (born Lillian Jen) was educated at Harvard, Stanford, and the University of Iowa. She has taught writing at Tufts University and the University of Massachusetts. Her awards and honors include a Henfield Foundation *Transatlantic Review* Award, 1983; resident, MacDowell Colony, 1985 and 1987; fellow, Radcliffe Bunting Institute, 1986; an NEA grant, 1988. Her fiction is represented in many anthologies including *Best American Short Stories of 1988, New Worlds of Literature,* and *Home to Stay: Asian American Women's Fiction.* Her first novel, *Typical American,* was published in 1991 to enthusiastic reviews. A.G. Mojtabai's comments in *The New York Times Book Review* also apply to "What Means Switch," the prize-winning story that follows here: "Migration and mutation form a persistent characterizing theme for our unsettling time [and] Gish Jen has engaged this theme with distinction. . . . No paraphrase could capture the intelligence of her prose, its epigrammatic sweep and swiftness." Like Amy Tan (page 242), Jen's fiction follows the hopeful and ambivalent lives of Chinese immigrants with bracing humor and unfailing sympathy. In "What Means Switch," Jen considers the theme of mixed races, intermarriage, whatever the name one gives to the tossing together of the pieces of the American mosaic. Her comic view of intermingled ethnicities bears an interesting comparison with the darker picture of such transformation rendered by Patricia Zelver (page 316).

❦

What Means Switch

❦

Gish Jen

There we are, nice Chinese family—father, mother,
two born-here girls. Where should we live next?
My parents slide the question back and forth like a
cup of ginseng neither one wants to drink. Until finally it
comes to them, what they really want is a milkshake (chocolate) and to go with it a house in Scarsdale. What else?
The broker tries to hint: the neighborhood, she says. Mon-
eyed. Many delis. Meaning rich and Jewish. But someone
has sent my parents a list of the top ten schools nation-wide
(based on the opinion of selected educators and others) and
so *many-deli* or not we nestle into a Dutch colonial on the
Bronx River Parkway. The road's windy where we are, very
charming; drivers miss their turns, plough up our flower
beds, then want to use our telephone. "Of course," my
mom tells them, like it's no big deal, we can replant. We're
the type to adjust. You know—the lady drivers weep, my
mom gets out the Kleenex for them. We're a bit down the
hill from the private plane set, in other words. Only in our
dreams do our jacket zippers jam, what with all the lift
tickets we have stapled to them, Killington on top of Sugar-
bush on top of Stowe, and we don't even know where the
Virgin Islands are—although certain of us do know that virgins are like priests and nuns, which there were a lot more
of in Yonkers, where we just moved from, than there are
here.

This is my first understanding of class. In our old neighborhood everybody knew everything about virgins and non-

virgins, not to say the technicalities of staying in-between. Or almost everybody, I should say; in Yonkers I was the laugh-along type. Here I'm an expert.

"You mean the man . . . ?" Pig-tailed Barbara Gugelstein spits a mouthful of Coke back into her can. "That is *so* gross!"

Pretty soon I'm getting popular for a new girl, the only problem is Danielle Meyers, who wears blue mascara and has gone steady with two boys. "How do *you* know," she starts to ask, proceeding to edify us all with how she French-kissed one boyfriend and just regular kissed another. ("Because, you know, he had braces.") We hear about his rubber bands, how once one popped right into her mouth. I begin to realize I need to find somebody to kiss too. But how?

Luckily, I just about then happen to tell Barbara Gugelstein I know karate. I don't know why I tell her this. My sister Callie's the liar in the family; ask anybody. I'm the one who doesn't see why we should have to hold our heads up. But for some reason I tell Barbara Gugelstein I can make my hands like steel by thinking hard. "I'm not supposed to tell anyone," I say.

The way she backs away, blinking, I could be the burning bush.

"I can't do bricks," I say—a bit of expectation management. "But I can do your arm if you want." I set my hand in chop position.

"Uhh, it's okay," she says. "I know you can, I saw it on TV last night."

That's when I recall that I too saw it on TV last night— in fact, at her house. I rush on to tell her I know how to get pregnant with tea.

"With *tea*?"

"That's how they do it in China."

She agrees that China is an ancient and great civilization that ought to be known for more than spaghetti and gunpowder. I tell her I know Chinese. *"Be-yeh fa-foon,"* I say. *"Shee-veh. Ji nu."* Meaning, "Stop acting crazy. Rice gruel. Soy sauce." She's impressed. At lunch the next day, Danielle Meyers and Amy Weinstein and Barbara's crush, Andy Kaplan, are all impressed too. Scarsdale is a liberal town, not like Yonkers, where the Whitman Road Gang used to throw crabapple mash at my sister Callie and me and tell us it would make our eyes stick shut. Here we're like permanent exchange students. In another ten years, there'll be so many Orientals we'll turn into Asians; a Japanese grocery will buy out that one deli too many. But for now, the mid-sixties, what with civil rights on TV, we're not so much accepted as embraced. Especially by the Jewish part of town—which, it turns out, is not all of town at all. That's just an idea people have, Callie says, and lots of them could take us or leave us same as the Christians, who are nice too; I shouldn't generalize. So let me not generalize except to say that pretty soon I've been to so many bar and bas mitzvahs, I can almost say myself whether the kid chants like an angel or like a train conductor, maybe they could use him on the commuter line. At seder I know to forget the bricks, get a good pile of that mortar. Also I know what is schmaltz. I know that I am a goy. This is not why people like me, though. People like me because I do not need to use deodorant, as I demonstrate in the locker room before and after gym. Also, I can explain to them, for example, what is tofu (*der-voo*, we say at home). Their mothers invite me to taste-test their Chinese cooking.

"Very authentic." I try to be reassuring. After all, they're nice people, I like them. "De-lish." I have seconds. On the question of what we eat, though, I have to admit, "Well, no, it's different than that." I have thirds. "What my mom makes is home style, it's not in the cookbooks."

Not in the cookbooks! Everyone's jealous. Meanwhile, the big deal at home is when we have turkey pot pie. My sister Callie's the one introduced them—Mrs. Wilder's, they come in this green-and-brown box—and when we have them, we both get suddenly interested in helping out in the kitchen. You know, we stand in front of the oven and help them bake. Twenty-five minutes. She and I have a deal, though, to keep it secret from school, as everybody else thinks they're gross. We think they're a big improvement over authentic Chinese home cooking. Ox-tail soup—now that's gross. Stir-fried beef with tomatoes. One day I say, "You know Ma, I have never seen a stir-fried tomato in any Chinese restaurant we have ever been in, ever."

"In China," she says, real lofty, "we consider tomatoes are a delicacy."

"Ma," I say. "Tomatoes are *Italian*."

"No respect for elders." She wags her finger at me, but I can tell it's just to try and shame me into believing her. "I'm tell you, tomatoes *invented* in China."

"*Ma.*"

"Is true. Like noodles. Invented in China."

"That's not what they said in *school.*"

"In *China,*" my mother counters, "we also eat tomatoes uncooked, like apple. And in summertime we slice them, and put some sugar on top."

"Are you sure?"

My mom says of course she's sure, and in the end I give in, even though she once told me that China was such a long time ago, a lot of things she can hardly remember. She said sometimes she has trouble remembering her characters, that sometimes she'll be writing a letter, just writing along, and all of a sudden she won't be sure if she should put four dots or three.

"So what do you do then?"

"Oh, I just make a little sloppy."

"You mean you *fudge*?"

She laughed then, but another time, when she was showing me how to write my name, and I said, just kidding, "Are you sure that's the right number of dots now?" she was hurt.

"I mean, of course you know," I said. "I mean, *oy.*"

Meanwhile, what *I* know is that in the eighth grade, what people want to hear does not include how Chinese people eat sliced tomatoes with sugar on top. For a gross fact, it just isn't gross enough. On the other hand, the fact that somewhere in China somebody eats or has eaten or once ate living monkey brains—now that's conversation.

"They have these special tables," I say, "kind of like a giant collar. With a hole in the middle, for the monkey's neck. They put the monkey in the collar, and then they cut off the top of its head."

"Whadda they use for cutting?"

I think. "Scalpels."

"*Scalpels?*" says Andy Kaplan.

"Kaplan, don't be dense," Barbara Gugelstein says. "The Chinese *invented* scalpels."

Once a friend said to me, You know, everybody is valued for something. She explained how some people resented

being valued for their looks; others resented being valued
for their money. Wasn't it still better to be beautiful and
rich than ugly and poor, though? You should be just glad,
she said, that you have something people value. It's like
having a special talent, like being good at ice-skating, or
opera-singing. She said, You could probably make a career
out of it.

Here's the irony: I am.

Anyway. I am ad-libbing my way through eighth grade,
as I've described. Until one bloomy spring day, I come in
late to homeroom, and to my chagrin discover there's a new
kid in class.

Chinese.

So what should I do, pretend to have to go to the girls'
room, like Barbara Gugelstein the day Andy Kaplan took
his ID back? I sit down; I am so cool I remind myself of
Paul Newman. First thing I realize, though, is that no one
looking at me is thinking of Paul Newman. The notes fly:

"*I* think he's cute."

"Who?" I write back. (I am still at an age, understand,
when I believe a person can be saved by aplomb.)

"I don't think he talks English too good. Writes it either."

"Who?"

"They might have to put him behind a grade, so don't
worry."

"He has a crush on you already, you could tell as soon
as you walked in, he turned kind of orangish."

I hope I'm not turning orangish as I deal with my mail, I
could use a secretary. The second round starts:

"What do you mean who? Don't be weird. Didn't you
see him??? Straight back over your right shoulder!!!!"

I have to look; what else can I do? I think of certain tips
I learned in Girl Scouts about poise. I cross my ankles. I
hold a pen in my hand. I sit up as though I have a crown
on my head. I swivel my head slowly, repeating to myself,
I could be Miss America.

"Miss Mona Chang."

Horror raises its hoary head.

"Notes, please."

Mrs. Mandeville's policy is to read all notes aloud.

I try to consider what Miss America would do, and see

myself, back straight, knees together, crying. Some inspiration. Cool Hand Luke, on the other hand, would, quick, eat the evidence. And why not? I should yawn as I stand up, and boom, the notes are gone. All that's left is to explain that it's an old Chinese reflex.

I shuffle up to the front of the room.

"One minute please," Mrs. Mandeville says.

I wait, noticing how large and plastic her mouth is.

She unfolds a piece of paper.

And I, Miss Mona Chang, who got almost straight A's her whole life except in math and conduct, am about to start crying in front of everyone.

I am delivered out of hot Egypt by the bell. General pandemonium. Mrs. Mandeville still has her hand clamped on my shoulder, though. And the next thing I know, I'm holding the new boy's schedule. He's standing next to me like a big blank piece of paper. "This is Sherman," Mrs. Mandeville says.

"Hello," I say.

"Non how a," I say.

I'm glad Barbara Gugelstein isn't there to see my Chinese in action.

"Ji nu," I say. *"Shee veh."*

Later I find out that his mother asked if there were any other Orientals in our grade. She had him put in my class on purpose. For now, though, he looks at me as though I'm much stranger than anything else he's seen so far. Is this because he understands I'm saying "soy sauce rice gruel" to him or because he doesn't?

"Sher-man," he says finally.

I look at his schedule card. Sherman Matsumoto. What kind of name is that for a nice Chinese boy?

(Later on, people ask me how I can tell Chinese from Japanese. I shrug. You just kind of know, I say. *Oy!*)

Sherman's got the sort of looks I think of as pretty-boy. Monsignor-black hair (not monk brown like mine), bouncy. Crayola eyebrows, one with a round bald spot in the middle of it, like a golf hole. I don't know how anybody can think of him as orangish; his skin looks white to me, with pink triangles hanging down the front of his cheeks like flags. Kind of delicate-looking, but the only truly uncool thing about him is that his spiral notebook has a picture of a kitty cat on it. A big white fluffy one, with a blue ribbon above each perky little ear. I get much opportunity to view this, as all the poor kid understands about life in junior high school is that he should follow me everywhere. It's embarrassing. On the other hand, he's obviously even more miserable than I am, so I try not to say anything. Give him a chance to adjust. We communicate by sign language, and by drawing pictures, which he's better at than I am; he puts in every last detail, even if it takes forever. I try to be patient.

A week of this. Finally I enlighten him. "You should get a new notebook."

His cheeks turn a shade of pink you mostly only see in hyacinths.

"Notebook." I point to his. I show him mine, which is psychedelic, with big purple and yellow stick-on flowers. I try to explain he should have one like this, only without the flowers. He nods enigmatically, and the next day brings me a notebook just like his, except that this cat sports pink bows instead of blue.

"Pret-ty," he says. "You."

He speaks English! I'm dumbfounded. Has he spoken it all this time? I consider: Pretty. You. What does that mean? Plus actually, he's said *plit-ty,* much as my parents would; I'm assuming he means pretty, but maybe he means pity. Pity. You.

"Jeez," I say finally.

"You are wel-come," he says.

I decorate the back of the notebook with stick-on flowers, and hold it so that these show when I walk through the halls. In class I mostly keep my book open. After all, the kid's so new; I think I really ought to have a heart. And for a livelong day nobody notices.

Then Barbara Gugelstein sidles up. "Matching notebooks, huh?"

I'm speechless.

"First comes love, then comes marriage, and then come chappies in a baby carriage."

"Barbara!"

"Get it?" she says. "Chinese Japs."

"Bar-*bra*," I say to get even.

"Just make sure he doesn't give you any *tea*," she says.

Are Sherman and I in love? Three days later, I hazard that we are. My thinking proceeds this way: I think he's cute, and I think he thinks I'm cute. On the other hand, we don't kiss and we don't exactly have fantastic conversations. Our talks *are* getting better, though. We started out, "This is a book." "Book." "This is a chair." "Chair." Advancing to, "What is this?" "This is a book." Now, for fun, he tests me.

"What is this?" he says.

"This is a book," I say, as if I'm the one who has to learn how to talk.

He claps. "Good!"

Meanwhile, people ask me all about him, I could be his press agent.

"No, he doesn't eat raw fish."

"No, his father wasn't a kamikaze pilot."

"No, he can't do karate."

"Are you sure?" somebody asks.

Indeed he doesn't know karate, but judo he does. I am hurt I'm not the one to find this out; the guys know from gym class. They line up to be flipped, he flips them all onto the floor, and after that he doesn't eat lunch at the girls' table with me anymore. I'm more or less glad. Meaning, when he was there, I never knew what to say. Now that he's gone, though, I seem to be stuck at the "This is a chair" level of conversation. Ancient Chinese eating habits have lost their cachet; all I get are more and more questions about me and Sherman. "I dunno," I'm saying all the time. *Are* we going out? We do stuff, it's true. For example, I take him to the department stores, explain to him who shops in Alexander's, who shops in Saks. I tell him my family's the type that shops in Alexander's. He says he's sorry. In Saks he gets lost; either that, or else I'm the lost one. (It's true I find him calmly waiting at the front door, hands behind his back, like a guard.) I take him to the candy store. I take him to the bagel store. Sherman is crazy about bagels. I explain to him that Lender's is gross, he should get his bagels from the bagel store. He says thank you.

"Are you going steady?" people want to know.

How can we go steady when he doesn't have an ID bracelet? On the other hand, he brings me more presents than I think any girl's ever gotten before. Oranges. Flowers. A little bag of bagels. But what do they mean? Do they mean thank you, I enjoyed our trip; do they mean I like you; do they mean I decided I liked the Lender's better even if they are gross, you can have these? Sometimes I think he's acting on his mother's instructions. Also I know at least a couple of the presents were supposed to go to our teachers. He told me that once and turned red. I figured it still might mean something that he didn't throw them out.

More and more now, we joke. Like, instead of "I'm thinking," he always says, "I'm sinking," which we both think is so funny, that all either one of us has to do is pretend to be drowning and the other one cracks up. And he tells me things—for example, that there are electric lights everywhere in Tokyo now.

"You mean you didn't have them before?"

"Everywhere now!" He's amazed too. "Since Olympics!"

"Olympics?"

"1960," he says proudly, and as proof, hums for me the Olympic theme song. "You know?"

"Sure," I say, and hum with him happily. We could be a picture on a UNICEF poster. The only problem is that I don't really understand what the Olympics have to do with the modernization of Japan, any more than I get this other story he tells me, about that hole in his left eyebrow, which is from some time his father accidentally hit him with a lit cigarette. When Sherman was a baby. His father was drunk, having been out carousing; his mother was very mad but didn't say anything, just cleaned the whole house. Then his father was so ashamed he bowed to ask her forgiveness.

"Your mother cleaned the house?"

Sherman nods solemnly.

"And your father *bowed*?" I find this more astounding than anything I ever thought to make up. "That is so weird," I tell him.

"Weird," he agrees. "This I no forget, forever. *Father* bow to *mother*!"

We shake our heads.

As for the things he asks me, they're not topics I ever discussed before. Do I like it here? Of course I like it here, I was born here, I say. Am I Jewish? Jewish! I laugh. *Oy!* Am I American? "Sure I'm American," I say. "Everybody who's born here is American, and also some people who convert from what they were before. You could become American." But he says no, he could never. "Sure you could," I say. "You only have to learn some rules and speeches."

"But I Japanese," he says.

"You could become American anyway," I say. "Like I *could* become Jewish, if I wanted to. I'd just have to switch, that's all."

"But you Catholic," he says.

I think maybe he doesn't get what means switch.

I introduce him to Mrs. Wilder's turkey pot pies. "Gross?" he asks. I say they are, but we like them anyway. "Don't tell anybody." He promises. We bake them, eat them. While we're eating, he's drawing me pictures.

"This American," he says, and he draws something that looks like John Wayne. "This Jewish," he says, and draws something that looks like the Wicked Witch of the West, only male.

"I don't think so," I say.

He's undeterred. "This Japanese," he says, and draws a fair rendition of himself. "This Chinese," he says, and draws what looks to be another fair rendition of himself.

"How can you tell them apart?"

"This way," he says, and he puts the picture of the Chinese so that it is looking at the pictures of the American and the Jew. The Japanese faces the wall. Then he draws another picture, of a Japanese flag, so that the Japanese has that to contemplate. "Chinese lost in department store," he says. "Japanese know how go." For fun, he then takes the Japanese flag and fastens it to the refrigerator door with magnets. "In school, in ceremony, we this way," he explains, and bows to the picture.

When my mother comes in, her face is so red that with the white wall behind her she looks a bit like the Japanese flag herself. Yet I get the feeling I better not say so. First she doesn't move. Then she snatches the flag off the refrigerator, so fast the magnets go flying. Two of them land on the stove. She crumples up the paper. She hisses at Sherman, *"This is the U. S. of A., do you hear me!"*

Sherman hears her.

"You call your mother right now, tell her come pick you up."

He understands perfectly. *I,* on the other hand, am stymied. How can two people who don't really speak English understand each other better than I can understand them? "But Ma," I say.

"Don't *Ma* me," she says.

Later on she explains that World War II was in China, too. "Hitler," I say. "Nazis. Volkswagens." I know the Japanese were on the wrong side, because they bombed Pearl Harbor. My mother explains about before that. The Napkin Massacre. *"Nan*-king," she corrects me.

"Are you sure?" I say. "In school, they said the war was about putting the Jews in ovens."

"Also about ovens."

"About both?"

"Both."

"That's not what they said in school."

"Just forget about school."

Forget about school? "I thought we moved here for the schools."

"We moved here," she says, "for your education."

Sometimes I have no idea what she's talking about.

"I like Sherman," I say after a while.

"He's nice boy," she agrees.

Meaning what? I would ask, except that my dad's just come home, which means it's time to start talking about whether we should build a brick wall across the front of the lawn. Recently a car made it almost into our livingroom, which was so scary, the driver fainted and an ambulance had to come. "We should have discussion," my dad said after that. And so for about a week, every night we do.

"Are you just friends, or more than just friends?" Barbara Gugelstein is giving me the cross-ex.

"Maybe," I say.

"Come on," she says, "I told you *everything* about me and Andy."

I actually *am* trying to tell Barbara everything about Sherman, but everything turns out to be nothing. Meaning, I can't locate the conversation in what I have to say. Sherman and I go places, we talk, one time my mother threw him out of the house because of World War II.

"I think we're just friends," I say.

"You think or you're sure?"

Now that I do less of the talking at lunch, I notice more what other people talk about—cheerleading, who likes who, this place in White Plains to get earrings. On none of these topics am I an expert. Of course, I'm still friends with Barbara Gugelstein, but I notice Danielle Meyers has spun away to other groups.

Barbara's analysis goes this way: To be popular, you have to have big boobs, a note from your mother that lets you use her Lord and Taylor credit card, and a boyfriend. On the other hand, what's so wrong with being unpopular? "We'll get them in the end," she says. It's what her dad tells her. "Like they'll turn out too dumb to do their own investing, and then they'll get killed in fees and then they'll have to move to towns where the schools stink. And my dad should know," she winds up. "He's a broker."

"I guess," I say.

But the next thing I know, I have a true crush on Sherman Matsumoto. *Mis*ter Judo, the guys call him now, with real respect; and the more they call him that, the more I don't care that he carries a notebook with a cat on it.

I sigh. "Sherman."

"I thought you were just friends," says Barbara Gugelstein.

"We were," I say mysteriously. This, I've noticed, is how Danielle Meyers talks; everything's secret, she only lets out so much, it's like she didn't grow up with everybody telling her she had to share.

And here's the funny thing: The more I intimate that Sherman and I are more than just friends, the more it seems we actually are. It's the old imagination giving reality a nudge. When I start to blush, he starts to blush; we reach a point where we can hardly talk at all.

"Well, there's first base with tongue, and first base without," I tell Barbara Gugelstein.

In fact, Sherman and I have brushed shoulders, which was equivalent to first base I was sure, maybe even second.

I felt as though I'd turned into one huge shoulder; that's all I was, one huge shoulder. We not only didn't talk, we didn't breathe. But how can I tell Barbara Gugelstein that? So instead I say, "Well there's second base and second base."

Danielle Meyers is my friend again. She says, "I know exactly what you mean," just to make Barbara Gugelstein feel bad.

"Like *what* do I mean?" I say.

Danielle Meyers can't answer.

"You know what I think?" I tell Barbara the next day. "I think Danielle's giving us a line."

Barbara pulls thoughtfully on one of her pigtails.

If Sherman Matsumoto is never going to give me an ID to wear, he should at least get up the nerve to hold my hand. I don't think he sees this. I think of the story he told me about his parents, and in a synaptic firestorm realize we don't see the same things at all.

So one day, when we happen to brush shoulders again, I don't move away. He doesn't move away either. There we are. Like a pair of bleachers, pushed together but not quite matched up. After a while, I have to breathe, I can't help it. I breathe in such a way that our elbows start to touch too. We are in a crowd, waiting for a bus. I crane my neck to look at the sign that says where the bus is going; now our wrists are touching. Then it happens: He links his pinky around mine.

Is that holding hands? Later, in bed, I wonder all night. One finger, and not even the biggest one.

Sherman is leaving in a month. Already! I think, well, I suppose he will leave and we'll never even kiss. I guess that's all right. Just when I've resigned myself to it, though, we hold hands all five fingers. Once when we are at the bagel shop, then again in my parents' kitchen. Then, when we are at the playground, he kisses the back of my hand.

He does it again not too long after that, in White Plains.

I invest in a bottle of mouthwash.

Instead of moving on, though, he kisses the back of my hand again. And again. I try raising my hand, hoping he'll make the jump from my hand to my cheek. It's like trying to wheedle an inchworm out the window. You know, *This way, this way.*

All over the world, people have their own cultures. That's what we learned in social studies.

If we never kiss, I'm not going to take it personally.

It is the end of the school year. We've had parties. We've turned in our textbooks. Hooray! Outside the asphalt already steams if you spit on it. Sherman isn't leaving for another couple of days, though, and he comes to visit every morning, staying until the afternoon, when Callie comes home from her big-deal job as a bank teller. We drink Kool-Aid in the backyard and hold hands until they are sweaty and make smacking noises coming apart. He tells me how busy his parents are, getting ready for the move. His mother, particularly, is very tired. Mostly we are mournful.

The very last day we hold hands and do not let go. Our palms fill up with water like a blister. We do not care. We talk more than usual. How much airmail is to Japan, that kind of thing. Then suddenly he asks, will I marry him?

I'm only thirteen.

But when old? Sixteen?

If you come back to get me.

I come. Or you can come to Japan, be Japanese.

How can I be Japanese?

Like you become American. Switch.

He kisses me on the cheek, again and again and again.

His mother calls to say she's coming to get him. I cry. I tell him how I've saved every present he's ever given me—the ruler, the pencils, the bags from the bagels, all the flower petals. I even have the orange peels from the oranges.

All?

I put them in a jar.

I'd show him, except that we're not allowed to go upstairs to my room. Anyway, something about the orange peels seems to choke him up too. *Mis*ter Judo, but I've gotten him in a soft spot. We are going together to the bathroom to get some toilet paper to wipe our eyes when poor tired Mrs. Matsumoto, driving a shiny new station wagon, skids up onto our lawn.

''Very sorry!''

We race outside.

"Very sorry!"

Mrs. Matsumoto is so short that about all we can see of her is a green cotton sun hat, with a big brim. It's tied on. The brim is trembling.

I hope my mom's not going to start yelling about World War II.

"Is all right, no trouble," she says, materializing on the steps behind me and Sherman. She's propped the screen door wide open; when I turn I see she's waving. "No trouble, no trouble!"

"No trouble, no trouble!" I echo, twirling a few times with relief.

Mrs. Matsumoto keeps apologizing; my mom keeps insisting she shouldn't feel bad, it was only some grass and a small tree. Crossing the lawn, she insists Mrs. Matsumoto get out of the car, even though it means trampling some lilies-of-the-valley. She insists that Mrs. Matsumoto come in for a cup of tea. Then she will not talk about anything unless Mrs. Matsumoto sits down, and unless she lets my mom prepare her a small snack. The coming in and the tea and the sitting down are settled pretty quickly, but they negotiate ferociously over the small snack, which Mrs. Matsumoto will not eat unless she can call Mr. Matsumoto. She makes the mistake of linking Mr. Matsumoto with a reparation of some sort, which my mom will not hear of.

"Please!"

"No no no no."

Back and forth it goes: "No no no no." "No no no no." "No no no no." What kind of conversation is that? I look at Sherman, who shrugs. Finally Mr. Matsumoto calls on his own, wondering where his wife is. He comes over in a taxi. He's a heavy-browed businessman, friendly but brisk—not at all a type you could imagine bowing to a lady with a taste for tie-on sunhats. My mom invites him in as if it's an idea she just this moment thought of. And would he maybe have some tea and a small snack?

Sherman and I sneak back outside for another farewell, by the side of the house, behind the forsythia bushes. We hold hands. He kisses me on the cheek again, and then—just when I think he's finally going to kiss me on the lips—he kisses me on the neck.

Is this first base?

He does it more. Up and down, up and down. First it tickles, and then it doesn't. He has his eyes closed. I close my eyes too. He's hugging me. Up and down. Then down. He's at my collarbone.

Still at my collarbone. Now his hand's on my ribs. So much for first base. More ribs. The idea of second base would probably make me nervous if he weren't on his way back to Japan and if I really thought we were going to get there. As it is, though, I'm not in much danger of wrecking my life on the shoals of passion; his unmoving hand feels more like a growth than a boyfriend. He has his whole face pressed to my neck skin so I can't tell his mouth from his nose. I think he may be licking me.

From indoors, a burst of adult laughter. My eyelids flutter. I start to try and wiggle such that his hand will maybe budge upward.

Do I mean for my top blouse button to come accidentally undone?

He clenches his jaw, and when he opens his eyes, they're fixed on that button like it's a gnat that's been bothering him for far too long. He mutters in Japanese. If later in life he were to describe this as a pivotal moment in his youth, I would not be surprised. Holding the material as far from my body as possible, he buttons the button. Somehow we've landed up too close to the bushes.

What to tell Barbara Gugelstein? She says, "Tell me what were his last words. He must have said something last."

"I don't want to talk about it."

"Maybe he said, Good-bye?" she suggests. "Sayonara?" She means well.

"I don't want to talk about it."

"Aw, come on, I told you everything about . . ."

I say, "Because it's private, excuse me."

She stops, squints at me as though at a far-off face she's trying to make out. Then she nods and very lightly places her hand on my forearm.

The forsythia seemed to be stabbing us in the eyes. Sherman said, more or less, *You will need to study how to switch.*

And I said, *I think you should switch. The way you do everything is weird.*

And he said, *You just want to tell everything to your friends. You just want to have boyfriend to become popular.*

Then he flipped me. Two swift moves, and I went sprawling through the air, a flailing confusion of soft human parts such as had no idea where the ground was.

It is the fall, and I am in high school, and still he hasn't written, so finally I write him.

I still have all your gifts, I write. *I don't talk so much as I used to. Although I am not exactly a mouse either. I don't care about being popular anymore. I swear. Are you happy to be back in Japan? I know I ruined everything. I was just trying to be entertaining. I miss you with all my heart, and hope I didn't ruin everything.*

He writes back, *You will never be Japanese.*

I throw all the orange peels out that day. Some of them, it turns out, were moldy anyway. I tell my mother I want to move to Chinatown.

"Chinatown!" she says.

I don't know why I suggested it.

"What's the matter?" she says. "Still boy-crazy? That Sherman?"

"No."

"Too much homework?"

I don't answer.

"Forget about school."

Later she tells me if I don't like school, I don't have to go everyday. Some days I can stay home.

"Stay home?" In Yonkers, Callie and I used to stay home all the time, but that was because the schools there were *waste of time.*

"No good for a girl be too smart anyway."

For a long time I think about Sherman. But after a while I don't think about him so much as I just keep seeing myself flipped onto the ground, lying there shocked as the Matsumotos get ready to leave. My head has hit a rock; my brain aches as though it's been shoved to some new place in my skull. Otherwise I am okay. I see the forsythia, all those whippy branches, and can't believe how many leaves there are on a bush—every one green and perky and durably itself. And past them, real sky. I try to remember about why the sky's blue, even though this one's gone the kind of indescribable grey you associate with the insides of old shoes. I smell grass. Probably I have grass stains all over my back. I hear my mother calling through the back door, "Mon-a! Everyone leaving now," and "Not coming to say goodbye?" I hear Mr. and Mrs. Matsumoto bowing as they leave—or at least I hear the embarrassment in my mother's voice as they bow. I hear their car start. I hear Mrs. Matsumoto directing Mr. Matsumoto how to back off the lawn so as not to rip any more of it up. I feel the back of my head for blood—just a little. I hear their chug-chug grow fainter and fainter, until it has faded into the whuzz-whuzz of all the other cars. I hear my mom singing, "*Mon*-a! *Mon*-a!" until my dad comes home. Doors open and shut. I see myself standing up, brushing myself off so I'll have less explaining to do if she comes out to look for me. Grass stains—just like I thought. I see myself walking around the house, going over to have a look at our churned-up yard. It looks pretty sad, two big brown tracks, right through the irises and the lilies of the valley, and that was a new dogwood we'd just planted. Lying there like that. I hear myself thinking about my father, having to go dig it up all over again. Adjusting. I think how we probably ought to put up that brick wall. And sure enough, when I go inside, no one's thinking about me, or that little bit of blood at the back of my head, or the grass stains. That's what they're talking about—that wall. Again. My mom doesn't think it'll do any good, but my dad thinks we should give it a try. Should we or shouldn't we? How high? How thick? What will the neighbors say? I plop myself down on a hard chair. And all I can think is, we are the complete only family that has to worry about this. If I could, I'd switch everything to be different. But since I can't, I might as well sit here at the table for a while, discussing what I know how to discuss. I nod and listen to the rest.

ANDREA LEE was born and grew up in a middle-class suburb of Philadelphia, the child of a Baptist minister and Civil Rights activist father and a school-teacher mother. Educated at Harvard, she has worked as a staff writer for *The New Yorker*. She is the author of *Russian Journal* (1981), a non-fictional account of her year in the Soviet Union which was nominated for an American Book Award and the autobiographical novel *Sarah Phillips* (1984) from which the following selection, "New African," is taken.

Unlike many narrator/heroines in fiction by African American women writers—Toni Morrison, Paule Marshall, Alice Walker, J. California Cooper, Terry McMillan—the autobiographical character Sarah Phillips grew up as a privileged child who became for a time an assimilated elitist with little interest in the cultural and historical past of her people. Eventually realizing the emptiness of her assimilation into white society, Sarah Phillips/Andrea Lee, in a series of fictionalized vignettes, reconstructs her childhood and adolescence with a detail and insight that bring her to a deeper understanding of herself and her heritage.

In "New African," Lee re-creates her ambivalent relationship as an adolescent with the Christian tradition of her family. Alienated by Christianity's scriptural and institutional privileging of the male sex, young Sairy refuses to be born again. With the "unstinting honesty and style at once simple and yet luminous" noted by reviewer Susan Richards Shreve, Lee brings to life the paradox of a religious tradition that at once limits and frees the individuals in the church pews and pulpit. Lee's insight into the legacy of freedom bestowed by the Baptist church in the person of her preacher-father brings to mind other American women writers who have explored—and reinvented—this paradoxical religious tradition: in the past there were Anne Bradstreet, Emily Dickinson, Harriet Beecher Stowe, Harriet Jacobs, and Sojourner Truth; more recently we have Lorene Cary's *Black Ice* (1991) and Shirley Abbott's *Womenfolks: Growing Up Down South* (1983). Unlike the Puritanism of Protestant New England, the story of Southern Christianity as it has been inscribed in the life and literature of both the black and white community is a comparatively neglected or unexplored narrative in the context of American cultural studies.

———————————

❧

New African
from *Sarah Phillips*

Andrea Lee

On a hot Sunday morning in the summer of 1963, I was sitting restlessly with my mother, my brother Matthew, and my aunts Lily, Emma, and May in a central pew of the New African Baptist Church. It was mid-August, and the hum of the big electric fans at the back of the church was almost enough to muffle my father's voice from the pulpit; behind me I could hear Mrs. Gordon, a stout, feeble old woman who always complained of dizziness, remark sharply to her daughter that at the rate the air-conditioning fund was growing, it might as well be for the next century. Facing the congregation, my father—who was Reverend Phillips to the rest of the world—seemed hot himself; he mopped his brow with a handkerchief and drank several glasses of ice water from the heavy pitcher on the table by the pulpit. I looked at him critically. He's still reading the text, I thought. Then he'll do the sermon, then the baptism, and it will be an hour, maybe two.

I rubbed my chin and then idly began to snap the elastic band that held my red straw hat in place. What I would really like to do, I decided, would be to go home, put on my shorts, and climb up into the tree house I had set up the day before with Matthew. We'd nailed an old bushel basket up in the branches of the big maple that stretched above the sidewalk in front of the house; it made a sort of crow's nest where you could sit comfortably, except for a few splinters, and read, or peer through the dusty leaves at the cars that passed down the quiet suburban road. There was shade and

wind and a feeling of high adventure up in the treetop, where
the air seemed to vibrate with the dry rhythms of the cica-
das; it was as different as possible from church, where the
packed congregation sat in a near-visible miasma of emotion and cologne, and trolleys passing in the city street outside set the stained-glass windows rattling.

I slouched between Mama and Aunt Lily and felt myself
going limp with lassitude and boredom, as if the heat had
melted my bones; the only thing about me with any character seemed to be my firmly starched eyelet dress. Below
the scalloped hem, my legs were skinny and wiry, the legs
of a ten-year-old amazon, scarred from violent adventures
with bicycles and skates. A fingernail tapped my wrist; it
was Aunt Emma, reaching across Aunt Lily to press a piece
of butterscotch into my hand. When I slipped the candy into
my mouth, it tasted faintly of Arpège; my mother and her
three sisters were monumental women, ample of bust and
slim of ankle, with a weakness for elegant footwear and
French perfume. As they leaned back and forth to exchange
discreet tidbits of gossip, they fanned themselves and me
with fans from the Byron J. Wiggins Funeral Parlor. The
fans, which were fluttering throughout the church, bore a
depiction of the Good Shepherd: a hollow-eyed blond Christ
holding three fat pink-cheeked children. This Christ resembled the Christ who stood among apostles on the stained-
glass windows of the church. Deacon Wiggins, a thoughtful
man, had also provided New African with a few dozen fans
bearing the picture of a black child playing, but I rarely saw
those in use.

There was little that was new or very African about the
New African Baptist Church. The original congregation had
been formed in 1813 by three young men from Philadelphia's
large community of free blacks, and before many generations
had passed, it had become spiritual home to a collection of
prosperous, conservative, generally light-skinned parishioners. The church was a gray Gothic structure, set on the
corner of a rundown street in South Philadelphia a dozen
blocks below Rittenhouse Square and a few blocks west of
the spare, clannish Italian neighborhoods that produced
Frankie Avalon and Frank Rizzo. At the turn of the century,
the neighborhood had been a tidy collection of brick houses

with scrubbed marble steps—the homes of a group of solid citizens whom Booker T. Washington, in a centennial address to
the church, described as "the ablest Negro businessmen of our
generation." Here my father had grown up aspiring to preach
to the congregation of New African—an ambition encouraged
by my grandmother Phillips, a formidable churchwoman. Here,
too, my mother and her sisters had walked with linked arms to
Sunday services, exchanging affected little catchphrases of
French and Latin they had learned at Girls' High.

In the 1950s many of the parishioners, seized by the national urge toward the suburbs, moved to newly integrated
towns outside the city, leaving the streets around New African to fill with bottles and papers and loungers. The big
church stood suddenly isolated. It had not been abandoned—on Sundays the front steps overflowed with members who had driven in—but there was a tentative feeling in
the atmosphere of those Sunday mornings, as if through the
middle of social change, the future of New African had become unclear. Matthew and I, suburban children, felt a
mixture of pride and animosity toward the church. On the
one hand, it was a marvelous private domain, a richly decorated and infinitely suggestive playground where we were
petted by a congregation that adored our father; on the other
hand, it seemed a bit like a dreadful old relative in the city,
one who forced us into tedious visits and who linked us to
a past that came to seem embarrassingly primitive as we
grew older.

I slid down in my seat, let my head roll back, and looked
up at the blue arches of the church ceiling. Lower than these,
in back of the altar, was an enormous gilded cross. Still
lower, in a semicircle near the pulpit, sat the choir, flanked
by two tall golden files of organ pipes, and below the choir
was a somber crescent of dark-suited deacons. In front, at
the center of everything, his bald head gleaming under the
lights, was Daddy. On summer Sundays he wore white
robes, and when he raised his arms, the heavy material fell
in curving folds like the ridged petals of an Easter lily. Usually when I came through the crowd to kiss him after the
service, his cheek against my lips felt wet and gravelly with
sweat and a new growth of beard sprouted since morning.
Today, however, was a baptismal Sunday, and I wouldn't
have a chance to kiss him until he was freshly shaven and

cool from the shower he took after the ceremony. The baptismal pool was in an alcove to the left of the altar; it had mirrored walls and red velvet curtains, and above it, swaying on a string, hung a stuffed white dove.

Daddy paused in the invocation and asked the congregation to pray. The choir began to sing softly:

> *Blessed assurance,*
> *Jesus is mine!*
> *Oh what a foretaste*
> *Of glory divine!*

In the middle of the hymn, I edged my head around my mother's cool, muscular arm (she swam every day of the summer) and peered at Matthew. He was sitting bolt upright holding a hymnal and a pencil, his long legs inside his navy-blue summer suit planted neatly in front of him, his freckled thirteen-year-old face that was so like my father's wearing not the demonic grin it bore when we played alone but a maddeningly composed, attentive expression. "Two hours!" I mouthed at him, and pulled back at a warning pressure from my mother. Then I joined in the singing, feeling disappointed: Matthew had returned me a glance of scorn. Just lately he had started acting very superior and tolerant about tedious Sunday mornings. A month before, he'd been baptized, marching up to the pool in a line of white-robed children as the congregation murmured happily about Reverend Phillips's son. Afterward Mrs. Pinkston, a tiny, yellow-skinned old woman with a blind left eye, had come up to me and given me a painful hug, whispering that she was praying night and day for the pastor's daughter to hear the call as well.

I bit my fingernails whenever I thought about baptism; the subject brought out a deep-rooted balkiness in me. Ever since I could remember, Matthew and I had made a game of dispelling the mysteries of worship with a gleeful secular eye: we knew how the bread and wine were prepared for Communion, and where Daddy bought his robes (Ekhardt Brothers, in North Philadelphia, makers also of robes for choirs, academicians, and judges). Yet there was an unassailable magic about an act as public and dramatic as baptism. I felt toward it the slightly exasperated awe a stagehand might feel on realizing that although he can identify with professional exactitude the minutest components of a show, there is still something indefinable in the power that makes it a cohesive whole. Though I could not have put it into words, I believed that the decision to make a frightening and embarrassing backward plunge into a pool of sanctified water meant that one had received a summons to Christianity as unmistakable as the blare of an automobile horn. I believed this with the same fervor with which, already, I believed in the power of romance, especially in the miraculous efficacy of a lover's first kiss. I had never been kissed by a lover, nor had I heard the call to baptism.

For a Baptist minister and his wife, my father and mother were unusually relaxed about religion; Matthew and I had never been required to read the Bible, and my father's sermons had been criticized by some older church members for omitting the word "sin." Mama and Daddy never tried to push me toward baptism, but a number of other people did. Often on holidays, when I had retreated from the noise of the family dinner table and sat trying to read in my favorite place (the window seat in Matthew's room, with the curtains drawn to form a tent), Aunt Lily would come and find me. Aunt Lily was the youngest of my mother's sisters, a kindergarten teacher with the fatally overdeveloped air of quaintness that is the infallible mark of an old maid. Aunt Lily hoped and hoped again with various suitors, but even I knew she would never find a husband. I respected her because she gave me wonderful books of fairy tales, inscribed in her neat, loopy hand; when she talked about religion, however, she assumed an anxious, flirtatious air that made me cringe. "Well, Miss Sarah, what are you scared of?" she would ask, tugging gently on one of my braids and bringing her plump face so close to mine that I could see her powder, which was, in accordance with the custom of fashionable colored ladies, several shades lighter than her olive skin. "God isn't anyone to be afraid of!" she'd continue as I looked at her with my best deadpan expression. "He's someone nice, just as nice as your daddy"—I had always suspected Aunt Lily of having a crush on my father—"and he loves you, in the same way your daddy does!"

"You would make us all so happy!" I was told at different times by Aunt Lily, Aunt Emma, and Aunt May. The only people who said nothing at all were Mama and Daddy, but I sensed in them a thoughtful, suppressed wistfulness that maddened me.

After the hymn, Daddy read aloud a few verses from the third chapter of Luke, verses I recognized in the almost instinctive way in which I was familiar with all of the well-traveled parts of the Old and New Testaments. "Prepare the way of the Lord, make his paths straight," read my father in a mild voice. "Every valley shall be filled, and every mountain and hill shall be brought low, and the crooked shall be made straight, and the rough paths made smooth, and all flesh shall see the salvation of God."

He had a habit of pausing to fix his gaze on part of the congregation as he read, and that Sunday he seemed to be talking to a small group of strangers who sat in the front row. These visitors were young white men and women, students from Philadelphia colleges, who for the past year had been coming to hear him talk. It was hard to tell them apart: all the men seemed to have beards, and the women wore their hair long and straight. Their informal clothes stood out in that elaborate assembly, and church members whispered angrily that the young women didn't wear hats. I found the students appealing and rather romantic, with their earnest eyes and timid air of being perpetually sorry about something. It was clear that they had good intentions, and I couldn't understand why so many of the adults in the congregation seemed to dislike them so much. After services, they would hover around Daddy. "Never a more beautiful civil rights sermon!" they would say in low, fervent voices. Sometimes they seemed to have tears in their eyes.

I wasn't impressed by their praise of my father; it was only what everyone said. People called him a champion of civil rights; he gave speeches on the radio, and occasionally he appeared on television. (The first time I'd seen him on Channel 5, I'd been gravely disappointed by the way he looked: the bright lights exaggerated the furrows that ran between his nose and mouth, and his narrow eyes gave him a sinister air; he looked like an Oriental villain in a Saturday afternoon thriller.) During the past year he had organized a boycott that integrated the staff of a huge frozen-food plant in Philadelphia, and he'd been away several times to attend marches and meetings in the South. I was privately embarrassed to have a parent who freely admitted going to jail in Alabama, but the students who visited New African seemed to think it almost miraculous. Their conversations with my father were peppered with references to places I had never seen, towns I imagined as being swathed in a mist of darkness visible: Selma, Macon, Birmingham, Biloxi.

Matthew and I had long ago observed that what Daddy generally did in his sermons was to speak very softly and then surprise everyone with a shout. Of course, I knew that there was more to it than that; even in those days I recognized a genius of personality in my father. He loved crowds, handling them with the expert good humor of a man entirely in his element. At church banquets, at the vast annual picnic that was held beside a lake in New Jersey, or at any gathering in the backyards and living rooms of the town where we lived, the sound I heard most often was the booming of my father's voice followed by shouts of laughter from the people around him. He had a passion for oratory; at home, he infuriated Matthew and me by staging absurd debates at the dinner table, verbal melees that he won quite selfishly, with a loud crow of delight at his own virtuosity. "Is a fruit a vegetable?" he would demand. "Is a zipper a machine?" Matthew and I would plead with him to be quiet as we strained to get our own points across, but it was no use. When the last word had resounded and we sat looking at him in irritated silence, he would clear his throat, settle his collar, and resume eating, his face still glowing with an irrepressible glee.

When he preached, he showed the same private delight. A look of rapt pleasure seemed to broaden and brighten the contours of his angular face until it actually appeared to give off light as he spoke. He could preach in two very different ways. One was the delicate, sonorous idiom of formal oratory, with which he must have won the prizes he held from his seminary days. The second was a hectoring, insinuating, incantatory tone, full of the rhythms of the South he had never lived in, linking him to generations of thunderous Baptist preachers. When he used this tone, as he was doing now, affectionate laughter rippled through the pews.

"I know," he said, looking out over the congregation and blinking his eyes rapidly, "that there are certain people in this room—oh, I don't have to name names or point a finger—who have ignored that small true voice, the voice that is the voice of Jesus calling out in the shadowy depths of the soul. And while you all are looking around and wondering just who those 'certain people' are, I want to tell you all a secret: they are you and me, and your brother-in-law, and every man, woman, and child in this room this morning. All of us listen to our bellies when they tell us it is time to eat, we pay attention to our eyes when they grow heavy from wanting sleep, but when it comes to the sacred knowledge our hearts can offer, we are deaf, dumb, blind, and senseless. Throw away that blindness, that deafness, that sulky indifference. When all the world lies to you, Jesus will tell you what is right. Listen to him. Call on him. In these times of confusion, when there are a dozen different ways to turn, and Mama and Papa can't help you, trust Jesus to set you straight. Listen to him. The Son of God has the answers. Call on him. Call on him. Call on him.''

The sermon was punctuated with an occasional loud "Amen!" from Miss Middleton, an excitable old lady whose eyes flashed defiantly at the reproving faces of those around her. New African was not the kind of Baptist church where shouting was a normal part of the service; I occasionally heard my father mock the staid congregation by calling it Saint African. Whenever Miss Middleton loosed her tongue (sometimes she went off into fits of rapturous shrieks and had to be helped out of the service by the church nurse), my mother and aunts exchanged grimaces and shrugged, as if confronted by incomprehensibly barbarous behavior.

When Daddy had spoken the final words of the sermon, he drank a glass of water and vanished through a set of red velvet curtains to the right of the altar. At the same time, the choir began to sing what was described in the church bulletin as a "selection." These selections were always arenas for the running dispute between the choirmaster and the choir. Jordan Grimes, the choirmaster, was a Curtis graduate who was partial to Handel, but the choir preferred artistic spirituals performed in the lush, heroic style of Paul Robeson. Grimes had triumphed that Sunday. As the choir gave a spirited but unwilling rendition of Agnus Dei, I watched old Deacon West smile in approval. A Spanish-American War veteran, he admitted to being ninety-four but was said to be older; his round yellowish face, otherwise unwrinkled, bore three deep, deliberate-looking horizontal creases on the brow, like carvings on a scarab. "That old man is as flirtatious as a boy of twenty!" my mother often said, watching his stiff, courtly movements among the ladies of the church. Sometimes he gave me a dry kiss and a piece of peppermint candy after the service; I liked his crackling white collars and smell of bay rum.

The selection ended; Jordan Grimes struck two deep chords on the organ, and the lights in the church went low. A subtle stir ran through the congregation, and I moved closer to my mother. This was the moment that fascinated and disturbed me more than anything else at church: the prelude to the ceremony of baptism. Deacon West rose and drew open the draperies that had been closed around the baptismal pool, and there stood my father in water to his waist. The choir began to sing:

> *We're marching to Zion,*
> *Beautiful, beautiful Zion,*
> *We're marching upward to Zion,*
> *The beautiful city of God!*

Down the aisle, guided by two church mothers, came a procession of eight children and adolescents. They wore white robes, the girls with white ribbons in their hair, and they all had solemn expressions of terror on their faces. I knew each one of them. There was Billy Price, a big, slow-moving boy of thirteen, the son of Deacon Price. There were the Duckery twins. There was Caroline Piggee, whom I hated because of her long, soft black curls, her dimpled pink face, and her lisp that ravished grownups. There was Georgie Battis and Sue Anne Ivory, and Wendell and Mabel Cullen.

My mother gave me a nudge. "Run up to the side of the pool!" she whispered. It was the custom for unbaptized children to watch the ceremony from the front of the church. They sat on the knees of the deacons and church mothers, and it was not unusual for a child to volunteer then and there for next month's baptism. I made my way quickly down the dark aisle, feeling the carpet slip under the smooth soles of my patent-leather shoes.

When I reached the side of the pool, I sat down in the

bony lap of Bessie Gray, an old woman who often took care of Matthew and me when our parents were away; we called her Aunt Bessie. She was a fanatically devout Christian whose strict ideas on child-rearing had evolved over decades of domestic service to a rich white family in Delaware. The link between us, a mixture of hostility and grudging affection, had been forged in hours of pitched battles over bedtimes and proper behavior. Her worshipful respect for my father, whom she called "the Rev," was exceeded only by her pride—the malice-tinged pride of an omniscient family servant—in her "white children," to whom she often unflatteringly compared Matthew and me. It was easy to see why my mother and her circle of fashionable matrons described Bessie Gray as "archaic"—one had only to look at her black straw hat attached with three enormous old-fashioned pins to her knot of frizzy white hair. Her lean, brown-skinned face was dominated by a hawk nose inherited from some Indian ancestor and punctuated by a big black mole; her eyes were small, shrewd, and baleful. She talked in ways that were already passing into history and parody, and she wore a thick orange face powder that smelled like dead leaves.

I leaned against her spare bosom and watched the other children clustered near the pool, their bonnets and hair ribbons and round heads outlined in the dim light. For a minute it was very still. Somewhere in the hot, darkened church a baby gave a fretful murmur; from outside came the sound of cars passing in the street. The candidates for baptism, looking stiff and self-conscious, stood lined up on the short stairway leading to the pool. Sue Anne Ivory fiddled with her sleeve and then put her fingers in her mouth.

Daddy spoke the opening phrases of the ceremony: "In the Baptist Church, we do not baptize infants, but believe that a person must choose salvation for himself."

I didn't listen to the words; what I noticed was the music of the whole—how the big voice darkened and lightened in tone, and how the grand architecture of the biblical sentences ennobled the voice. The story, of course, was about Jesus and John the Baptist. One phrase struck me newly each time: "This is my beloved son, in whom I am well pleased!" Daddy sang out these words in a clear, triumphant tone, and the choir echoed him. Ever since I could understand it, this phrase had made me feel melancholy; it seemed to expose a hard knot of disobedience that had always lain inside me. When I heard it, I thought enviously of Matthew, for whom life seemed to be a sedate and ordered affair: he, not I, was a child in whom a father could be well pleased.

Daddy beckoned to Billy Price, the first baptismal candidate in line, and Billy, ungainly in his white robe, descended the steps into the pool. In soft, slow voices the choir began to sing:

> *Wade in the water,*
> *Wade in the water, children,*
> *Wade in the water,*
> *God gonna trouble*
> *The water.*

In spite of Jordan Grimes's efforts, the choir swayed like a gospel chorus as it sang this spiritual; the result was to add an eerie jazz beat to the minor chords. The music gave me gooseflesh. Daddy had told me that this was the same song that the slaves had sung long ago in the South, when they gathered to be baptized in rivers and streams. Although I cared little about history, and found it hard to picture the slaves as being any ancestors of mine, I could clearly imagine them coming together beside a broad muddy river that wound away between trees drooping with strange vegetation. They walked silently in lines, their faces very black against their white clothes, leading their children. The whole scene was bathed in the heavy golden light that meant age and solemnity, the same light that seemed to weigh down the Israelites in illustrated volumes of Bible stories, and that shone now from the baptismal pool, giving the ceremony the air of a spectacle staged in a dream.

All attention in the darkened auditorium was now focused on the pool, where between the red curtains my father stood holding Billy Price by the shoulders. Daddy stared into Billy's face, and the boy stared back, his lips set and trembling. "And now, by the power invested in me," said Daddy, "I baptize you in the name of the Father, the Son, and the Holy Ghost." As he pronounced these words, he conveyed a tenderness as efficient and impersonal as a phy-

sician's professional manner; beneath it, however, I could
see a strong private gladness, the same delight that transformed his face when he preached a sermon. He paused to
flick a drop of water off his forehead, and then, with a single
smooth, powerful motion of his arms, he laid Billy Price
back into the water as if he were putting an infant to bed. I
caught my breath as the boy went backward. When he came
up, sputtering, two church mothers helped him out of the
pool and through a doorway into a room where he would
be dried and dressed. Daddy shook the water from his hands
and gave a slight smile as another child entered the pool.

One by one, the baptismal candidates descended the steps.
Sue Anne Ivory began to cry and had to be comforted. Caroline Piggee blushed and looked up at my father with such
a coquettish air that I jealously wondered how he could stand
it. After a few baptisms my attention wandered, and I began
to gnaw the edge of my thumb and to peer at the pale faces
of the visiting college students. Then I thought about Matthew, who had punched me in the arm that morning and had
shouted, "No punchbacks!" I thought as well about a collection of horse chestnuts I meant to assemble in the fall,
and about two books, one whose subject was adults and
divorces, and another, by E. Nesbit, that continued the adventures of the Bastable children.

After Wendell Cullen had left the water (glancing uneas-
ily back at the wet robe trailing behind him), Daddy stood
alone among the curtains and the mirrors. The moving reflections from the pool made the stuffed dove hanging over
him seem to flutter on its string. "Dear Lord," said Daddy,
as Jordan Grimes struck a chord, "bless these children who
have chosen to be baptized in accordance with your teaching, and who have been reborn to carry out your work. In
each of them, surely, you are well pleased." He paused,
staring out into the darkened auditorium. "And if there is
anyone out there—man, woman, child—who wishes to be
baptized next month, let him come forward now." He
glanced around eagerly. "Oh, do come forward and give
Christ your heart and give me your hand!"

Just then Aunt Bessie gave me a little shake and whispered sharply, "Go on up and accept Jesus!"

I stiffened and dug my bitten fingernails into my palms.
The last clash of wills I had had with Aunt Bessie had been

when she, crazily set in her old southern attitudes, had tried
to make me wear an enormous straw hat, as her "white
children" did, when I played outside in the sun. The old
woman had driven me to madness, and I had ended up
spanked and sullen, crouching moodily under the dining-
room table. But this was different, outrageous, none of her
business, I thought. I shook my head violently and she took
advantage of the darkness in the church to seize both of my
shoulders and jounce me with considerable roughness,
whispering, "Now, listen, young lady! Your daddy up there
is calling you to Christ. Your big brother has already offered
his soul to the Lord. Now Daddy wants his little girl to step
forward."

"No, he doesn't." I glanced at the baptismal pool, where
my father was clasping the hand of a strange man who had
come up to him. I hoped that this would distract Aunt Bessie, but she was tireless.

"Your mama and your aunt Lily and your aunt May all
want you to answer the call. You're hurting them when you
say no to Jesus."

"No, I'm not!" I spoke out loud and I saw the people
nearby turn to look at me. At the sound of my voice, Daddy,
who was a few yards away, faltered for a minute in what he
was saying and glanced over in my direction.

Aunt Bessie seemed to lose her head. She stood up
abruptly, pulling me with her, and, while I was still frozen
in a dreadful paralysis, tried to drag me down the aisle toward my father. The two of us began a brief struggle that
could not have lasted for more than a few seconds but that
seemed an endless mortal conflict—my slippery patent-
leather shoes braced against the floor, my straw hat sliding
cockeyed and lodging against one ear, my right arm twisting
and twisting in the iron circle of the old woman's grip, my
nostrils full of the dead-leaf smell of her powder and black
skirts. In an instant I had wrenched my arm free and darted
up the aisle toward Mama, my aunts, and Matthew. As I
slipped past the pews in the darkness, I imagined that I
could feel eyes fixed on me and hear whispers. "What'd
you do, dummy?" whispered Matthew, tugging on my sash
as I reached our pew, but I pushed past him without an-
swering. Although it was hot in the church, my teeth were
chattering: it was the first time I had won a battle with a

grownup, and the earth seemed to be about to cave in beneath me. I squeezed in between Mama and Aunt Lily just as the lights came back on in the church. In the baptismal pool, Daddy raised his arms for the last time. "The Lord bless you and keep you," came his big voice. "The Lord be gracious unto you, and give you peace."

What was curious was how uncannily subdued my parents were when they heard of my skirmish with Aunt Bessie. Normally they were swift to punish Matthew and me for misbehavior in church and for breaches in politeness toward adults; this episode combined the two, and smacked of sacrilege besides. Yet once I had made an unwilling apology to the old woman (as I kissed her she shot me such a vengeful glare that I realized that forever after it was to be war to the death between the two of us), I was permitted, once we had driven home, to climb up into the green shade of the big maple tree I had dreamed of throughout the service. In those days, more than now, I fell away into a remote dimension whenever I opened a book; that afternoon, as I sat with rings of sunlight and shadow moving over my arms and legs, and winged yellow seeds plopping down on the pages of *The Story of the Treasure Seekers,* I felt a vague uneasiness floating in the back of my mind—a sense of having misplaced something, of being myself misplaced. I was holding myself quite aloof from considering what had happened, as I did with most serious events, but through the adventures of the Bastables I kept remembering the way my father had looked when he'd heard what had happened. He hadn't looked severe or angry, but merely puzzled, and he had regarded me with the same puzzled expression, as if he'd just discovered that I existed and didn't know what to do with me. "What happened, Sairy?" he asked, using an old baby nickname, and I said, "I didn't want to go up there." I hadn't cried at all, and that was another curious thing.

After that Sunday, through some adjustment in the adult spheres beyond my perception, all pressure on me to accept baptism ceased. I turned twelve, fifteen, then eighteen without being baptized, a fact that scandalized some of the congregation; however, my parents, who openly discussed everything else, never said a word to me. The issue, and the episode that had illuminated it, was surrounded by a clear ring of silence that, for our garrulous family, was something close to supernatural. I continued to go to New African—in fact, continued after Matthew, who dropped out abruptly during his freshman year in college; the ambiguousness in my relations with the old church gave me at times an inflated sense of privilege (I saw myself as a romantically isolated religious heroine, a sort of self-made Baptist martyr) and at other times a feeling of loss that I was too proud ever to acknowledge. I never went up to take my father's hand, and he never commented upon that fact to me. It was an odd pact, one that I could never consider in the light of day; I stored it in the subchambers of my heart and mind. It was only much later, after he died, and I left New African forever, that I began to examine the peculiar gift of freedom my father—whose entire soul was in the church, and in his exuberant, bewitching tongue—had granted me through his silence.

DIANE LEVENBERG grew up in New Haven, Connecticut and New York and now lives in Israel and teaches English at Kutztown University. "The Ilui," the story that follows, was included in *Prize Stories: The 1991 O. Henry Awards*. The author has provided the autobiographical background of her story: like its main character, Schoen, she writes, "I, too, attended the Beth Jacob School for Girls, and like Schoen, the idea of an *ilui*—either to be one or to attract one, has affected the direction of my life. I began to write at seventeen, not stories but poems, and in 1980 Doubleday published *Out of the Desert*. Eventually, wanting the challenge of sustained longer work, I also wrote stories, publishing them in *Midstream, Response,* and *The Sojourner*. I now live in Jerusalem, a city of light and *iluim*. I spend my days on my front porch, in the Jerusalem sun, working on a collection of stories and a novel. On the story itself: "The Ilui" was probably rejected thirty times. But the story was important to me and I wanted to see it published. There was a Davidson in my life. Perhaps I have found the *ilui* from within; the *ilui* from without still eludes me."

This story reflects the concern with the past and with both the liberating and confining effects of Jewish tradition, characteristics of Jewish-American fiction discussed by Irving Howe in his Introduction to *Jewish-American Stories*. Levenberg joins company with other Jewish-American women writers—Cynthia Ozick, Grace Paley, Tillie Olsen, Vivian Gornick, and Anzia Yezierska (see page 301)—all of whom have written with great force of growing up female, at once secure and rebellious within the enclosure of their ethnic families and communities. What Irving Howe does not discuss is how these women writers respond to the gender-exclusiveness of their Jewish-American immigrant and second-generation experience, with its patriarchal bias rooted in an ancient religious tradition. As Levenberg's Schoen learns: "Girls shouldn't learn Talmud."

The Ilui

❦

Diane Levenberg

Her father, a young widower, had studied in one of the great yeshivas of Eastern Europe. When she was a little girl he had often recited to her tales of the *iluim* with whom he had studied. These were young geniuses who were still able to carry on the Jewish tradition of the Oral Law—who could perform prodigious feats of memory.

"Were you an *ilui*?" she asked.

"Well, in my day," he said modestly, "I could also memorize—books of the Bible, tractates, pages of the Talmud. But not the entire *Mishnah*, not an entire volume of the Talmud. To be an *ilui*," he spread his hands wide, "one might wish for it, but one is either born such a genius or one isn't."

On a late Sabbath afternoon, a week after she had scored a 98 on her geometry Regents, her father was, in sing-song fashion, studying a page from one of his huge leather-bound volumes of the Talmud. His comforting *nigun* promised to pry open the secrets of the universe. She begged him to teach her.

"All right," he agreed. "This is *Gemorah Baba Bathra.* The *Mishnah* reads: 'Carrion, graves and tanyards must, because of the bad smell, be kept fifty cubits from a town. Rabbi Akiba says a tanyard can be kept on any side except the west. How do we know which side is the west?' The rabbis then go on to discuss specific directions and the general shape of the world.

"Rabbi Eliezer says that the north side of the world is not enclosed and so when the sun reaches the northwest corner, it turns back and returns to the east above the firmament. Rabbi Joshua, however, says that the world is like a tent—completely enclosed—and the sun must go around it till it reaches the east."

"And who is right?" she asked, hoping that the *Gemorah,* contrary to Copernicus, was on to something.

"Well, let's see," said her father. "Sometimes, when the *Gemorah* is not sure, it ends *Teku.* Let it stand until the prophet Elijah comes to solve the difficulty—"

As he pored down the end of the long page, she heard a knock at the door. It was Mr. Bernstein.

"Good Shabbos, Mr. Schoen. Sorry to interrupt. We need a *minyan* for *Ma'ariv.* Could you join us?"

"Sure, sure," said her father. "I was just trying to teach my daughter a little Talmud. But that can wait. The evening star, on the other hand, cannot. Let's go."

Years later, she realized that her father agreed with her teachers—girls shouldn't learn Talmud. He had begun with a confusing but tantalizing passage and, confounded, she lost interest. But not in the idea of an *ilui.*

And women, she asked her father, carrying in another steaming plate of noodle pudding. Could a woman be an *ilui*? Was Bruriah, one of the only women mentioned in the Talmud, an *ilui*?

A good question, he said. He wasn't sure.

Somewhere, she believed, rattling around, hovering above the firmament, was an unmoored, extra soul, destined for her. An *ilui,* a man who could commit volumes to memory. A man who might have the patience to teach her the answers before the advent of Elijah.

To her father, brilliant but distracted girls, with their messy hair and unironed dresses, were a mystery. Her *ilui* would study with her, appreciate her poetry, and perhaps even try to explore with her her precociously complicated psyche.

At the Beth Jacob High School for Girls, "studiers" were not popular. The teachers, however, most of them impoverished Holocaust survivors from Poland or Hungary, happily put the studiers in the first two rows where they were called on by their last names. Schoen, pronounced with a

Hungarian accent, became "Shoin." Hearing herself called that way always made her jump. It sounded very much like the Yiddish word for "already" as in "*nu shoin* let's have the answer." In this way she was trained to think fast. And to have time left over to dream of her soul mate.

In her senior year, her prospects brightened. Her class was dating and even the dumbest girl wanted a boy who was adept at studying, one who liked, as it was said, to sit and learn. Schoen started the class joke—as soon as a girl started to discuss her latest "beau" Schoen would wisecrack, "And what yeshiva is he the best in?"

Hiding *Dr. Zhivago* behind her volume devoted to the Laws of Modesty, Schoen longed to visit a yeshiva dedicated to producing an *ilui*. The Princeton of boys' yeshivas was also to be found in New Jersey—Lakewood. On several weekend visits, Schoen quickly discovered the disagreeable fate of Lakewood wives. They had babies, tried to support their husbands by selling Avon or Tupperware, and waddled into middle age by the time they hit twenty-five. The system, Schoen discovered, designed by men, was for men only.

A Lakewood scholar never worked—he learned until the day came when his "*rosh yeshiva*" decided he was ready to start a microcosmic Lakewood somewhere in the hinterlands of America. And then the cycle would begin again. He would administer his yeshiva, raise the money for his salary, and his wife would stretch their dollars. And bear more junior *iluim*.

Schoen realized that while her desires were clear to her, her capacity for such sacrifice was almost nil. In her senior year, she had the thickest glasses, the largest library of secular books and the fewest dates.

Finally, a relative fixed her up with a scholar from the Baltimore yeshiva. He was dressed in the uniform—navy blue coat, navy blue suit, black hat with a dark red feather saluting from its hat band. She wore a black velvet suit, her first Salon St. Honore hairdo, and her new fur-collared black coat. In the lobby of the Americana Hotel he kept his hat on, she kept her glasses in her clutch bag. They talked about food, family, and philosophy. She thought him very sophisticated when he bought her a drink at the bar. Then she grew tired and put her glasses on. He adjusted his hat and took her home. He hadn't called a month later. Her cousin told her that he wanted a taller girl with a shorter nose. Years later, Schoen was attending an education conference and met him again—her first *ilui*. To her amusement, his wife was shorter than her by several inches, her nose prominently longer.

She had endless dates—one at Idlewild Airport to watch the planes take off, one in a Greenwich Village bookstore, one in the first kosher Italian restaurant where the pareve chicken parmesan turned black. He wore a black hat with a dark green feather. She forgot to remove her glasses. They talked about family, philosophy, and God. Why college? Why wasn't her father sending her to secretarial school?, asked the young scholar. Would God love her more, if she, after marriage, wore a wig and hated herself?, she asked. He removed his hat, checked to see that his yarmulka was still lining it, and rose to take her home. She watched the sorbet, like her hopes, melt away.

She would have to go it alone, her way. She told her guidance counsellor she wanted to attend Yeshiva University, but because it taught biblical criticism her transcript was not sent there.

She hated City College's messy urban campus, but she loved the sound of its clipped academic dialogue. Reading alone, she thought that Yeats might rhyme with Keats. Sitting on the lawn were boys with longish hair, and thick glasses, suggesting that Dostoevsky's imprisonment in Siberia had been good for his soul and arguing whether, indeed, the worst are full of passionate intensity.

Another group was debating Marxist theory. In the student lounge, the girls were reading Emma Goldman, Simone de Beauvoir, and wishing they, too, like Emily Dickinson, could write their letters to the world. Schoen spent the afternoon listening, feeling as though she were in an adult toy store and they were giving away whatever she might want to play with.

She met Sarah, her one close high school friend. "What are you doing here?" she asked in shocked surprise. "You mean at this college? I got into Barnard, but with my brother still at Harvard we couldn't afford it. Actually, this is a scholar's paradise. I'm finally learning that an iamb isn't part of the verb to be. And, it's free. Sit down, have a cup of coffee. I'll show you something.''

Schoen opened the catalogue describing the new creative writing program and her mind was made up. "You're right," she said. "This catalogue is as seductive as *Glamour*'s September issue. Could we take some courses together?''

Schoen enrolled in a special program at City which seemed to have attracted some of the most creative minds at the college. She had a double major—writing and literature. She was surprised at the number of boys in her class, long-haired, serious-looking types, trying hard to emulate their wealthy Columbia "brothers.''

Schoen believed that boys didn't read fiction, let alone write it. To her, a real man was still someone who knew how to learn. But these City College boys studied writing the way her father learned Talmud. They never let a writing instructor get away with anything.

When Prof. Brick, well-known for his own satirical short stories, tried to tear apart the work of the intense and brilliant Davidson (it was rumored that he had already spent a semester at Oxford), Davidson retaliated. He had read all of Brick's work and knew which stories the critics had panned. "Listen, Brick, you're too tight-assed to let a spontaneous image emerge. Too afraid to expand for fear you'll bleed upon the page,'' he said quoting I.J. Howard for deadly emphasis. Brick unbuttoned his shirt, loosened his tie and called for a coffee break.

Davidson went to the window and lit a cigarette. She stood nearby. The old radiator hissed and thumped and they heard the faint cries of the children in the playground across the street. Schoen had never tried one before but she knew he was smoking a joint. His hands were shaking. He offered her a puff and she tried to imitate the way he drew it into his lungs.

"I have to admire the way you got to him, but that was nasty.'' Schoen focused on the playground, watching one boy push another onto the concrete. Davidson pulled out his shirttail and wiped his glasses. It was a gesture which endeared him to her. "Two months I spend on that piece,'' he said, holding his glasses up to the light, "and all he has to say is that I don't have an ear for dialogue." Schoen noticed that his hands were still trembling. "Where the hell does that bastard WASP hang out? On the ersatz Welsh walkways trod by the Philistines of Mainline Philadelphia? In Brooklyn, walking up and down the ghetto's graveolent replica of the Champs Elysées, that's the way people speak. In his stories no one talks. He should call his collection, 'Mute Man, Aphasic Woman.' "

"I liked your story very much," she said. "The young painter who lives alone and has his vision in Brighton Beach—I could relate to that. I . . ."

"You could? Where are you from?"

"Brooklyn. Believe me. I know how hard it is to have an epiphany in Crown Heights. Brighton Beach was the right touch. And I think you're right. That's how people speak when their desires far exceed their grasp."

Davidson's eyes were shining. He was obviously pretty high. He grabbed her arm.

"Look, I've had enough of this class for today. Do you want to go downtown? I know a great cafe near my apartment. We can have some coffee, and continue this. I've never heard you read in class. Maybe I can look at some of your work."

Schoen giggled. She hoped the marijuana wouldn't make her sound too dumb. She'd had her eye fixed on Davidson for a long time.

"Sure," she said. "Let's go. I'd like to talk to you some more about your story. I don't have anything of mine on me that I'm up to sharing."

"That's all right. I have my entire binder right here in my bag."

In the dimly lit but cozy cafe, Davidson explained that the new critics "are reactionary and elitist. They are totally out of touch with what my, our, generation of writers is trying to express. The absurdists, on the other hand, like Pynchon, are too far ahead of their time." He stared into her empty teacup. "Schoen's your name, right? Nice. It means nice. I met a woman once who could read your future in these grummels of tea leaves. Myself," he added, swilling down his fifth cup of coffee, "I'm a Blake man. Northrop Frye and I have been writing letters to each other for years. He keeps encouraging me to write my own book on

Blake. If I survive this damn writing program, I'll probably
write my thesis on *Songs of Innocence*." By the end of the
evening, Schoen was ready to change her definition of the
word *ilui*. Davidson was the sort of scholar she had spent
hundreds of high school hours dreaming about.

In class a few days later, Davidson sat next to her, biting
down on an unlit cigarette while Brick attacked another student's latest story. During the break, he walked to the window and finally lit it. Schoen stood next to him wishing that
she also smoked so she could break his silence by asking
for a light.

He spoke without looking at her. "This time that bastard
was right. That guy had no business reading that yet. It
needs too much work."

"We're not professionals, you know. We're here to learn.
Where else can you take these kinds of risks?"

That night Schoen rewrote her own story for the fourth
time. She was afraid to face Davidson's scorn. She needn't
have worried. Davidson never again returned to class. Over
the years she wondered about him, occasionally scanning
the better literary magazines for his name and the criticism
sections of the bookstores for his book on Blake. She was
sure she would hear about him, but when she did it wasn't
because his name had appeared in print.

Pollack was on the phone again for the third time that
day. Schoen bit down hard on her pencil, but she couldn't
hang up on him. Pollack was her current link to true suffering—a survivor of Auschwitz, with dreams and fantasies of
making it in New York, but who was usually too depressed
to put any workable plan into action.

Today he sounded almost cheerful. "How would you like
to meet an interesting fellow?" he asked. "My friend just
got back to New York. He wants to meet an interesting
woman. Immediately, of course, I thought of you. You and
he have a lot in common. He writes poetry, loves literature,
film, art."

"Pollack, you sound like you're reading from one of the
personals in the *Village Voice*. I'm in the middle of a difficult section of my dissertation. I don't have time for this."

"What do you mean you don't have time? Don't you want
to meet a man who is fascinating, cosmopolitan, who un-

derstands my jokes, has an intelligent face? An intellectual who talks—he could help you with that damn dissertation. You've been writing it since I was a child.''

"Pollack, you were never a child. Besides, I think my advisor likes a woman who takes her time.''

"Well, so does Davidson.''

"Davidson?''

"Yah. This fellow I want you to meet.''

"Is his first name Chaim?''

"Chaim? Can't you imagine a human being who comes with a normal English name? No. His name is Mark.''

"Oh. I thought I might have known him. A long time ago. In a writing class.''

"I don't think Davidson would take a writing course. He prides himself on being an autodidact.''

"How long have you known him?''

"A few years. We met at a conference on the Holocaust. Look, if you once knew him you'll jump off that bridge when you get to it. I have to run up to the lab at Columbia. Why don't you have coffee with him. I'll give him your number, o.k.?''

"O.k.,'' said Schoen, smiling. She had worked steadily for a month on her chapter without even seeing a movie. "I almost wish his name was Chaim Davidson. I still have the story I wrote just to impress him. In fact, I published it.''

Pollack chuckled. "The story of your story sounds like just the kind of story Davidson adores. Tell him about it. You'll have a good time. So long.''

She had ridden her bike home at top speed. Even so, she was a few minutes late. He was there sitting on the steps of her apartment building. The years, she thought, had caressed him. He was even wearing the same beige scarf, wrapped around a rather worn Harris tweed jacket. But his hair was combed, his beard was trimmed, and his shirt was clean.

Schoen smiled. "Mark Davidson, how nice to meet you.''

He looked up from the book he was reading. He rose and they shook hands. She noticed that now his grip was firm and sure. "Same here,'' he said. "Derrida,'' he said, slapping his book. "You know why the French have to be so intellectual? Because they're short. Seriously, this guy is brilliant. Say," he said. "You look slightly familiar. Did you by any chance go to City College?"

"Yes," she said. "Sorry I'm late. Let's go up." She wheeled the bike ahead of her and he followed her in. She had short curly hair now. At City, she had been twenty pounds thinner, her hair had been long, and she had been afraid to try contact lenses. Still, she must have made a dent in his memory. They had spent only one afternoon together and, like her high school teachers, he had never called her by her first name.

"Now I remember," he said. "You were the girl who thought I was too hard on the other writing students."

"Woman," she said, smiling.

"Woman. Yes. Right."

"And you were the guy who was going to write a book on Blake. Your name was Chaim then."

"Yeah. Well, I thought Mark went better with Blake. But that never worked out." He turned to wander around the living room and check out her library. "Does it pass?" she asked.

"You have all the required reading matter for a City College graduate," he said. "And I won't insult you by asking whether or not you've read all these. In fact, I trust that like Johnson you've read some of them twice. Myself, I'm a collector. I love purchasing books almost as much as I love perusing them."

"It's hard having a big library in a Manhattan apartment."

"Well, fortunately, my parents are illiterate. They own a house in the cultural wasteland of Queens. I live away, and when my books crowd me out, I move myself and my library back to their little house on the Philistine prairie."

They ate in a popular Upper West Side Chinese restaurant. After her first cup of Chinese tea, Schoen could no longer contain her curiosity. "Where did you go when you left our class?" she asked. Between forksful of cold sesame noodles, Davidson wove his tale.

"Dropped out of City. Went to Los Angeles to peddle a screenplay I'd written for a film class. No luck there but an agent hired me to read scripts. Tried that for two years, had enough of it and UCLA's night school, and ended up in the

creative writing program at the University of Iowa. Before
my three-year fellowship ran out, I had finished a novel.''

"How was it there at Iowa? I've always heard such good
stories about the place."

"As the epicenter of contemporary American writing, it's
rather quiescent and uninspiring. And very ugly. The campus is comprised of converted Quonset huts. There's no
view—just flat land rolling out to the horizon. A good place
for writing though—there were no distractions. I hunkered
over my typewriter, a grateful prisoner of my own imagination. After Iowa, New York looks good.'' He smiled at
her.

Schoen remained silent, but something didn't ring true.
She thought she remembered hearing that the University of
Iowa had a scenic campus.

"Then what?'' she asked.

"Then back to New York teaching at Brooklyn College.
Tried to peddle my novel. Probably poetic bromides extoll-
ing shaving lotion have more appeal. Some lowly editor at
Knopf is slowly reading it. A good sign I'm told, unless,
condemned to some Sisyphean torture, she can't make it
past the first ten pages. Hope they decide soon. My money's
disappearing.''

"Would you like some more of this wonderful tea?'' she
asked, wondering if she had grown into the sort of woman
with whom he might want to sleep.

"No. I'm full. How would you like to repair to the Thalia
to see *Rashomon*?''

"Sounds wonderful. Somehow I've never seen it.''

They met again the following week and Davidson offered
to come up and massage her back. He had somewhere
learned the art of shiatsu.

"Was that kiss part of the technique?'' asked Schoen.

"Not really. You know what the yogis say. You can judge
the age of a person by the flexibility of his or her spine.
Now that I've made you younger, back to our City College
days, and eased all the tension out of your body, I think we
should make love.''

Schoen lay snuggled comfortably against Davidson and
the last event-filled decade of her life unreeled before her
in haunting images—the first man who had made love to her

as she lay trembling in the shadow of their Sabbath candles, standing with Sarah in front of the White House chanting anti-war slogans, her husband, on their wedding night, undressing down to his father's baggy underwear, the rabbi asking her if she really wanted this divorce, and teaching her first literature class at City College.

After that night, Davidson just stayed. A week later she saw his valise in the living room. Shirts and pants lay in a tangled pile begging her to give them a home. She was preparing a new course and Davidson seemed to have nothing to do but wait for a phone call from Knopf. A phone call to his father invariably produced an envelope of cash. While she was at the library he would roast a chicken in garlic, lemon juice and whatever spices he fancied at the moment. He cooked intuitively, and the food was always superb. But once she made him throw out a delicious chicken and rice dish when she found the Perdue wrapper in the garbage. In a hurry, he had bought the unkosher chicken at the nearest supermarket.

"I'm sorry. It won't happen again. I was in a rush."

"You know this house is kosher. How could you do such a thing?"

"I didn't think. I'm sorry. Are you sure Frank Perdue isn't really a southern shochet? Come on, let's forget it." And they did, the next night, while visiting Schoen's friend, the author of a bestselling book on sexuality, in the hills of Litchfield, Connecticut. In the hot tub, his resonant voice taking her back to that afternoon years before, in the Hungarian Cafe. Davidson recited from memory, T.S. Eliot's "The Love Song of J. Alfred Prufrock." That was the moment, that ten years later, she fell in love with him.

Back in her New York apartment, Davidson read a-book-a-day and Schoen envied him. She had an eight o'clock class to teach and three others on alternate afternoons. When he was stoned or just after making love, Davidson swore he would look for work—advertising, public relations, something in which he would be forced, once again, to put pen to paper. He made calls and set up interviews. But no one ever called him back a second time. She didn't really understand it. He signed up for more shiatsu courses. He shopped, he cooked, and sometimes he even cleaned. He asked to see her dissertation chapter.

"You really should explain more about how the Jewish family in the shtetl breaks down when they arrive in America," he said.

"But this is a study of literature."

"Still, the phenomenology of the family is what your advisor will need to understand."

She rewrote it as he suggested. But he didn't take as well to her comments. After she gently criticized one of his chattier job letters, he stopped writing them. He was reading scores of books, lying in bed until way past noon.

"I need inspiration so that I can begin my new novel before I find full time work."

"You look like Huckleberry Finn," she said, brushing the hair away from his eyes. "Whiling away the morning. Fishing for an idea."

"I'm taking a break from job hunting. Right now, I want to write another novel." He set his battered Olivetti on the dining room table, but except for a paragraph on Decoding Blake's "The Little Black Boy," all his pages remained blank. It seemed to Schoen that the more pages Davidson couldn't write, the more his desire for sex increased. When she gave in to him, too tired to continue writing her dissertation, and too weak to refuse him, Davidson would bring fresh French rolls, brie, wine and Blake to bed and keep her there with him till nightfall. She asked him about the novel he had written at Iowa.

"It wasn't good enough for them," he said. "And I had to leave before I rewrote. They did like some of my short stories, though."

"I'd like to see them."

"They're in the basement at home. I'll bring them back next time I go visit my folks." But he never did. What he brought back was an ounce of marijuana. Or maybe it was hash. This time he smoked three or four pipefuls a day and Schoen was worried. He grew contentious. When she asked him to rinse out the tub after he had left a ring of grime around its sides, he raised his hand and she thought he might hit her. Instead, he scratched his head, stepped back, brought his clenched fist to his chest, turned on his heel and left the house. He didn't return until morning. She opened her eyes to the smell of fresh coffee and bagels still warm from the oven. "My breakfast guilt offering," he said.

* * *

Her old friend Dan was in town and they were having lunch at The Library, one of their favorite Upper West Side haunts. Suddenly, Schoen remembered that Dan had spent a semester at the Iowa Workshop.

"I can forgive his eccentricities," she said, "because the guy's a genius. His stories, when we were at City, were masterpieces. He says he spent a semester at Iowa. Did you know him?"

"No. What's he doing now?"

"Not much. Reading. Looking for work."

"Is he writing?"

"Not really. But he says he's warming up."

"Too bad. New York is not as beautiful nor as peaceful as Iowa, but he's sharing your place, you're buying the food, and if I may say so, you're a great lady with a generous spirit. This would be an ideal situation for any writer."

"Thanks," she said smiling. "What was Iowa like?" she asked.

"Didn't he tell you? Rolling hills, modern buildings, a long river roiling right through town. Students hate to graduate."

"The way he described it it sounded like an old army camp."

"The guy should start writing again. He sounds like he has a great imagination. The place is a writer's paradise. My first day there I thought I died and woke up in heaven."

That night she brought home a large bottle of Soave for dinner. He drank most of it. After dinner he lit a joint and handed it to her. When he was high, either on wine or grass, he was always affectionate. She lay in his lap and he stroked her hair. She sat up and gently kissed him on the mouth. Being high gave her courage. "Chaim, after City where did you go? Tell me the truth."

He pushed her away. "So, you don't believe me. Don't kiss me. Chaim. I hate that name. Call me Mark. Where did I go? Not to Los Angeles. That comes out of my own private script. But I did go to Iowa. The Iowa I believed in where the instructors were good writers who might have something to teach me. I was accepted to the Writers' Workshop, but I never made it past the second class at the instructor's home. I don't think you want to hear this . . . a nice upright middle-class Jewish girl like you. If I remember correctly you spent your formative years in some hole-in-the-wall girl's yeshiva. . . .''

"If I remember correctly, you spent those same years at the Brooklyn Torah Academy.''

"Well, I broke out. I'm not sure you did.''

"Look, I've had to learn to trust that from now on you'll buy kosher chickens. Trust me just a little. Where did you go?''

"Outside of town, at the local bar. I met a woman. Two women. Two men. We were all finished with the Workshop. We drove half the night and I joined their commune in Madison. We did every drug ever invented. Except heroin. They wouldn't dare to shoot up. So I had to be the first. And, I liked it. A lot.'' He took another long deep drag. "This isn't pretty.'' He searched her face for a sign that he should continue.

"It's all right, Mark. I'm with you. Really I am.''

"It took a month and then I was, as they say, hooked. I told the lies I had to tell to get money for more stuff until finally my parents came out to see for themselves. Eventually, I ended up back East on a drug farm. One of those places where they detox you. I spent about two years on that project—back and forth to the funny farm just to get back to the place I had once been. A healthy kid who wanted to write just one good novel.'' He turned to her. "In case you're worried, I'm off the junk now.''

"What do you take?''

"Besides grass? Just Valium. A little Valium to get me through the day. I've got to take something. I've never had a permanent job and I don't seem to be able to write anymore. I thought perhaps that living here would inspire me to get my act together. It's inspired me to something. Let's drop this and go back to bed.''

"No,'' she said. "It doesn't solve anything. You're using me the way you use your drug-filled pipe. I won't be your escape.''

"Okay,'' he said sadly. "But don't force me to leave. Just give me a little more time.'' He pulled her towards him.

"All right,'' she said, suddenly aware of how very tired she was. "I don't want you to leave. At least not now.''

"Your dissertation. You're on the wrong track. I want to help you make it brilliant."

Something told her that trying to write a brilliant dissertation would keep her "hooked" to a project she really wanted to wrap up as soon as possible. But she didn't say anything. He needed his dignity—a way to stay with her and give her something back. He could, at times, with indefatigable energy sit with her for hours helping her to refine her ideas. And his memory! If he read it once, he could recall it at will. She told him he ought to start a hotline for students in crisis. "They could call you up and get a bibliography right off the top of your head."

"Schoen, baby, I'm not for sale." He developed insomnia and she awoke to find him sitting in his jeans and pajama top, reading, smoking his water pipe, drinking Southern Comfort ("It's not Southern and it offers none but real men drink it neat"). He shot her a guilty look. "Have some," he offered. "It will help you fall back to sleep."

Another time, she saw him vigorously rubbing the sole of his foot, a book spread across his lap. "Reflexology," he said. "Did you know you could activate all the energy centers of the body by doing this? Uh. Oh. I hit the wrong one. Now I want you."

And he held her and kissed her, until ever so sweetly she fell back to sleep.

One night, he called to tell her that he and Pollack were visiting a writer, who in the fifties, had enjoyed a sort of cult following. "Hope you don't mind," he said. "You know, sort of boys' night out. I won't be home too late."

At six in the morning, he jumped on top of her wanting to make love. "Where were you? Mark, where the hell did you disappear? I've been going crazy worrying. Pollack's been home since eleven and he told me not to call your folks."

"I had some business to take care of." He grabbed her again. "Come on, Schoen. Don't be a spoil sport. I want you."

She jumped out of bed and headed for the bathroom. She ran the bath water as hot as she could stand it. This way she could keep the door locked, soak in the tub and calm down. When she came out he was fast asleep. When he didn't get up ten hours later, she called Pollack. He came running over and checked his pulse.

"It sounds weak," he said. "I'm no doctor but I think you should call an ambulance."

"What about his parents," she asked dialing the nearest hospital.

"Them too."

Two days later, Davidson was sitting up, grinning weakly. He buried his nose in the dozen red tulips she had brought him. "Their redness talks to/my wound, it corresponds," he quoted softly. "I blew it, didn't I?" he said, finally looking up. "Yes. You almost died. Heroin, grass, Valium and wine." She shook her head. "They make a potent cocktail."

"I have let things slip." He was forlorn and pleading. "It's over, now, isn't it?"

"Pollack told me that you left that night to score. Why, Mark? You've been off heroin for years."

"Why? Because an old pal had some. Because I was starting to lose myself. And because that writer we went to see is so damn good and no one cares. I looked at him and knew that even if I sold my novel, what's the use?"

"You care. Pollack cares. Literature is what you live for."

"It's not enough. You are and . . ."

"And that isn't enough?" she asked mournfully.

"No." He was crying and she would not let go of him.

"Schoen, baby, I really love you. It's myself I can't stand. It's time for me to go away again."

She held him harder, unable to control her own soundless weeping.

"By the way," he said, when she finally sat up, "your dissertation is a fine piece of work. It always was. Finish it. It's almost . . ."

"Brilliant?"

"Yes. So far good enough to hand in." He turned on his side. "Go home, Schoen," he said, beginning to cry again. "Let me go through this alone."

She walked home, carrying all the way the weight of her loneliness. Without drugs, without sex, without the guidance of her *ilui*, she would finish her last chapter.

JOYCE MAYNARD, born in 1953, was a freshman at Yale when her article "An Eighteen-Year-Old Looks Back at Life" appeared in the Sunday magazine of *The New York Times*. She was hailed immediately as the spokesperson for her age group, which she described as a "generation of unfulfilled expectations." An expanded version of the article, *Looking Back: A Chronicle of Growing Up Old in the Sixties*, was published in 1973. Maynard also published the novel *Baby Love* in 1981, which focused on the impact of parenthood on several teenage mothers. The following selection, "Mary Emmet," taken from Maynard's recently published novel *To Die For*, takes us into the mind of a pregnant teenager and shows us the world of the moment when Mary Emmet chooses to become a mother. Maynard's vision of teenage motherhood, as elaborated throughout the grim and tragic New England world of her novel, is the opposite of Beverly Donofrio's experience as it unfolds in her memoir of teenage motherhood, *Riding in Cars With Boys* (page 67). These two selections, both of them excerpts from longer works, make interesting companion pieces.

Mary Emmet
from *To Die For*

❦

Joyce Maynard

I was supposed to have an abortion. Sixteen years old, Eddy off to Woodbury with no forwarding address two days after he got the news, my mother and dad on unemployment, calling me a whore. No way I was going to get to keep this baby. I had the appointment all set up. I even got a ride over to the clinic that morning. "Don't come home without blood in your underpants," my mom told me. A real softie, that one.

We got there early, so I told Patty, my friend that drove me, to drop me off a couple blocks away. I'd walk the rest. It was May. A real sunny day and the black flies hadn't come out yet. I stopped at a park—not even a park, just a playing field—where this Little League team was practicing. A bunch of little squirt boys and a coach that looked like he was somebody's dad. And over on this bench a little ways away, the moms sitting by a cooler, handing out Hi-C and calling out to their kid when it was his turn at bat. Some of them had littler kids too, playing in the dirt. This one mother was pregnant, only not like me. She was showing. Wearing this shirt with an arrow pointing down at her stomach that said FUTURE ALL-STAR. They were all laughing and talking. One had a baby in her lap and it looked like she was nursing him. I guess she was married to the coach, because he came over to her one time, when the kids were taking a break, and gave her a kiss. Not a french kiss or anything, like Eddy used to. This was the type kiss a husband and wife give each other. Just a peck on the cheek, but I saw that and I thought to myself: He doesn't just want sex out of her. He loves her. They're a family.

I knew it wasn't likely that this little amoeba or whatever that I had in my stomach was going to be some big baseball player, or some guy that discovers the cure for cancer. But one thing was for sure. He was my best shot at somebody that would always love me. And he'd be all mine.

There I am. A total fuckup at school. My parents hate me and you know Eddy wishes I'd jump off a bridge. I'm not smart and I'm not pretty, and I'll never get further than sponging ketchup off the tables at some fast-food restaurant. This baby I got is the most precious thing I ever had, and I'm going to let somebody stick a tube in that sucks it out of me and flush it down the toilet? I must be an even bigger idiot than my father tells me.

I tell myself there are people that have a million dollars, but they can't have a baby. They fly all over the country having operations, getting sperm donors, hiring women to have one for them, getting doctors to try and fertilize their eggs in a test tube. And here I am, I pulled it off without even trying. It's the most important thing I ever did or ever will do, most likely.

I sat down on the bench, behind the mothers. I guess I sat there a long time. Thinking about all the same stuff I'd been over a million times already: How am I supposed to pay for the diapers and stuff? How will I ever get another boyfriend if I have a baby? What happens if my dad kicks me out of the house? It's not like I'm going to be driving some station wagon and talking about trips to Disney World like these mothers. I don't even have the money to buy my kid a baseball glove. Who am I kidding, thinking I could be someone's mother?

This little guy with real thick glasses comes up to bat. He's a shrimp. The batting helmet keeps falling down over his face and he's all choked up on the bat. Then I see something's wrong with one of his arms. It's shriveled up and it looks like some of the fingers are missing. You can tell the kids on the team aren't that wild about him either. The mother that's keeping score or whatever mutters something about how his father was drunk when he dropped this kid off. One of the others says he's always sticking his hands down his pants and she wouldn't make any bets on him wearing underwear. Lucky her son wears a batting glove. "You'd think it was enough we had him for soccer," she says.

Frankie, his name was. A little guy that had less than nothing going for him.

OK, I say to myself. It's up to you, Frankie. Strike out, I'm heading straight over to that clinic to plunk down my two hundred dollars. Get on base and I'm having the baby.

First pitch they throw him, Frankie swings and misses. Second pitch, same thing. Then he lets maybe a dozen good pitches go by. Just stands there grinning, while you can see the dad that's pitching getting pretty fed up. "Come on now, Frankie," he says. "Other kids need to get a turn."

It's like he doesn't hear. He keeps waiting as one perfectly good ball after another sails across the plate. Nice easy balls. Ten, maybe fifteen more pitches.

The kids are yelling at him now. "Funky," they call him. Mothers shaking their heads, looking at their watches. Me, I'm barely breathing.

"OK, Frankie," says the coach. "This is your last shot." He releases the ball. Not even a good pitch like those others. It's way outside. No way is Funky connecting with this one. In my head I'm already climbing up on the table, putting my feet in the stirrups.

He does this little dance, and then he swings like no swing you ever saw, dips the bat low. Taps the ball. Just barely, mind you. You figured the pitcher had to get it, the way the ball wobbled over to him, only it bounced off his glove and past him. Fell to the ground and rolled right between the second baseman's legs.

So I skipped my appointment at the clinic. Decided then and there to have my baby. And that was my son Jimmy.

But here's the trick life hands you. You get this kid all right. You love him to death. And just like you figured, he loves you too. You weren't wrong when you figured this child was going to be the most precious thing you'd ever be handed in your life.

But the joke's on you. Because once you get this child, what can you do about it but wake up every morning, waiting to see what dreams won't come true today? Before long, you stop having the dreams altogether. If you're smart you do.

Jimmy was three weeks old before I could bring him home from the hospital on account of how little he was. Four pounds, two ounces, when he was born. They had him in an incubator.

I'd stand there in the nursery, holding him in my hands, him with this little shirt on that came off my old Tiny Tears doll. His skin was almost transparent, with these blue veins showing through. Legs like chicken wings. No hair, no eyelashes. Fingernails barely sprouted. He was so little he couldn't even cry. Just made these little squeaking sounds, more like a puppy than a kid.

It was no picnic. My folks wouldn't let me come back home, so I moved in at Patty's, put Jimmy in day care when he was five weeks old, got my job at Wendy's, the three-to-eleven shift.

You think about all this stuff you'll do when you have a kid. Taking them to the carnival to ride in those little boats. Get their picture taken with Santa, make sand castles at the beach. You picture yourself being one of those mothers pushing the stroller down the street, pushing your kid on the swings. Passing out the Hi-C at baseball games. It never works out like how you pictured. You only have enough tickets for him to ride the little boats four times, and then you got to take him home only he's crying for another turn. He's scared of Santa. Your one afternoon off all week to take him to the beach it rains. Or you're just so tired by the time you get home, you got barely enough energy to stick the frozen pizza in the microwave and turn on the TV.

He was always a good boy, Jimmy. Nights I'd be at work, he'd fix himself supper, get himself to bed even. He learned pretty young not to ask for much, so I hardly ever had to say no. I mean he always loved dogs, but he always knew we couldn't have a puppy.

Third grade, he wanted to join Little League. Not that he knew the first thing about baseball. It's not like this was a boy that got to play catch with his dad every night after supper. He just watched games on TV and got the idea in his head that this was his sport. What could be so tricky about running around the bases, you know?

So we signed up for the league. I paid my registration

money. We bought him a glove and a bat and I even took
him down to this field near our apartment to throw him
some balls. Not that I could throw worth beans. But you
did the best you could.

Comes the Saturday morning of the tryouts, he takes a
bath, wets his hair down, changes his T-shirt three times,
he's so excited. Down at the field, when I fill out the papers
on him, and they ask who he played for last year, I write
down "Never been on a team before." The guy in charge
looks surprised. "Most boys his age already have some experience," he says.

"Well this one doesn't," I say. You got to start somewhere.

I see a couple of the mothers rolling their eyes, like
"What kind of people are these?" and you know they take
one look at me and figure out my whole story: She got
knocked up when she was a teenager. No dad in the picture.
Kid's a loser.

When Jimmy's turn comes to bat, they throw him all these
pitches, and he never manages to hit one. Finally they set
up the T for him, and he kind of taps it. They tag him out.
One of the mothers on the bench that doesn't know this is
my son says, "Jesus, let's hope the Orioles don't get that
one."

Jimmy stuck it out that season, but he never signed up
for a sport again, and we never discussed it.

I should've known, that day on the ballpark, heading over
to the abortion clinic. Frankie got on base all right. But
what happened next was the real story. Next batter up hits
a single, and Frankie's an easy out at second. No way that
kid was ever going to score in baseball or in life.

The game's rigged. Doesn't everybody know that yet?

SUSAN MINOT grew up in Manchester-by-the-Sea, Massachusetts, and now lives in New York City. She received a Bachelor of Arts degree at Brown University and a Master of Fine Arts at Columbia. She has worked as a waitress, a bookstore clerk, an editorial assistant, an assistant editor, a teacher of writing workshops, and an adjunct professor. Her stories have appeared in *Grand Street, The New Yorker,* and *The Paris Review,* and also in the *Pushcart Prize IX* collection and *The Best American Short Stories 1984* and *1985.* Her first novel, *Monkeys,* about growing up in a large New England, Roman Catholic family, was published to high praise in 1986. Reviewers compared the gifted Minot to Evelyn Waugh, John Irving, and J.D. Salinger.

"Lust," the award-winning story that follows, is the title story of the collection published in 1989. James Robison, writing in *The New York Times Book Review,* praised the "disarming clarity and lyrical directness" of the volume's twelve stories. "Ms. Minot's book," he wrote, "is as timeless as its subject, as timeless as midnight swims, dinner-party gossip, a night kiss on a city street. . . . The book accumulates its truest sense and strength when read straight through, for its meanings assemble themselves, story by story, and its wisdom and overall restraint come to full flower as the tales mount up. This is a superbly organized, poignant and profound collection." Reviewer Elizabeth Stevens's comment in the *Women's Review of Books* applies especially to the story "Lust": "These brief, beautifully written stories employ economical prose and an elegiac mood to portray young women yearning for something more than short-term sex." As Minot's narrator says in "Lust," evoking the sense of loss and sadness that runs through all her fiction, "Teenage years. You know just what you're doing and don't see the things that start to get in the way." The story provokes questions about the effects of the sexual

revolution on the liberation of women from sexual stereotyping. It also addresses the nature of the sexual experience
itself for males and females and the effect of adolescent
sexual experience on identity formation. In the prestigious
prep-school world of Minot's story, the effect of teenage
promiscuity on the female narrator's sense of self is that she
loses whatever budding identity she has developed. After
sex, she says, "You're gone. . . . You seem to have disappeared."

Lust

❦

Susan Minot

Leo was from a long time ago, the first one I ever saw nude. In the spring before the Hellmans filled their pool, we'd go down there in the deep end, with baby oil, and like that. I met him the first month away at boarding school. He had a halo from the campus light behind him. I flipped.

Roger was fast. In his illegal car, we drove to the reservoir, the radio blaring, talking fast, fast, fast. He was always going for my zipper. He got kicked out sophomore year.

By the time the band got around to playing "Wild Horses," I had tasted Bruce's tongue. We were clicking in the shadows on the other side of the amplifier, out of Mrs. Donovan's line of vision. It tasted like salt, with my neck bent back, because we had been dancing so hard before.

Tim's line: "I'd like to see you in a bathing suit." I knew it was his line when he said the exact same thing to Annie Hines.

You'd go on walks to get off campus. It was raining like hell, my sweater as sopped as a wet sheep. Tim pinned me to a tree, the woods light brown and dark brown, a white house half-hidden with the lights already on. The water was as loud as a crowd hissing. He made certain comments about my forehead, about my cheeks.

We started off sitting at one end of the couch and then our feet were squished against the armrest and then he went over to turn off the TV and came back after he had taken off his shirt and then we slid onto the floor and he got up again to close the door, then came back to me, a body waiting on the rug.

You'd try to wipe off the table or to do the dishes and Willie would untuck your shirt and get his hands up under in front, standing behind you, making puffy noises in your ear.

He likes it when I wash my hair. He covers his face with it and if I start to say something, he goes, "Shush."

For a long time, I had Philip on the brain. The less they noticed you, the more you got them on the brain.

My parents had no idea. Parents never really know what's going on, especially when you're away at school most of the time. If she met them, my mother might say, "Oliver seems nice" or "I like that one" without much of an opinion. If she didn't like them, "He's a funny fellow, isn't he?" or "Johnny's perfectly nice but a drink of water." My father was too shy to talk to them at all, unless they played sports and he'd ask them about that.

The sand was almost cold underneath because the sun was long gone. Eben piled a mound over my feet, patting around my ankles, the ghostly surf rumbling behind him in the dark. He was the first person I ever knew who died, later that summer, in a car crash. I thought about it for a long time.

"Come here," he says on the porch.

I go over to the hammock and he takes my wrist with two fingers.

"What?"

He kisses my palm then directs my hand to his fly.

Songs went with whichever boy it was. "Sugar Magnolia" was Tim, with the line "Rolling in the rushes/down by the riverside." With "Darkness Darkness," I'd picture Philip with his long hair. Hearing "Under my Thumb" there'd be the smell of Jamie's suede jacket.

We hid in the listening rooms during study hall. With a record cover over the door's window, the teacher on duty couldn't look in. I came out flushed and heady and back at the dorm was surprised how red my lips were in the mirror.

One weekend at Simon's brother's, we stayed inside all day with the shades down, in bed, then went out to Store 24 to get some ice cream. He stood at the magazine rack and read through *MAD* while I got butterscotch sauce, craving something sweet.

I could do some things well. Some things I was good at, like math or painting or even sports, but the second a boy put his arm around me, I forgot about wanting to do anything else, which felt like a relief at first until it became like sinking into a muck.

It was different for a girl.

When we were little, the brothers next door tied up our ankles. They held the door of the goat house and wouldn't let us out till we showed them our underpants. Then they'd forget about being after us and when we played whiffle ball, I'd be just as good as them.

Then it got to be different. Just because you have on a short skirt, they yell from the cars, slowing down for a while and if you don't look, they screech off and call you a bitch.

"What's the matter with me?" they say, point-blank.

Or else, "Why won't you go out with me? I'm not asking you to get married," about to get mad.

Or it'd be, trying to be reasonable, in a regular voice, "Listen, I just want to have a good time."

So I'd go because I couldn't think of something to say back that wouldn't be obvious, and if you go out with them, you sort of have to do something.

I sat between Mack and Eddie in the front seat of the pickup. They were having a fight about something. I've a feeling about me.

Certain nights you'd feel a certain surrender, maybe if you'd had wine. The surrender would be forgetting yourself and you'd put your nose to his neck and feel like a squirrel, safe, at rest, in a restful dream. But then you'd start to slip from that and the dark would come in and there'd be a cave. You make out the dim shape of the windows and feel yourself become a cave, filled absolutely with air, or with a sadness that wouldn't stop.

Teenage years. You know just what you're doing and don't see the things that start to get in the way.

Lots of boys, but never two at the same time. One was plenty to keep you in a state. You'd start to see a boy and something would rush over you like a fast storm cloud and you couldn't possibly think of anyone else. Boys took it differently. Their eyes perked up at any little number that walked by. You'd act like you weren't noticing.

The joke was that the school doctor gave out the pill like aspirin. He didn't ask you anything. I was fifteen. We had a picture of him in assembly, holding up an IUD shaped like a T. Most girls were on the pill, if anything, because they couldn't handle a diaphragm. I kept the dial in my top drawer like my mother and thought of her each time I tipped out the yellow tablets in the morning before chapel.

If they were too shy, I'd be more so. Andrew was nervous. We stayed up with his family album, sharing a pack of Old Golds. Before it got light, we turned on the TV. A man was explaining how to plant seedlings. His mouth jerked to the side in a tic. Andrew thought it was a riot and kept imitating him. I laughed to be polite. When we finally dozed off, he dared to put his arm around me but that was it.

You wait till they come to you. With half fright, half swagger, they stand one step down. They dare to touch the button on your coat then lose their nerve and quickly drop their hand so you—you'd do anything for them. You touch their cheek.

The girls sit around in the common room and talk about boys, smoking their heads off.

"What are you complaining about?" says Jill to me when we talk about problems.

"Yeah," says Giddy. "You always have a boyfriend."

I look at them and think, As if.

I thought the worst thing anyone could call you was a cockteaser. So, if you flirted, you had to be prepared to go through with it. Sleeping with someone was perfectly normal once you had done it. You didn't really worry about it. But there were other problems. The problems had to do with something else entirely.

Mack was during the hottest summer ever recorded. We were renting a house on an island with all sorts of other people. No one slept during the heat wave, walking around the house with nothing on which we were used to because of the nude beach. In the living room, Eddie lay on top of a coffee table to cool off. Mack and I, with the bedroom door open for air, sweated and sweated all night.

"I can't take this," he said at 3 A.M. "I'm going for a

swim.'' He and some guys down the hall went to the beach.
The heat put me on edge. I sat on a cracked chest by the
open window and smoked and smoked till I felt even worse,
waiting for something—I guess for him to get back.

One was on a camping trip in Colorado. We zipped our sleeping
bags together, the coyotes' hysterical chatter far away. Other couples murmured in other tents. Paul was up before sunrise, starting
a fire for breakfast. He wasn't much of a talker in the daytime. At
night, his hand leafed about in the hair at my neck.

There'd be times when you overdid it. You'd get carried away.
All the next day, you'd be in a total fog, delirious, absent-minded,
crossing the street and nearly getting run over.

The more girls a boy has, the better. He has a bright look,
having reaped fruits, blooming. He stalks around, sure-
shouldered, and you have the feeling he's got more in him,
a fatter heart, more stories to tell. For a girl, with each boy
it's like a petal gets plucked each time.

Then you start to get tired. You begin to feel diluted, like
watered-down stew.

Oliver came skiing with us. We lolled by the fire after
everyone had gone to bed. Each creak you'd think was
someone coming downstairs. The silver-loop bracelet he
gave me had been a present from his girlfriend before.

On vacations, we went skiing, or you'd go south if someone invited you. Some people had apartments in New York
that their families hardly ever used. Or summer houses, or
older sisters. We always managed to find someplace to go.

We made the plan at coffee hour. Simon snuck out and
met me at Main Gate after lights-out. We crept to the chapel
and spent the night in the balcony. He tasted like onions
from a submarine sandwich.

The boys are one of two ways: either they can't sit still or they
don't move. In front of the TV, they won't budge. On weekends
they play touch football while we sit on the sidelines, picking
blades of grass to chew on, and watch. We're always watching
them run around. We shiver in the stands, knocking our boots
together to keep our toes warm and they whizz across the ice,
chopping their sticks around the puck. When they're in the rink,
they refuse to look at you, only eyeing each other beneath low
helmets. You cheer for them but they don't look up, even if it's a
face-off when nothing's happening, even if they're doing drills
before any game has started at all.

Dancing under the pink tent, he bent down and whispered in my ear. We slipped away to the lawn on the other side of the hedge. Much later, as he was leaving the buffet with two plates of eggs and sausage, I saw the grass stains on the knees of his white pants.

Tim's was shaped like a banana, with a graceful curve to it. They're all different. Willie's like a bunch of walnuts when nothing was happening, another's as thin as a thin hot dog. But it's like faces, you're never really surprised.

Still, you're not sure what to expect.

I look into his face and he looks back. I look into his eyes and they look back at mine. Then they look down at my mouth so I look at his mouth, then back to his eyes then, backing up, at his whole face. I think, Who? Who are you? His head tilts to one side.

I say, "Who are you?"

"What do you mean?"

"Nothing."

I look at his eyes again, deeper. Can't tell who he is, what he thinks.

"What?" he says. I look at his mouth.

"I'm just wondering," I say and go wandering across his face. Study the chin line. It's shaped like a persimmon.

"Who are you? What are you thinking?"

He says, "What the hell are you talking about?"

Then they get mad after when you say enough is enough. After, when it's easier to explain that you don't want to. You wouldn't dream of saying that maybe you weren't really ready to in the first place.

Gentle Eddie. We waded into the sea, the waves round and plowing in, buffalo-headed, slapping our thighs. I put my arms around his freckled shoulders and he held me up, buoyed by the water, and rocked me like a seashell.

I had no idea whose party it was, the apartment jam-packed, stepping over people in the hallway. The room with the music was practically empty, the bare floor, me in red shoes. This fellow slides onto one knee and takes me around the waist and we rock to jazzy tunes, with my toes pointing heavenward, and waltz and spin and dip to "Smoke Gets in Your Eyes" or "I'll Love You Just for Now." He puts his head to my chest, runs a sweeping hand down my inside thigh and we go loose-limbed and sultry and as smooth as silk and I stamp my red heels and he takes me into a swoon. I never saw him again after that but I thought, I could have loved that one.

You wonder how long you can keep it up. You begin to feel like you're showing through, like a bathroom window that only lets in gray light, the kind you can't see out of.

They keep coming around. Johnny drives up at Easter vacation from Baltimore and I let him in the kitchen with everyone sound asleep. He has friends waiting in the car.

"What are you crazy? It's pouring out there," I say.

"It's okay," he says. "They understand."

So he gets some long kisses from me, against the refrigerator, before he goes because I hate those girls who push away a boy's face as if she were made out of Ivory soap, as if she's that much greater than he is.

The note on my cubby told me to see the headmaster. I had no idea for what. He had received complaints about my amorous displays on the town green. It was Willie that spring. The headmaster told me he didn't care what I did but that Casey Academy had a reputation to uphold in the town. He lowered his glasses on his nose. "We've got twenty acres of woods on this campus," he said. "If you want to smooch with your boyfriend, there are twenty acres for you to do it out of the public eye. You read me?"

Everybody'd get weekend permissions for different places, then we'd all go to someone's house whose parents were away. Usually there'd be more boys than girls. We raided the liquor closet and smoked pot at the kitchen table and you'd never know who would end up where, or with whom. There were always disasters. Ceci got bombed and cracked her head open on the banister and needed stitches. Then there was the time Wendel Blair walked through the picture window at the Lowe's and got slashed to ribbons.

He scared me. In bed, I didn't dare look at him. I lay back with my eyes closed, luxuriating because he knew all sorts of expert angles, his hands never fumbling, going over my whole body, pressing the hair up and off the back of my head, giving an extra hip shove, as if to say *There*. I parted my eyes slightly, keeping the screen of my lashes low because it was too much to look at him, his mouth loose and pink and parted, his eyes looking through my forehead, or kneeling up, looking through my throat. I was ashamed but couldn't look him in the eye.

You wonder about things feeling a little off-kilter. You begin to feel like a piece of pounded veal.

At boarding school, everyone gets depressed. We go in and see the housemother, Mrs. Gunther. She got married when she was eighteen. Mr. Gunther was her high-school sweetheart, the only boyfriend she ever had.

"And you knew you wanted to marry him right off?" we ask her.

She smiles and says, "Yes."

"They always want something from you," says Jill, complaining about her boyfriend.

"Yeah," says Giddy. "You always feel like you have to deliver something."

"You do," says Mrs. Gunther. "Babies."

After sex, you curl up like a shrimp, something deep inside you ruined, slammed in a place that sickens at slamming, and slowly you fill up with an overwhelming sadness, an elusive gaping worry. You don't try to explain it, filled with the knowledge that it's nothing after all, everything filling up finally and absolutely with death. After the briskness of loving, loving stops. And you roll over with death stretched out alongside you like a feather boa, or a snake, light as air, and you . . . you don't even ask for anything or try to say something to him because it's obviously your own damn fault. You haven't been able to—to what? To open your heart. You open your legs but can't, or don't dare anymore, to open your heart.

It starts this way:

You stare into their eyes. They flash like all the stars are out. They look at you seriously, their eyes at a low burn and their hands no matter what starting off shy and with such a gentle touch that the only thing you can do is take that tenderness and let yourself be swept away. When, with one attentive finger they tuck the hair behind your ear, you—

You do everything they want.

Then comes after. After when they don't look at you. They scratch their balls, stare at the ceiling. Or if they do turn, their gaze is altogether changed. They are surprised. They turn casually to look at you, distracted, and get a mild distracted surprise. You're gone. Their blank look tells you that the girl they were fucking is not there anymore. You seem to have disappeared.

GLORIA NAYLOR was born and grew up in New York City, graduating from Brooklyn College in 1981. She has worked as a missionary for Jehovah's Witnesses and done graduate work at Yale University.

Her first novel *The Women of Brewster Place: A Novel in Seven Stories* received the 1982 American Book Award for best first novel. The book concerns seven women residents of a ghetto housing project. Although their personal situations differ, they collectively share the problems of the African-American female at various stages of life. Each chapter reads like a short story and focuses on one character and her interaction with the others. Critics unanimously praised the novel's narrative control and Naylor's lyrical, passionate prose. On the strength of this award-winning debut, Naylor has won a place, in the words of Mari Evans, "in the ongoing pantheon of Black women writers whose creativity continues to blossom." Reviewer Annie Gottlieb, writing in *The New York Times Book Review,* observed, "*The Women of Brewster Place* isn't realistic fiction—it is mythic. Nothing supernatural happens in it, yet its vivid, earthy characters . . . seem constantly on the verge of breaking out into magical powers." Another reviewer wrote that the novel is more than a simple celebration of female solidarity. Essentially, it is about motherhood. Each of Naylor's women is a surrogate child or mother to the next.

An interesting companion piece to the majestic speech of Kiswana Browne's mother in the story that follows here is the recent and highly acclaimed "A Letter To My Sons" in the memoir *The Measure of Our Success* by Marian Wright Edelman. Both Ms. Edelman and the fictional mother of Kiswana, née Melanie, preach the pride of the generations, the commitment to others at the core of family survival, a perception strong in the bones of motherhood. Such narratives (and along these lines others come to mind—Paule Marshall's *Brown Girl, Brownstones,* Lorene Cary's *Black Ice,* Andrea Lee's *Sarah Phillips*) reflect the truth of critic Mary Helen Washington's view that "the story of family has inspired some of the very best writing by black writers, and surely that is because the family is integral to black traditions.'' Washington's thoughts about family, expressed in her introduction to her anthology *Memory of Kin: Stories About Family By Black Writers*, have a special resonance after the summer of the 1992 Republican Convention in Houston: ''I know how the idea of family has been used to oppress women, especially black women. Fundamentalists can conjure up so-called 'family values' whenever they want to assert male domination and canonize female subordination. Almost every effort on the part of women to achieve equality in this society has been associated with the loss of these so-called 'family values' . . . a book that takes family as its major subject needs to be aware of the ideological traps that underlie the construction of family.''

The story that follows here shows the character of the daughter, who is trying to grow up on her own terms, not on her mother's or her mother's culture, gradually re-visioning where in the adult world the traps lie and where the freedoms. This selection, in its conflict between generations and the values of the different generations, bears interesting comparison with the selection in this anthology by Andrea Lee (page 161).

In her comments to *Contemporary Authors* about the sources of her inspiration, Naylor writes:

> I wanted to become a writer because I felt that my presence as a black woman and my perspective as a woman in general had been underrepresented in American literature. My first novel grew out of a desire to respond to a trend that I had noticed in the black and white critical establishment. There has been a tendency on the part of both to assume that a black writer's work should be ''definitive'' of black experience. This type of critical stance denies the vast complexity of black existence. . . . One book or even one literary career . . . could never represent the vast array of lifestyles that have been lumped into an anonymous mass labeled ''the black experience.''

❧

Kiswana Browne

from *The Women Of Brewster Place*

❦

Gloria Naylor

From the window of her sixth-floor studio apartment, Kiswana could see over the wall at the end of the street to the busy avenue that lay just north of Brewster Place. The late-afternoon shoppers looked like brightly clad marionettes as they moved between the congested traffic, clutching their packages against their bodies to guard them from sudden bursts of the cold autumn wind. A portly mailman had abandoned his cart and was bumping into indignant window-shoppers as he puffed behind the cap that the wind had snatched from his head. Kiswana leaned over to see if he was going to be successful, but the edge of the building cut him off from her view.

A pigeon swept across her window, and she marveled at its liquid movements in the air waves. She placed her dreams on the back of the bird and fantasized that it would glide forever in transparent silver circles until it ascended to the center of the universe and was swallowed up. But the wind died down, and she watched with a sigh as the bird beat its wings in awkward, frantic movements to land on the corroded top of a fire escape on the opposite building. This brought her back to earth.

Humph, it's probably sitting over there crapping on those folks' fire escape, she thought. Now, that's a safety hazard. . . . And her mind was busy again, creating flames and smoke and frustrated tenants whose escape was being hindered because they were slipping and sliding in pigeon shit. She watched their cussing, haphazard descent on the fire escapes until they had all reached the bottom. They were milling around, oblivious to their burning apartments, angrily planning to march on the mayor's office about the pigeons. She materialized placards and banners for them, and they had just reached the corner, boldly sidestepping fire hoses and broken glass, when they all vanished.

A tall copper-skinned woman had met this phantom parade at the corner, and they had dissolved in front of her long, confident strides. She plowed through the remains of their faded mists, unconscious of the lingering wisps of their presence on her leather bag and black fur-trimmed coat. It took a few seconds for this transfer from one realm to another to reach Kiswana, but then suddenly she recognized the woman.

"Oh, God, it's Mama!" She looked down guiltily at the forgotten newspaper in her lap and hurriedly circled random job advertisements.

By this time Mrs. Browne had reached the front of Kiswana's building and was checking the house number against a piece of paper in her hand. Before she went into the building she stood at the bottom of the stoop and carefully inspected the condition of the street and the adjoining property. Kiswana watched this meticulous inventory with growing annoyance but she involuntarily followed her mother's slowly rotating head, forcing herself to see her new neighborhood through the older woman's eyes. The brightness of the unclouded sky seemed to join forces with her mother as it highlighted every broken stoop railing and missing brick. The afternoon sun glittered and cascaded across even the tiniest fragments of broken bottle, and at that very moment the wind chose to rise up again, sending unswept grime flying into the air, as a stray tin can left by careless garbage collectors went rolling noisily down the center of the street.

Kiswana noticed with relief that at least Ben wasn't sitting in his usual place on the old garbage can pushed against the far wall. He was just a harmless old wino, but Kiswana knew her mother only needed one wino or one teenager with a reefer within a twenty-block radius to decide that her daughter was living in a building seething with dope factories and hang-outs for derelicts. If she had seen Ben, nothing would have made her believe that practically every apartment contained a family, a Bible, and a dream that one day enough could be scraped from those meager Friday night paychecks to make Brewster Place a distant memory.

As she watched her mother's head disappear into the building, Kiswana gave silent thanks that the elevator was broken. That would give her at least five minutes' grace to straighten up the apartment. She rushed to the sofa bed and hastily closed it without smoothing the rumpled sheets and blanket or removing her nightgown. She felt that somehow the tangled bedcovers would give away the fact that she had not slept alone last night. She silently apologized to Abshu's memory as she heartlessly crushed his spirit between the steel springs of the couch. Lord, that man was sweet. Her toes curled involuntarily at the passing thought of his full lips moving slowly over her instep. Abshu was a foot man, and he always started his lovemaking from the bottom up. For that reason Kiswana changed the color of the polish on her toenails every week. During the course of their relationship she had gone from shades of red to brown and was now into the purples. I'm gonna have to start mixing them soon, she thought aloud as she turned from the couch and raced into the bathroom to remove any traces of Abshu from there. She took up his shaving cream and razor and threw them into the bottom drawer of her dresser beside her diaphragm. Mama wouldn't dare pry into my drawers right in front of me, she thought as she slammed the drawer shut. Well, at least not the *bottom* drawer. She may come up with some sham excuse for opening the top drawer, but never the bottom one.

When she heard the first two short raps on the door, her eyes took a final flight over the small apartment, desperately seeking out any slight misdemeanor that might have to be defended. Well, there was nothing she could do about the crack in the wall over that table. She had been after the landlord to fix it for two months now. And there had been no time to sweep the rug, and everyone knew that off-gray always looked dirtier than it really was. And it was just too damn bad about the kitchen. How was she expected to be out job-hunting every day and still have time to keep a kitchen that looked like her mother's, who didn't even work and still had someone come in twice a month for general cleaning. And besides . . .

Her imaginary argument was abruptly interrupted by a second series of knocks, accompanied by a penetrating, "Melanie, Melanie, are you there?"

Kiswana strode toward the door. She's starting before she even gets in here. She knows that's not my name anymore.

She swung the door open to face her slightly flushed mother. "Oh, hi, Mama. You know, I thought I heard a knock, but I figured it was for the people next door, since no one hardly ever calls me Melanie." Score one for me, she thought.

"Well, it's awfully strange you can forget a name you answered to for twenty-three years," Mrs. Browne said, as she moved past Kiswana into the apartment. "My, that was a long climb. How long has your elevator been out? Honey, how do you manage with your laundry and groceries up all those steps? But I guess you're young, and it wouldn't bother you as much as it does me." This long string of questions told Kiswana that her mother had no intentions of beginning her visit with another argument about her new African name.

"You know I would have called before I came, but you don't have a phone yet. I didn't want you to feel that I was snooping. As a matter of fact, I didn't expect to find you home at all. I thought you'd be out looking for a job." Mrs. Browne had mentally covered the entire apartment while she was talking and taking off her coat.

"Well, I got up late this morning. I thought I'd buy the afternoon paper and start early tomorrow."

"That sounds like a good idea." Her mother moved toward the window and picked up the discarded paper and glanced over the hurriedly circled ads. "Since when do you have experience as a fork-lift operator?"

Kiswana caught her breath and silently cursed herself for her stupidity. "Oh, my hand slipped—I meant to circle file clerk." She quickly took the paper before her mother could see that she had also marked cutlery salesman and chauffeur.

"You're sure you weren't sitting here moping and daydreaming again?" Amber specks of laughter flashed in the corner of Mrs. Browne's eyes.

Kiswana threw her shoulders back and unsuccessfully tried to disguise her embarrassment with indignation.

"Oh, God, Mama! I haven't done that in years—it's for kids. When are you going to realize that I'm a woman now?" She sought desperately for some womanly thing to do and settled for throwing herself on the couch and crossing her legs in what she hoped looked like a nonchalant arc.

"Please, have a seat," she said, attempting the same tones and gestures she'd seen Bette Davis use on the late movies.

Mrs. Browne, lowering her eyes to hide her amusement, accepted the invitation and sat at the window, also crossing her legs. Kiswana saw immediately how it should have been done. Her celluloid poise clashed loudly against her mother's quiet dignity, and she quickly uncrossed her legs. Mrs. Browne turned her head toward the window and pretended not to notice.

"At least you have a halfway decent view from here. I was wondering what lay beyond that dreadful wall—it's the boulevard. Honey, did you know that you can see the trees in Linden Hills from here?"

Kiswana knew that very well, because there were many lonely days that she would sit in her gray apartment and stare at those trees and think of home, but she would rather have choked than admit that to her mother.

"Oh, really, I never noticed. So how is Daddy and things at home?"

"Just fine. We're thinking of redoing one of the extra bedrooms since you children have moved out, but Wilson insists that he can manage all that work alone. I told him that he doesn't really have the proper time or energy for all that. As it is, when he gets home from the office, he's so tired he can hardly move. But you know you can't tell your father anything. Whenever he starts complaining about how stubborn you are, I tell him the child came by it honestly. Oh, and your brother was by yesterday," she added, as if it had just occurred to her.

So that's it, thought Kiswana. That's why she's here.

Kiswana's brother, Wilson, had been to visit her two days ago, and she had borrowed twenty dollars from him to get her winter coat out of layaway. That son-of-a-bitch probably ran straight to Mama—and after he swore he wouldn't say anything. I should have known, he was always a snotty-nosed sneak, she thought.

"Was he?" she said aloud. "He came by to see me, too, earlier this week. And I borrowed some money from him because my unemployment checks hadn't cleared in the bank, but now they have and everything's just fine." There, I'll beat you to that one.

"Oh, I didn't know that," Mrs. Browne lied. "He never mentioned you. He had just heard that Beverly was expecting again, and he rushed over to tell us."

Damn. Kiswana could have strangled herself.

"So she's knocked up again, huh?" she said irritably.

Her mother started. "Why do you always have to be so crude?"

"Personally, I don't see how she can sleep with Willie. He's such a dishrag."

Kiswana still resented the stance her brother had taken in college. When everyone at school was discovering their blackness and protesting on campus, Wilson never took part; he had even refused to wear an Afro. This had outraged Kiswana because, unlike her, he was dark-skinned and had the type of hair that was thick and kinky enough for a good "Fro." Kiswana had still insisted on cutting her own hair, but it was so thin and fine-textured, it refused to thicken even after she washed it. So she had to brush it up and spray it with lacquer to keep it from lying flat. She never forgave Wilson for telling her that she didn't look African, she looked like an electrocuted chicken.

"Now that's some way to talk. I don't know why you have an attitude against your brother. He never gave me a restless night's sleep, and now he's settled with a family and a good job."

"He's an assistant to an assistant junior partner in a law firm. What's the big deal about that?"

"The job has a future, Melanie. And at least he finished school and went on for his law degree."

"In other words, not like me, huh?"

"Don't put words into my mouth, young lady. I'm perfectly capable of saying what I mean."

Amen, thought Kiswana.

"And I don't know why you've been trying to start up with me from the moment I walked in. I didn't come here to fight with you. This is your first place away from home, and I just wanted to see how you were living and if you're doing all right. And I must say, you've fixed this apartment up very nicely.''

''Really, Mama?'' She found herself softening in the light of her mother's approval.

''Well, considering what you had to work with.'' This time she scanned the apartment openly.

''Look, I know it's not Linden Hills, but a lot can be done with it. As soon as they come and paint, I'm going to hang my Ashanti print over the couch. And I thought a big Boston Fern would go well in that corner, what do you think?''

''That would be fine, baby. You always had a good eye for balance.''

Kiswana was beginning to relax. There was little she did that attracted her mother's approval. It was like a rare bird, and she had to tread carefully around it lest it fly away.

''Are you going to leave that statue out like that?''

''Why, what's wrong with it? Would it look better somewhere else?''

There was a small wooden reproduction of a Yoruba goddess with large protruding breasts on the coffee table.

''Well,'' Mrs. Browne was beginning to blush, ''it's just that it's a bit suggestive, don't you think? Since you live alone now, and I know you'll be having male friends stop by, you wouldn't want to be giving them any ideas. I mean, uh, you know, there's no point in putting yourself in any unpleasant situations because they may get the wrong impressions and uh, you know, I mean, well . . .'' Mrs. Browne stammered on miserably.

Kiswana loved it when her mother tried to talk about sex. It was the only time she was at a loss for words.

''Don't worry, Mama.'' Kiswana smiled. ''That wouldn't bother the type of men I date. Now maybe if it had big feet . . .'' And she got hysterical, thinking of Abshu.

Her mother looked at her sharply. ''What sort of gibberish is that about feet? I'm being serious, Melanie.''

''I'm sorry, Mama.'' She sobered up. ''I'll put it away in the closet,'' she said, knowing that she wouldn't.

''Good,'' Mrs. Browne said, knowing that she wouldn't either. ''I guess you think I'm too picky, but we worry about you over here. And you refuse to put in a phone so we can call and see about you.''

"I haven't refused, Mama. They want seventy-five dollars for a deposit, and I can't swing that right now."

"Melanie, I can give you the money."

"I don't want you to be giving me money—I've told you that before. Please, let me make it by myself."

"Well, let me lend it to you, then."

"No!"

"Oh, so you can borrow money from your brother, but not from me."

Kiswana turned her head from the hurt in her mother's eyes. "Mama, when I borrow from Willie, he makes me pay him back. You never let me pay you back," she said into her hands.

"I don't care. I still think it's downright selfish of you to be sitting over here with no phone, and sometimes we don't hear from you in two weeks—anything could happen—especially living among these people."

Kiswana snapped her head up. "What do you mean, *these people*. They're my people and yours, too, Mama—we're all black. But maybe you've forgotten that over in Linden Hills."

"That's not what I'm talking about, and you know it. These streets—this building—it's so shabby and rundown. Honey, you don't have to live like this."

"Well, this is how poor people live."

"Melanie, you're not poor."

"No, Mama, *you're* not poor. And what you have and I have are two totally different things. I don't have a husband in real estate with a five-figure income and a home in Linden Hills—*you* do. What I have is a weekly unemployment check and an overdrawn checking account at United Federal. So this studio on Brewster is all I can afford."

"Well, you could afford a lot better," Mrs. Browne snapped, "if you hadn't dropped out of college and had to resort to these dead-end clerical jobs."

"Uh-huh, I knew you'd get around to that before long." Kiswana could feel the rings of anger begin to tighten around her lower backbone, and they sent her forward onto the couch. "You'll never understand, will you? Those bourgie schools were counterrevolutionary. My place was in the streets with my people, fighting for equality and a better community."

"Counterrevolutionary!" Mrs. Browne was raising her voice. "Where's your revolution now, Melanie? Where are all those black revolutionaries who were shouting and demonstrating and kicking up a lot of dust with you on that campus? Huh? They're sitting in wood-paneled offices with their degrees in mahogany frames, and they won't even drive their cars past this street because the city doesn't fix potholes in this part of town."

"Mama," she said, shaking her head slowly in disbelief, "how can you—a black woman—sit there and tell me that what we fought for during the Movement wasn't important just because some people sold out?"

"Melanie, I'm not saying it wasn't important. It was damned important to stand up and say that you were proud of what you were and to get the vote and other social opportunities for every person in this country who had it due. But you kids thought you were going to turn the world upside down, and it just wasn't so. When all the smoke had cleared, you found yourself with a fistful of new federal laws and a country still full of obstacles for black people to fight their way over—just because they're black. There was no revolution, Melanie, and there will be no revolution."

"So what am I supposed to do, huh? Just throw up my hands and not care about what happens to my people? I'm not supposed to keep fighting to make things better?"

"Of course, you can. But you're going to have to fight within the system, because it and these so-called 'bourgie' schools are going to be here for a long time. And that means that you get smart like a lot of your old friends and get an important job where you can have some influence. You don't have to sell out, as you say, and work for some corporation, but you could become an assemblywoman or a civil liberties lawyer or open a freedom school in this very neighborhood. That way you could really help the community. But what help are you going to be to these people on Brewster while you're living hand-to-mouth on file-clerk jobs waiting for a revolution? You're wasting your talents, child."

"Well, I don't think they're being wasted. At least I'm here in day-to-day contact with the problems of my people. What good would I be after four or five years of a lot of white brainwashing in some phony, prestige institution, huh? I'd be like you and Daddy and those other educated blacks sitting over there in Linden Hills with a terminal case of middle-class amnesia.''

"You don't have to live in a slum to be concerned about social conditions, Melanie. Your father and I have been charter members of the NAACP for the last twenty-five years.''

"Oh, God!" Kiswana threw her head back in exaggerated disgust. "That's being concerned? That middle-of-the-road, Uncle Tom dumping ground for black Republicans!''

"You can sneer all you want, young lady, but that organization has been working for black people since the turn of the century, and it's still working for them. Where are all those radical groups of yours that were going to put a Cadillac in every garage and Dick Gregory in the White House? I'll tell you where.''

I knew you would, Kiswana thought angrily.

"They burned themselves out because they wanted too much too fast. Their goals weren't grounded in reality. And that's always been your problem.''

"What do you mean, my problem? I know exactly what I'm about.''

"No, you don't. You constantly live in a fantasy world— always going to extremes—turning butterflies into eagles, and life isn't about that. It's accepting what is and working from that. Lord, I remember how worried you had me, putting all that lacquered hair spray on your head. I thought you were going to get lung cancer—trying to be what you're not.''

Kiswana jumped up from the couch. "Oh, God, I can't take this anymore. Trying to be something I'm not—trying to be something I'm not, Mama! Trying to be proud of my heritage and the fact that I was of African descent. If that's being what I'm not, then I say fine. But I'd rather be dead than be like you—a white man's nigger who's ashamed of being black!''

Kiswana saw streaks of gold and ebony light follow her mother's flying body out of the chair. She was swung around by the shoulders and made to face the deadly stillness in the angry woman's eyes. She was too stunned to cry out from the pain of the long fingernails that dug into her shoulders, and she was brought so close to her mother's face that she saw her reflection, distorted and wavering, in the tears that stood in the older woman's eyes. And she listened in that stillness to a story she had heard from a child.

"My grandmother," Mrs. Browne began slowly in a whisper,

"was a full-blooded Iroquois, and my grandfather a free black from a long line of journeymen who had lived in Connecticut since the establishment of the colonies. And my father was a Bajan who came to this country as a cabin boy on a merchant mariner."

"I know all that," Kiswana said, trying to keep her lips from trembling.

"Then, know this." And the nails dug deeper into her flesh. "I am alive because of the blood of proud people who never scraped or begged or apologized for what they were. They lived asking only one thing of this world—to be allowed to be. And I learned through the blood of these people that black isn't beautiful and it isn't ugly—black is! It's not kinky hair and it's not straight hair—it just is.

"It broke my heart when you changed your name. I gave you my grandmother's name, a woman who bore nine children and educated them all, who held off six white men with a shotgun when they tried to drag one of her sons to jail for 'not knowing his place.' Yet you needed to reach into an African dictionary to find a name to make you proud.

"When I brought my babies home from the hospital, my ebony son and my golden daughter, I swore before whatever gods would listen—those of my mother's people or those of my father's people—that I would use everything I had and could ever get to see that my children were prepared to meet this world on its own terms, so that no one could sell them short and make them ashamed of what they were or how they looked—whatever they were or however they looked. And Melanie, that's not being white or red or black—that's being a mother."

Kiswana followed her reflection in the two single tears that moved down her mother's cheeks until it blended with them into the woman's copper skin. There was nothing and then so much that she wanted to say, but her throat kept closing up every time she tried to speak. She kept her head down and her eyes closed, and thought, Oh, God, just let me die. How can I face her now?

Mrs. Browne lifted Kiswana's chin gently. "And the one lesson I wanted you to learn is not to be afraid to face anyone, not even a crafty old lady like me who can outtalk you." And she smiled and winked.

"Oh, Mama, I . . ." and she hugged the woman tightly.

"Yeah, baby." Mrs. Browne patted her back. "I know."

She kissed Kiswana on the forehead and cleared her

throat. "Well, now, I better be moving on. It's getting late, there's dinner to be made, and I have to get off my feet—these new shoes are killing me."

Kiswana looked down at the beige leather pumps. "Those are really classy. They're English, aren't they?"

"Yes, but, Lord, do they cut me right across the instep." She removed the shoe and sat on the couch to massage her foot.

Bright red nail polish glared at Kiswana through the stockings. "Since when do you polish your toenails?" she gasped. "You never did that before."

"Well . . ." Mrs. Browne shrugged her shoulders, "your father sort of talked me into it, and, uh, you know, he likes it and all, so I thought, uh, you know, why not, so . . ." And she gave Kiswana an embarrassed smile.

I'll be damned, the young woman thought, feeling her whole face tingle. Daddy's into feet! And she looked at the blushing woman on her couch and suddenly realized that her mother had trod through the same universe that she herself was now traveling. Kiswana was breaking no new trails and would eventually end up just two feet away on that couch. She stared at the woman she had been and was to become.

"But I'll never be a Republican," she caught herself saying aloud.

"What are you mumbling about, Melanie?" Mrs. Browne slipped on her shoe and got up from the couch.

She went to get her mother's coat. "Nothing, Mama. It's really nice of you to come by. You should do it more often."

"Well, since it's not Sunday, I guess you're allowed at least one lie."

They both laughed.

After Kiswana had closed the door and turned around, she spotted an envelope sticking between the cushions of her couch. She went over and opened it up; there was seventy-five dollars in it.

"Oh, Mama, darn it!" She rushed to the window and started to call to the woman, who had just emerged from the building, but she suddenly changed her mind and sat down in the chair with a long sigh that caught in the upward draft of the autumn wind and disappeared over the top of the building.

❦

R. A. SASAKI, a third-generation San Franciscan, has a B.A. from the University of California at Berkeley, and an M.A. in Creative Writing from San Francisco State University. Winner of the 1983 American Japanese National Literary Award, she has published her stories in the *Short Story Review* and in *Making Waves: An Anthology of Writing by Asian-American Women*. *The Loom and Other Stories* is her first published collection. Each of its nine stories, but especially the title story, ''The Loom,'' is extraordinary, among the best of the last decade. Together they comprise a beautiful portrait of three generations of Japanese-Americans trying to assimilate within the fabric of American society and wishing, too, to keep intact their original cultural identities. The stories resonate with the tension bred by conflicted understandings of personal identity and also with the wisdom that comes from accepting complexity as the emotional and historical fact of the American experience. In ''First Love,'' the story that follows, the conflict converges on the complexities of young love to enact the drama of a smart and funny adolescent growing up to think and act for herself.

Of her own coming of age, the author writes: ''I wandered ghostlike amidst the mainstream of America, treading unaware on a culture that lay buried like a lost civilization beneath my feet, unaware of the cultural amnesia inflicted on my parents' generation by the internment and the atomic bomb.'' Of her eventual discoveries as a woman and artist, Gus Lee, author of *China Boy*, writes: ''Ruth Sasaki writes with great self-knowledge, with a sensitivity born of examined experience, and with a wonderfully humorous insight of the American ethnic experience.''

❦

First Love

❦

R. A. Sasaki

It was William Chin who started the rumor. He had been crossing California Street on a Saturday afternoon in December when he was almost struck down by two people on a Suzuki motorcycle. As if it weren't enough to feel the brush of death on the sleeve of his blue parka, a split second before the demon passed, he had looked up and caught sight of two faces he never would have expected to see on the same motorcycle—one of which he wouldn't have expected to see on a motorcycle at all. No one would have imagined these two faces exchanging words, or thought of them in the same thought even; yet there they were, together not only in physical space, but in their expressions of fiendish abandon as they whizzed by him. He was so shaken, first by his nearness to death, then by seeing an F.O.B. hood like Hideyuki "George" Sakamoto in the company of a nice girl like Joanne Terasaki, that it was a full five minutes before he realized, still standing in amazement on the corner of California and Fourth, that Joanne had been driving.

When William Chin's story got around, there was a general sense of outrage among the senior class of Andrew Jackson High—the boys, because an upstart newcomer like George Sakamoto had done what they were too shy to do (that is, he had gotten Joanne to like him), and the girls, because George Sakamoto was definitely cool and Joanne Terasaki, as Marsha Aquino objected with utter contempt, "doesn't even like to dance." Joanne's friends remained loyal and insisted that Jo would come to her senses by graduation. George's motorcycle cronies were less generous. "Dude's fuckin' crazy," was their cryptic consensus. Opinions differed as to which of the two lovers had completely lost their minds; however, it was unanimously held that the pairing was unsuitable.

And indeed, the two were from different worlds.

Hideyuki Sakamoto ("George" was his American name) was Japanese, a conviction that eight years, or half his life, in the States had failed to shake. He had transferred into Jackson High's senior class that year from wherever it was that F.O.B.s (immigrants fresh off the boat) transferred from; and though perhaps in his case the "fresh" no longer applied, the fact that he had come off the boat at one time or another was unmistakable. It lingered—rather, persisted—in his speech, which was ungrammatical and heavily accented, and punctuated by a mixture of exclamations commonly used on Kyushu Island and in the Fillmore District.

An F.O.B. at Jackson High could follow one of two routes: he could be quietly good at science or mathematics, or he could be a juvenile delinquent. Both options condemned him to invisibility. George hated math. His sympathies tended much more toward the latter option; however, he was not satisfied to be relegated to that category either. One thing was certain, and that was that George wanted no part of invisibility. As soon as his part-time job at Nakamura Hardware in Japantown afforded him the opportunity, he went out and acquired a second-hand Suzuki chopper (most hoods dreamed of owning a Harley, but George was Japanese and proud of it). He acquired threads which, when worn on his tall, wiry frame, had the effect—whether from admiration, derision, or sheer astonishment—of turning all heads, male and female alike. He had, in a short span of time, established a reputation as a "swinger." So when William Chin's story got around about George Sakamoto letting Joanne Terasaki drive his bike, the unanimous reaction among the girls who thought of themselves as swingers was voiced by Marsha Aquino: "God dog, what a waste."

Joanne Terasaki, or "Jo," as she preferred to be called, was, in popular opinion, a "brain." Although her parents were living in Japantown when she was born, soon afterwards her grandparents had died and the family moved out to "the Avenues." Jo was a product of the middle-class, ethnically mixed Richmond District. She had an air of breeding that came from three generations of city living, one college-educated parent, and a simple belief in the illusion so carefully nurtured by her parents' generation, who had been through the war, that she was absolutely Mainstream. No one, however, would have thought of her in conjunction with the word "swing," unless it was the playground variety. Indeed, there was a childlike quality about her, a kind of functional stupidity that was surprising in a girl so intelligent in other respects. She moved slowly, as if her mind were always elsewhere, a habit that boys found mysterious and alluring at first, then exasperating. Teachers found it exasperating as well, even slightly insulting, as she earned As in their classes almost as an afterthought. Her attention was like a dim but powerful beacon, slowly sweeping out to sea for—what? Occasionally it would light briefly on the world at hand, and Jo would be quick, sharp, formidable. Then it would turn out to faraway places again. Perhaps she was unable to reconcile the world around her, the world of Jackson High, with the fictional worlds where her love of reading took her. In her mind, she was Scarlett O'Hara, Lizzy Bennet, Ari Ben Canaan. Who would not be disoriented to find oneself at one moment fleeing the Yankees through a burning Atlanta, and the next moment struggling across the finish line in girls' P.E.? Tart repartee with Mr. Darcy was far more satisfying than the tongue-tied and painful exchanges with boys that occurred in real life. Rebuffed boys thought Jo a snob, a heartless bitch. The world of Andrew Jackson High was beneath her, that was it—a passing annoyance to be endured until she went out into the wider world and entered her true element. It must be on this wider world, this future glory, that her vision was so inexorably fixed.

Or perhaps it was fixed on a point just across San Francisco Bay, on the imposing campanile of the Berkeley campus of the University of California. She had always known she would go there, ever since, as a child, she had often gone to her mother's dresser and surreptitiously opened the top drawer to take out the fuzzy little golden bear bearing the inscription in blue letters, "CAL." It was one of the few "heirlooms" that her mother had salvaged from the wartime relocation. She had taken it with her to internment camp in the Utah desert, an ineffectual but treasured symbol of a shattered life. The government could take away her rights, her father's business, her home, but they could never take away the fact that she was U.C. Berkeley, Class of '39. Jo would have that, too. People often said of Jo that she was a girl who was going places; and they didn't mean on the back (or front) of George Sakamoto's bike.

Only love or drama could bring together two people cast in such disparate roles. When auditions began for the play that was traditionally put on by the senior class before graduation, Jo, tired of being typecast as a brain, tried out for the part most alien to her image—that of the brazen hussy who flings herself at the hero in vain. For a brief moment she stood before her fellow classmates and sang her way out of the cramped cage that their imaginations had fashioned for her. The moment was indeed brief. Marsha Aquino got the part.

"You have to admit, Jo," said William Chin apologetically, "Marsha's a natural." And Jo agreed, somewhat maliciously, that Marsha was.

George, for his part, went for the lead. It was unheard of for a hood (and an F.O.B., at that) to aspire to the stage, much less the leading part. So thoroughly did George's aspect contradict conventional expectations of what a male lead should be, that the effect was quite comic. His good-natured lack of inhibition so charmed his audience that they almost overlooked the fact that his lines had been unintelligible. At the last moment, a voice of reason prevailed, and George was relegated to a nonspeaking part as one of six princes in a dream ballet, choreographed by Jo's friend Ava.

And so the two worlds converged.

"Grace," Ava was saying. "And—flair." She was putting the dream princes and princesses through their paces. "This is a ballet."

The dancers shuffled about self-consciously. After hours of work the princes and princesses, trained exclusively in soul, were managing to approximate a cross between a square dance and a track-and-field event.

"You've got to put more energy into it, or something," Jo, who was a princess, observed critically as a sheepish

William Chin and Ed Bakowsky leaped halfheartedly across the floor.

"Like this, man!" George yelled suddenly, covering the stage in three athletic leaps. He landed crookedly on one knee, arms flung wide, whooping in exhilaration. There was an embarrassed silence.

"Yeah," Jo said. "Like that."

"Who is that?" she asked Ava after the rehearsal.

"I don't know," Ava said, "but what a body."

"That's George Sakamoto," said Marsha Aquino, who knew about everyone. "He's bad."

Jo, unfamiliar with the current slang, took her literally.

"Well, he seems all right to me. If it wasn't for him, our dream ballet would look more like 'The Funeral March.' Is he new?"

"He transferred from St. Francis," Marsha said. "That's where all the F.O.B.s go."

Jo had always had a vague awareness of Japanese people as being unattractively shy and rather hideously proper. Nothing could have been further from this image than George. Jo and her friends, most of whom were of Asian descent, were stunned by him, as a group of domesticated elephants born and bred in a zoo might have been upon meeting their wild African counterpart for the first time. George was a revelation to Jo, who, on the subject of ethnic identity, had always numbered among the ranks of the sublimely oblivious.

George, meanwhile, was already laying his strategy. He was not called "*Sukebe* Sakamoto" by his friends for nothing.

"This chick is the door-hanger type," he told his friend Doug. "You gotta move real slow."

"Yeah," Doug said. "Too slow for you."

"You watch, sucker."

He called her one weekend and invited her and Ava to go bowling with him and Doug. Jo was struck dumb on the telephone.

"Ha-ro, is Jo there?"

"This is Jo."

"Hey, man. This is George."

"Who?"

"George, man. Sakamoto."

"Oh." Then she added shyly, "Hi."

The idea of bowling was revolting, but Jo could bowl for love.

She told her mother that she had a date. Her mother mentally filed through her list of acquaintances for a Sakamoto.

"Is that the Sakamoto that owns the cleaner on Fillmore?"

"I don't think so," Jo said.

"Well, if Ava's going, I guess it's all right."

When George came to pick her up, Jo introduced him to her father, who was sitting in the living room watching television.

"Ha-ro," George said, cutting a neat bow to her startled father.

"Was that guy Japanese?" her father asked later when she returned.

"Yeah," Jo said, chuckling.

There was an unspoken law of evolution which dictated that in the gradual march toward Americanization, one did not deliberately regress by associating with F.O.B.s. Jo's mother, who was second generation, had endured much criticism from her peers for "throwing away a college education" and marrying Jo's father, who had graduated from high school in Japan. Even Jo's father, while certainly not an advocate of this law, assumed that most people felt this way. George, therefore, was a shock.

On their second date, Jo and George went to see Peter O'Toole in a musical. From then on, they decided to dispense with the formalities, a decision owing only in part to the fact that the musical had been wretched. The main reason was that they were in love.

They would drive out to the beach, or to the San Bruno hills, and sit for hours, talking. In the protective shell of George's mother's car they found a world where they were not limited by labels. They could be complex, vulnerable. He told her about his boyhood in Kyushu, about the sounds that a Japanese house makes in the night. He had been afraid of ghosts. His mother had always told him ghost stories. She would make her eyes go round and utter strange sounds: "*Ka-ra* . . . *ko-ro* . . . *ka-ra* . . . *ko-ro* . . ."—the sound made by the wooden sandals of an approaching ghost. Jap-

anese ghosts were different from American ghosts, he said.
They didn't have feet.

"If they don't have feet," Jo asked curiously, "how could
they wear sandals?"

George was dumbfounded. The contradiction had never
occurred to him.

They went for motorcycle rides along the roads that
wound through the Presidio, at the edge of cliffs overlook-
ing the Golden Gate. Then, chilled by the brisk winter fog,
they would stop at his house in Japantown for a cup of green
tea.

He lived in an old Victorian flat on the border between
Japantown and the Fillmore, with his mother and grandmother and cat. His mother worked, so it was his grandmother who came from the kitchen to greet them. (But this
was later. At first, George made sure that no one would be
home when they went. He wanted to keep Jo a secret until
he was sure of her.)

The Victorian kitchen, the green tea, all reminded Jo of
her grandparents' place, which had stood just a few blocks
away from George's house before it was torn down. Jo had
a vague memory of her grandmother cooking fish in the
kitchen. She couldn't remember her grandfather at all. The
war had broken his spirit, taken his business, forced him to
do day work in white people's homes, and he had died when
Jo was two. After that, Jo's family moved out of Japantown,
and she had not thought about the past until George's house
reminded her. It was so unexpected, that the swinger, the
hood, the F.O.B. George Sakamoto should awaken such
memories.

But they eventually had to leave the protective spaces that
sheltered their love. Then the still George of the parked car
and Victorian kitchen, the "real" George, Jo wanted to believe, evolved, became the flamboyant George, in constant
motion, driven to maintain an illusion that would elude the
cages of other people's limited imaginations.

He took her to dances Jo had never known existed. Jo
had been only to school dances, where everyone stood
around too embarrassed to dance. The dances that George
took her to were dark, crowded. Almost everyone was
Asian. Jo knew no one. Where did all these people come
from? They were the invisible ones at school, the F.O.B.s.

They *dressed* (unlike Jo and her crowd, who tended toward corduroy jeans). And they danced.

George was in his element here. In his skintight striped slacks flared at the calf, black crepe shirt open to the navel, billowing sleeves and satiny white silk scarf, he shimmered like a mirage in the strobe lights that cut the darkness. Then, chameleonlike, he would appear in jeans and a white T-shirt, stocking the shelves of Nakamura Hardware. At school, George shunned the striped shirts and windbreaker jackets that his peers donned like a uniform. He wore turtleneck sweaters under corduroy blazers, starched shirts in deep colors with cuff links. When he rode his bike, he was again transformed, a wild knight in black leather.

"The dudes I ride with," George confided to Jo in the car, "see me working in the store, and they say, 'Hey, what is this, man? You square a-sup'm?' Then the guys in the store, they can't believe I hang out with those suckers on bikes. 'Hey George,' they say, 'you one crazy son-of-a-bitch.' In school, man, these straight suckers can't believe it when I do good on a test. I mean, I ain't no hot shit at English, but I ain't no dumb sucker neither. 'Hey George,' they say, 'you tryin' to get into college a-sup'm?' 'Hey, why not, man?' I say. They can't take it if you just a little bit different, you know? All them dudes is like that—'cept you."

Jo was touched, and tried to be the woman of George's dreams. It was a formidable endeavor. Nancy Sinatra was the woman of George's dreams. For Christmas Jo got a pair of knee-high black boots. She wore her corduroy jeans tighter in the crotch.

"Hey, George," Doug said. "How's it goin' with Slow Jo?"

"None of your fuckin' business, man," George snapped.

"Oh-oh. Looks bad."

On New Year's Eve Jo discovered French kissing and thought it was "weird." She got used to it, though.

"You tell that guy," her father thundered, "that if he's gonna bring that motorcycle, he doesn't have to come around here anymore!"

"Jesus Christ!" Jo wailed, stomping out of the room. "I can't wait to get out of here!"

Then they graduated, and Jo moved to Berkeley in the spring.

The scene changed from the narrow corridors of Andrew Jackson High to the wide steps and manicured lawns of the university. George was attending a junior college in the city. He came over on weekends.

"Like good ice cream," he said. "I want to put you in the freezer so you don't melt."

"What are you talking about?"

They were sitting outside Jo's dormitory in George's car. Jo's roommate was a blonde from Colusa who had screamed the first time George walked into the room with Jo. ("Hey, what's with that chick?" George had later complained.)

"I want to save you," George said.

"From what?" Jo asked.

He tried another analogy. "It's like this guy got this fancy shirt, see? He wants to wear it when he goes out, man. He don't want to wear it every day, get it dirty. He wears an old T-shirt when he works under the car—get grease on it, no problem. It don't matter. You're like the good shirt, man."

"So who's the old T-shirt?" Jo asked, suddenly catching on.

"Hey, nobody, man. Nobody special. You're special. I want to save you."

"I don't see it that way," Jo said. "When you love someone, you want to be with them and you don't mind the grease."

"Hey, outasight, man."

So he brought her to his room.

George's room was next to the kitchen. It was actually the dining room converted into a young man's bedroom. It had the tall, narrow Victorian doors and windows, and a sliding door to the living room, which was blocked by bookshelves and a stereo. The glass-doored china cabinet, which should have housed Imari bowls, held tapes of soul music, motorcycle chains, Japanese comic books, and Brut. In Jo's grandparents' house there had been a black shrine honoring dead ancestors in the corner of the dining room. The same corner in George's room was decorated by a life-sized poster of a voluptuous young woman wearing skintight leather pants and an equally skintight (but bulging) leather jacket, unzipped to the waist.

George's mother and grandmother were delighted by Jo. In their eyes she was a "nice Japanese girl," something they never thought they would see, at least in conjunction with George. George had had a string of girlfriends before Jo, which had dashed their hopes. Jo was beyond their wildest expectations. It didn't seem to matter that this "nice Japanese girl" didn't understand any Japanese; George's grandmother spoke to her anyway, and gave her the benefit of the doubt when she smiled blankly and looked to George for a translation. They were so enthusiastic that George was embarrassed, and tried to sneak Jo in and out to spare her their effusions.

They would go to his room and turn up the stereo and make love to the lush, throbbing beat of soul. At first Jo was mortified, conscious of what her parents would say, knowing that "good girls" were supposed to "wait." But in the darkness of George's room, all of that seemed very far away.

So her first experiences of love were in a darkened room filled with the ghosts of missing Japanese heirlooms; in the spaces between the soul numbers with which they tried to dispel those ghostlike shadows, sounds filtered in from the neighboring kitchen: samurai music from the Japanese program on television, the ancient voice of his grandmother calling to the cat, the eternal shuffle of slippers across the kitchen floor. When his mother was home and began to worry about what they were doing in his room, he installed a lock; and when she began pounding on the door, insisting that it was getting late and that George really should take Jo home, George would call out gruffly, "Or-righ! Or-righ!"

But there was that other world, Jo's weekday world, a world of classical buildings, bookstores, coffee shops, and tear gas (for the United States had bombed Cambodia).

Jo flitted like a ghost between the two worlds so tenuously linked by a thin span of steel suspended over San Francisco Bay. She wanted to be still, and at home, but where? On quiet weekday mornings, reading in an empty courtyard with the stillness, the early morning sun, the language of Dickens, she felt her world full of promise and dreams. Then

the sun rose high, people came out, and Jo and her world
disappeared in a cloak of invisibility, like a ghost.

"Her English is so good," Ava's roommate remarked to
Ava. "Where did she learn it?"

"From my parents," Jo said. "In school, from friends.
Pretty much the same way most San Franciscans learn it, I
guess."

Ava's roommate was from the East Coast, and had never
had a conversation with an "Oriental" before.

"She just doesn't know any better," Ava apologized later.

"Well where has that chick been all her life?" Jo fumed.

Then she would long for George, and he would come on
the weekend to take her away. Locked together on George's
bike, hurtling back and forth between two worlds, they
found a place where they could be still and at peace.

George tried to be the man of her dreams. They went on
hikes now instead of soul dances. He would appear in jeans
and a work shirt, and he usually had an armload of books.
He was learning to type, and took great pains over his es-
says for Remedial English.

But they began to feel the strain. It began to bother George
that Jo made twenty-five cents an hour more at her part-time
job in the student dining room than he did at the hardware
store. He had been working longer. He needed the money.
Jo, on the other hand, never seemed to buy anything. Just
books. Although her parents could afford to send her to
college, her high-school record had won her a scholarship
for the first year. She lived in a dream world. She had it so
easy.

He asked to borrow fifty dollars, he had to fix his car,
and she lent it to him immediately. But he resented it, resented his need, resented her for having the money, for parting with it so easily. Everything, so easily. And he tortured
her.

"Hey, is something wrong, man?" George asked suddenly, accusing, over the phone.

"Wrong?" Jo was surprised. "What do you mean?"

"You sound funny."

"What do you mean, funny?"

"You sound real cold, man," George said. His voice was
flat, dull.

"There's nothing wrong!" Jo protested, putting extra emphasis in her voice to convince him, then hating herself for doing so. "I'm fine."

"You sound real far away," George went on, listlessly.

"Hey, is something bothering *you*?"

"No," George said. "You just sound funny to me. Real cold, like you don't care." He wanted her to be sympathetic, remorseful.

And at first she was—repentant, almost hysterical. Then she became impatient. Finally, she lapsed into indifference.

"I have the day off tomorrow," George said over the phone. "Can I come?"

Jo hesitated.

"I have to go to classes," she warned.

"That's okay," he said. "I'll come with you."

There was another long pause. "Well . . . we'll see," she said.

As soon as she saw him the next day, her fears were confirmed. He had gone all out. He wore a silky purple shirt open halfway to his navel, and skintight slacks that left nothing to the imagination. There was something pathetic and vulnerable about the line of his leg so thoroughly revealed by them. As they approached the campus, George pulled out a pair of dark shades and put them on.

He was like a character walking into the wrong play. He glowed defiantly among the faded jeans and work shirts of the Berkeley campus.

Jo's first class was Renaissance Literature.

"If you want to do something else," she said, "I can meet you after class."

"That's okay, man," George said happily. "I want to see what they teaching you."

"It's gonna be real boring," she said.

"That's okay," he said. "I have my psych book."

"If you're going to study," Jo said carefully, "maybe you should go to the library."

"Hey," George said, "you tryin' to get rid of me?"

"No," Jo lied.

"Then let's go."

They entered the room. It was a seminar of about ten people, sitting in a circle. They joined the circle, but after a few minutes of discussion about *Lycidas,* George opened his psychology textbook and began to read.

Jo was mortified. The woman sitting on the other side of George was looking curiously, out of the corner of her eye, at the diagram of the human brain in George's book.

"Would you care to read the next stanza aloud?" the lecturer asked suddenly. "You—the gentleman with the dark glasses."

There was a horrible moment as all eyes turned to George, bent over his psychology textbook. He squirmed and sank down into his seat, as if trying to become invisible.

"I think he's just visiting," the woman next to George volunteered. "I'll read."

Afterwards, Jo was brutal. Why had he come to the class if he was going to be so rude? Why hadn't he sat off in the corner, if he was going to study? Or better yet, gone to the library as she had suggested? Didn't he know how inappropriate his behavior was? Didn't he care if they thought that Japanese people were boors? Didn't he know? Didn't he care?

No, he didn't know. He was oblivious. It was the source of his confidence, and that was what she had loved him for.

And so the curtain fell on their little drama, after a predictable denouement—agreeing that they would date others, then a tearful good-bye one dark night in his car, parked outside her apartment. Jo had always thought it somewhat disturbing when characters who had been left dead on the set in the last act, commanding considerable emotion by their demise, should suddenly spring to life not a minute later, smiling and bowing, and looking as unaffected by tragedy as it is possible to look. She therefore hoped she would not run into George, who would most certainly be smiling and bowing and oblivious to tragedy. She needn't have worried. Their paths had never been likely to cross.

Jo was making plans to study in New York when she heard through the grapevine that George was planning a trip to Europe. He went that summer, and when he returned, he brought her parents a gift. Jo's parents, who had had enough complaints about George when Jo was seeing him, were touched, and when Christmas came around Jo's mother, in true Japanese fashion, prepared a gift for George to return his kindness. Jo, of course, was expected to deliver it.

She had had no contact with him since they had broken up. His family was still living in Japantown, but the old

Victorian was soon going to be torn down for urban renewal, and they were planning to move out to the Avenues, the Richmond District where Jo's parents lived.

As Jo's dad drove her to George's house, Jo hoped he wouldn't be home, hoped she could just leave the gift with his mother. She was thankful that she was with her father, who had a habit of gunning the engine as he sat waiting in the car for deliveries to be made, and was therefore the ideal person with whom to make a quick getaway.

George's grandmother opened the door. When she saw who it was, her face changed and she cried out with pleasure. Jo was completely unprepared for the look of happiness and hope on her face.

"Jo-chan!" George's grandmother cried; then, half-turning, she called out Jo's name twice more, as if summoning the household to her arrival.

Jo was stunned.

"This is for George," she said, thrusting the gift at George's grandmother, almost throwing it at her in her haste. "Merry Christmas."

She turned and fled down those stairs for the last time, away from the doomed Victorian and the old Japanese woman who stood in the doorway still, calling her name.

AMY TAN was born in Oakland, California in 1952, two and a half years after her parents immigrated to the United States. They anticipated that she would become a neurosurgeon by trade and a concert pianist by hobby, an expectation reflected in the selection that follows here. Instead she became a consultant to programs for disabled children, and later a freelance writer. *The Joy Luck Club*, reminiscent of Maxine Hong Kingston's *The Woman Warrior* in its vivid depiction of Chinese-American women, is her first book. Orville Schell, writing in *The New York Times Book Review* in 1989, observed that ''in the hands of a less talented writer such thematic material might easily have become overly didactic, and the characters might have seemed like cutouts from a Chinese-American knockoff of *Roots*. But in the hands of Amy Tan, who has a wonderful eye for what is telling, a fine ear for dialogue, a deep empathy for her subject matter and a guilelessly straightforward way of writing, they sing with a rare fidelity and beauty. She has written a jewel of a book.'' Especially moving and memorable in the following excerpt is the adolescent narrator's double-edged sensitivity: she knows and feels her mother's needs, shaped by history, at the same time as she possesses her own self-knowledge and its rhythms.

Amy Tan lives now in San Francisco with her husband. Her second novel, *The Kitchen God's Wife,* was published to hats-off reviews in 1992.

Two Kinds
from *the Joy Luck Club*

❦

Amy Tan

My mother believed you could be anything you wanted to be in America. You could open a restaurant. You could work for the government and get good retirement. You could buy a house with almost no money down. You could become rich. You could become instantly famous.

"Of course you can be prodigy, too," my mother told me when I was nine. "You can be best anything. What does Auntie Lindo know? Her daughter, she is only best tricky."

America was where all my mother's hopes lay. She had come here in 1949 after losing everything in China: her mother and father, her family home, her first husband, and two daughters, twin baby girls. But she never looked back with regret. There were so many ways for things to get better.

We didn't immediately pick the right kind of prodigy. At first my mother thought I could be a Chinese Shirley Temple. We'd watch Shirley's old movies on TV as though they were training films. My mother would poke my arm and say, "*Ni kan*"—You watch. And I would see Shirley tapping her feet, or singing a sailor song, or pursing her lips into a very round O while saying, "Oh my goodness."

"*Ni kan*," said my mother as Shirley's eyes flooded with tears. "You already know how. Don't need talent for crying!"

Soon after my mother got this idea about Shirley Temple,

she took me to a beauty training school in the Mission district and put me in the hands of a student who could barely hold the scissors without shaking. Instead of getting big fat curls, I emerged with an uneven mass of crinkly black fuzz. My mother dragged me off to the bathroom and tried to wet down my hair.

"You look like Negro Chinese," she lamented, as if I had done this on purpose.

The instructor of the beauty training school had to lop off these soggy clumps to make my hair even again. "Peter Pan is very popular these days," the instructor assured my mother. I now had hair the length of a boy's, with straight-across bangs that hung at a slant two inches above my eyebrows. I liked the haircut and it made me actually look forward to my future fame.

In fact, in the beginning, I was just as excited as my mother, maybe even more so. I pictured this prodigy part of me as many different images, trying each one on for size. I was a dainty ballerina girl standing by the curtains, waiting to hear the right music that would send me floating on my tiptoes. I was like the Christ child lifted out of the straw manger, crying with holy indignity. I was Cinderella stepping from her pumpkin carriage with sparkly cartoon music filling the air.

In all of my imaginings, I was filled with a sense that I would soon become *perfect*. My mother and father would adore me. I would be beyond reproach. I would never feel the need to sulk for anything.

But sometimes the prodigy in me became impatient. "If you don't hurry up and get me out of here, I'm disappearing for good," it warned. "And then you'll always be nothing."

Every night after dinner, my mother and I would sit at the Formica kitchen table. She would present new tests, taking her examples from stories of amazing children she had read in *Ripley's Believe It or Not,* or *Good Housekeeping, Reader's Digest,* and a dozen other magazines she kept in a pile in our bathroom. My mother got these magazines from people whose houses she cleaned. And since she cleaned many houses each week, we had a great assortment.

She would look through them all, searching for stories about remarkable children.

The first night she brought out a story about a three-year-old boy who knew the capitals of all the states and even most of the European countries. A teacher was quoted as saying the little boy could also pronounce the names of the foreign cities correctly.

"What's the capital of Finland?" my mother asked me, looking at the magazine story.

All I knew was the capital of California, because Sacramento was the name of the street we lived on in Chinatown. "Nairobi!" I guessed, saying the most foreign word I could think of. She checked to see if that was possibly one way to pronounce "Helsinki" before showing me the answer.

The tests got harder—multiplying numbers in my head, finding the queen of hearts in a deck of cards, trying to stand on my head without using my hands, predicting the daily temperatures in Los Angeles, New York, and London.

One night I had to look at a page from the Bible for three minutes and then report everything I could remember. "Now Jehoshaphat had riches and honor in abundance and . . . that's all I remember, Ma," I said.

And after seeing my mother's disappointed face once again, something inside of me began to die. I hated the tests, the raised hopes and failed expectations. Before going to bed that night, I looked in the mirror above the bathroom sink and when I saw only my face staring back—and that it would always be this ordinary face—I began to cry. Such a sad, ugly girl! I made high-pitched noises like a crazed animal, trying to scratch out the face in the mirror.

And then I saw what seemed to be the prodigy side of me—because I had never seen that face before. I looked at my reflection, blinking so I could see more clearly. The girl staring back at me was angry, powerful. This girl and I were the same. I had new thoughts, willful thoughts, or rather thoughts filled with lots of won'ts. I won't let her change me, I promised myself. I won't be what I'm not.

So now on nights when my mother presented her tests, I performed listlessly, my head propped on one arm. I pretended to be bored. And I was. I got so bored I started counting the bellows of the foghorns out on the bay while my mother drilled me in other areas. The sound was comforting and reminded me of the cow jumping over the moon. And the next day, I played a game with myself, seeing if my mother would give up on me before eight bellows. After a while I usually counted only one, maybe two bellows at most. At last she was beginning to give up hope.

Two or three months had gone by without any mention of my being a prodigy again. And then one day my mother was watching *The Ed Sullivan Show* on TV. The TV was old and the sound kept shorting out. Every time my mother got halfway up from the sofa to adjust the set, the sound would go back on and Ed would be talking. As soon as she sat down, Ed would go silent again. She got up, the TV broke into loud piano music. She sat down. Silence. Up and down, back and forth, quiet and loud. It was like a stiff embraceless dance between her and the TV set. Finally she stood by the set with her hand on the sound dial.

She seemed entranced by the music, a little frenzied piano piece with this mesmerizing quality, sort of quick passages and then teasing lilting ones before it returned to the quick playful parts.

"*Ni kan,*" my mother said, calling me over with hurried hand gestures, "Look here."

I could see why my mother was fascinated by the music. It was being pounded out by a little Chinese girl, about nine years old, with a Peter Pan haircut. The girl had the sauciness of a Shirley Temple. She was proudly modest like a proper Chinese child. And she also did this fancy sweep of a curtsy, so that the fluffy skirt of her white dress cascaded slowly to the floor like the petals of a large carnation.

In spite of these warning signs, I wasn't worried. Our family had no piano and we couldn't afford to buy one, let alone reams of sheet music and piano lessons. So I could be generous in my comments when my mother bad-mouthed the little girl on TV.

"Play note right, but doesn't sound good! No singing sound," complained my mother.

"What are you picking on her for?" I said carelessly. "She's pretty good. Maybe she's not the best, but she's trying hard." I knew almost immediately I would be sorry I said that.

"Just like you," she said. "Not the best. Because you

not trying." She gave a little huff as she let go of the sound dial and sat down on the sofa.

The little Chinese girl sat down also to play an encore of "Anitra's Dance" by Grieg. I remember the song, because later on I had to learn how to play it.

Three days after watching *The Ed Sullivan Show*, my mother told me what my schedule would be for piano lessons and piano practice. She had talked to Mr. Chong, who lived on the first floor of our apartment building. Mr. Chong was a retired piano teacher and my mother had traded housecleaning services for weekly lessons and a piano for me to practice on every day, two hours a day, from four until six.

When my mother told me this, I felt as though I had been sent to hell. I whined and then kicked my foot a little when I couldn't stand it anymore.

"Why don't you like the way I am? I'm *not* a genius! I can't play the piano. And even if I could, I wouldn't go on TV if you paid me a million dollars!" I cried.

My mother slapped me. "Who ask you be genius?" she shouted. "Only ask you be your best. For you sake. You think I want you be genius? Hnnh! What for! Who ask you!"

"So ungrateful," I heard her mutter in Chinese. "If she had as much talent as she has temper, she would be famous now."

Mr. Chong, whom I secretly nicknamed Old Chong, was very strange, always tapping his fingers to the silent music of an invisible orchestra. He looked ancient in my eyes. He had lost most of the hair on top of his head and he wore thick glasses and had eyes that always looked tired and sleepy. But he must have been younger than I thought, since he lived with his mother and was not yet married.

I met Old Lady Chong once and that was enough. She had this peculiar smell like a baby that had done something in its pants. And her fingers felt like a dead person's, like an old peach I once found in the back of the refrigerator; the skin just slid off the meat when I picked it up.

I soon found out why Old Chong had retired from teaching piano. He was deaf. "Like Beethoven!" he shouted to me. "We're both listening only in our head!" And he would start to conduct his frantic silent sonatas.

Our lessons went like this. He would open the book and point to different things, explaining their purpose: "Key! Treble! Bass! No sharps or flats! So this is C major! Listen now and play after me!"

And then he would play the C scale a few times, a simple chord, and then, as if inspired by an old, unreachable itch, he gradually added more notes and running trills and a pounding bass until the music was really something quite grand.

I would play after him, the simple scale, the simple chord, and then I just played some nonsense that sounded like a cat running up and down on top of garbage cans. Old Chong smiled and applauded and then said, "Very good! But now you must learn to keep time!"

So that's how I discovered that Old Chong's eyes were too slow to keep up with the wrong notes I was playing. He went through the motions in half-time. To help me keep rhythm, he stood behind me, pushing down on my right shoulder for every beat. He balanced pennies on top of my wrists so I would keep them still as I slowly played scales and arpeggios. He had me curve my hand around an apple and keep that shape when playing chords. He marched stiffly to show me how to make each finger dance up and down, staccato like an obedient little soldier.

He taught me all these things, and that was how I also learned I could be lazy and get away with mistakes, lots of mistakes. If I hit the wrong notes because I hadn't practiced enough, I never corrected myself. I just kept playing in rhythm. And Old Chong kept conducting his own private reverie.

So maybe I never really gave myself a fair chance. I did pick up the basics pretty quickly, and I might have become a good pianist at that young age. But I was so determined not to try, not to be anybody different that I learned to play only the most ear-splitting preludes, the most discordant hymns.

Over the next year, I practiced like this, dutifully in my own way. And then one day I heard my mother and her friend Lindo Jong both talking in a loud bragging tone of voice so others could hear. It was after church, and I was leaning against the brick wall wearing a dress with stiff white petticoats. Auntie Lindo's daughter, Waverly, who was about my age, was standing farther down the wall about five feet away. We had grown up together and shared all the closeness of two sisters squabbling over crayons and dolls. In other words, for the most part, we hated each other. I thought she was snotty. Waverly Jong had gained a certain amount of fame as "Chinatown's Littlest Chinese Chess Champion."

"She bring home too many trophy," lamented Auntie Lindo that Sunday. "All day she play chess. All day I have no time do nothing but dust off her winnings." She threw a scolding look at Waverly, who pretended not to see her.

"You lucky you don't have this problem," said Auntie Lindo with a sigh to my mother.

And my mother squared her shoulders and bragged: "Our problem worser than yours. If we ask Jing-mei wash dish, she hear nothing but music. It's like you can't stop this natural talent."

And right then, I was determined to put a stop to her foolish pride.

A few weeks later, Old Chong and my mother conspired to have me play in a talent show which would be held in the church hall. By then, my parents had saved up enough to buy me a secondhand piano, a black Wurlitzer spinet with a scarred bench. It was the showpiece of our living room.

For the talent show, I was to play a piece called "Pleading Child" from Schumann's *Scenes from Childhood*. It was a simple, moody piece that sounded more difficult than it was. I was supposed to memorize the whole thing, playing the repeat parts twice to make the piece sound longer. But I dawdled over it, playing a few bars and then cheating, looking up to see what notes followed. I never really listened to what I was playing. I daydreamed about being somewhere else, about being someone else.

The part I liked to practice best was the fancy curtsy: right foot out, touch the rose on the carpet with a pointed foot, sweep to the side, left leg bends, look up and smile.

My parents invited all the couples from the Joy Luck Club to witness my debut. Auntie Lindo and Uncle Tin were there. Waverly and her two older brothers had also come. The first two rows were filled with children both younger and older than I was. The littlest ones got to go first. They recited simple nursery rhymes, squawked out tunes on miniature violins, twirled Hula Hoops, pranced in pink ballet tutus, and when they bowed or curtsied, the audience would sigh in unison, "Awww," and then clap enthusiastically.

When my turn came, I was very confident. I remember my childish excitement. It was as if I knew, without a doubt, that the prodigy side of me really did exist. I had no fear whatsoever, no nervousness. I remember thinking to myself, This is it! This is it! I looked out over the audience, at my mother's blank face, my father's yawn, Auntie Lindo's stiff-lipped smile, Waverly's sulky expression. I had on a white dress layered with sheets of lace, and a pink bow in my Peter Pan haircut. As I sat down I envisioned people jumping to their feet and Ed Sullivan rushing up to introduce me to everyone on TV.

And I started to play. It was so beautiful. I was so caught up in how lovely I looked that at first I didn't worry how I would sound. So it was a surprise to me when I hit the first wrong note and I realized something didn't sound quite right. And then I hit another and another followed that. A chill started at the top of my head and began to trickle down. Yet I couldn't stop playing, as though my hands were bewitched. I kept thinking my fingers would adjust themselves back, like a train switching to the right track. I played this strange jumble through two repeats, the sour notes staying with me all the way to the end.

When I stood up, I discovered my legs were shaking. Maybe I had just been nervous and the audience, like Old Chong, had seen me go through the right motions and had not heard anything wrong at all. I swept my right foot out, went down on my knee, looked up and smiled. The room was quiet, except for Old Chong, who was beaming and shouting, "Bravo! Bravo! Well done!" But then I saw my mother's face, her stricken face. The audience clapped weakly, and as I walked back to my chair, with my whole face quivering as I tried not to cry, I heard a little boy whisper loudly to his mother, "That was awful," and the mother whispered back, "Well, she certainly tried."

And now I realized how many people were in the audience, the whole world it seemed. I was aware of eyes burning into my back. I felt the shame of my mother and father as they sat stiffly throughout the rest of the show.

We could have escaped during intermission. Pride and some strange sense of honor must have anchored my parents to their chairs. And so we watched it all: the eighteen-year-old boy with a fake mustache who did a magic show and juggled flaming hoops while riding a unicycle. The breasted girl with white makeup who sang from *Madama Butterfly* and got honorable mention. And the eleven-year-old boy who won first prize playing a tricky violin song that sounded like a busy bee.

After the show, the Hsus, the Jongs, and the St. Clairs from the Joy Luck Club came up to my mother and father.

"Lots of talented kids," Auntie Lindo said vaguely, smiling broadly.

"That was somethin' else," said my father, and I wondered if he was referring to me in a humorous way, or whether he even remembered what I had done.

Waverly looked at me and shrugged her shoulders. "You aren't a genius like me," she said matter-of-factly. And if I hadn't felt so bad, I would have pulled her braids and punched her stomach.

But my mother's expression was what devastated me: a quiet, blank look that said she had lost everything. I felt the same way, and it seemed as if everybody were now coming up, like gawkers at the scene of an accident, to see what parts were actually missing. When we got on the bus to go home, my father was humming the busy-bee tune and my mother was silent. I kept thinking she wanted to wait until we got home before shouting at me. But when my father unlocked the door to our apartment, my mother walked in and then went to the back, into the bedroom. No accusations. No blame. And in a way, I felt disappointed. I had been waiting for her to start shouting, so I could shout back and cry and blame her for all my misery.

I assumed my talent-show fiasco meant I never had to play the piano again. But two days later, after school, my mother came out of the kitchen and saw me watching TV.

"Four clock," she reminded me as if it were any other day. I was stunned, as though she were asking me to go through the talent-show torture again. I wedged myself more tightly in front of the TV.

"Turn off TV," she called from the kitchen five minutes later.

I didn't budge. And then I decided. I didn't have to do what my mother said anymore. I wasn't her slave. This wasn't China. I had listened to her before and look what happened. She was the stupid one.

She came out from the kitchen and stood in the arched entryway of the living room. "Four clock," she said once again, louder.

"I'm not going to play anymore," I said nonchalantly. "Why should I? I'm not a genius."

She walked over and stood in front of the TV. I saw her chest was heaving up and down in an angry way.

"No!" I said, and I now felt stronger, as if my true self had finally emerged. So this was what had been inside me all along.

"No! I won't!" I screamed.

She yanked me by the arm, pulled me off the floor, snapped off the TV. She was frighteningly strong, half pulling, half carrying me toward the piano as I kicked the throw rugs under my feet. She lifted me up and onto the hard bench. I was sobbing by now, looking at her bitterly. Her chest was heaving even more and her mouth was open, smiling crazily as if she were pleased I was crying.

"You want me to be someone that I'm not!" I sobbed. "I'll never be the kind of daughter you want me to be!"

"Only two kinds of daughters," she shouted in Chinese. "Those who are obedient and those who follow their own mind! Only one kind of daughter can live in this house. Obedient daughter!"

"Then I wish I wasn't your daughter. I wish you weren't my mother," I shouted. As I said these things I got scared. It felt like worms and toads and slimy things crawling out of my chest, but it also felt good, as if this awful side of me had surfaced, at last.

"Too late change this," said my mother shrilly.

And I could sense her anger rising to its breaking point. I wanted to see it spill over. And that's when I remembered the babies she had lost in China, the ones we never talked about. "Then I wish I'd never been born!" I shouted. "I wish I were dead! Like them."

It was as if I had said the magic words. Alakazam!—and

her face went blank, her mouth closed, her arms went slack, and she backed out of the room, stunned, as if she were blowing away like a small brown leaf, thin, brittle, lifeless.

It was not the only disappointment my mother felt in me. In the years that followed, I failed her so many times, each time asserting my own will, my right to fall short of expectations. I didn't get straight As. I didn't become class president. I didn't get into Stanford. I dropped out of college.

For unlike my mother, I did not believe I could be anything I wanted to be. I could only be me.

And for all those years, we never talked about the disaster at the recital or my terrible accusations afterward at the piano bench. All that remained unchecked, like a betrayal that was now unspeakable. So I never found a way to ask her why she had hoped for something so large that failure was inevitable.

And even worse, I never asked her what frightened me the most: Why had she given up hope?

For after our struggle at the piano, she never mentioned my playing again. The lessons stopped. The lid to the piano was closed, shutting out the dust, my misery, and her dreams.

So she surprised me. A few years ago, she offered to give me the piano, for my thirtieth birthday. I had not played in all those years. I saw the offer as a sign of forgiveness, a tremendous burden removed.

"Are you sure?" I asked shyly. "I mean, won't you and Dad miss it?"

"No, this your piano," she said firmly. "Always your piano. You only one can play."

"Well, I probably can't play anymore," I said. "It's been years."

"You pick up fast," said my mother, as if she knew this was certain. "You have natural talent. You could been genius if you want to."

"No I couldn't."

"You just not trying," said my mother. And she was neither angry nor sad. She said it as if to announce a fact that could never be disproved. "Take it," she said.

But I didn't at first. It was enough that she had offered it to me. And after that, every time I saw it in my parents' living room, standing in front of the bay windows, it made me feel proud, as if it were a shiny trophy I had won back.

Last week I sent a tuner over to my parents' apartment and had the piano reconditioned, for purely sentimental reasons. My mother had died a few months before and I had been getting things in order for my father, a little bit at a time. I put the jewelry in special silk pouches. The sweaters she had knitted in yellow, pink, bright orange—all the colors I hated—I put those in moth-proof boxes. I found some old Chinese silk dresses, the kind with little slits up the sides. I rubbed the old silk against my skin, then wrapped them in tissue and decided to take them home with me.

After I had the piano tuned, I opened the lid and touched the keys. It sounded even richer than I remembered. Really, it was a very good piano. Inside the bench were the same exercise notes with handwritten scales, the same second-hand music books with their covers held together with yellow tape.

I opened up the Schumann book to the dark little piece I had played at the recital. It was on the left-hand side of the page, "Pleading Child." It looked more difficult than I remembered. I played a few bars, surprised at how easily the notes came back to me.

And for the first time, or so it seemed, I noticed the piece on the right-hand side. It was called "Perfectly Contented." I tried to play this one as well. It had a lighter melody but the same flowing rhythm and turned out to be quite easy. "Pleading Child" was shorter but slower; "Perfectly Contented" was longer, but faster. And after I played them both a few times, I realized they were two halves of the same song.

❦

JUDY TROY was born in Chicago and grew up in northwest Indiana. She attended Indiana University and finished her undergraduate education at the University of Illinois. She was part-owner of a bar in southern Indiana, later attended graduate school at Indiana University and received an M.A. in creative writing. She writes, ''I lived in the country, outside of Bloomington, for thirteen years. I was public relations director for a school, an artist-in-residence in the Indiana schools, and was, and still am, the fiction editor for *Crazyhorse,* the literary magazine of the University of Arkansas.'' She is currently visiting professor at the University of Missouri.

The story that follows, ''The Way Things Will Be,'' originally published in *The New Yorker,* is included in her forthcoming collection of stories *Mourning Doves* (1993). This selection shows her gift for conjuring the marvelous from the mundane, stirring the reader without ever resorting to sentimentality or excess. In her fictional world of blue-collar American families, the difficulties of just getting by are offset by the healing power of love. The voice of the twelve-year-old narrator Jean has a calm and observant honesty that calls to mind other young narrators in this collection: Paulette Childress White's Minerva Blue (page 289), Elizabeth Cullinan's Aileen Driscoll (page 35), Katherine Dunn's Jean (page 81), and Linda Hogan's Sis (page 117). Each of these girls is wise and sometimes sad beyond her years on the subject of the suffering of women within families and other closed communities; this very awareness delivers each of them from resignation, from the death of spirit and hope they observe in the lives of older men and women.

❦

The Way Things Will Be

❦

Judy Troy

On our way to Florida in the winter of 1965, Eddie, the older of my two brothers, had an appendicitis attack and was operated on in a hospital in Nashville. My parents didn't have much money—we were moving from South Bend, Indiana, to Key West, where my aunt and uncle owned a motel. My father's idea was for us to live in one of the units while he and my uncle started a fishing business. My father had been a car salesman in South Bend, and before that he had worked in a dairy, and before that he had sold suits in a department store. He said that people he worked for didn't like him. He said that he was the kind of person who should have his own business, because he was independent-minded and good at making decisions. My mother said she thought it took a lot of money to start a business of your own, but my father said no, it just took courage and intelligence, and a family that was willing to stand behind you.

In Nashville, while Eddie was being operated on, my other brother, Lee, and I slept on couches in the lobby. We had been up all night in the car. Eddie had been crying, and my parents had been arguing about what to do. My father had wanted to wait until morning to see if Eddie felt better, and my mother wanted to find a hospital immediately. In the middle of the night, as they were shouting at one another, my father took his hand off the steering wheel and slapped her. There was suddenly silence. As far as my brothers and I knew, my father had never hit her before, and he seemed as shocked as anyone. As soon as he could, he stopped at a gas station and got out of the car. He walked to the edge of the pavement, which bordered a field. His shoulders were hunched over, and he was looking down at his feet. He was standing just outside the circle of light that separated the gas station from the darkness.

My mother got out of the car, too. "If it weren't for Eddie I wouldn't get back in," she said, loudly enough for him to hear. "I'd find a bus and go back to South Bend." Lee started to cry. He was seven, and Eddie was ten, and I was twelve. My mother got in the back seat with us, and after a few minutes my father came over to the car and put his hands on the hood, as though he didn't want the car ever to move again. My mother told him to drive to a hospital.

After Eddie's operation was over, my father drove Lee and me to a motel on the outskirts of the city, because it was cheaper, and he gave us money to buy hamburgers at a restaurant next door. He said that he would be back before too long. "I'm putting you in charge, Jean," he said. "Take care of Lee." I made Lee take a bath, and I took a bath, and I unpacked clean clothes for us. It was raining, and we ran to the restaurant, which was a diner on a road that ran parallel to the highway. It was noon, and the restaurant was crowded with truckers. I ate my hamburger quickly and wrapped up Lee's to take with us. He had brought a toy car with him, and instead of eating his lunch he pushed the car back and forth across the table, crashing it into the sugar bowl.

At the motel, Lee fell asleep and I lay down next to him and imagined shapes of faces in the patterns that the streaks of rain were making on the window. There wasn't a TV in the room, and most of our books and games were in the car. There wasn't even a clock, and I couldn't tell how much time was going by until it began to get dark outside, late in the afternoon, and then I became really frightened. Lee was up by then, and he kept asking me when our parents were coming back. He didn't cry, but when I put my arms around him I could feel him shaking. I tried to make my voice sound normal. I invented games for us to play, and after it stopped raining we stood outside, even though it was cold, so that we could watch for the headlights of our parents' car as it turned in to the motel. When our parents finally came,

I was so relieved that I didn't feel angry until later, when I was in bed, trying to fall asleep. I thought about how scared I'd been all afternoon, and how happy I'd acted to see them, and I felt as though I'd been tricked.

They weren't speaking to one another—at least my mother wasn't speaking to my father. It seemed that he hadn't shown up at the hospital for a long time after he'd left us; he had stopped for a beer and got into a conversation with someone. My father liked talking to strangers. That morning, just before he'd driven Lee and me to the motel, he'd had a conversation with a nurse in the hospital lobby. "She thought we lived here in Nashville," he said cheerfully on the way to the motel, which made the motel seem even shabbier and lonelier than it was when we pulled up in front.

My mother sat on one of the beds with me and Lee. She told us what Eddie had said after he woke up, and what his roommate was like, and what she had eaten at the hospital cafeteria. My father was unpacking his clothes, but all of his attention was focussed on her. Even when he wasn't looking at her I felt that he was listening unusually hard, that he was waiting for her to say something especially meant for him. She didn't, though. She sent him out to bring us back some dinner, and later slept in bed with me.

In the morning, my parents took us to the hospital with them—they didn't have enough money to stay in the motel again. We brought our Monopoly game in with us and set it up on a table in the lobby. My father was in charge of the bank. Each time Lee or I asked for anything he would say, "I'm not sure. What have you done to deserve it?" He tried to joke this way once with my mother and she took the money out of his hand without saying a word. After that we played the game as seriously as if the outcome of it would change our lives. I hadn't wanted to go to Florida to begin with, but now I felt as though I would do anything to get there, so that we could at least stay in one place. I started to think, This is the way things will be from now on— nothing planned.

After lunch, my father took Lee and me for a walk. We passed a pawnshop and a liquor store and a big vacant lot. It was winter weather, but warm compared to South Bend. The wind was pushing dry leaves and scraps of paper down the street, and dark clouds were flying across the sky. We could hear thunder in the distance. "Are we going to live here?" Lee asked. He was holding my father's hand.

"We're going to live in Florida," my father said. "You'll see the ocean every day, and it will always be warm outside. It will never snow."

"Why not?" Lee asked.

"Because it's too far south," my father told him. "It's where the birds in Indiana fly to in the winter."

He bought us ice-cream bars at a candy store and we walked back to the hospital. When my mother saw us, the expression on her face changed from serious to happy. My father put his arm around her and she didn't pull away, and we sat down on a couch in the lobby. They discussed what we were going to do. Eddie had to stay in the hospital three more days, and if we stayed in a motel again we wouldn't have enough money to get to Florida, and my parents didn't know how they were going to pay the hospital bill. My father didn't seem worried now that my mother had stopped being angry with him. "I think you should call your dad," he said to her. "He can wire us money, and when things are going well for us in Florida we can pay him back."

My mother said no at first, but changed her mind. As a result, late that afternoon we checked into a nicer motel—with TV. It was in downtown Nashville, across the street from a park. We ate dinner in the coffee shop, and afterward my parents decided to go to the motel bar, which had a band and dancing. My mother pushed back the curtains in our room and showed us where it was—in front of the motel, just across the parking lot. It was a small, low building with red lights around the windows and a flashing neon sign. "Dad and I will sit next to the window and keep an eye on you, so you don't have to worry," my mother said. "And if you need us for any reason, just come out and get us. But watch out for cars."

"O.K.," we said. Lee was watching TV, but when our parents left he went to the window and watched them walk across the parking lot and disappear into the bar. "We could go over there now and ask them to come back," I told him. He shook his head; his eyes were on the TV again.

At nine o'clock we both got ready for bed and I made Lee lie down. I turned out the light and went into the bathroom and sat on the floor to read *Black Beauty*. I had prob-

ably read it twenty times before. I was reading the part
where Black Beauty is made to gallop with one shoe missing
when I heard my parents' voices. I went outside in my
nightgown. The stormy weather had ended, and now it was
colder and there was a bright moon. Because my mind was
still on my book, I was feeling waves of pity for both Black
Beauty and myself. I had been crying, and my mother noticed the tears on my face. "I'm sorry we didn't come back
sooner, honey," she said. She gave my father an angry look
and walked me inside. My father hesitated in the doorway.
Just in front of where he was standing the door to the bathroom was open, and the light was on. He picked up *Black
Beauty* without looking at it and put it on top of a luggage
rack in the open closet.

"Go back over to the bar if you want," my mother told
him.

"Why should I?" he said. He closed the door. "Why
should I do something I don't want to do?"

My mother helped me into bed, next to Lee. "I was reading a sad part of *Black Beauty,* I told her. "That's why I
was crying."

"We're back now," my mother said. "Go to sleep. Everything's fine." I closed my eyes and listened to my parents undressing.

"May," my father whispered a little later.

"I don't want to talk now," my mother whispered back.
I opened my eyes and saw that they were lying just at the
edges of the bed, as far apart as if I had been lying in the
middle between them.

"May, just put your arms around me," I heard my father
say. After a few minutes my mother moved closer to him.
"Things will be better when we get to Florida," my father
whispered.

"You're always looking on the bright side," my mother
said.

The next morning, my father took Lee and me to the park
while my mother slept; we had woken up early. It was cold
outside, and there were high white clouds drifting across
the sky. We had Eddie's football with us, which we passed
around—my father to Lee to me to my father. About every
five minutes Lee would try to tackle one of us. We were the

only people in the park. But gradually more traffic appeared in the streets and buses began delivering people to work. My father seemed depressed all of a sudden. "Let's get Mom," he said. We walked across the street to the motel.

My mother was already awake and dressed. "I was watching you from here," she said. "I was spying on you."

We all went out to the car; we were going to have breakfast at the hospital cafeteria. "We have a flat," my mother said. She was standing next to the front passenger door, looking at the tire. She squatted down in her high heels and touched it.

My father came around the car. He rested his hand on my mother's shoulder. "We have nothing but bad luck," he said. "We don't have a spare."

My mother stood up. "How can you tell me something like that now?" she said.

"Can't we buy a tire or get it fixed?" I asked. Neither of them paid attention to me. They were looking at each other. They were having a conversation without words. I took Lee's hand and walked across the parking lot, and then across the street to the park. I was careful and crossed at the light, but I knew my parents would be nervous watching us cross a street this busy. By the time they called us back, though, we were halfway across. "It's O.K.," I told Lee. "They won't be mad at us."

We sat on a bench in the sun. After a few minutes, Lee got up to look at something shiny in the grass which turned out to be a dime. I watched my parents standing next to the car, arguing. I wasn't afraid that my father would hit my mother. I didn't think that would happen again unless, as in a "Twilight Zone" episode, we had to relive that night in the car all over again, just as it took place the first time. But I could see now that my parents were not going to be any happier in Florida.

I called to Lee, and he looked up at me. "Come over here and sit still for five minutes," I told him.

By this time, our parents were crossing the street. But they got caught in the middle by a yellow light and were stranded together on the concrete strip that separated the lanes of traffic. From where we were sitting we could hardly see the concrete strip—just their heads, which looked as small as flowers, above a steady stream of cars. "They shouldn't be standing there," Lee said.

"They'll be all right," I told him. The light changed, and they crossed the street without looking at anything except us.

❧

DONNA TRUSSELL now lives in the Midwest, but grew up a fifth-generation Texan. "Every year," she writes, "we attended the family reunion, which was a sober event because my grandmother came from teetotaling Baptist stock—an East Texas farm family with eleven children. My grandmother married a college professor twice her age, and was widowed while still a young woman. She then became a museum director. To this day, my favorite job is the one she gave me when I was sixteen: giving tours of the Steamboat House, old and steeped in tales about the day Sam Houston died. His last words were 'Margaret' and 'Texas,' I dutifully recited."

Donna Trussell's grandmother was one of the inspirations for "Fishbone," which first appeared in *TriQuarterly* in 1989, and was reprinted in their anthology *Fiction of the Eighties* and in Algonquin's *New Stories From the South 1990*. The story was a finalist for *Best American Short Stories*.

The author writes a film column for a Kansas City newspaper. Her poems can be found in *Poetry*, *The Quarterly*, and other journals.

❧

Fishbone

❦

Donna Trussell

The other girls from my senior class were off at college or working. Not me. I stayed alone in my room and played The Game of Life. Mama didn't like it. "Wanda, are you on drugs?" she said.

I shook my head. I spun the plastic wheel—it made a ratchet sound—and moved the blue car two spaces, up on a hill. The great thing about The Game of Life was all the plastic hills and valleys. No other game had such realism.

"You need a change," Mama said. "You're going to Meemaw's."

My bus was leaving early the next morning, so I had to pack in a hurry. But I took the time to put a matchbook in my purse. I don't smoke, but I thought it might come in handy if I needed to send a message to the bus driver: Hijacker, ninth row, submachine gun under his coat.

The sky was overcast, and it was a slow, pale trip. The only rest stop was in Centerville, where I got a fish sandwich at the Eat It and Beat It.

Meemaw was waiting for me at the station. She smelled of cold cream and lilacs.

Ed grabbed my suitcase. "Yo," he said.

"Yo," I said back.

Ed's pickup was full of old *Soldier of Fortune*s. I rested my feet on top of a picture of a tank. Meemaw's life sure had changed since she married Ed.

"My little girl," she said. She patted my knee the way a kid flattens Play-Doh.

"She's not your girl," Ed said. "She's your granddaughter."

"She *is* my little girl."

A chain link fence now surrounded Meemaw's garden. "Keeps dogs out," she said. The fence made her farm look even less farmish than it had, with its green shack for a barn and refrigerator toppled on its side out back and giant new house modeled after the governor's mansion.

Meemaw fussed over me at supper: Wanda, can I get you some more roast, would you like another helping of butter beans, how about some corn bread?

Ed had three cups of coffee with supper. He poured the coffee into his saucer and blew on it. I asked him why he drank his coffee that way.

He didn't answer. Finally Meemaw said, "To cool it down."

Ed's cup and saucer were monogrammed in gold. My plate too.

"Meemaw, where's your dishes?" I asked. "The ones with purple ribbons and grapes?"

"Well, we have Ed's china now."

He slurped his coffee, staring straight ahead. He might as well have been talking to the curtains when he said, "I'm glad you're here, Wanda, because I've been wanting to ask you something. All day I've been wondering—who paid the hospital when you had that baby? The taxpayers?"

I smashed a butter bean with my fork. "Excuse me," I said and went outside.

I looked out across the pine trees, dark green. I used to believe trees had people inside them. I wished some God would change me into a tree. That wouldn't be a bad life— sun, rain, birds. Kids looking for pine cones. Me shaking my branches for them.

The peat moss in the garden was warm. I lay down and pulled a watermelon close.

After a while Meemaw came out and sat down near my head, in the snapdragons and cucumbers. Meemaw planted vegetables and flowers together, except for the gladiolas, off by themselves. Pink, peach, yellow, white—a million baby shoes, shifting in the wind.

She smoothed my hair and talked about exercise and how important it was.

"Meemaw, what happened to your strawberries?"

"Birds. But that's all right. Plenty for the birds too."

Every morning we'd go out to pull weeds, and she'd tell me uplifting stories about people she knew. Trials they'd had. A young man wanted to commit suicide because law school was so hard. Once a week his mother wrote him letters full of encouraging words.

"What kind of encouraging words?"

"Oh, 'Don't give up.' That sort of thing."

When he graduated he found out she'd been dead for a month. She'd known she was dying, and had written the last letters ahead of time.

Meemaw knew lots of stories about people who "took the path of least resistance" and ended up sick or poor. I got back at her by asking personal questions.

"Meemaw, have you ever had an orgasm?"

Yes, she said. Once. "I was glad to know what it is that causes so much of human behavior." She smiled and handed me a bunch of gladiolas.

Afternoons I stayed in my room. Mama wouldn't let me bring The Game of Life. I lay on the bed a lot. The light fixture had leaves and berries molded in the glass. Once I wrapped my arms around the chest of drawers and put my head down on the cool marble top.

Meemaw would call me to supper. There wasn't much discussion at the table. If anyone said anything, it was Ed talking to Meemaw or Meemaw talking to me. Except for once, when I went to the stove to get some salt. Ed told me I'd done it all wrong. "You don't bring the *plate* to the salt. You bring the *salt* to the plate."

After supper Meemaw and I went down to the barn. She milked Sissy. I fed the chickens. I'd throw a handful of feed and they'd move in at eighty miles an hour.

Ed never came with us. He hates Sissy, Meemaw told me. "He's jealous."

"Jealous of a cow?"

"Why, of course. I spend so much of my time with her."

Evenings Ed watched *Walking Tall* on his VCR. Or he went inside his toolshed. He never worked on anything. He looked at catalogs and ordered tools, and when they came he hung them on the walls. He read books about the end of the world: the whole state of Colorado was going to turn into Jell-O, and people will drown. "You've got five years to live, young lady," he told me. "*Five years.*"

He had guns—a whole case-full. Once I saw him polishing them when I was standing in the hall by his study.

"What do you think you're doing?" he said.

I walked away. He shut the door.

One day when I was watching Meemaw through a little diamond shape made of my thumbs and two fingers, Ed said, "You planning on sitting on your butt all summer?"

"I haven't thought about it."

"Start thinking."

Meemaw knew a man in town who was looking for help. She knew everybody in town.

"It's a photography studio," Meemaw said.

"I don't know anything about photography."

"He's willing to train someone. It's a nice place. There's another studio in town, but everybody says Mr. Lamont's is the one that puts on the finishing touch."

She made the phone call. Ed was smiling behind his magazine. I *knew* he was.

I drove Meemaw's old Fairmont into town. First Ed showed me all the things I had to do to it, because "service stations don't do a damned thing anymore." He showed me the oil stick and the radiator. He told me to check the windshield-wiper blades once a week. He was just about to make me measure the air in the tires when I said I'd be late for my interview if I didn't get going.

Mr. Lamont wore glasses and a pair of green doubleknit pants that were stretched about as far as they could go.

"Wanda, you put here that your last job was back in December. What have you been doing since then?"

"Nothing."

"Nothing?"

"Nothing you'd want to know about."

"But I would like to know."

"O.K. I was in love with this guy. We were going to get married, but then we didn't. And then I had a baby boy."

"Oh."

"He's been adopted."

"I see." Mr. Lamont tried to look neutral, but I could

see little bursts of energy flying from the corners of his mouth.

"I can't pay minimum wage," he said.

"Whatever." I might as well be here, I thought, as out on the farm with Ed.

After supper Ed gave me a lecture about jobs and responsibility and attitude. People don't think, they just don't *think*. World War III is coming, and no one's prepared. All the goddamned niggers will try to steal their chickens.

"But I'm ready for them," he said. "I've been stocking up on hollow points. They blow a hole in a man as big as a barrel." He punched his fist in the air. Meemaw sort of jumped, but she didn't say anything. She clanked the dishes and sang "Rock of Ages" a little louder.

I went to bed with the pamphlet Mr. Lamont gave me, *The Fine Art of Printing Black and White*. The paper is very sensitive, it said.

The next day Mr. Lamont showed me the safelight switch. "See that gouge? I did that so I could feel for it in the dark."

He did a test strip. "Agitate every few seconds," he said, rocking the developer tray.

He let me print a picture of a kid holding a trophy. "Make it light," he said. "The newspaper adds contrast. Look how this one came out." He showed me a clipping of a bunch of Shriners. They looked like they had some kind of skin disease.

After a week I got the hang of it, and Mr. Lamont left me in charge of black and white. I liked the darkroom. No phones. No people, except for the faces that slowly developed before me. Women and their fiancés. Sometimes the man stood behind the woman and put both arms around her waist.

Jimmy used to do that.

He held me like that at the senior picnic. It was windy. Big rocks nailed down the corners of each tablecloth. Blue gingham. The white tablecloths had to be returned because the principal thought they'd remind the students of bedsheets. Jimmy and I laughed; we'd been making love for weeks. We got careless, in the tall grasses by Cedar Creek Lake. Night birds called across the water.

When I was two weeks late, I told him. He looked away.

There's a clinic, he said, in Dallas. I covered his lips with my fingers.

At Western Auto they said they'd take him on, weekends and nights. At the Sonic, too, for the morning shift. Jimmy and I looked at an apartment on Burning Tree Drive, southwest of town. A one-bedroom. He stared at the ceiling. Jimmy? I said.

Goodbye, goodbye, I told the mirror long before I really said it.

I read every book I could find about babies and their tadpole bodies. I gave up Coke and barbecue potato chips. My breasts swelled. I felt great. Hormones, the doctor said.

At first my baby was just a rose petal, sleeping, floating. At eight months I played him records, Mama's *South Pacific* and Daddy's "Seventy-six Trombones." I stood right next to the stereo, and he talked to me with thumps of his feet.

You want to feel him kick? I asked. Mama shook her head and kept on ironing. Daddy left the room.

I didn't get a baby shower. Mama told everyone I was putting it up for adoption. "It," she called him. I made up different names for him. Fishbone, one week. Logarithm, the next.

Mama bought me a thin gold wedding band to wear to the hospital. Girls don't do that anymore, I told her. Some girls even keep their babies, these days.

Not here in Grand Saline, she said. Not girls from good families.

My little Fishbone got so big two nurses had to help push him out. Breathe, they said. Pant hard.

Please let me hold him, I said. *Please.*

Now, Wanda, Mama said. You know what's best.

He cried. Then he slipped away, down the hall. The room caved in on me, with its green walls and white light. Mama held me down, saying, we've been through this. We decided.

At the nurse's station Jimmy left me a get-well card. Good luck, he wrote. That's all.

Mama took me home to a chocolate cake, and we never talked about Fishbone again. She never mentioned Jimmy's name.

Sometimes now, before driving home to Meemaw, I stopped at the trailer court at the edge of town. I watched people. A woman would frown and I'd think: that's me heating up a bottle for Fishbone and the formula got too hot. A man takes off his cowboy boots and props his feet on the coffee table. A woman tucks herself next to him. He kisses her hair, her neck.

I remembered love. I remembered it all. Now I felt thick and dull, something to be tossed away in the basement.

"How's the passport picture coming?" Mr. Lamont asked, knocking on my door.

"Don't come in. Paper exposed."

"That man going to New Guinea is back."

The man had worried about his eyes. I've got what they call raccoon eyes, he'd said, is there any way you can lighten it up around the eyes?

He looked disappointed when I gave him the picture. "I know you did the best you could," he said. He smiled. He didn't look like a criminal when he smiled.

When I got home, Meemaw was cutting up chicken wire and putting it over holes in the coop. Making it "snake proof," she said. I took over the cutting. I'd never used wire cutters before. Everything is just paper in their path.

"It's so bare in the chicken coop," I said. "Why don't you put down an old blanket or something?"

"You know, Wanda, I did that very thing one time, when I had a batch of baby chicks. I put down a carpet scrap, so they'd be warm. And they died. Every single one! I was just heartbroken. And do you know what I found out? They'd eaten the carpet."

"How'd you find that out?"

"I did an autopsy."

"Ooooo, Meemaw! How awful."

She shrugged. "Nothing awful about it. I wanted to know."

"I could never be a doctor," I said.

I read somewhere that these psychologists asked a bunch of surgeons why they became doctors, and they all said they wanted to help people. And then they did psychological tests on them and found out they were part sadists. They liked knives.

"How about a photographer?" Meemaw said. "I hear

they teach photography in college now. I would pay for you to go.''

I rolled up the leftover chicken wire and put it away in the barn. Meemaw came in after me.

"Time to milk Sissy, isn't it?" I said. I went to get the milk pail.

"What do you want to do with your life, Wanda?"

"You promised not to ask me that anymore."

She laughed and patted me on the back. "Yes, I did." She set the pail under Sissy, and then turned to face me again. "But what *are* you going to do?"

"I don't know, Meemaw."

Lately I'd been thinking about the homeless on TV, and how they live. I live in the gutter, I could say. It has a nice ring to it.

"Wanda, I once read a book where the first page had a quotation from the Bible. I thought it was the most beautiful of any Bible verse I'd ever read. It said the Lord will restore unto you the years the locusts have eaten."

She paused. When I didn't say anything, she waved her arms, saying, "Isn't that beautiful?"

"Uh huh."

The barn door swung open. Ed.

"How many times do I have to tell you not to leave the wheelbarrow out? It's been sitting there in the garden since morning."

"I told her it was O.K.," Meemaw said. "It doesn't hurt anything."

"The hell it doesn't. If you leave it out, it rusts. If it rusts, you have to buy a new one."

"I don't think it'll rust for ten years at least."

"Either you use the tools or they use you. That's all I have to say about it."

He stomped off.

Meemaw rubbed my arm. "Don't worry about it. Ed's just upset because yesterday you left his mail in the glove compartment instead of bringing it in to him. He's afraid somebody could have stolen his pension check."

"Who would steal it out here in the middle of nowhere? Who'd even know it's there?"

Meemaw went back to milking Sissy. I always thought milking a cow would be fun, till I tried it. The milk comes

out in tiny streams, about the size of dental floss. It takes
forever.

"You know how Ed is."

"Yeah, I know. Why did you marry him, anyway?"

"He needed me."

"But why not marry someone you needed?"

"I don't need anybody. I just need to be needed. They
say money is the root of all evil, but I say selfishness is.
Selfishness, and lack of exercise."

That got her started.

"Sweetie," she said, "I once read about a mental hospital for rich movie stars. It costs a powerful lot of money
to go there. And you know what the doctors make those
ladies do? Run in circles. Why, one movie star had to cut
wood for two hours."

I thought about that on the way back to the house, but I
couldn't see how cutting wood would make a difference.

That night I wrote a letter to Jimmy: "I hope you like it
at college. Do you ever think about our baby? Whenever I
take a shower, I think I hear him crying. Do you have this
problem?"

I signed it, "Your friend, Wanda," and sent the letter in
care of his parents.

"Let sleeping dogs lie," Mama wrote. "Think of the
future. Pastor Dobbins will be needing a new receptionist
at the church, and he told me he's willing to interview you.
It's very big of him, considering."

I dropped the letter into the pigpen. The next day I could
only see one corner, and after that it was gone.

I did Dwayne Zook, his sister Tracy Zook, and then I
was finally done with the high-school-annual pictures. Mr.
Lamont asked me to sit at the front desk to answer the phone
and give people their proofs.

"Lovely," they'd say. Or, "Your boss surely does a fine
job." Mr. Lamont told me to answer everything with: "He
had a lot to work with." There was this one girl, though,
who looked like Ted Koppel. I didn't know what to say to
her.

We had lots of brides, even in August. I patted their faces
dry and gave them crushed ice to eat. I spread their dresses
in perfect circles around their feet.

One day Mr. Lamont asked if I'd like to come into his darkroom to see how he did color.

"It looks like pink," he said, "but we call it magenta." He held up another filter. "What would you call that?"

"Turquoise?"

"Cyan," he said.

"Sigh-ann."

He let me do one, a baby sitting with its mother on the grass. The picture turned out too yellow, so I did another one.

"Perfect," he said. "You learn real quick."

"Thanks."

We goofed off the rest of the day. He showed me some wedding pictures that were never picked up. "A real shame," he said. "That's the best shot of the getaway car I've ever done."

He started going down to Food Heaven to get lunch for both of us. We'd eat Crescent City Melts and talk. He teased me about Ed, asking if it was true that he got kicked in the head by a mule when he was a kid.

"Does he really have two Cadillacs?"

"Three. They just sit out back. He drives his pickup truck everywhere."

Sometimes Mr. Lamont would come into my darkroom. He'd check on my supply of stop bath or Panalure. Then he'd lean in the corner and watch me work. He never touched me. We'd just stand there in the cool darkness.

He told me about his mother and why he couldn't leave her. "Cataracts," he said. "I read to her."

I told him about the book I got at the library, *The Songwriter's Book of Rhymes*. Also-ran rhymed with Peter Pan, Marianne, caravan, Yucatan, lumberman, and about two hundred other words.

In *Discovering Your America* every state was pale pink, green or yellow. Nebraska had tiny bundles of wheat in one corner, and New Mexico had Indian headdresses. That night I dreamed I was high above Texas, watching the whole pink state come alive. Oil wells gushed. Fish flopped high in the air. Little men in hard hats danced around.

"I don't want to go to photography school," I told Meemaw the next morning. "I want to buy a car and drive to West Texas. Or maybe California."

"You can't do that," Meemaw said. "A young girl, alone."

"Why not?"

"It's just not done."

"Why can't *I* be the first to do it?"

"Oh, Wanda."

Meemaw believes in Good and Evil. She doesn't understand how lonely people are. Anyone who tried to hurt me, I would talk to him. I would listen to his tales of old hotels and wide-hipped women who left him.

On my seventy-seventh day at Meemaw's I came home and found Ed filling up the lawnmower.

"It's about time you earned your keep," he said.

"What about supper?"

"Forget supper. You're going to mow the lawn."

"Oh, is that so?"

"Yes, ma'am, you betcha that's so." He sat down on a lawn chair. "Get started."

A vat of green Jell-O swallowed him up, chair and all.

While I mowed, I thought of another fate for him—a giant cheese grater with arms and legs. Ed ran and ran, and then stumbled. The cheese grater stood over him and laughed as Ed tried to crawl away.

I didn't get to the big finale because the lawnmower made a crunching sound and stopped. Ed came running over, asking how come I didn't comb the yard first, how come I can't do anything right? "You're as lazy as a Mexican housecat."

His red, puffy face pushed into mine. In the folds of his skin I could see the luxury Meemaw had given him, her flowers and food and love. He just lapped it up.

He followed me into the house. Young people! Welfare! Good-for-nothings!

"You're a fine one to talk," I said, turning to face him. "I've never seen you lift a finger around here."

He moved towards me, and then stopped. He was so close I could see his eyes roll up into his head, and his eyelids quiver. The room was silent. I heard the hands on the clock move.

"You ungrateful bitch," he said. "Your grandmother thinks you're different, but I told her. I told her what you are."

It got dark while he told me what I was. He must have been rehearsing. I heard words I knew he got out of a dictionary. Meemaw twirled yarn and cried.

He got my suitcase and threw it at my feet.

"Get out. Now." He turned to Meemaw. "If she's here when I come back, I'll send for my things."

He slammed the door. His truck roared out, spitting gravel into the night.

"He's a child," Meemaw said. "A grown-up child, and I can't do anything about it." She held my face in her hands. "My little girl. My sweetie. What are we going to do?"

She put my head on her shoulder. We stood there, rocking.

"I named my baby Fishbone," I said. "Did you know that?" She shushed me and patted my back.

He'd be eight months old now. In twenty years he'll come looking for me. We'll have iced tea and wonder how to act. I wanted you, I'll tell him, but I was young. I didn't know I was strong.

"There's a bus to Grand Saline in the morning," Meemaw said. "I'll call your mother."

We rode a taxi into town. Meemaw got me a room at the motel. She brushed my hair and put me in bed.

"You can go home now, Meemaw."

"Yes, I suppose I can."

She wouldn't leave until I pretended I was asleep. But I couldn't sleep at all. I found a *Weekly World News* under the bed. I read every story in it. Then the ads, about releasing the secret power within you and True Ranches for sale and the Laffs Ahoy Klown Kollege in Daytona Beach.

At five A.M. I went for a walk. The air was cool and clear as October. I breathed deep.

Waffle Emporium was open. Something about dawn at a coffee shop gets to me. Pink tabletops, and people too sleepy to talk. New things around the corner. Carlsbad Caverns. White Sands.

I thought about what I was going to do next. I had eight hundred dollars inside my shoes. I could go anywhere. San Francisco, to work at the Believe It or Not Museum. Or Miami—I could take care of dolphins. I thought about Indian reservations. Gas stations in the desert. Snake farms. The owner would be named Chuck, probably, or Buzz.

I walked to the bus station and read the destination board. I said each city twice, to see how it felt on my tongue.

YOSHIKO UCHIDA was born in California in 1921. She graduated from the University of California and received a Master's in Education from Smith College before her first book, *The Dancing Kettle,* was published in 1949. In 1952, Uchida began a two-year foreign-study research fellowship in Japan, where she gathered material for books and articles on Japanese folk art. Many of her more than 28 titles, including *The Best Bad Thing, A Jar of Dreams, Picture Bride, Desert Exile,* and *Journey to Topaz,* reflect the Japanese-American experience. During World War II, Uchida's family was incarcerated in West Coast internment camps, first in a horse stall at Tanforan Race Track and then in the barracks of a concentration camp in Topaz, Utah. Uchida died in Berkeley, California on June 21, 1992.

In "Tears of Autumn," the story that follows here, the themes of marriage and immigration converge to show both experiences as acts of exile from the native place and people and leaps toward the other, toward a new and strange identity, language, and culture. The metaphor of the mosaic applies to both experiences: in marriage, as in the assimilation of immigrants in the United States, each person or culture retains individual characteristics while at the same time creating the complexity and richness of the new family and country. Like the convergences of ethnic identities, some family mosaics take form more successfully than others. At the end of Uchida's story, the possibilities of the marriage and assimilation of Hana Omiya seem limited but open. Marriage in the backgrounds of other stories of passage in this volume—Cullinan's (page 35), Troy's (page 256), Donofrio's (page 67), Zelver's (page 316)—looks more enclosed, if not dead-end. Considering how prominently marriage looms on the horizons of many adolescent girls (like the New World—America as Promised Land—for emigrating Asians, Europeans, Latinas), one can interpret both goals, as they appear to children and the inexperienced, as dreams. That is the state of consciousness evoked in Yezierska's ''The Miracle'' (page 301). But the words of Joyce Carol Oates come closer to the reality of many metaphorical mosaics: ''I believe,'' she said in an interview, ''that we achieve our salvation, or our ruin, by the marriages we contract . . . because people are mortal, most of the marriages they go into are mistakes of some kind, misreadings of themselves.''

Tears of Autumn

❦

Yoshiko Uchida

Hana Omiya stood at the railing of the small ship that shuddered toward America in a turbulent November sea. She shivered as she pulled the folds of her silk kimono close to her throat and tightened the wool shawl about her shoulders.

She was thin and small, her dark eyes shadowed in her pale face, her black hair piled high in a pompadour that seemed too heavy for so slight a woman. She clung to the moist rail and breathed the damp salt air deep into her lungs. Her body seemed leaden and lifeless, as though it were simply the vehicle transporting her soul to a strange new life, and she longed with childlike intensity to be home again in Oka Village.

She longed to see the bright persimmon dotting the barren trees beside the thatched roofs, to see the fields of golden rice stretching to the mountains where only last fall she had gathered plum white mushrooms, and to see once more the maple trees lacing their flaming colors through the green pine. If only she could see a familiar face, eat a meal without retching, walk on solid ground, and stretch out at night on a *tatami* mat instead of in a hard narrow bunk. She thought now of seeking the warm shelter of her bunk but could not bear to face the relentless smell of fish that penetrated the lower decks.

Why did I ever leave Japan? she wondered bitterly. Why did I ever listen to my uncle? And yet she knew it was she herself who had begun the chain of events that placed her on this heaving ship. It was she who had first planted in her uncle's mind the thought that she would make a good wife for Taro Takeda, the lonely man who had gone to America to make his fortune in Oakland, California.

It all began one day when her uncle had come to visit her mother.

"I must find a nice young bride," he had said, startling Hana with this blunt talk of marriage in her presence. She blushed and was ready to leave the room when her uncle quickly added, "My good friend Takeda has a son in America. I must find someone willing to travel to that far land."

This last remark was intended to indicate to Hana and her mother that he didn't consider this a suitable prospect for Hana, who was the youngest daughter of what once had been a fine family. Her father, until his death fifteen years ago, had been the largest landholder of the village and one of its last samurai. They had once had many servants and field hands, but now all that was changed. Their money was gone. Hana's three older sisters had made good marriages, and the eldest remained in their home with her husband to carry on the Omiya name and perpetuate the homestead. Her other sisters had married merchants in Osaka and Nagoya and were living comfortably.

Now that Hana was twenty-one, finding a proper husband for her had taken on an urgency that produced an embarrassing secretive air over the entire matter. Usually, her mother didn't speak of it until they were lying side by side on their quilts at night. Then, under the protective cover of darkness, she would suggest one name and then another, hoping that Hana would indicate an interest in one of them.

Her uncle spoke freely of Taro Takeda only because he was so sure Hana would never consider him. "He is a conscientious, hardworking man who has been in the United States for almost ten years. He is thirty-one, operates a small shop, and rents some rooms above the shop where he lives." Her uncle rubbed his chin thoughtfully. "He could provide well for a wife," he added.

"Ah," Hana's mother said softly.

"You say he is successful in this business?" Hana's sister inquired.

"His father tells me he sells many things in his shop—clothing, stockings, needles, thread, and buttons—such things as that. He also sells bean paste, pickled radish, bean cake, and soy sauce. A wife of his would not go cold or hungry.''

They all nodded, each of them picturing this merchant in varying degrees of success and affluence. There were many Japanese emigrating to America these days, and Hana had heard of the picture brides who went with nothing more than an exchange of photographs to bind them to a strange man.

''Taro San is lonely,'' her uncle continued. ''I want to find for him a fine young woman who is strong and brave enough to cross the ocean alone.''

''It would certainly be a different kind of life,'' Hana's sister ventured, and for a moment, Hana thought she glimpsed a longing ordinarily concealed behind her quiet, obedient face. In that same instant, Hana knew she wanted more for herself than her sisters had in their proper, arranged, and loveless marriages. She wanted to escape the smothering strictures of life in her village. She certainly was not going to marry a farmer and spend her life working beside him planting, weeding, and harvesting in the rice paddies until her back became bent from too many years of stooping and her skin was turned to brown leather by the sun and wind. Neither did she particularly relish the idea of marrying a merchant in a big city as her two sisters had done. Since her mother objected to her going to Tokyo to seek employment as a teacher, perhaps she would consent to a flight to America for what seemed a proper and respectable marriage.

Almost before she realized what she was doing, she spoke to her uncle. ''Oji San, perhaps I should go to America to make this lonely man a good wife.''

''You, Hana Chan?'' Her uncle observed her with startled curiosity. ''You would go all alone to a foreign land so far away from your mother and family?''

''I would not allow it.'' Her mother spoke fiercely. Hana was her youngest and she had lavished upon her the attention and latitude that often befall the last child. How could she permit her to travel so far, even to marry the son of Takeda who was known to her brother?

But now, a notion that had seemed quite impossible a moment before was lodged in his receptive mind, and Hana's uncle grasped it with the pleasure that comes from an unexpected discovery.

"You know," he said looking at Hana, "it might be a very good life in America."

Hana felt a faint fluttering in her heart. Perhaps this lonely man in America was her means of escaping both the village and the encirclement of her family.

Her uncle spoke with increasing enthusiasm of sending Hana to become Taro's wife. And the husband of Hana's sister, who was head of their household, spoke with equal eagerness. Although he never said so, Hana guessed he would be pleased to be rid of her, the spirited younger sister who stirred up his placid life with what he considered radical ideas about life and the role of women. He often claimed that Hana had too much schooling for a girl. She had graduated from Women's High School in Kyoto, which gave her five more years of schooling than her older sister.

"It has addled her brain—all that learning from those books," he said when he tired of arguing with Hana.

A man's word carried much weight for Hana's mother. Pressed by the two men, she consulted her other daughters and their husbands. She discussed the matter carefully with her brother and asked the village priest. Finally, she agreed to an exchange of family histories and an investigation was begun into Taro Takeda's family, his education, and his health, so they would be assured there was no insanity or tuberculosis or police records concealed in his family's past. Soon Hana's uncle was devoting his energies entirely to serving as go-between for Hana's mother and Taro Takeda's father.

When at last an agreement to the marriage was almost reached, Taro wrote his first letter to Hana. It was brief and proper and gave no more clue to his character than the stiff formal portrait taken at his graduation from middle school. Hana's uncle had given her the picture with apologies from his parents, because it was the only photo they had of him and it was not a flattering likeness.

Hana hid the letter and photograph in the sleeve of her kimono and took them to the outhouse to study in private. Squinting in the dim light and trying to ignore the foul odor, she read and reread Taro's letter, trying to find the real man somewhere in the sparse unbending prose.

By the time he sent her money for her steamship tickets, she had received ten more letters, but none revealing much more of the man than the first. In none did he disclose his loneliness or his need, but Hana understood this. In fact, she would have recoiled from a man who bared his intimate thoughts to her so soon. After all, they would have a lifetime together to get to know one another.

So it was that Hana had left her family and sailed alone to America with a small hope trembling inside of her. Tomorrow, at last, the ship would dock in San Francisco and she would meet face to face the man she was soon to marry. Hana was overcome with excitement at the thought of being in America, and terrified of the meeting about to take place. What would she say to Taro Takeda when they first met, and for all the days and years after?

Hana wondered about the flat above the shop. Perhaps it would be luxuriously furnished with the finest of brocades and lacquers, and perhaps there would be a servant, although he had not mentioned it. She worried whether she would be able to manage on the meager English she had learned at Women's High School. The overwhelming anxiety for the day to come and the violent rolling of the ship were more than Hana could bear. Shuddering in the face of the wind, she leaned over the railing and became violently and wretchedly ill.

By five the next morning, Hana was up and dressed in her finest purple silk kimono and coat. She could not eat the bean soup and rice that appeared for breakfast and took only a few bites of the yellow pickled radish. Her bags, which had scarcely been touched since she boarded the ship, were easily packed, for all they contained were her kimonos and some of her favorite books. The large willow basket, tightly secured by a rope, remained under the bunk, untouched since her uncle had placed it there.

She had not befriended the other women in her cabin, for they had lain in their bunks for most of the voyage, too sick to be company to anyone. Each morning Hana had fled the closeness of the sleeping quarters and spent most of the day huddled in a corner of the deck, listening to the lonely songs of some Russians also travelling to an alien land.

As the ship approached land, Hana hurried up to the deck

to look out at the gray expanse of ocean and sky, eager for a first glimpse of her new homeland.

"We won't be docking until almost noon," one of the deckhands told her.

Hana nodded. "I can wait," she answered, but the last hours seemed the longest.

When she set foot on American soil at last, it was not in the city of San Francisco as she had expected, but on Angel Island, where all third-class passengers were taken. She spent two miserable days and nights waiting, as the immigrants were questioned by officials, examined for trachoma and tuberculosis, and tested for hookworm by a woman who collected their stools on tin pie plates. Hana was relieved she could produce her own, not having to borrow a little from someone else, as some of the women had to do. It was a bewildering, degrading beginning, and Hana was sick with anxiety, wondering if she would ever be released.

On the third day, a Japanese messenger from San Francisco appeared with a letter for her from Taro. He had written it the day of her arrival, but it had not reached her for two days.

Taro welcomed her to America, and told her that the bearer of the letter would inform Taro when she was to be released so he could be at the pier to meet her.

The letter eased her anxiety for a while, but as soon as she was released and boarded the launch for San Francisco, new fears rose up to smother her with a feeling almost of dread.

The early morning mist had become a light chilling rain, and on the pier black umbrellas bobbed here and there, making the task of recognition even harder. Hana searched desperately for a face that resembled the photo she had studied so long and hard. Suppose he hadn't come. What would she do then?

Hana took a deep breath, lifted her head and walked slowly from the launch. The moment she was on the pier, a man in a black coat, wearing a derby and carrying an umbrella, came quickly to her side. He was of slight build, not much taller than she, and his face was sallow and pale. He bowed stiffly and murmured, "You have had a long trip, Miss Omiya. I hope you are well."

Hana caught her breath. "You are Takeda San?" she asked.

He removed his hat and Hana was further startled to see that he was already turning bald.

"You are Takeda San?" she asked again. He looked older than thirty-one.

"I am afraid I no longer resemble the early photo my parents gave you. I am sorry."

Hana had not meant to begin like this. It was not going well.

"No, no," she said quickly. "It is just that I . . . that is, I am terribly nervous. . . ." Hana stopped abruptly, too flustered to go on.

"I understand," Taro said gently. "You will feel better when you meet my friends and have some tea. Mr. and Mrs. Toda are expecting you in Oakland. You will be staying with them until . . ." He couldn't bring himself to mention the marriage just yet and Hana was grateful he hadn't.

He quickly made arrangements to have her baggage sent to Oakland then led her carefully along the rain-slick pier toward the streetcar that would take them to the ferry.

Hana shuddered at the sight of another boat, and as they climbed to its upper deck she felt a queasy tightening of her stomach.

"I hope it will not rock too much," she said anxiously. "It is many hours to your city?"

Taro laughed for the first time since their meeting, revealing the gold fillings of his teeth. "Oakland is just across the bay," he explained. "We will be there in twenty minutes."

Raising a hand to cover her mouth, Hana laughed with him and suddenly felt better. I am in America now, she thought, and this is the man I came to marry. Then she sat down carefully beside Taro, so no part of their clothing touched.

PAULETTE CHILDRESS WHITE was born in 1948 and grew up in Ecorse, Michigan, a small segregated suburb of Detroit. Of her adult life she writes: "Married for the second time, I have five sons. At the age of 31, I began college and am currently pursuing a Ph.D. in English at Wayne State University. I teach at Henry Ford Community College in Dearborn, Michigan and at Wayne State. I continue to write short stories and hope to publish my first novel soon—as soon as I complete my doctoral program. My short fiction has been published in *Redbook, Essence, The Harbor Review, The Michigan Quarterly Review* and in several anthologies: *Midnight Birds, Memory of Kin,* and *Sturdy Black Bridges.*" In "Getting the Facts of Life," the story that follows, Paulette Childress White shows the nexus of poverty, racism, and the lives of women and children. The welfare office is the perfect setting for her revelation of the failure of justice for poor, black women and their families as well as of the democracy established to enable the pursuit of justice. In her essay "Place In Fiction," Eudora Welty writes: "The moment the place in which the novel (or story) happens is accepted as true, through it will begin to glow, in a kind of recognizable glory, the feelings and thought that inhabited the novel (or story) in the author's head and animated the whole of his work." In the details and voices of the welfare office, White creates the humanly empty and ironically salvific core of the neighborhood (and larger urban world) Minerva and her mother pass through. What Minerva learns about growing up female, black, and poor is the lesson of the welfare office and its surrounding neighborhood: physical dependency is a curse of a woman's body, and of poverty, and of racism. But at the end of the story, the young girl and the mother are undaunted. On their way back home, the men along the way "could see in the way we walked that we weren't afraid." Her long afternoon's

experience of the facts of life has empowered the protagonist. Life at the helping heart of the American democracy
has been demystified. Minerva, the reader guesses, will
grow up to avoid the traps of empty optimism, idealism,
and illusions that often make slaves of women in their sexual and political alliances. Political realism that centers on
the distribution of wealth in the lives of oppressed people
inspires a sense of personal liberation in Minerva, a wised-
up woman-child at the age of twelve. In the course of one
long, thirsty afternoon of filial duty, she has felt and seen
the triple bind of race, gender, and class.

Getting the Facts of Life

❧

Paulette Childress White

The August morning was ripening into a day that promised to be a burner. By the time we'd walked three blocks, dark patches were showing beneath Momma's arms, and inside tennis shoes thick with white polish, my feet were wet against the cushions. I was beginning to regret how quickly I'd volunteered to go.

"Dog. My feet are getting mushy," I complained.

"You should've wore socks," Momma said, without looking my way or slowing down.

I frowned. In 1961, nobody wore socks with tennis shoes. It was bare legs, Bermuda shorts and a sleeveless blouse. Period.

Momma was chubby but she could really walk. She walked the same way she washed clothes—up-and-down, up-and-down until she was done. She didn't believe in taking breaks.

This was my first time going to the welfare office with Momma. After breakfast, before we'd had time to scatter, she corralled everyone old enough to consider and announced in her serious-business voice that someone was going to the welfare office with her this morning. Cries went up.

Junior had his papers to do. Stella was going swimming at the high school. Dennis was already pulling the *Free Press* wagon across town every first Wednesday to get the surplus food—like that.

"You want clothes for school, don't you?" That landed. School opened in two weeks.

"I'll go," I said.

"Who's going to baby-sit if Minerva goes?" Momma asked.

Stella smiled and lifted her small golden nose. "I will," she said. "I'd rather baby-sit than do *that*."

That should have warned me. Anything that would make Stella offer to baby-sit had to be bad.

A small cheer probably went up among my younger brothers in the back rooms where I was not too secretly known as "The Witch" because of the criminal licks I'd learned to give on my rise to power. I was twelve, third oldest under Junior and Stella, but I had long established myself as first in command among the kids. I was chief baby-sitter, biscuit-maker and broom-wielder. Unlike Stella, who'd begun her development at ten, I still had my girl's body and wasn't anxious to have that changed. What would it mean but a loss of power? I liked things just the way they were. My interest in bras was even less than my interest in boys, and that was limited to keeping my brothers—who seemed destined for wildness—from taking over completely.

Even before we left, Stella had Little Stevie Wonder turned up on the radio in the living room, and suspicious jumping-bumping sounds were beginning in the back. They'll tear the house down, I thought, following Momma out the door.

We turned at Salliotte, the street that would take us straight up to Jefferson Avenue where the welfare office was. Momma's face was pinking in the heat, and I was huffing to keep up. From here, it was seven more blocks on the colored side, the railroad tracks, five blocks on the white side and there you were. We'd be cooked.

"Is the welfare office near the Harbor Show?" I asked. I knew the answer, I just wanted some talk.

"Across the street."

"Umm. Glad it's not way down Jefferson somewhere."

Nothing. Momma didn't talk much when she was outside. I knew that the reason she wanted one of us along when she had far to go was not for company but so she wouldn't have to walk by herself. I could understand that. To me, walking alone was like being naked or deformed—everyone seemed to look at you harder and longer. With Momma, the feeling was probably worse because you knew people were wondering if she were white, Indian maybe or really colored. Having one of us along, brown and clearly hers, probably helped define that. Still, it was like being a little parade, with Momma's pale skin and straight brown hair turning heads like the clang of cymbals. Especially on the colored side.

"Well," I said, "here we come to the bad part."

Momma gave a tiny laugh.

Most of Salliotte was a business street, with Old West-looking storefronts and some office places that never seemed to open. Ecorse, hinged onto southwest Detroit like a clothes closet, didn't seem to take itself seriously. There were lots of empty fields, some of which folks down the residential streets turned into vegetable gardens every summer. And there was this block where the Moonflower Hotel raised itself to three stories over the poolroom and Beaman's drugstore. Here, bad boys and drunks made their noise and did an occasional stabbing. Except for the cars that lined both sides of the block, only one side was busy—the other bordered a field of weeds. We walked on the safe side.

If you were a woman or a girl over twelve, walking this block—even on the safe side—could be painful. They usually hollered at you and never mind what they said. Today, because it was hot and early, we made it by with only one weak *Hey baby* from a drunk sitting in the poolroom door.

"Hey baby yourself," I said but not too loudly, pushing my flat chest out and stabbing my eyes in his direction.

"Minerva girl, you better watch your mouth with grown men like that," Momma said, her eyes catching me up in real warning though I could see that she was holding down a smile.

"Well, he can't do nothing to me when I'm with you, can he?" I asked, striving to match the rise and fall of her black pumps.

She said nothing. She just walked on, churning away under a sun that clearly meant to melt us. From here to the tracks it was mostly gardens. It felt like the Dixie Peach I'd used to help water-wave my hair was sliding down with the sweat on my face, and my throat was tight with thirst. Boy, did I want a pop. I looked at the last little store before we crossed the tracks without bothering to ask.

Across the tracks, there were no stores and no gardens. It was shady, and the grass was June green. Perfect-looking houses sat in unfenced spaces far back from the street. We walked these five blocks without a word. We just looked and hurried to get through it. I was beginning to worry about the welfare office in earnest. A fool could see that in this part of Ecorse, things got serious.

We had been on welfare for almost a year. I didn't have any strong feelings about it—my life went on pretty much the same. It just meant watching the mail for a check instead of Daddy getting paid, and occasional visits from a social worker that I'd always managed to miss. For Momma and whoever went with her, it meant this walk to the office and whatever went on there that made everyone hate to go. For Daddy, it seemed to bring the most change. For him, it meant staying away from home more than when he was working and a reason not to answer the phone.

At Jefferson, we turned left and there it was, halfway down the block. The Department of Social Services. I discovered some strong feelings. That fine name meant nothing. This was the welfare. The place for poor people. People who couldn't or wouldn't take care of themselves. Now I was going to face it, and suddenly I thought what I knew the others had thought, *What if I see someone I know?* I wanted to run back all those blocks to home.

I looked at Momma for comfort, but her face was closed and her mouth looked locked.

Inside, the place was gray. There were rows of long benches like church pews facing each other across a middle aisle that led to a central desk. Beyond the benches and the desk, four hallways led off to a maze of partitioned offices. In opposite corners, huge fans hung from the ceiling, humming from side to side, blowing the heavy air for a breeze.

Momma walked to the desk, answered some questions, was given a number and told to take a seat. I followed her through, trying not to see the waiting people—as though that would keep them from seeing me.

Gradually, as we waited, I took them all in. There was no one there that I knew, but somehow they all looked familiar. Or maybe I only thought they did, because when your eyes connected with someone's, they didn't quickly look away and they usually smiled. They were mostly women and children, and a few low-looking men. Some of them were white, which surprised me. I hadn't expected to see them in there.

Directly in front of the bench where we sat, a little girl with blond curls was trying to handle a bottle of Coke. Now and then, she'd manage to turn herself and the bottle around and watch me with big gray eyes that seemed to know quite well how badly I wanted a pop. I thought of asking Momma for fifteen cents so I could get one from the machine in the back but I was afraid she'd still say no so I just kept planning more and more convincing ways to ask. Besides, there was a water fountain near the door if I could make myself rise and walk to it.

We waited three hours. White ladies dressed like secretaries kept coming out to call numbers, and people on the benches would get up and follow down a hall. Then more people came in to replace them. I drank water from the fountain three times and was ready to put my feet up on the bench before us—the little girl with the Coke and her momma got called—by the time we heard Momma's number.

"You wait here," Momma said as I rose with her.

I sat down with a plop.

The lady with the number looked at me. Her face reminded me of the librarian's at Bunch school. Looked like she never cracked a smile. "Let her come," she said.

"She can wait here," Momma repeated, weakly.

"It's OK. She can come in. Come on," the lady insisted at me.

I hesitated, knowing that Momma's face was telling me to sit.

"Come on," the woman said.

Momma said nothing.

I got up and followed them into the maze. We came to a small room where there was a desk and three chairs. The woman sat behind the desk and we before it.

For a while, no one spoke. The woman studied a folder open before her, brows drawn together. On the wall behind her there was a calendar with one heavy black line drawn slantwise through each day of August, up to the twenty-first. That was today.

"Mrs. Blue, I have a notation here that Mr. Blue has not reported to the department on his efforts to obtain employment since the sixteenth of June. Before that, it was the tenth of April. You understand that department regulations require that he report monthly to this office, do you not?" Eyes brown as a wren's belly came up at Momma.

"Yes," Momma answered, sounding as small as I felt.

"Can you explain his failure to do so?"

Pause. "He's been looking. He says he's been looking."

"That may be. However, his failure to report those efforts here is my only concern."

Silence.

"We cannot continue with your case as it now stands if Mr. Blue refuses to comply with departmental regulations. He is still residing with the family, is he not?"

"Yes, he is. I've been reminding him to come in . . . he said he would."

"Well, he hasn't. Regulations are that any able-bodied man, head-of-household and receiving assistance who neglects to report to this office any effort to obtain work for a period of sixty days or more is to be cut off for a minimum of three months, at which time he may reapply. As of this date, Mr. Blue is over sixty days delinquent, and officially, I am obliged to close the case and direct you to other sources of aid."

"What is that?"

"Aid to Dependent Children would be the only source available to you. Then, of course, you would not be eligible unless it was verified that Mr. Blue was no longer residing with the family."

Another silence. I stared into the gray steel front of the desk, everything stopped but my heart.

"Well, can you keep the case open until Monday? If he comes in by Monday?"

"According to my records, Mr. Blue failed to come in May and such an agreement was made then. In all, we allowed him a period of seventy days. You must understand that what happens in such cases as this is not wholly my decision." She sighed and watched Momma with hopeless eyes, tapping the soft end of her pencil on the papers before her. "Mrs. Blue, I will speak to my superiors on your be-

half. I can allow you until Monday next . . . that's the''—
she swung around to the calendar—''twenty-sixth of August, to get him in here.''

''Thank you. He'll be in,'' Momma breathed. ''Will I be able to get the clothing order today?''

Hands and eyes searched in the folder for an answer before she cleared her throat and tilted her face at Momma. ''We'll see what we can do,'' she said, finally.

My back touched the chair. Without turning my head, I moved my eyes down to Momma's dusty feet and wondered if she could still feel them, my own were numb. I felt bodyless—there was only my face, which wouldn't disappear, and behind it, one word pinging against another in a buzz that made no sense. At home, we'd have the house cleaned by now, and I'd be waiting for the daily appearance of my best friend, Bernadine, so we could comb each other's hair or talk about stuck-up Evelyn and Brenda. Maybe Bernadine was already there, and Stella was teaching her to dance the bop.

Then I heard our names and ages—all eight of them—being called off like items in a grocery list.

''Clifford, Junior, age fourteen.'' She waited.

''Yes.''

''Born? Give me the month and year.''

''October 1946,'' Momma answered, and I could hear in her voice that she'd been through these questions before.

''Stella, age thirteen.''

''Yes.''

''Born?''

''November 1947.''

''Minerva, age twelve.'' She looked at me. ''This is Minerva?''

''Yes.''

No. I thought, no this is not Minerva. You can write it down if you want to, but Minerva is not here.

''Born?''

''December 1948.''

The woman went on down the list, sounding more and more like Momma should be sorry or ashamed, and Momma's answers grew fainter and fainter. So this was welfare. I wondered how many times Momma had had to do this. Once before? Three times? Every time?

More questions. How many in school? Six. Who needs
shoes? Everybody.

"Everybody needs shoes? The youngest two?"

"Well, they don't go to school . . . but they walk."

My head came up to look at Momma and the woman.
The woman's mouth was left open. Momma didn't blink.

The brown eyes went down. "Our allowances are based on
the median costs for moderately priced clothing at Sears, Roe-
buck." She figured on paper as she spoke. "That will mean
thirty-four dollars for children over ten . . . thirty dollars for
children under ten. It comes to one hundred ninety-eight dollars. I can allow eight dollars for two additional pairs of shoes."

"Thank you."

"You will present your clothing order to a salesperson at
the store, who will be happy to assist you in your selections.
Please be practical as further clothing requests will not be
considered for a period of six months. In cases of necessity,
however, requests for winter outerwear will be considered
beginning November first."

Momma said nothing.

The woman rose and left the room.

For the first time, I shifted in the chair. Momma was
looking into the calendar as though she could see through
the pages to November first. Everybody needed a coat.

I'm never coming here again, I thought. If I do, I'll stay
out front. Not coming back in here. Ever again.

She came back and sat behind her desk. "Mrs. Blue, I must
make it clear that, regardless of my feelings, I will be forced to
close your case if your husband does not report to this office by
Monday, the twenty-sixth. Do you understand?"

"Yes. Thank you. He'll come. I'll see to it."

"Very well." She held a paper out to Momma.

We stood. Momma reached over and took the slip of paper. I moved toward the door.

"Excuse me, Mrs. Blue, but are you pregnant?"

"What?"

"I asked if you were expecting another child."

"Oh. No, I'm not," Momma answered, biting down on her
lips.

"Well, I'm sure you'll want to be careful about a thing
like that in your present situation."

"Yes."

I looked quickly to Momma's loose white blouse. We'd never known when another baby was coming until it was almost there.

"I suppose that eight children are enough for anyone," the woman said, and for the first time her face broke into a smile.

Momma didn't answer that. Somehow, we left the room and found our way out onto the street. We stood for a moment as though lost. My eyes followed Momma's up to where the sun was burning high. It was still there, blazing white against a cloudless blue. Slowly, Momma put the clothing order into her purse and snapped it shut. She looked around as if uncertain which way to go. I led the way to the corner. We turned. We walked the first five blocks.

I was thinking about how stupid I'd been a year ago, when Daddy lost his job. I'd been happy.

"You-all better be thinking about moving to Indianapolis," he announced one day after work, looking like he didn't think much of it himself. He was a welder with the railroad company. He'd worked there for eleven years. But now, "Company's moving to Indianapolis," he said. "Gonna be gone by November. If I want to keep my job, we've got to move with it."

We didn't. Nobody wanted to move to Indianapolis—not even Daddy. Here, we had uncles, aunts and cousins on both sides. Friends. Everybody and everything we knew. Daddy could get another job. First came unemployment compensation. Then came welfare. Thank goodness for welfare, we said, while we waited and waited for the job that hadn't yet come.

The problem was that Daddy couldn't take it. If something got repossessed or somebody took sick or something was broken or another kid was coming, he'd carry on terribly until things got better—by which time things were always worse. He'd always been that way. So when the railroad left, he began to do everything wrong. When he was home, he was so grouchy we were afraid to squeak. Now when we saw him coming, we got lost. Even our friends ran for cover.

At the railroad tracks, we sped up. The tracks were as far across as a block was long. Silently, I counted the rails by the heat of the steel bars through my thin soles. On the other side, I felt something heavy rise up in my chest and I knew that I wanted to cry. I wanted to cry or run or kiss the dusty ground. The little houses with their sun-scorched lawns and backyard gardens were mansions in my eyes. "Ohh, Ma . . . look at those collards!"

"Umm-humm," she agreed, and I knew that she saw it too. "Wonder how they grew so big?"

"Cow dung, probably. Big Poppa used to put cow dung out to fertilize the vegetable plots, and everything just grew like crazy. We used to get tomatoes this big"—she circled with her hands—"and don't talk about squash or melons."

"I bet y'all ate like rich people. Bet y'all had everything you could want."

"We sure did," she said. "We never wanted for anything when it came to food. And when the cash crops were sold, we could get whatever else that was needed. We never wanted for a thing."

"What about the time you and cousin Emma threw out the supper peas?"

"Oh! Did I tell you about that?" she asked. Then she told it all over again. I didn't listen. I watched her face and guarded her smile with a smile of my own.

We walked together, step for step. The sun was still burning, but we forgot to mind it. We talked about an Alabama girlhood in a time and place I'd never know. We talked about the wringer washer and how it could be fixed, because washing every day on a scrub-board was something Alabama could keep. We talked about how to get Daddy to the Department of Social Services.

Then we talked about having babies. She began to tell me things I'd never known, and the idea of womanhood blossomed in my mind like some kind of suffocating rose.

"Momma," I said, "I don't think I can be a woman."

"You can," she laughed, "and if you live, you will be. You gotta be some kind of woman."

"But it's hard," I said, "sometimes it must be hard."

"Umm-humm," she said, "sometimes it is hard."

When we got to the bad block, we crossed to Beaman's drugstore for two orange crushes. Then we walked right through the groups of men standing in the shadows of the poolroom and the Moonflower Hotel. Not one of them said a word to us. I supposed they could see in the way we walked that we weren't afraid. We'd been to the welfare office and back again. And the facts of life, fixed in our minds like the sun in the sky, were no burning mysteries.

ANZIA YEZIERSKA was born in 1885 in Poland in a poor family of nine children. In the 1890s, they emigrated to America, settling on the Lower East Side of New York City. Like many immigrants, Yezierska sought liberation from poverty and the ghetto by attending night school, an auto-biographical detail in the story that follows. In her preface to the new edition of *Hungry Hearts* (1985) from which "The Miracle" is taken, her daughter Louise Levitas Henriksen presents the background of Yezierska's re-emergence in American literature:

> Houghton Mifflin first published *Hungry Hearts* in 1920, after one of its stories, "The Fat of the Land," appearing in a magazine the year before, was named the Best Short Story of 1919 by Edward J. O'Brien. *Hungry Hearts* earned for Anzia . . . an overnight fortune (more than $10,000, a dazzling sum in those days) when it brought her to Hollywood to work on the silent film Samuel Goldwyn's company made from her book. Her second book, *Salome of the Tenements,* also sold to the movies—for a larger sum, $15,000. For the next ten years, during which she wrote four more books, Anzia was a celebrity. Newspapers frequently retold the fairy tale of how my mother rose from New York's Lower East Side ghetto to literary stardom. But with the Depression of the 1930s, she lost her audience and her money as well. . . . Anzia has [now] been rediscovered by feminists and social historians during the past ten years. . . . I regret that this began to happen only after her death in 1970.

For all her popularity in Women's Studies courses and the attention paid her by Gilbert and Gubar in *The Norton Anthology of Literature By Women* and by Mary Dearborn in her study of ethnic female literature, *Pocahontas's Daughters*, Yezierska was not included in Irving Howe's collection *Jewish-American Stories* (1977) and is seldom found in anthologies of American short fiction. Whatever the reason for such neglect, in her work we find Jewish immigrant culture imprinted with an ecstasy of yearning and vision, a unique combination of Old World mysticism, and American (and adolescent) romanticism. For her, education has a redemptive power. The New Land is a place of despair and promise. In "The Miracle," the passion of Jewish-American aspiration in the heart of a young woman comes across with the one-shot force of a transforming dream.

❧

The Miracle

❧

Anzia Yezierska

Like all people who have nothing, I lived on dreams. With nothing but my longing for love, I burned my way through stone walls till I got to America. And what happened to me when I became an American is more than I can picture before my eyes, even in a dream.

I was a poor Melamid's daughter in Savel, Poland. In my village, a girl without a dowry was a dead one. The only kind of a man that would give a look on a girl without money was a widower with a dozen children, or someone with a hump or on crutches.

There was the village water-carrier with red, teary eyes, and warts on his cracked lip. There was the janitor of the bath-house, with a squash nose, and long, black nails with all the dirt of the world under them. Maybe one of these uglinesses might yet take pity on me and do me the favor to marry me. I shivered and grew cold through all my bones at the thought of them.

Like the hunger for bread was my hunger for love. My life was nothing to me. My heart was empty. Nothing I did was real without love. I used to spend nights crying on my pillow, praying to God: "I want love! I want love! I can't live—I can't breathe without love!"

And all day long I'd ask myself: "Why was I born? What is the use of dragging on day after day, wasting myself eating, sleeping, dressing? What is the meaning of anything without love?" And my heart was so hungry I couldn't help feeling and dreaming that somehow, somewhere, there must be a lover waiting for me. But how and where could I find my lover was the one longing that burned in my heart by day and by night.

Then came the letter from Hanneh Hayyeh, Zlata's daughter, that fired me up to go to America for my lover.

"America is a lover's land," said Hanneh Hayyeh's letter. "In America millionaires fall in love with poorest girls. Matchmakers are out of style, and a girl can get herself married to a man without the worries for a dowry."

"God from the world!" began knocking my heart. "How grand to live where the kind of a man you get don't depend on how much money your father can put down! If I could only go to America! There—there waits my lover for me."

That letter made a holiday all over Savel. The butcher, the grocer, the shoemaker, everybody stopped his work and rushed to our house to hear my father read the news from the Golden Country.

"Stand out your ears to hear my great happiness," began Hanneh Hayyeh's letter. "I, Hanneh Hayyeh, will marry myself to Solomon Cohen, the moss from the shirtwaist factory, where all day I was working sewing on buttons. If you could only see how the man is melting away his heart for me! He kisses me after each step I walk. The only wish from his heart is to make me for a lady. Think only, he is buying me a piano! I should learn piano lessons as if I were from millionaires."

Fire and lightning burst through the crowd. "Hanneh Hayyeh a lady!" They nudged and winked one to the other as they looked on the loose fatness of Zlata, her mother, and saw before their eyes Hanneh Hayyeh, with her thick, red lips, and her shape so fat like a puffed-out barrel of yeast.

"In America is a law called 'ladies first,'" the letter went on. "In the cars the men must get up to give their seats to the women. The men hold the babies on their hands and carry the bundles for the women, and even help with the dishes. There are not enough women to go around in America. And the men run after the women, and not like in Poland, the women running after the men."

Gewalt! What an excitement began to burn through the whole village when they heard of Hanneh Hayyeh's luck!

The ticket agents from the ship companies seeing how

Hanneh Hayyeh's letter was working like yeast in the air for America, posted up big signs by all the market fairs: "Go to America, the New World. Fifty rubles a ticket."

"Fifty rubles! Only fifty rubles! And there waits your lover!" cried my heart.

Oi weh! How I was hungering to go to America after that! By day and by night I was tearing and turning over the earth, how to get to my lover on the other side of the world.

"Nu, Zalmon?" said my mother, twisting my father around to what I wanted. "It's not so far from sense what Sara Reisel is saying. In Savel, without a dowry, she had no chance to get a man, and if we got to wait much longer she will be too old to get one anywhere."

"But from where can we get together the fifty rubles?" asked my father. "Why don't it will itself in you to give your daughter the moon?"

I could no more think on how to get the money than they. But I was so dying to go, I felt I could draw the money out from the sky.

One night I could not fall asleep. I lay in the darkness and stillness, my wild, beating heart on fire with dreams of my lover. I put out my hungry hand and prayed to my lover through the darkness: "Oh, love, love! How can I get the fifty rubles to come to you?"

In the morning I got up like one choking for air. We were sitting down to eat breakfast, but I couldn't taste nothing. I felt my head drop into my hands from weakness.

"Why don't you try to eat something?" begged my mother, going over to me.

"Eat?" I cried, jumping up like one mad. "How can I eat? How can I sleep? How can I breathe in this deadness? I want to go to America. I *must* go, and I *will* go!"

My mother began wringing her hands. "Oi weh! Mine heart! The knife is on our neck. The landlord is hollering for the unpaid rent, and it wills itself in you America?"

"Are you out of your head?" cried my father.

"What are you dreaming of golden hills on the sky? How can we get together the fifty rubles for a ticket?"

I stole a look at Yosef, my younger brother. Nothing that was sensible ever laid in his head to do; but if there was anything wild, up in the air that willed itself in him, he could break through stone walls to get it. Yosef gave a look around the house. Everything was old and poor, and not a thing to get money on—nothing except father's Saifer Torah—the Holy Scrolls—and mother's silver candlesticks, her wedding present from our grandmother.

"Why not sell the Saifer Torah and the candlesticks?" said Yosef.

Nobody but my brother would have dared to breathe such a thing.

"What? A Jew sell the Saifer Torah or the Sabbath candlesticks?" My father fixed on us his burning eyes like flaming wells. His hands tightened over his heart. He couldn't speak. He just looked on the Saifer Torah, and then on us with a look that burned like live coals on our naked bodies. "What?" he gasped. "Should I sell my life, my soul from generation and generation? Sell my Saifer Torah? Not if the world goes under!"

There was a stillness of thunder about to break. Everybody heard everybody's heart beating.

"Did I live to see this black day?" moaned my father, choking from quick breathing. "Mine own son, mine Kadish—mine Kadish tells me to sell the Holy Book that our forefathers shed rivers of blood to hand down to us."

"What are you taking it so terrible?" said my brother. "Doesn't it stand in the Talmud that to help marry his daughter a man may sell the holiest thing—even the Holy Book?"

"*Are there miracles in America*? Can she yet get there a man at her age and without a dowry?"

"If Hanneh Hayyeh, who is older than Sara Reisel and not half as good-looking," said my brother, "could get a boss from a factory, then whom cannot Sara Reisel pick out? And with her luck all of us will be lifted over to America."

My father did not answer. I waited, but still he did not answer.

At last I burst out with all the tears choking in me for years: "Is your old Saifer Torah that hangs on the wall dearer to you than that I should marry? The Talmud tells you to sell the holiest thing to help marry your daughter, but you—you love yourself more than your own child!"

Then I turned to my mother. I hit my hands on the table and cried in a voice that made her tremble and grow fright-

ened: "Maybe you love your silver candlesticks more than
your daughter's happiness? To whom can I marry myself
here, I ask you, only—to the bath janitor, to the water-
carrier? I tell you I'll kill myself if you don't help me get
away! I can't stand no more this deadness here. I must get
away. And you must give up everything to help me get away.
All I need is a chance. I can do a million times better than
Hanneh Hayyeh. I got a head. I got brains. I feel I can
marry myself to the greatest man in America."

My mother stopped crying, took up the candlesticks from
the mantelpiece and passed her hands over them. "It's like
a piece from my flesh," she said. "We grew up with this,
you children and I, and my mother and my mother's mother.
This and the Saifer Torah are the only things that shine up
the house for the Sabbath."

She couldn't go on, her words choked in her so. I am
seeing yet how she looked, holding the candlesticks in her
hands, and her eyes that she turned on us. But then I didn't
see anything but to go to America.

She walked over to my father, who sat with his head in
his hands, stoned with sadness. "Zalmon!" she sobbed.
"The blood from under my nails I'll give away, only my
child should have a chance to marry herself well. I'll give
away my candlesticks—"

Even my brother Yosef's eyes filled with tears, so he quick
jumped up and began to whistle and move around. "You
don't have to sell them," he cried, trying to make it light
in the air. "You can pawn them by Moisheh Itzek, the usu-
rer, and as soon as Sara Reisel will get herself married,
she'll send us the money to get them out again, and we'll
yet live to take them over with us to America."

I never saw my father look so sad. He looked like a man
from whom the life is bleeding away. "I'll not stand myself
against your happiness," he said, in a still voice. "I only
hope this will be to your luck and that you'll get married
quick, so we could take out the Saifer Torah from the
pawn."

In less than a week the Saifer Torah and the candlesticks
were pawned and the ticket bought. The whole village was
ringing with the news that I am going to America. When I
walked in the street people pointed on me with their fingers
as if I were no more the same Sara Reisel.

Everybody asked me different questions.

"Tell me how it feels to go to America? Can you yet sleep nights like other people?"

"When you'll marry yourself in America, will you yet remember us?"

God from the world! That last Friday night before I went to America! Maybe it is the last time we are together was in everybody's eyes. Everything that happened seemed so different from all other times. I felt I was getting ready to tear my life out from my body.

Without the Saifer Torah the house was dark and empty. The sun, the sky, the whole heaven shined from that Holy Book on the wall, and when it was taken out it left an aching emptiness on the heart, as if something beautiful passed out of our lives.

I yet see before me my father in the Rabbi's cap, with eyes that look far away into things; the way he sang the prayer over the wine when he passed around the glass for everyone to give a sip. The tears rolled out from my little sister's eyes down her cheeks and fell into the wine. On that my mother, who was all the time wiping her tears, burst out crying. "Shah! Shah!" commanded my father, rising up from his chair and beginning to walk around the room. "It's Sabbath night, when every Jew should be happy. Is this the way you give honor to God on His one day that He set aside for you?"

On the next day, that was Sabbath, father as if held us up in his hands, and everybody behaved himself. A stranger coming in couldn't see anything that was going on, except that we walked so still and each one by himself, as if somebody dying was in the air over us.

On the going-away morning, everybody was around our house waiting to take me to the station. Everybody wanted to give a help with the bundles. The moving along to the station was like a funeral. Nobody could hold in their feelings any longer. Everybody fell on my neck to kiss me, as if it was my last day on earth.

"Remember you come from Jews. Remember to pray every day," said my father putting his hands over my head, like in blessing on the day of Atonement.

"Only try that we should be together soon again," were

the last words from my mother as she wiped her eyes with the corner of her shawl.

"Only don't forget that I want to study, and send for me as quick as you marry yourself," said Yosef, smiling good-bye with tears in his eyes.

As I saw the train coming, what wouldn't I have given to stay back with the people in Savel forever! I wanted to cry out: "Take only away my ticket! I don't want any more America! I don't want any more my lover!"

But as soon as I got into the train, although my eyes were still looking back to the left-behind faces, and my ears were yet hearing the good-byes and the partings, the thoughts of America began stealing into my heart. I was thinking how soon I'd have my lover and be rich like Hanneh Hayyeh. And with my luck, everybody was going to be happy in Savel. The dead people will stop dying and all the sorrows and troubles of the world will be wiped away with my happiness.

I didn't see the day. I didn't see the night. I didn't see the ocean. I didn't see the sky. I only saw my lover in America, coming nearer and nearer to me, till I could feel his eyes bending on me so near that I got frightened and began to tremble. My heart ached so with the joy of his nearness that I quick drew back and turned away, and began to talk to the people that were pushing and crowding themselves on the deck.

Nu, I got to America.

Ten hours I pushed a machine in a shirt-waist factory, when I was yet lucky to get work. And always my head was drying up with saving and pinching and worrying to send home a little from the little I earned. All that my face saw all day long was girls and machines—and nothing else. And even when I came already home from work, I could only talk to the girls in the working-girls' boarding-house, or shut myself up in my dark, lonesome bedroom. No family, no friends, nobody to get me acquainted with nobody! The only men I saw were what passed me by in the street and in cars.

"Is this 'lovers' land'?" was calling in my heart. "Where are my dreams that were so real to me in the old country?"

Often in the middle of the work I felt like stopping all the machines and crying out to the world the heaviness that pressed on my heart. Sometimes when I walked in the street I felt like going over to the first man I met and cry out to him: "Oh, I'm so lonely! I'm so lonely!"

One day I read in the Jewish "Tageblatt" the advertisement from Zaretzky, the matchmaker. "What harm is it if I try my luck?" I said to myself. "I can't die away an old maid. Too much love burns in my heart to stand back like a stone and only see how other people are happy. I want to tear myself out from my deadness. I'm in a living grave. I've got to lift myself up. I have nobody to try for me, and maybe the matchmaker will help."

As I walked up Delancey Street to Mr. Zaretzky, the street was turning with me. I didn't see the crowds. I didn't see the pushcart peddlers with their bargains. I didn't hear the noises or anything. My eyes were on the sky, praying: "Gottuniu! Send me only the little bit of luck!"

"Nu? Nu? What need you?" asked Mr. Zaretzky when I entered.

I got red with shame in the face the way he looked at me. I turned up my head. I was too proud to tell him for what I came. Before I walked in I thought to tell him everything. But when I looked on his face and saw his hard eyes, I couldn't say a word. I stood like a yok unable to move my tongue. I went to the matchmaker with my heart, and I saw before me a stone. The stone was talking to me—but—but— he was a stone!

"Are you looking for a shidduch?" he asked.

"Yes," I said, proud, but crushed.

"You know I charge five dollars for the stepping in," he bargained.

"I got cold by my heart. It wasn't only to give him the five dollars, nearly a whole week's wages, but his thick-skinness for being only after the money. But I couldn't help myself—I was like in his fists hypnotized. And I gave him the five dollars.

I let myself go to the door, but he called me back. "Wait, wait. Come in and sit down. I didn't question you yet."

"About what?"

"I got to know how much money you got saved before I can introduce you to anybody."

"Oh—h—h! Is it only depending on the *money*?"

"Certainly. No move in this world without money," he said, taking a pinch of snuff in his black, hairy fingers and sniffing it up in his nose.

I glanced on his thick neck and greasy, red face. "And to him people come looking for love," I said to myself, shuddering. Oh, how it burned in my heart, but still I went on, "Can't I get a man in America without money?"

He gave a look on me with his sharp eyes. Gottuniu! What a look! I thought I was sinking into the floor.

"There are plenty of *young* girls with money that are begging themselves the men to take them. So what can you expect? *Not young, not lively, and without money, too?* But, anyhow, I'll see what I can do for you."

He took out a little book from his vest-pocket and looked through the names.

"What trade do you go on your hands?" he asked, turning to me. "Sometimes a dressmaker or a hairdresser that can help make a living for a man, maybe—"

I couldn't hear any more. It got black before my eyes, my voice stopped inside of me.

"If you want to listen to sense from a friend, so I have a good match for you," he said, following me to the door. "I have on my list a widower with no more than five or six children. He has a grand business, a herring-stand on Hester Street. He don't ask for no money, and he don't make an objection if the girl is in years, so long as she knows how to cook well for him."

How I got myself back to my room I don't know. But for two days and for two nights I lay still on my bed, unable to move. I looked around on my empty walls, thinking, thinking, "Where am I? Is this the world? Is this America?"

Suddenly I sprang up from bed. "What can come from pitying yourself?" I cried. "If the world kicks you down and makes nothing of you, you bounce yourself up and make something of yourself." A fire blazed up in me to rise over the world because I was downed by the world.

"Make a person of yourself," I said. "Begin to learn English. Make yourself for an American if you want to live in America. American girls don't go to matchmakers. American girls don't run after a man: if they don't get a husband they don't think the world is over; they turn their mind to something else.

"Wake up!" I said to myself. "You want love to come to you? Why don't you give it out to other people? Love the women and children, everybody in the street and the shop. Love the rag-picker and the drunkard, the sad and the ugly. All those whom the world kicks down you pick up and press to your heart with love."

As I said this I felt wells of love that choked in me all my life flowing out of me and over me. A strange, wonderful light like a lover's smile melted over me, and the sweetness of lover's arms stole around me.

The first night I went to school I felt like falling on everybody's neck and kissing them. I felt like kissing the books and the benches. It was such great happiness to learn to read and write the English words.

Because I started a few weeks after the beginning of the term, my teacher said I might stay after the class to help me catch up with my back lessons. The minute I looked on him I felt that grand feeling: "Here is a person! Here is America!" His face just shined with high thoughts. There was such a beautiful light in his eyes that it warmed my heart to steal a look on him.

At first, when it came my turn to say something in the class, I got so excited the words stuck and twisted in my mouth and I couldn't give out my thoughts. But the teacher didn't see my nervousness. He only saw that I had something to say, and he helped me say it. How or what he did I don't know. I only felt his look of understanding flowing into me like draughts of air to one who is choking.

Long after I already felt free and easy to talk to him alone after the class, I looked at all the books on his desk. "Oi weh!" I said to him, "if I only knew half of what is in your books, I couldn't any more sit still in the chair like you. I'd fly in the air with the joy of so much knowledge."

"Why are you so eager for learning?" he asked me.

"Because I want to make a person of myself," I answered. "Since I got to work for low wages and I can't be young any more, I'm burning to get among people where it's not against a girl if she is in years and without money."

His hand went out to me. "I'll help you," he said. "But you must first learn to get hold of yourself."

Such a beautiful kindness went out of his heart to me with his words! His voice, and the goodness that shone from his

eyes, made me want to burst out crying, but I choked back
my tears till I got home. And all night long I wept on my
pillow: "Fool! What is the matter with you? Why are you
crying?" But I said, "I can't help it. He is so beautiful!"

My teacher was so much above me that he wasn't a man
to me at all. He was a God. His face lighted up the shop
for me, and his voice sang itself in me everywhere I went.
It was like healing medicine to the flaming fever within me
to listen to his voice. And then I'd repeat to myself his
words and live in them as if they were religion.

Often as I sat at the machine sewing the waists I'd forget
what I was doing. I'd find myself dreaming in the air.
"Ach!" I asked myself, "what was that beautifulness in his
eyes that made the lowest nobody feel like a somebody?
What was that about him that when his smile fell on me I
felt lifted up to the sky away from all the coldness and the
ugliness of the world? Gottunui!" I prayed, "if I could only
always hold on to the light of high thoughts that shined from
him. If I could only always hear in my heart the sound of
his voice I would need nothing more in life. I would be
happier than a bird in the air.

"Friend," I said to him once, "if you could but teach
me how to get cold in the heart and clear in the head like
you are!"

He only smiled at me and looked far away. His calmness
was like the sureness of money in the bank. Then he turned
and looked on me, and said: "I am not so cold in the heart
and clear in the head as I make-believe. I am bound. I am
a prisoner of convention."

"You make-believe—you bound?" I burst out. "You who
do not have foreladies or bosses—you who do not have to
sell yourself for wages—you who only work for love and
truth—you a prisoner?"

"True, I do not have bosses just as you do," he said.
"But still I am not free. I am bound by formal education
and conventional traditions. Though you work in a shop,
you are really freer than I. You are not repressed as I am
by the fear and shame of feeling. You could teach me more
than I could teach you. You could teach me how to be natural."

"I'm not so natural like you think," I said. "I'm afraid."

He smiled at me out of his eyes. "What are you afraid of?"

"I'm afraid of my heart," I said, trying to hold back the blood rushing to my face. "I'm burning to get calm and sensible like the born Americans. But how can I help it? My heart flies away from me like a wild bird. How can I learn to keep myself down on earth like the born Americans?"

"But I don't want you to get down on earth like the Americans. That is just the beauty and the wonder of you. We Americans are too much on earth; we need more of your power to fly. If you would only know how much you can teach us Americans. You are the promise of the centuries to come. You are the heart, the creative pulse of America to be."

I walked home on wings. My teacher said that I could help him; that I had something to give to Americans. "But how could I teach him?" I wondered; "I who had never had a chance to learn anything except what he taught me. And what had I to give to the Americans, I who am nothing but dreams and longings and hunger for love?"

When school closed down for vacation, it seemed to me all life stopped in the world. I had no more class to look forward to, no more chance of seeing my teacher. As I faced the emptiness of my long vacation, all the light went out of my eyes, and all the strength out of my arms and fingers.

For nearly a week I was like without air. There was no school. One night I came home from the shop and threw myself down on the bed. I wanted to cry, to let out the heavy weight that pressed on my heart, but I couldn't cry. My tears felt like hot, burning sand in my eyes.

"Oi-i-i! I can't stand it no more, this emptiness," I groaned. "Why don't I kill myself? Why don't something happen to me? No consumption, no fever, no plague or death ever comes to save me from this terrible world. I have to go on suffering and choking inside myself till I grow mad."

I jumped up from the bed, threw open the window, and began fighting with the deaf-and-dumb air in the air-shaft.

"What is the matter with you?" I cried. "You are going out of your head. You are sinking back into the old ways from which you dragged yourself out with your studies.

Studies! What did I get from all my studies? Nothing. Nothing. I am still in the same shop with the same shirt-waists. A lot my teacher cares for me once the class is over.''

A fire burned up in me that he was already forgetting me. And I shot out a letter to him:

"You call yourself a teacher? A friend? How can you go off in the country and drop me out of your heart and out of your head like a read-over book you left on the shelf of your shut-down classroom? How can you enjoy your vacation in the country while I'm in the sweatshop? You learned me nothing. You only broke my heart. What good are all the books you ever gave me? They don't tell me how to be happy in a factory. They don't tell me how to keep alive in emptiness, or how to find something beautiful in the dirt and ugliness in which I got to waste away. I want life. I want people. I can't live inside my head as you do.''

I sent the letter off in the madness in which I wrote it, without stopping to think; but the minute after I dropped it in the mail-box my reason came again to my head. I went back tearing my hair. "What have I done? Meshugeneh!''

Walking up the stairs I saw my door open. I went in. The sky is falling to the earth! Am I dreaming? There was my teacher sitting on my trunk! My teacher come to see me? Me, in my dingy room? For a minute it got blind before my eyes, and I didn't know where I was any more.

"I had to come,'' he said, the light of heaven shining on me out of his eyes. "I was so desolate without you. I tried to say something to you before I left for my vacation, but the words wouldn't come. Since I have been away I have written you many letters, but I did not mail them, for they were like my old self from which I want to break away.''

He put his cool, strong hand into mine. "You can save me,'' he said. "You can free me from the bondage of age-long repressions. You can lift me out of the dead grooves of sterile intellectuality. Without you I am the dry dust of hopes unrealized. You are fire and sunshine and desire. You make life changeable and beautiful and full of daily wonder.''

I couldn't speak. I was so on fire with his words. Then, like whirlwinds in my brain, rushed out the burning words of the matchmaker: "Not young, not lively, and without money, too!''

''You are younger than youth,'' he said, kissing my hands.
''Every day of your unlived youth shall be relived with love,
but such a love as youth could never know.''

And then how it happened I don't know; but his arms
were around me. ''Sara Reisel, tell me, do you love me,''
he said, kissing me on my hair and on my eyes and on my
lips.

I could only weep and tremble with joy at his touch. ''The
miracle!'' cried my heart; ''the miracle of America come
true!''

—————— 🍂 ——————

PATRICIA ZELVER was born in California, and grew up in Medford, Oregon. She has an M.A. from Stanford and now lives in Portola Valley, California, with her husband and two sons. She has published two novels, *The Honey Bunch* and *The Happy Family* and a recent collection *A Man of Middle Age,* which includes "My Father's Jokes." She has been included in the *Esquire* anthology, *All Our Secrets Are the Same, The Pushcart Prize, The Random Review,* and has won O. Henry short story awards. She is now working on a novel.

—————— 🍂 ——————

My Father's Jokes

❦

Patricia Zelver

The Horrible Hairy Spider was dangling over Cissy's
head.

"Jello, again, this is Jack Benny," said Jack
Benny.

Cissy was sitting on the rug—the Peck hooked rug, made
by our New England great-grandmother on my mother's
side; her golden corkscrew curls spilled down her back. Father sat in his faded sprung armchair. A Ryan armchair.
Grand Rapids, Mother called it, which meant that it was not
an antique, which meant that it was common. I sat on the
Peck Boston rocker; I sat very straight, as if I were hanging
my head from a string in order not to grow up to be a
hunchback. I was eleven; Cissy, six.

Mother? Mother was down with one of her Spells. She
often had these Spells, which had something to do with a
New England conscience.

"Thank God I don't have a New England conscience,"
Father used to say.

Was it a disease? I often wondered. If so, would I inherit
it?

The Horrible Hairy Spider (revolting, nearly five inches
across; fat rubber body with long hairy legs, fifteen cents)
dropped lower; it hung menacingly near Cissy's forehead,
just above her large, long-lashed baby-blue eyes. Ryan eyes,
like Father's. Father's eyes were choirboy blue. They were
uplifted, now, toward Heaven. Father was one, once—a
choirboy. There was a photograph of him in a lacy robe,

holding a candle snuffer—that same sweet, sly expression in his choirboy eyes. That was before he stopped being Catholic.

"It's the only church if you go to church," he sometimes said. "They know how to do things up right," he said, with a touch of vanity in his voice, which aggravated Mother. There was no one, really, less vain than Father. Why, then, I wondered, was he vain about having once been Catholic, when decent people, according to Mother, would be ashamed?

> He only does it to annoy
> Because he knows it teases—

Father loved Mother. On her last birthday he had given her a peek-a-boo blouse and a transparent purple nightie, which hung in her closet, unworn, except when Cissy played Dress Up. Father was also concerned about Mother's Spells. Mother wore her long chestnut hair in a tight bun at the back of her neck. Could it be that she was exerting too much strain upon her scalp? Father asked her. Perhaps, he said, if she let her hair down, let it fall more loosely, it would ease her suffering. His suggestion had no effect. Every year, it seemed, Mother drew her hair tighter; no loose wave or tendril was permitted to escape. Still, he continued to urge her. Such lovely hair, he said. Hair like yours should be displayed for people to admire.

"Beauty," said Mother, "is as Beauty does."

Father loved Mother, whatever love was. I was not sure. But the absolute token of his affection was that he liked to tease her. Father always teased the people he loved.

He liked to tease Cissy, most of all. He seldom teased me, any more. Did this mean that he loved Cissy more, or did it mean that I had grown too old for most of his jokes? Or, possibly, too dignified? Was love undignified? No. Mother had great dignity, and Mother loved Father.

"We are One," she used to say. "When two people marry, they become One."

Why then did she suffer so? Why did she grieve? Why did she feel that our home, at 43 North Elm, in Norton, was not truly her home, that her marriage had forced her into some sort of awful exile? Why did she never laugh at

Father's jokes? It was her pride, her terrible Peck pride. Those were my thoughts, as I watched, with an ill-disguised, adolescent scorn, the descent of the Horrible Hairy Spider.

"Oh yes, they do things up right," Mother said, when Father talked about having been Catholic. "All that mumbo jumbo! It's for people who have nothing else, who want to crawl on their knees in front of the Pope and kiss his feet. Crawl!" she added, with a shudder.

Father's hands were folded, *innocently,* in his lap, in a kind of prayerful attitude. But I knew what was in them. The Secret Control Ring! I tensed my body for what was about to occur.

Another jerk! The Spider dropped, swaying to and fro, in front of Cissy's eyes. Ryan eyes, like Father's. Cissy shrieked. Oh, that shriek! Even though I had prepared myself, it went through me like an electric shock.

Father? Father was looking at Cissy with a deep concern. What dreadful thing can have happened to this little girl? What had caused her to cry out in such an anguished manner? Was she in some sort of awful peril? Oh me! Oh my! Poor Cissy!

Then Cissy caught on. She got it. If she were in the funny papers, a shimmering light bulb would have appeared over her head.

"Oh, Dad—dee!" cried Cissy. She plucked the Horrible Hairy Spider out of the air and examined it; she giggled; she stared at Father with unabashed admiration. "Oh, Dad—dee," she said again.

Father's eyes lost their innocent look; they twinkled. The little laugh wrinkles around his eyes and mouth erupted. His chest, beneath his old coat sweater, heaved, and chuckles exploded out of his mouth—little "heh, heh, heh's," like the "heh, heh, heh's" in the balloons over funny paper people. Father and Cissy were funny paper people. "Did you see *Father and Cissy* today? Wasn't the Spider *funny*?"

"She's the perfect fall guy, isn't she?" said Father, winking at me, as if I were a co-conspirator.

I refused to be implicated; I did not acknowledge the wink. I was not a funny paper person, could not have been, even if I tried. I was Emily Peck Ryan, more Peck than Ryan, everyone said.

If Justice ruled the World, which I had, by then, learned

it did not, my name would have been Charity Peck Ryan, instead.

> Charity Peck is my name; in peaceful Warren born
> In Sorrow's School my Infant Mind was pierced with a Thorn,
> In Wisdom's Ways, I'll spend my Days,
> Humility be with me
> Should Fortune frown or Friends disown,
> Divine Support can't leave me.

That was the verse Great-Great-Grandmother Charity had embroidered on the Sampler at the age of nine, following the death of her father. Above the verse she had stitched three rows of the alphabet and numbers up to ten in different calligraphic design in order to demonstrate her skill at needlework. Below the verse, a tombstone presided over by a Grieving Angel, such as the one in the Peck Plot of the old IOOF cemetery in Metropolis, which the Reverend Gideon Freeland Peck, owner and publisher of *The Democratic Christian Evangelist* ("Southern Oregon's first newspaper," it said on the historical plaque), had copied from the one he remembered in the Warren cemetery.

Below the tombstone were these lines:

> Phineas Peck departed this life at a meeting of the Citizens of Warren on July the Fourth, 1831, following the discharge of a cannon.

"Why would a man step in front of a cannon at a Fourth of July celebration?" asked Father, one Sunday afternoon, as he stood in the parlor of my grandmother's house in Metropolis, five miles from Norton, the house where Mother had grown up and which was known by all the right people and even some of the wrong ones as the Old Peck Place. Father was examining the Sampler on the parlor wall. He gazed innocently at Granny, at Aunt Dee, at Uncle Gideon, at Mother. "Unless," he said, "he was perhaps not quite sober?"

Uncle Gideon, who was mixing Granny's before-dinner martini—the most important thing, perhaps the only thing, he learned at Harvard, Father sometimes said—shook the frosted cocktail shaker more vigorously than usual; Aunt Dee bustled out of the room to see to dinner; Granny, an Abbot, not a Peck, and whose reaction, therefore, did not matter, smiled; Cissy giggled; Mother was silent. A silence fraught with meaning, I thought. I had just learned "fraught." A fraught-with-meaning silence. A silence, meaningfully fraught. This was how so many of Mother's silences were.

"It was only an idle question, to satisfy a point concerning which I have often been curious," said Father.

When I was born, there was already a Charity Peck Ryan, a year older than I, who was now known as Poor Charity; she died, when I was three, of scarlet fever and now lay under the left wing of the angel in Metropolis. Mother's sorrow impaired her delicate Nervous System. Dr. Conroy prescribed warm baths, brisk walks, and no more babies. Both Mother and Father were deeply concerned over Mother's Nervous System; neither would have wilfully disobeyed Dr. Conroy's orders. What had happened? I should never know.

> "Where did you come from Baby dear?
> Out of the Nowhere into the Here.
> Where did you get those eyes so blue?
> God gave them to me, as He did you."

This was how Mother responded when Cissy asked Where She Came From, at an age when she was too little to comprehend. I knew, of course, that babies were the result of the most intimate physical expression of the deepest spiritual love between one man and one woman. Cissy had been told this, now, too, but Heaven only knew if Cissy "got" it. Heaven only knew what went on in Cissy's head. "Out of the Nowhere into the Here," though hardly a scientific explanation, seemed to me, on the whole, the best explanation for Cissy's existence.

Cissy, by being born in mysterious violation of the Doctor's Orders, had stolen my Rights of Primogeniture, in more ways than one. Being named "Charity," she would inherit the Peck Sampler. Would she spend her days wisely and humbly? Should Fortune frown and Friends disown, would she be able to count on Divine Support? Knowing Cissy, it seemed to me unlikely.

Father and Cissy were a Team. Like Jack Benny and Rochester. Like Edgar Bergen and Charley. Like George Burns and Gracie Allen. John C. Ryan and His Little Daughter, Cissy. John C. Ryan and His Bag of Magical Tricks and Practical Jokes. Little Cissy, the Perfect Fall Guy! Watch her "fall" for all the Tricks, no matter how many times performed.

Father: "Adam and Eve and Pinch Me
Went down to the Water to swim
Adam and Eve were drowned-ed
And who do you think was saved?"
Cissy: Pinch Me.
Father: (pinches Cissy)
Cissy: (squealing) Oh, Dad—dee!

Father: I can row a boat, canoe?
Mother: Oh, John, not again.
Emily: It's a pun, stupid. A pun on *words*. (One of the lowest forms of humor, despite Shakespeare's use of it, Miss Wilson, her seventh-grade teacher had said.) One of the lowest forms of humor.
Cissy: Boat! Can-you? I get it! (giggles)

Mother: Old Mr. Henry died last night in his sleep.
Father: Mr. Henry is with Barnum and Bailey.
Cissy: What's Barnum and Bailey?
Emily: (who knows her History) It was a famous circus, with Buffalo Bill.
Cissy: Why is Mr. Henry with them?
Emily: Barnum and Bailey are dead, stupid.
Cissy: (silence) (giggle) Oh!

Watch Cissy perform, too. A Chip Off the Old Block. Enjoy her Impersonation of Shirley Temple, singing "The Good Ship, Lollypop." A Mimic. A Great Little Trouper. Can really strut her stuff.

Mother: Not now, Cissy, Judge and Mrs. Blair want to talk.

Judge Blair: It isn't every day that an old man is enter-
               tained by a pretty little girl. Let's hear your
               song, sweetheart.

Jack Benny was over. They were playing the Theme Song.
Father turned off the Zenith. "I better go look in on poor
Mama," he said.

Cissy's response to this was to stand on her head; her
dress fell over her shoulders, revealing her pink panties;
then she dropped, plop, in a giggling, quivering heap upon
the rug.

"When I was a little girl, I always went to bed the moment Jack Benny was over," said Father.

Cissy looked up at Father, blue eyes big. Silence. Then,
"Oh, Dad—dee, you were never a little girl!"

Father picked up Cissy and threw her over his shoulder,
marched out of the room with a shrieking Cissy, dimpled
legs kicking at the air.

I rose and went into the dining room and sat down at the
round oak table (Grand Rapids, Ryan) and prepared to begin
my seventh-grade Original Research paper.

"Why don't you write about Old Metropolis?" said Miss
Emmeline Trowbridge, my friend and head librarian of the
Norton Public Library, when I had consulted her about the
theme. "After all," she said, "you are a Peck. Your Grand-
mother and your Uncle Gideon are filled with information.
You must pick a particular subject. The journey of your
Great-Grandfather from Massachusetts to Metropolis. The
Gold Rush. Your Great-Grandfather's Temperance Crusade,
the visit of Rutherford B. Hayes—"

I had decided to write about the Railroad. If it had not
been for the Railroad, all Pecks would have been rich today.
Not that Pecks cared about material wealth, in itself. It was
the respect that went with it.

If it had not been for a man named Norton, who bought
up one thousand acres of land in the fertile valley below
Metropolis, who bribed the S.P.—

"It was flatter land; it was easier to lay track," said Father.

"He *bribed* them," said Mother, said Uncle Gideon, said
Aunt Dee.

History, I sometimes thought, consisted as much, if not more, of what did not happen as what did.

Father was a lawyer in a small Oregon town. John C. Ryan, Atty-at-Law, it said in curly gold-leaf letters on the window of the Union Building, where he had his office. He had never finished law school; he had gone to World War I, instead. After the war, they made a law that veterans who had left college to enlist could get their degree by passing a formal examination. Father traveled to Salem and was interviewed by the Chief Justice. This is the story he liked to tell concerning the interview:

"The Chief Justice asked me a question, which I wasn't able to answer. Then he asked me another question, which I wasn't able to answer. Then he said, 'You are now admitted to the practice of law in the State of Oregon.' "

Father enjoyed being a lawyer in a small town. He was not ambitious, either for money or fame. You don't have to be if you have the rare privilege of enjoying your work. He was a popular man among people of every social and economic level. He was unassuming, courtly, gentle, genial, honest. He spent little time in court. By temperament, he was a "settler," not a litigator.

Outside of his work and his family, to whom he was devoted, he fished, gardened, and, after age fifty, played gin rummy every Saturday afternoon at the University Club in town. Outside of the Bar Association, this was his only affiliation; he was not a joiner. Once, someone talked him into the Kiwanis Club, because it would be "good for business." He went to one meeting and found it too serious.

He enjoyed his liquor, but drank like a gentleman. He smoked too much; his rumpled clothes were covered with cigarette ash. His other vice—if you can call it that—was his addiction to practical jokes. He kept *The Catalogue of Magical Tricks and Practical Jokes* on top of the toilet tank. The jokes, which he sent away for, were the only things he ever bought for himself, outside of necessities. This story is about my father's jokes.

THE RUBBER POINTED PENCIL

Looks like Lead

Fools and annoys 'em.

Mother: This pencil doesn't work, John. This pencil—
          is this one of your *jokes*, John? Will you be so
          kind as to find me a proper pencil, please?

THE FAKE FLY

Sticks to almost any surface.
Put it on your lapel, on the butter dish.
On Mrs. Social Register's lace tablecloth.
Watch 'em try to brush it off.
Confound your hostess.

Miss Singer: (County Recorder at the Courthouse to
               Cissy and Emily, who are waiting for Fa-
               ther in her office) Well, if there's anything
               I can't tolerate, it's a nasty, filthy fly. I
               tried to brush it off and it wouldn't move.
               It just—stuck. I should have guessed! He
               was going all over the courthouse last
               week with his squirting flower in his but-
               tonhole. Well, we all know your dad! He
               makes life just a bit brighter for everyone.
               No, things are never dull when your dad's
               around!

THE JUMPING SPOON

Greatest Laugh Producer ever invented.
A startling after-dinner trick. The performer
places one of the teaspoons to be found on the
dinner table into an ordinary drinking glass.
In a few seconds, the spoon jumps out of the
glass! This is really surprising and funny.

Mrs. Blair: (wife of Judge Blair) It was really surprising
              and funny. I couldn't believe my eyes; it
              just *jumped* out of the glass!
                         * * *

THE LIVE MYSTERY MOUSE

Miss Jost: (Elevator operator in Union Building. To
              Cissy and Emily) Going to see your dad?

              (The elevator is like an iron cage; through
              the bars of the cage one sees the cables
              move past as the elevator rises. Miss Jost
              has fixed up the interior of the cage like a
              miniature living room. She sits in an old
              chintz slipper chair; her knees are covered
              with a multicolored afghan; her knitting is
              on her lap. Taped to one of the bars is a
              photograph of her nephew, Carl, who lost
              an arm in the service of his country; taped
              to another bar is a postcard—a pretty rural
              scene of Denmark, where Miss Jost's par-
              ents grew up. Above this, a calendar with a
              photograph of the Norton Valley with the
              pear blossoms in bloom, courtesy of the
              Norton Groceteria.)

              "Fifth floor, Miss Jost," he says. (Creak-
              ing and grinding of chains, as she pulls the
              wheel.)

              Every morning, every noon—"Fifth floor,
              please." (The Union Building only has two
              floors.) He fooled me with that mouse of
              his, last week. "Could that be a *mouse* in
              your elevator, Miss Jost?" he says. I looked
              down and let out a frightful scream. "Don't
              worry, Miss Jost, I'll get the rascal," he
              says, and he leans down and picks it up and
              puts it in his pocket. Very solemnlike. Very
              calm. You would think he was accustomed
              to picking up mice everyday! Oh, Mr. Ryan,
              you almost gave me a heart attack! I said.
              You really shouldn't, Mr. Ryan!—But you
              know your dad. There's no stopping him.
              Heaven only knows what he'll think up next!

THE MECHANICAL HAND VIBRATOR
Startle your friends with a "friendly" handshake.

Miss Porter: (Father's stenographer. To Cissy and Emily) My hand was still tingling in bed last night.

(Miss Porter is Mother's age. An old maid. They knew each other, *slightly,* at Norton High. Miss Porter lives very quietly in the Kingscote Arms, with her widowed mother. She is the only person Emily and Cissy know who lives "downtown." Miss Porter wears too much rouge. She has her dyed hair done once a week at the Fountain of Beauty; every six months she gets a permanent. She plucks her eyebrows to a fine line and dresses in frilly frocks and sheer silk hose.) "It's a pity someone can't tell her how to dress suitable for an office," says Mother. "I'm sure it must give a bad impression when she meets the Public." Miss Porter is short and plump. Her freckled flesh is so soft it looks as if it would dent if you touched her. She has a soft voice and a slight stammer and is extremely meticulous. Since Mother doesn't drive—"I don't care to run around like other women," Mother says—she often asks Emily to phone the office and give Miss Porter a shopping list for Father. If Emily says, "One dozen oranges," Miss Porter will say, "What sort of oranges, dear? Does your mother prefer juice oranges or eating oranges?" This is the part of her meticulousness, which, though appropriate for legal stenography, irritates Mother. (Emily is not sure *why.*) "Miss Porter wants to know if you want juice or eating oranges?" Emily says. "Oh, isn't that just like her! Tell her either kind will do!" Mother's cavalier attitude toward oranges, or, perhaps her cavalier attitude toward Miss Porter, imposes a burden on Emily. "You better say *which*," she tells Mother. "Juice, then! Tell her *juice!*—or, *eating*. Tell her eating! Tell her anything you like." "Juice, please," Emily says. Then Miss Porter inquires after Mother's health. "How is your mother feeling today?" she says. Or, "Is your mother feeling better today?" "Yes, better, thank you," says Emily, no matter how Mother is feeling. She senses that it is not proper to go into more personal details, that neither Miss Porter nor Mother would care for that. Mother, in fact, would prefer that Miss Porter not inquire after her health at all.

Mother never phones, herself, if she can avoid it. Having known Miss Porter, *slightly,* in high school, where they called each other by their first names, it is awkward to phone and say, "This is Mrs. Ryan." On the other hand, it will not do to say, "This is Jean." When it is necessary, for one reason or another to call, herself, Mother says, "Is this Vera?" Then she waits for Miss Porter to recognize her voice, which Miss Porter always does. Miss Porter, recognizing Mother's voice, says, "Oh, how are you?" "Very well, thank you. And you?" says Mother. "I can't complain," says Miss Porter, or, "Chipper, I'm always chipper," she says. Then she says, "I bet you'd like to talk to the Boss." "Yes, please, if he's not occupied," says Mother. "I think I can arrange for you to speak to him," says Miss Porter. "I'll just put a little flea in his ear."

(Mother does not care for Miss Porter calling Father, "the Boss," nor does she care for the expression, "a little flea in his ear." But it does solve the awkward social problem for both of them. In all the ten years in which Miss Porter has worked for Father, she has, somehow, managed never to call Mother either Mrs. Ryan, or Jean.)

Miss Porter: That dreadful vibrator! It sent funny little shivers all through me. (She gives Cissy a box of paperclips to make into a chain; she gives Emily a stack of magazines—*The Elks Magazine, Field and Stream,* an old copy of *The Saturday Evening Post,* to entertain them while they wait for Father to drive them home from the dentist's. She opens the drawer of her desk and takes out a small tin box and opens it and offers them hard little white mints called "pastelles.")

Cissy: (listening to the story of the Vibrator, giggles)

Emily: (finds story embarrassing. Why would Father shake Miss Porter's hand, she wonders. That soft plump freckled hand. Sending little shivers through her soft plump body. Making Miss Porter tingle. She does not want to think of Miss Porter in bed. Tingling. She does not want to think of Miss Porter as having any existence at all, outside of her duties as Father's stenographer. She looks up from the *Post* and scowls at Cissy for giggling. Cissy, she thinks, lacks the Peck's innate good taste and proud reserve.)

"Isn't Miss Porter beautiful?" Cissy said one night, when we were in our beds in the upstairs bedroom we shared at 43 North Elm.

"Beautiful?" I said scornfully. "What could possibly make you think she is beautiful?"

But Cissy was already asleep.

* * *

Father: (driving our Buick on the way to the Peck
            House in Metropolis)
                As I was driving to Salt Lake
                I met a little rattlesnake
                I fed it some jellycake,
                It got a little bellyache.

Mother: (in front seat, holding Father's jacket and tie on
            her lap; flowers, in a Mason jar, for the Peck
            Plot, at her feet) Tummy, not belly!

Cissy: (sitting between Mother and Father, because
            she *claims* to get car sick. Giggles.)

Father: It got a little tummyache, not a bellyache, after
            all.

Emily: (alone in back seat) It says "belly" in the Bi-
            ble. (She agrees with Mother, but possesses a
            fund of knowledge she feels obliged to dem-
            onstrate.)

Mother: The language of the Bible and the language of
            everyday life are two different things alto-
            gether.

Father: Your mother is correct, as always. The lan-
            guage of the Bible is not appropriate language
            for everyday speech.

Mother: (ignoring Father) Drive slowly when we go
            through Metropolis, so Emily can take notes
            for her theme.

Cissy: My belly feels fun—ny.

            (Consternation! Should they stop? Let Cissy
            out? Roll down the window? Buy her some
            chewing gum? It is decided to drive *fast* through
            Metropolis and go straight to the Peck Plot,
            where she can run about among the tombstones
            in the fresh air. This, of course, takes prece-
            dence over Emily's Original Research.)

I got an "A" anyhow. "Emily has Literary Tendencies,"
Mrs. Wilson wrote across my theme, which I brought home
to show to Mother and Father. They were both proud of me.
The phrase: "Literary Tendencies" was taken up by them,
and then by others.

"Emily has Literary Tendencies," people would say. They didn't mean it, I suppose, but they always made "Literary Tendencies" sound as if it were—not so much a disease, maybe, as a kind of morbidity, a lack of normal health. They may have been right. I don't know. Perhaps it was like the New England Conscience, which as it turned out, I did inherit from Mother.

Certainly, Cissy didn't inherit it. The way she climbed upon gentlemen's laps, for example; climbed up and burrowed in and snuggled down, as if she were some sort of little animal; made a nest and curled up, peacefully, as long as she was being cuddled, patted, stroked—but, should the gentleman reach for a drink or a cigarette, or, simply pause for a moment, the burrowing and squirming began again to remind him of his neglect and did not stop until the neglect was rectified.

"Cissy, don't pester Judge Blair," or, "Cissy, I think Mr. Hefflinger would be happier if you were to get down at once," Mother would say.

"Oh, Cissy's my girl, aren't you, Cissy?"

"It isn't every day an old codger like myself can hold a pretty blonde on his lap."

The pet names she was called. Cissy. Missy Cissy. Cissy-Pie. Later, scrawled upon the Angel—a famous necking spot for the students at Norton High: "Hot Pants Cissy." This was, fortunately, after Mother's breakdown. Aunt Dee took rubbing alcohol and scrubbed it off.

It was Father's fault. He spoiled her. Mother often said so.

THE DOGGIE DOO DOO

> Latex. Fantastically realistic imitation.
> Nauseating. Put on your hostess's best rug.
> Watch her chide poor Fido.

Mrs. Hefflinger: (mother of Jimmy Hefflinger, with whom Emily is secretly in love, who has invited the Ryan family to visit them at their cabin at the Lake) Oh, no!

Father: (innocent expression in choir-blue eyes) Is something the matter, Mil?

Mrs. Hefflinger: (to Mr. Hefflinger) Carl!

Father: Perhaps I can be of assistance?

Mrs. Hefflinger: No, no, it's all right. I'm sorry, Bingo's
          made a mess. Where *is* Bingo? Carl? I'll get paper
          towels—

Cissy: (looks at Doggie Doo Doo; looks at Father.
          Giggles.)

Emily: (silent, dying of shame)

Mother: John! John, you didn't—!

Mr. Hefflinger: Well, I guess we better clean it up.

Mrs. Hefflinger: I'll do it. You men take the girls down
          to the Lake. They want to go out in the boat. I'm
          afraid Bingo's been a very naughty dog.

Mother: (pale-faced, weakly) John?

Father: I, for one, intend to stay and help Milly. (picks
          up Doggie Doo Doo, puts it casually in pocket)

Jimmy Hefflinger: Hey—that's neat. Let's see it!

Emily: Let's go out in the boat!

Cissy: Show it to Jimmy, Daddy.

Mother: John!

Mrs. Hefflinger: (laughing) Oh, John, it's one of your
          jokes!

Father: You know I never joke, Mil. (takes out Doggie
          Doo Doo from pocket and hands it, proudly, to
          Jimmy. Jimmy and Cissy examine Doggie Doo
          Doo.)

Mrs. Hefflinger: You certainly fooled me this time.

Jimmy: (turning Doggie Doo Doo over in his hand)
          Hey, this is great. (to Cissy) Where'd your fa-
          ther get it?

Cissy: (giggling, looking up at Jimmy with big blue
          eyes) He has this catalogue. (coquettishly) I'll
          show it to you, sometime. It's got lots of neat
          stuff. Come on, you promised to take us for a
          boat ride.

Emily: (forever shamed, forever unable to forget her
          shame when she sees Jimmy Hefflinger at
          school) I don't think I'll go. I brought a book
          to read.

* * *

(Jimmy and Cissy run off, down to the dock.
Mrs. Hefflinger fixes gin fizzes for the adults.
Mother declines hers. She has a sudden headache, perhaps it is the run, perhaps she had
better lie down for a time with a cool wet washcloth on her forehead. Father fetches a cool wet
washcloth, returns from the bedroom. Emily
sits down with her book.)

Father: I've been told my—ah—joke—was not in the
            best of taste.
Mrs. Hefflinger: Nonsense! You wouldn't be John Ryan
            without your jokes. I'm going to tell her to come
            back out here.
Father: Better wait a bit, Mil.
Mrs. Hefflinger: Well, you know best. (looks at Emily)
            Emily is quite a little bookworm, isn't she?
Father: (proudly) Her teacher says she has Literary
            Tendencies.

SNOW

(7:00 A.M. February morning. Emily is sixteen; Cissy, eleven. Mother, that winter, has
"taken to her bed," a phrase of Aunt Dee's,
taken up by others. Father sleeps on a cot, in
the hallway, in order to be near her in the night.
Cissy and Emily are still asleep. Father enters
their bedroom.)

Father: Girls! Wake up! We're going to give Mother a
            nice surprise.
Emily: (always an early riser, already awake, sits up,
            gets out of bed)
Cissy: (burrows under covers. To Father) Go 'way.
            (Father pulls covers off Cissy's bed. Cissy
            shrieks. Both girls follow Father, reluctantly,
            arms across chests, shivering, in their flannel
            nighties. Father leads them into Mother's room.
            Mother is lying on her back, eyes open. She
            seems to be looking at something beyond, or
            perhaps through her visitors.)

Father:	(to Mother) Surprise! Surprise! We have a little surprise for you this morning. (goes to window, peeps behind drawn curtain; faces Mother again) Ready? (clears throat, assumes theatrical stance) Presto chango! (pulls curtain) Snow! (Father twinkles, beams)
Mother:	(looks at snow, expression does not change; she seems to be looking at something beyond, or perhaps through this sudden Winter Wonderland)
Cissy:	(marveling at the magical metamorphosis produced by Father) Oh, Dad—dee!
Father:	(to Mother, trying again) Now we see it. (draws curtain) Now we don't. (pulls curtain) Presto chango—Snow!
Mother:	It's very nice, but the light hurts my eyes. Would you mind closing the curtain, again, please, John?

In 1949, I returned from Reed College, to attend my mother's funeral. She had taken, it seemed, too many pills all at once. The funeral was private, but Miss Porter showed up, anyhow. Her sobs spoiled the lovely simplicity of the words from the Book of Common Prayer—the service Uncle Gideon had arranged. I considered her presence in the worst of taste.

After the funeral, Father, Cissy, and I sat in the living room at 43 North Elm. Father was pale, solemn, still. The laugh lines in his face were etched more deeply; perhaps they were no longer laugh lines, anymore. He chain-smoked, dropping ashes on the Peck hooked rug. I fetched an ashtray.

Father said, "Well, I guess Mama is with Barnum and Bailey." Cissy giggled, then burst into tears. Father wept with her. I stood, holding the ashtray—apart, alone, dry-eyed. Being more Peck than Ryan, I could neither laugh nor weep.

This story is about my father's jokes. Father joked. Cissy was his Fall Guy. Mother had her pride. I have Literary Tendencies. I am writing this story. Everyone has his or her way of coping.

A Selected List of Secondary Sources on the Theme of
Growing Up Female In Multicultural America

Bataille, Gretchen M. and Kathleen Mullen Sands. *American Indian Woman: Telling Their Lives*. Lincoln: Univ. of Nebraska Press, 1984.

Busby, Margaret, ed. *Daughters of Africa: An International Anthology of Words and Writings by Women of African Descent from the Ancient Egyptian to the Present*. New York: Pantheon, 1992.

Dearborn, Mary. *Pocahontas's Daughters: Gender and Ethnicity in American Culture*. New York: Oxford Univ. Press, 1986.

Edelman, Marian Wright. *The Measure of Our Success: A Letter to My Children and Yours*. Boston: Beacon Press, 1992.

Evans, Mari, ed. *Black Women Writers: A Critical Evaluation*. New York: Anchor Books, 1984.

Gilbert, Sandra M. and Susan Gubar, eds. *The Norton Anthology of Literature By Women*. New York: Norton, 1985.

Gilligan, Carol and Lyn Mikel Brown. *Meeting at the Crossroads: Women's Psychology and Girls' Development*. Cambridge, Mass.: Harvard Univ. Press, 1992.

Hirsch, Marianne. *The Mother/Daughter Plot: Narrative, Psychoanalysis, Feminism*. Bloomington: Indiana Univ. Press, 1991.

Jordan, Judith V., Alexandra G. Kaplan, Jean Baker Miller, Irene P. Stiver, and Janet L. Surrey. *Women's Growth In Connection: Writings From The Stone Center*. New York: The Guilford Press, 1991.

Moers, Ellen. *Literary Women: The Great Writers*. New York, Oxford Univ. Press, 1985.

Spacks, Patricia Meyer. *The Female Imagination*. New York: Avon Books, 1975.

ACKNOWLEDGMENTS

"Trespass" by Julia Alvarez from *How The Garcia Girls Lost Their Accents*, Copyright © 1991 by Julia Alvarez. First published in hardcover by Algonquin Books of Chapel Hill. Published in paperback by Plume, an imprint of New American Library, a division of Penguin USA, Inc. Reprinted by permission of Susan Bergholz Literary Services, New York.

"My Lucy Friend Who Smells Like Corn" by Sandra Cisneros from *Woman Hollering Creek*. Copyright © by Sandra Cisneros. First published in *Story*. Published in the United States by Random House, Inc. and simultaneously in Canada by Random House of Canada Ltd., Toronto. Reprinted by permission of Susan Bergholz Literary Services, New York.

"Sins Leave Scars" by J. California Cooper from *A Piece of Mine* by J. California Cooper. Copyright © 1984 by J. California Cooper. Reprinted by permission of Doubleday, a division of Bantam Doubleday Dell Publishing Group, Inc.

"The Power of Prayer" from *The Time of Adam* by Elizabeth Cullinan. First published in *The New Yorker*. Published in the United States by Houghton Mifflin & Company. Copyright © 1971 by Elizabeth Cullinan. Reprinted by permission of the author.

"Aimlessness" from *Lakota Woman* by Mary Crow Dog with Richard Erdoes. Copyright © 1990 by Mary Crow Dog and Richard Erdoes. Reprinted by permission of Grove Press, Inc.

From *Riding in Cars With Boys: Confessions of a Bad Girl Who Makes Good* by Beverly Donofrio. Copyright © 1990 by Beverly Donofrio. Reprinted by permission of William Morrow & Company, Inc.

From *Truck* by Katherine Dunn. Copyright © 1971 by Katherine Dunn. First published by Harper & Row Publishers, Inc. Reprinted by permission of HarperCollins Publishers, Inc.

"Vito Loves Geraldine" by Janice Eidus from *Vito Loves Geraldine*. Copyright © 1989 by Janice Eidus. First appeared in *The Village Voice Literary Supplement*. Reprinted by permission of City Lights Publishers.

"Aunt Moon's Young Man" by Linda Hogan first appeared in *Missouri Review*, and also in *Best American Short Stories* published by Houghton Mifflin, 1989. Reprinted by permission of the author.

"What Means Switch" by Gish Jen. Copyright © 1990 by Gish Jen. First published in *The Atlantic*. Reprinted by permission of the author.